OF KNIGHTS AND MONSTERS

COMPLETE SERIES

CORINNE M. KNIGHT

Written and published by Corinne M. Knight

Edited by Karen Sanders Editing

Alpha Read by Alpha Reading by TS Arthur

Cover by Geka at Grafico Espacio

BLURB

The Order of the Dragon casts a dark shadow over Europe, manipulating supernatural beings for their sinister purposes. Within the hallowed halls of Roslyn Academy, a group of brave individuals rises to challenge the oppressive Order.

Vampires, demons and formidable supernaturals come together across six books to challenge the heroes as they battle their way across Europe in their attempts to overthrow the Order's reign of terror.

Betrayal, kidnap, and dangerous alliances threaten not only their quest against evil, but their very lives. Join them in a tale of courage, sacrifice and epic battles as they face the tightening grip of a malevolent enemy in an unyielding fight for freedom against the backdrop of supernatural intrigue and treachery.

Of Knights and Monsters is a Supernatural Paranormal Fantasy series set in Roslyn Academy and various places across Europe, and features secret societies, supernatural creatures, demonic activity and action-packed adventure with a side of perilous journeys, forbidden love and battles between good and evil.

THE DARK HEIR

CHAPTER 1

Roslyn Academy

Tick tock. Tick tock.

Lucien de Winter was sitting in the headmaster's office, watching the mechanical cuckoo clock swing its pendulum from side to side.

He was waiting for the elderly man to finish reading a document he had brought from the Order. While Mr Brunner took his time, almost like he was doing it on purpose, Lucien found the workings of the machinery fascinating.

"Your file says you're twenty-one, Mr de Winter."

"Yes, sir. I'll be twenty-two next summer."

"Very well. You look about eighteen to me, which is to your advantage."

The young man nodded in understanding. He knew his youthful appearance, more than his combat skills or attractiveness, was the reason he stood out from other talented candidates. While he wasn't fond of looking much younger than his age, it gave him an edge in blending in and investigating violations against the Order and various supernatural occurrences.

"So, why here?" the headmaster enquired. "Why Roslyn Academy?"

"I can't divulge much, sir," Lucien explained, his tone guarded. "They've assigned me to this task with the strictest confidentiality. You're the sole individual authorised to be aware of my true identity, granted access by my credentials and the letter from the organisation's head. Any further details are strictly on a need-to-know basis."

"You should give me something to work with. I demand to be informed of what I'm dealing with here," the headmaster snapped, his nostrils flaring. "What division of the Order are you from?"

"I'm a knight. A high-ranking member. Disciples get this by training most of their lives."

"Then you're no novice. Tell me, should I be worried?"

Lucien grinned. "Old man, I suggest you start praying. If the rumours hold any truth, you'll be dealing with some demonic activities. But if I discover you're involved, no deity will come to your aid."

"Mr. de Winter, you seem to have misunderstood. I recommend that you conduct a thorough investigation before assigning blame. Despite your claims of expertise as a knight, you appear to be inexperienced, akin to a novice on his maiden assignment."

Lucien was certain the headmaster had something to do with the demonic activity. He'd used this cheap tactic to unnerve him, and it worked. The fool fell right into his trap. The man before him was hiding something. He didn't know what it was, but it had a connection to the issue at hand.

“Let’s pray you’re right, then, for the sake of the students. It would be a shame to skin you alive.” He chuckled.

“Until tomorrow, Mr de Winter.” The headmaster dismissed the knight.

“See you tomorrow, Mr Brunner.” Lucien got up from the chair and made his way to the exit.

He opened the heavy wooden-panelled door carved with an intricate pattern as he heard the older man shout after him. “Don’t forget to pick up your uniform from my secretary, Mr de Winter.”

How could I forget such an important detail? He laughed. Blending in was his speciality. Countless missions and hundreds of hours of training made him who he was today. A killing machine trained to do the bidding of his higher-ups, all in the Order’s name.

As he ventured into the hallway, Lucien collided with a brunette girl who appeared to be a student, judging by her uniform. Her blue blazer, white shirt, black tie, blue pleated skirt, and high ponytail suggested as much. However, he couldn’t help but notice how short her skirt was, a detail that struck him as indecent. He gazed at her, his throat tightening. Despite her petite and delicate appearance, she exuded an air of danger akin to a cursed rose adorned with poisonous thorns—beautiful yet deadly.

The girl’s looks disarmed Lucien. She had long, raven hair, with loose tendrils framing her face. Dark, sparkling eyes—which weren’t the usual European shape—enhanced her beauty. He coughed, composing himself.

She was standing in one of those spots that echo every sound in a room. How did he know that? He used the same trick on the old man moments before stepping into his office.

“Did nobody tell you it’s not polite to listen to people’s conversations?” he chided her. She clearly needed to be taught a lesson.

The girl’s pretty mouth turned into an ‘o’, then she smiled.

“I just got here.” An expression of satisfaction played in her eyes. “Rumour has it you’re the new student, and I wanted to see what the fuss was all about. Tell me, what brings you here? Where did you study before?”

She fired off questions left and right, catching him off guard. His eyes couldn’t help but stray to her rosy, plump lips as she talked. Part of him wished she’d just leave, but another part enjoyed having her around.

"I'll give you an answer, but only if you spill the deets on what brings you here," Lucien replied nonchalantly. Did she get sent to spy on him by his higher-ups? No, that wasn’t possible. Someone as young as her wouldn’t be an agent of the Order, would they?

“You’re used to getting your way, aren’t you?” She sighed. “Very well. My friend told me a good-looking guy walked into the headmaster’s office. I had to see if it was true.”

“Is that so?” Lucien asked, an eyebrow lifted in curiosity. Was she attracted to him? Suddenly, his task became much more intriguing.

“Nah, but you’ll do.” She laughed, and it wasn’t a nervous cackle. The girl looked smug with confidence, like she knew something he didn’t.

“I’ll do? That’s quite bold of you, little girl.” His eyes sparkled with irritation. Just who did she think she was? He had nearly tripped over her when he exited the headmaster’s office, all thanks to her carelessness.

One, two, three, and calm down. She’s just a vexing student. You’ve seen her type before.

“Hey, listen. There’s a big party tonight at the usual spot

where everyone hangs out. Want to come?" She flashed him a delighted grin. Something was off. Why didn't she have a witty response to his remark?

Despite finding her personality somewhat grating, the chance to do a bit of sleuthing was too good to miss. He decided it was time to turn the tables on her. With a smile, he prepared to play his part.

"I'll be there. Who would say no to that?" Lucien replied, giving her an overly flirtatious look.

"Just so we're clear, this isn't a date, all right? I'm doing you a favour. It's going to be packed with some of the academy's top students. You don't strike me as the nerd type," she retorted, her eyes narrowing.

"If you say so." He stepped closer, reducing the space between them. Leaning in, he trifled with the idea of kissing her, curious about her reaction. His gaze lingered on her, his heart skipping a beat. "Make sure to dress up; I'll ensure you have a good time." He flashed her a wink.

"You're such a moron," she muttered, rolling her eyes but smiling slightly. "So, where am I picking you up? I heard you're without wheels." She gave a casual shrug. "Gossip flies around here."

Her extensive knowledge about him before their first encounter disconcerted him. This student was proving to be quite the enigma. Lucien found himself genuinely captivated, a feeling he hadn't known in a while, and he relished the focus on him.

"Saint Augustine's Street. The Old Church," he told her.

"The rundown church?" she enquired, her confusion clear.

"It's been in my family for generations. You're not getting cold feet, are you?" he teased, closing the distance until she was backed against the wall. "I'm pretty sure you'll be too distracted by my company to notice any spookiness." Lucien framed her in his arms, effectively trapping her.

I have you exactly where I want you, he thought, raising an eyebrow as he locked eyes with her.

"I wouldn't be caught dead in there," she breathed out, clearly flustered.

"Don't be too sure," Lucien chuckled. "I have a feeling you might change your mind."

She let out an exasperated sigh. "Just the arrogant type I'd expect from this academy. Well done on fitting right in. You'll probably thrive here."

After a moment's glare, Lucien stepped back. "And who are you to label me?" he challenged.

"Avery Darmon, notorious for being a pain to many here. My father supports this academy. I've grown up around it, so I'm familiar with your kind."

"Ah, Avery," he said with a grin. "Seems you've misjudged me. I'm Lucien. And I'm determined to prove you wrong."

CHAPTER 2

Lucien ended up walking home to clear his head. Avery, with her endless questions and that undeniable charm, somehow managed to both annoy and intrigue him at the same time. How did she do that?

As a knight, Lucien was supposed to be tough, trained for anything. But Avery threw him for a loop. Why did he get all warm and fuzzy when he saw her? He thought about his family's history. Seemed like falling hard for someone was in his genes, but it never ended well.

His life was usually all about hunting demons and keeping the peace. No time for personal stuff. Relationships? Just simple, no-fuss flings. No complicated feelings, no remembering dates, no dealing with someone who wanted more. He preferred keeping things straightforward and drama-free. Why bother with the mess of a serious relationship?

Lucien closed the ancient, creaky gate behind him and paused to examine his new residence. The Old Church, now converted into a house, appeared eerie from the exterior, echoing Avery's description. However, Lucien remained unperturbed. He pushed open the weathered wooden door, grimacing at the groan it emitted.

The place was all set up for him by the Order. Stocked cupboards, a dust-free environment, and even his bedroom with its four-poster bed, boasted freshly laundered sheets. Glancing around, Lucien felt a surprising fondness for his new home. It had an indefinable allure with its French, antique furniture that seemed centuries old yet perfectly preserved. It had the vibe of a neglected manor, its gothic appeal enhanced by the stained-glass windows.

Light danced through the church's colourful stained glass, casting vibrant patterns across the room. Lucien headed to the library, carelessly tossed his coat and tie onto an armchair, loosened a few shirt buttons, and settled at his desk.

There was so much to tackle in so little time. The slightest hint of demonic activity at the Order's top academy could wreak havoc. His bosses wanted quick answers.

Firing up his laptop, Lucien tapped into Roslyn Academy's servers, easily accessing student files thanks to the outdated security system. He didn't need to hack his way in for hours like before.

He started sifting through the top students' profiles, guided by the hunch that these bright minds, likely bored by standard lessons, might dabble in the forbidden out of curiosity.

But after hours of digging, Lucien was no closer to identifying the culprit. It was clear a deeper, more direct investigation was needed.

Lucien pondered for a moment. This didn't seem like a straightforward defiance against the Order's rule. Had the teachers been part of it, the summoning would have been on a grander scale, with more demons to manage, making them tougher to rein in. Yet, something nudged him towards believing the headteacher played a role, either directly or by shielding someone else.

He planned to comb the academy grounds, hunting for traces of the magic that brought these dark beings into their realm. His best chance was tomorrow night, after classes, when the dormitories were quiet and everyone was asleep. Stealth was crucial; he needed to research without drawing any attention. This discreet approach was necessary to avoid tipping off whoever was behind this.

THE DOORBELL'S CHIME SNAPPED LUCIEN BACK TO REALITY, and he rose to see who it was. He half-expected an ambush. But it wasn't an enemy that greeted him—it was Avery, surprisingly, back so soon. A lump formed in his throat. This spelled trouble. What did she want this time?

"Why did it take you ages to open the door?"

"To be honest, I wasn't expecting company, especially not you. Missed me already?" he joked, masking his surprise. Typical, he thought; women often tried to get involved in his life, especially when he was knee-deep in a case. He usually sent them on their way, but Avery was different. He actually needed her help to keep up appearances.

"Just bored at home, and a friend suggested checking out this new spot before the big bash tonight. Thought you might want to join," she suggested, a hint of mischief in her tone.

"A pre-party? Sounds perfect. Give me a sec to change. You can stick around for the show if you want," he teased, smirking at the thought.

The notion of spending time together before the party

piqued his interest, although he harboured doubts about whether they would even make it there if she accepted his invitation. Confirming she was of age, Lucien saw no harm in making things interesting if she was willing. Clad in his suit, he was well aware of his appeal.

"Gross." Avery burst out laughing. "I'd rather bleach my eyeballs, thanks. Hurry, will you? Or I might ditch you."

Her humour struck him; she certainly knew how to hold her own, looking quite pleased with herself.

Changing quickly, Lucien opted for jeans and a dark blue t-shirt boasting "Hotter than Hell". It was just a midweek party, and Avery was his only connection there. Confident in his looks, he knew he'd turn heads. A quick tousle with styling wax gave him the perfect messy look.

Joining Avery in her car, they were met with a sudden silence, marking the beginning of an unpredictable night.

AVERY HAD BEEN HANGING AROUND FOR A BIT WHEN Lucien finally showed up, leaving her speechless. She hadn't expected him to ditch the suit and still look stunningly hot.

In his laid-back clothes, he shed the polished, rich-kid vibe he had at school. Back then, his posh British accent had thrown her off, making her think of him as some kind of nobility. But royalty didn't just wander the English countryside, did they?

His outfit might have been simple, but Lucien was anything but. His t-shirt brought out the blue in his eyes, his hair was perfectly dishevelled, and those jeans. They did his legs justice. Absolutely breath-taking. He looked like he could give angels a run for their money.

"Why did you drag your feet getting here?" Avery managed to say, playing it cool despite being floored by his looks.

"I had to make sure I looked my best for you, baby, didn't I? You're the one who invited me," Lucien quipped with a smirk.

"Cut the 'baby' stuff. I'm not your date. Just a placeholder until I find someone hotter at the party," she shot back, her glare sharp. Despite his knockout appearance, his arrogance was all too familiar, just like every other entitled guy at the academy.

"Oh, I promise tonight will be unforgettable," Lucien countered, his smile somehow enhancing his already considerable allure.

"And how do you plan to manage that?" Avery prodded, curious despite herself. She was playing it tough, but deep down, she was already drawn to him. Her dad hadn't warned her enough about Lucien. Sure, she'd heard about him, but none of those rumours mentioned just how good-looking he was.

"Just wait and see. Now, are we driving, or would you rather stay back at mine?" He looked at her with a playful glint in his eye.

"Not happening," Avery said with a head shake and an eye roll, trying to hide her growing interest.

CHAPTER 3

LUCIEN AND AVERY HIT THE CLUB JUST AFTER NINE. Lucien, taken aback, quickly steered Avery aside to avoid curious glances.

"Why didn't you say we were heading here?" he asked, a bit rattled. "I'm going to stand out."

"Just own it. You always do," Avery shot back with a laugh.

"Is that supposed to make me feel better?" he replied, visibly annoyed. Avery could be a handful, but this situation was pushing it.

He was fuming. They'd walked straight into a vampire hangout, on the invite of one of Avery's friends. Supernatural beings had a knack for messing with humans, and this friend was a supernatural creature or someone who enjoyed living dangerously.

Lucien had raided places like this before while working for the Order. Vampires could spot a knight a mile off, and right then, they were all too aware of their presence, forming a protective circle around their boss.

Facing them head-on would be a death wish. Lucien's

priority was to keep both Avery and himself safe, blending in and not drawing attention to themselves as much as possible to make it through the night.

Then, a towering vampire with a commanding presence rose from his chair. Lucien recognised him instantly – Lóthurr, a vampire he'd once nearly defeated on the Order's command. That day, Lucien had seen the darkness of his actions reflected in Lóthurr's eyes and had let him go, turning him into the organisation's most wanted.

"Now, Lucien de Winter in my club, that's something," boomed Lóthurr from across the room. "And you've brought a guest. Do come closer."

"Lóthurr, my friend, long time no see," Lucien greeted, masking his tension.

"We're hardly friends. A little respect, please."

"I guess 'saviour' will have to do," Lucien muttered.

"Here to make peace? Do you have any idea how tough it's been dodging the Order since you let me go? A Norse descendant, brought to shame," Lóthurr said, his anger palpable.

"I'm here to toast to your long life, nothing more," Lucien responded, hitting a nerve.

"Still as cocky, I see. But I'll take that toast," Lóthurr sneered, a smile breaking through his stern facade.

A busty waitress dressed in a black and white leather corset and mini skirt brought up a tray with glasses and a bottle of whiskey.

It's going to be a long night, Lucien thought. Why did they have to come here? He had a lot going on with the task the Order gave him; he didn't have time to deal with the vampire. And to get out alive, he required a lot of cunning.

"Come forth and sit with us. I see you brought a lovely friend." Lóthurr licked his lips and curled them into a grin, watching the girl curiously.

With a sigh, Lucien began walking towards the table, keeping Avery tight by his side, silently wishing his old acquaintance wouldn't cause a scene over her being human.

"What's your whiskey preference?" Lóthurr enquired.

"On the rocks," Lucien answered, keeping a wary eye on the vampire.

"Come sit here, beautiful," Lóthurr gestured to Avery as a chair was promptly brought over and positioned beside him.

"Thanks, but I'd rather stand," Avery said haughtily.

Lucien shook his head, sensing trouble brewing. He regretted coming here. If it weren't for the Order and their need to close the investigation soon, he wouldn't have needed her to blend in with the other students.

"I'm afraid you have no other choice, little girl. People here do what I tell them to." He motioned to one of his subordinates, who promptly grabbed Avery's elbow and forced her into the chair.

She scowled and rubbed her arm. "There's no need to act so uncivilised."

The Norseman burst into laughter, clearly taken aback by Avery's boldness. Despite being the most formidable being in the room, Avery's courage didn't waver. Lucien, watching the scene unfold, silently shook his head at her, hoping she'd dial it back. The vampire caught that exchange and grinned.

"I came here to share a drink, not to watch you pick on someone half your size," Lucien taunted, drawing Lóthurr's attention to himself as he took the seat next to Avery.

"No worries, my friend. There's always room for you at the table of misfits," the Norseman replied, lifting his glass in a toast.

"So, what's been keeping you occupied lately?" Lucien enquired, putting on an act of curiosity. His interest in the vampire's doings was nil, yet he knew that maintaining the charade was essential for both his and Avery's wellbeing.

"I've been dedicating myself to building my legacy. Being immortal sure helps with that. How about you? What drags a renowned demon slayer to our little gathering?"

Avery's eyes widened in surprise, turning to Lóthurr. "That can't be right. He's just a new guy at my school."

"Oh, he hasn't filled you in, then," Lóthurr said, shaking his head in mock pity, a sly grin on his face. "He's with the Order of the Dragon, a demon hunter by trade. And not just demons—he's taken on all sorts of supernatural beings. His family ties go back to Prince Vlad Drakulya of Wallachia, a key figure in founding their esteemed Order."

"He's around my age, though. The organisation doesn't usually scout from the academy, does it?" Avery's shock hadn't faded, despite the revelation.

"They don't. High-ranking members like him are born into the role. They're raised to take on these missions, silently dealing with anything amiss, all while keeping under the radar."

With his cover blown, Lucien pondered over Lóthurr's angle by outing him to Avery. There had to be more to his motives.

"Kind of like a secret society?" Avery murmured.

"Precisely," he confirmed with a grin.

Avery burst out laughing. "You're too easy. Of course I knew who he was. I'm from Roslyn Academy, remember? Anyone with a bit of sense knows about the de Winter lineage, their noble blood, and their legendary battles with the supernatural."

"Cut the crap!" Lucien exploded, his frustration clear. "What's your angle, Lóthurr? You didn't summon us to chat about the Order. There's something you're after, and I'm itching to figure it out. Looking for some kind of payback? You think I owe you?"

"If revenge was my goal, you'd have been a goner the moment you walked in. But you're onto something; I'm after more," Lóthurr said, his gaze shifting slyly towards Avery.

"Spill it then," Lucien demanded, feeling a knot form in his stomach, anticipating his next words.

"I want her as my mate." No sooner had Lóthurr spoken than his goons moved in, pulling Avery towards him. "I could turn her into one of us in no time, and there's nothing you could do to stop me. We've got you outnumbered. You've got no way out."

"Like hell!" Avery protested fiercely. "I'd rather die!"

Lucien, while sceptical of Lóthurr's claim, couldn't ignore their precarious situation. He shot a disdainful look at the vampire, taking a swig of his drink, plotting his next move with utmost caution.

"Come on, you're not the type to get worked up over a mortal," Lucien joked, though a sense of foreboding gripped him. He might just agree to whatever Lóthurr proposed if it meant keeping Avery safe. He cursed his soft spot for playing the hero.

"Thought I'd give it a shot. But really, I need your expertise. Once I heard you were around, it was just a matter of time before our paths crossed," Lóthurr admitted, looking pleased.

"In a small town like this, it was inevitable," Lucien remarked, on alert for any vampire mischief.

"I require a favour from you. Fulfil it, and you're at liberty to depart with the girl. All I ask is that the job is completed."

"What is it?" Lucien pressed, wary of his capricious nature. The vampire had a reputation for lethal impulsiveness.

"I want you to retrieve the original Manual of Demonic Magic. There are whispers that it might hold secrets to our origins and possibly a way to revert vampires back to humans, thanks to hidden spells," Lóthurr revealed.

"That's a tall order. That book's under tight security at the Bavarian State Library," Lucien countered.

"They've got a decoy on display. The real deal was locked away in their vault. There was a heist back in the 1850s, but I'm sure you can piece together the rest," the vampire hinted with a sly smile.

"Who's been filling your head with these fairy tales? You seriously believe in some mythical book's power to change your nature?" Lucien couldn't hide his scepticism. He'd heard rumours about Lóthurr's desperation to turn human but dismissed them as just talk.

"If there's even a slim chance at a cure, I'd rather have it than let it fall into the wrong hands. I'll pay whatever it takes," Lóthurr insisted, slamming his hand on the table.

"Money's no motivation for me," Lucien replied, not keen on becoming a supernatural errand boy.

"Then let's talk about the girl. What does she mean to you? Help me, and I guarantee her safety," Lóthurr proposed, grinning.

Lucien's mind raced. He felt compelled to protect Avery, despite their brief acquaintance. He knew she'd be trouble but couldn't stand by and do nothing. Fraternising with a vampire was against the Order's rules, risking his expulsion and wiping his memory. Everything he worked for would vanish.

"You're ready to gamble with lives over what might be only hearsay. I wonder what the Order would do if they found out about this." Lucien tried another angle.

"Never use them to intimidate me, de Winter! You're no threat to me," Lóthurr retorted, visibly angered.

Lóthurr had the upper hand, and Lucien knew better than to push his luck. Any further provocation could end badly.

"We've got to tread lightly," Lucien murmured, leaning in. "Let's not forget the stakes if the Order catches wind of this. You'd lose your best shot at finding that book. Our cooperation stays under wraps."

"You have my assurance," the supernatural agreed.

"Deal," Lucien said, rising. "We'll leave now. Expect my call when I have news."

He quickly guided Avery out, eager to leave before Lóthurr reconsidered. Back in the safety of their car, Lucien allowed himself to relax with a heavy sigh.

"You owe me a ton of answers," Avery began, disbelief in her eyes.

"Seriously? You're saying you've never encountered a vampire before? What are they even teaching you at that supernatural academy?" Lucien teased.

Roslyn Academy wasn't just any school. It was a melting pot for supernatural beings and magically gifted humans, secretly linked to the Order of the Dragon, and a hub for training in various combat techniques.

"Sorry for not having a vampire handy for a chat," Avery retorted. "And here I was, fooled by a demon hunter who's too good at blending in. Got distracted by your charm, I suppose."

Lucien cupped her face, feeling a twinge of guilt for keeping her in the dark. There was something about Avery that compelled him to protect her.

"Don't kick yourself over it. My mission was classified, known only to the headmaster. I'm sorry for all the secrecy. I hope you can look past it."

"It's behind us," Avery said with a forgiving smile, then leaned in for a kiss.

Alarm bells were going off like crazy in Lucien's mind. He had feelings for the woman, a strong desire to shield her from all harm, including the dangers that came with his own life as a knight, surrounded by foes on every side.

He gently pulled away from Avery and stared into the distance, avoiding her gaze. "We should make a move before Lóthurr decides he wants more from us to ensure your safety," he suggested, his voice fading.

"So, where are we headed?" her voice carried a hint of disappointment.

"To my place," he reluctantly admitted. It was the only safe haven for her, under the Order's protection, where vampires feared to tread.

"I really don't like that old church; it's creepy," Avery said with a forced laugh.

"It's our only option. I need to dive into some research, and you're involved now. We can't risk Lóthurr using you against me," Lucien explained, firm yet gentle.

Resigned, she agreed. "Let's go."

Their drive was unusually silent, a stark contrast to Avery's typically vibrant chatter.

Arriving at the Old Church, Avery visibly tensed but followed Lucien inside. Despite its eerie exterior, the interior was a beautifully preserved piece of history.

Feeling compelled to explain, Lucien shared, "This place is a family legacy. Not my first choice, but it's ours." His tone was laced with nostalgia in such a personal space with someone other than family stirred emotions he'd long suppressed.

"I would love to see you guys do Christmas together," Avery blurted.

Avery's casual mention of family holidays elicited a bittersweet smile from Lucien. "You wouldn't have enjoyed it," he reflected. "It was all about duty over warmth. But you know, family isn't something you choose."

Her comment on Christmas evoked memories of longing for a sense of belonging and joy, something his duty-focused family seldom provided. Only his sister remained as a beacon of familial love.

Trying to shake off those thoughts, Lucien suggested, "Let's not linger. School tomorrow, remember?"

"Don't tell me the big bad knight is afraid of the headteacher," Avery teased him.

Avery's casual comment elicited a weary eye roll from Lucien. Keeping a distance was crucial, especially after their recent intimate moment. He did not expect to become so emotionally invested in her, and now it felt uncomfortably natural.

Watching her in the present moment, Lucien couldn't deny his attraction. Avery's authenticity, her laughter, her openness—each aspect of her stirred a desire within him that he hadn't foreseen.

Yet, the dread of surrendering control, of succumbing to his desires, was daunting. Yielding to his emotions for Avery could unravel everything he believed in. Investigating Roslyn was now intertwined with navigating his feelings, complicating his mission. "Fear isn't part of my vocabulary," Lucien stated, partly to reassure Avery, partly to affirm his own resolve. "Let's focus on why we're here."

CHAPTER 4

Avery left just before eleven, leaving Lucien poring over his computer, searching for leads on the Manual of Demonic Magic's location. After numerous online searches, he stumbled upon a hint. He needed to confront a particularly troublesome vampire clan leader whose ancestors reportedly had the manuscript a hundred years back. The book was mentioned briefly in the records, then vanished without further details.

He arranged a rendezvous for later that night in the local cemetery, conveniently close to where he was staying.

Anyone concerned for their wellbeing, or just plain sensible, might have armed themselves with holy water or an amulet charged with protective magic. Lucien, however, deemed the elderly vampire no real danger, viewing the encounter as merely a formal meeting. He figured as long as he didn't provoke the vampire, he'd walk away unharmed.

Lucien made his way along the narrow path leading to the cemetery's edge, carrying his demon-slaying Katana. This weapon, a gift from his father on his nineteenth birthday, was believed to be Oshigata, once wielded by the legendary Japanese warlord Oda Nobunaga. The sword was enchanted with a unique form of black magic capable of ensnaring demons upon contact. A mere scratch on a demon-possessed human with this blade could transfer the demon inside it. Its insatiable appetite for the souls of the damned made Lucien unparalleled in his field.

The cemetery was eerily quiet, devoid of the usual nighttime sounds like the flutter of bats or distant barking dogs. The air was motionless. Lucien couldn't shake off the feeling that something was amiss. A chill of apprehension crept up his spine, and he fought to control his rising panic. As a knight, he knew the importance of composure; any sign of fear could betray his presence to lurking dangers.

"Look who we have here, our very own knight," came a voice, as a figure stepped out from the shadow of a tomb.

Bathed in moonlight, the figure's ghostly pallor stood out starkly. Though his appearance was unnerving, the man's wavy dark hair, piercing blue eyes, and strikingly red lips lent him an air of eerie attractiveness.

"Count Alec de Rosier, I appreciate you making time for this meeting," Lucien greeted, trying to gauge the supernatural. Despite his otherworldly presence, the Count didn't immediately appear notably menacing to him.

"It's my pleasure to assist a member of the Order of the Dragon. How have you been finding our little town?" the vampire enquired, his manner almost overly cordial.

Lucien sensed a layer of deceit beneath the Count's gracious facade.

"Thank you. Everything's been great. Now, regarding why I asked to meet..." Lucien began.

"Ah, right to the point. Your English father would have been proud. You're just like him. But thanks to your French mother's influence, there's still a bit of France in you, Monsieur de Winter," the Count mused.

"You overlook a critical detail, Count de Rosier. I'm related to the infamous Prince Vlad of Wallachia. Don't provoke me further, or I won't hesitate to end you for dishonouring my heritage. Despite the historic animosity between our countries, I choose to rise above it."

"A test, my dear knight." The Count quickly backtracked, his gaze sharpening as he smiled, revealing his fangs.

"Enough with the theatrics. Are you going to help me or not?" Lucien pressed, frustration mounting. He had no time for the Count's evasive manoeuvres.

"Regrettably, I cannot assist. The artefact you seek was sold many years ago," the Count confessed.

"To whom?"

"That is not information for your ears. But I can let you in on another little secret. The Order has decreed that you become one of us." The supernatural laughed.

As soon as he finished talking, what seemed like hundreds of vampires started walking out of the shadows.

"The organisation will hear of this," Lucien hissed. There were way too many, and his sword did not affect their kind. They would heal before significant damage was done. Even if he cut off the heads of one or two, he would soon be overwhelmed. That was what he got for being too trusting.

"And when they do, it will be too late. You'll no longer be a knight of the Order; you will have become a creature of the night, like the very monsters you hunt."

A sudden blow to the head knocked Lucien out cold.

LUCIEN REGAINED CONSCIOUSNESS HOURS LATER, SPRAWLED across the stone floor of a decrepit mausoleum. Brushing off the layers of dust and cobwebs clinging to him, he seethed with anger, promising retribution.

Struggling to rise, he felt an overwhelming weakness. A sudden, dreadful realisation struck him, and he inspected his neck, discovering two small puncture wounds near his jugular.

This is bad.

"Damn it! That idiot wasn't bluffing," Lucien cursed under his breath.

Had he remained unconscious for much longer, the marks would have vanished, leaving him oblivious until an insatiable thirst for blood revealed the truth. Thankfully, he'd awakened in time to understand his peril.

After pausing to gather his strength, Lucien tried standing again. He estimated he had a few hours until dawn to make it back to the safety of the church. While sunlight didn't reduce vampires to ashes as myths suggested, it caused severe burns and agony—a fate he had no intention of testing first-hand.

Rushing home, Lucien was determined not to succumb to his newfound nature. He resolved not to feed; his lineage might trace back to Prince Vlad, but he didn't inherit the infamous Dracula's thirst.

Rumours about Dracula's fate were varied—some believed he was slain, others speculated he descended into madness, and a few fancied he found true love and vanished. Regardless, Lucien refused to embrace the darkness.

He understood the transformation required a significant

amount of blood, often leaving the donor on the brink of death. Survivors were rare, and Lucien wasn't eager to gamble.

Finally steadying himself, he took one painstaking step, then another, cursing his slow progress. Surviving this ordeal, he vowed vengeance against Alec. No matter the vampire's ancient lineage, he had signed his death warrant.

The urgency to locate the Manual of Demonic Magic had never been clearer. If the prospect of saving another's life wasn't motivation enough, preserving his own certainly was. Now the test subject for reversing the curse, Lucien faced a grim outlook. His quest might well end in his own demise.

Feeling like he'd been trudging for an eternity, Lucien finally made it back. He slipped through his door just as the first rays of sunlight began to kiss the grass.

With leaden steps, he moved to his room, swiftly closing all the curtains to block out any slivers of daylight. Curiosity led him to grab a handheld mirror from the dresser, eager yet apprehensive to inspect the vampire's craftsmanship. The reflection that greeted him was a shadow of his former self—his complexion ashen, his eyes dimmed of their usual vitality, his lips a stark, unnatural red against his pallid skin, and small fangs peeking out among his teeth.

Tears welled up, spilling over as he hurled the mirror against the wall, where it shattered, fragments scattering across the floor.

Time dragged on, and Lucien remained cloistered in his room, lost in thought, until the shrill ring of the phone cut through the silence. Wiping away his tears, he answered.

"Hey, Avery. How's it going?"

"I'm fine, thanks. And you? You skipped school today. Everything all right?" Avery's voice was laden with questions, her curiosity unyielding.

"Yeah, I'm just not feeling up to par today. I'll catch up with you in a bit," Lucien managed to say, realising he needed to keep his distance lest she become the first to suffer his newfound thirst.

"What's happening, Lucien? We had plans to research together. Are you ditching me now?"

Lucien sighed, irritation mounting. "Look, Avery, I've caught a cold. You're not planning to play nurse, are you?" he joked half-heartedly.

"Stop hiding, Lucien de Winter. I'm coming over."

"I told you to stay away," he replied, his voice icy.

"It's too late for that. We're in this together, remember? We need to find that book."

"The door's open. I'll be in the library," Lucien conceded before hanging up.

Reluctantly, he made his way downstairs, lighting candles to bathe the chamber in a forgiving gloom, hoping it would mask his altered appearance.

He positioned himself behind his desk, an imposing mahogany piece adorned with Celtic designs, surrounded by towering stacks of books and papers. Feeling decades older than when Avery last saw him, he braced for her arrival, dreading and expecting it in equal measure.

When Avery entered the chamber, Lucien gulped. The scent of her blood was exhilarating. Now he understood why newly turned vampires always killed their first victim in a frenzy. For the first time in his life, he was happy he had developed his self-discipline. It took a lot of willpower not to act on his impulses and pounce on her.

Tightening his fists to suppress the craving, he was besieged by images of himself pressing Avery against the flowery wallpaper of the library. His gaze raked over her hungrily. He remained motionless, fixating on her eyes, tantalizing her with anticipation. As she drew closer, he shut his eyes and breathed in her fragrance. She exuded the scents of raspberry, roses, and vanilla, which he found irresistible. Lowering himself, he captured her soft lips.

Lucien let out a frustrated sigh, trying in vain to banish the troublesome thoughts swirling in his mind. Avery's presence promised nothing but complications.

"Do you want the lights on?" Avery's voice came from the doorway, tentative.

"Keep them off. Just find a spot and start looking around, but don't disturb me. Time's running out, and I need to concentrate," he said, his voice strained, fighting to maintain control.

"You seem off. Didn't you get any rest? You look exhausted. About last night..."

Inviting her here was clearly a lapse in judgment. Fielding her barrage of questions was one thing, but suppressing his newfound, darker urges around her was another battle entirely. His gaze involuntarily drifted from her lips to the pulsing vein in her neck, torn between desire and a thirst he dared not quench.

"Avery." He cut her off sharply. "This was a mistake. You shouldn't be involved in this mess. It's best you return to your normal life and forget everything you've witnessed."

His hand trembled uncontrollably; he quickly hid it, hoping she hadn't noticed.

"I want answers," she demanded, brushing off his attempt to dismiss her.

"Why should I explain anything? This is my house, and

you're practically a stranger. Our kiss changes nothing," he snapped back, his tone harsher than intended.

"Why are you acting like this? Yesterday, we were allies, and you promised to protect me. Now, suddenly, you're pushing me away. Remember, my safety is on the line here," Avery countered, stepping closer to his desk.

Lucien kept his gaze fixed on the open pages before him, deliberately avoiding eye contact. He feared his resolve would crumble if he looked at her directly.

Yet, she continued to approach him.

"Halt. I've already asked you to sit down and leave me be if you insist on staying," he uttered, his voice tinged with irritation.

"And why is that? I don't see any reason for your coldness."

"This is the reason!" In a swift motion, he pushed the books aside, clenched his fists, and slammed them down on the desk before finally raising his head to reveal his changed visage. "This! Are you happy now? They've turned me into a monster. Is this the moment you run scared?" His laugh was bitter, filled with despair.

"I will not run. I've been drawn to you since the day you arrived at the academy. Your being a knight, or now, a vampire, changes nothing for me," she declared, standing dangerously close.

He silently pleaded with her to keep her distance.

"Perhaps you should consider returning to Roslyn. Who's to guarantee I won't cause you harm? I could easily overpower you, leaving you on the brink of death, only to resurrect you as one of my kind, binding you to me eternally. Would that please you?"

The turmoil within him intensified. His new vampiric instincts twisted his fondness for her into a dark craving. Her presence wasn't just tantalising; it was maddening. Why did she have to be so obstinate?

"Finding that manuscript Lóthurr spoke of might revert you to your former self," Avery murmured, her face inches from his, her breath warm against his skin.

He looked at her profile once again. She seemed unmoved by his speech or even his threat. He wanted to believe she would help, but his mind kept wandering to the fact that if he allowed her to stay, there would be nobody to keep her safe from him. Why did Avery want to aid him even though they hardly knew each other?

Lucien's thoughts were a whirlwind of dark possibilities and desperate hopes. There was a part of him that toyed with the idea of drawing Avery into the shadowy embrace of his new existence. Together, they could vanish into the night, forever beyond the Order's reach, entwined in an eternal dance of darkness.

"Why does fear not touch you?" he whispered.

Avery stood her ground, her aura undimmed by the gloom surrounding them. "Because I see the man beneath the curse, Lucien. Your solitary path as a knight doesn't define you. My time at the academy has shown me the myriad shades of evil that lurk in our world, but you, you're not among them. You fight against it."

Frustration and resignation mingled in Lucien's gesture as he passed a hand through his hair. "Your faith in me is... misguided. Yet, should our quest fail, I face a grim deadline. I refuse to sustain myself on blood; I will not embrace my new nature."

"We'll find a way, Lucien. We must."

Time seemed to slow as Lucien's strength ebbed away, the call of the blood growing ever more insistent. Avery's presence, a beacon of warmth in the growing cold, tempted him with promises of forbidden sustenance. He cursed the fates that brought them to this precipice.

"Your being here is a risk," he finally admitted, the battle within him raging. "My hunger grows stronger by the moment."

"Then rest," Avery proposed, her voice a soothing balm. "Let me shoulder this burden for now."

He agreed, though the thought of leaning on her chafed against his pride. Lucien sighed, a sound heavy with the weight of unspoken fears. Perhaps this nightmarish chapter of their lives was not yet destined to close.

AVERY'S SUPPORT WAS BOTH A PHYSICAL AND EMOTIONAL cradle for Lucien as they navigated the short distance to his bedroom. Her pulse quickened with the closeness, a rare feeling of connection in their shadow-veiled existence bringing a sliver of warmth to the chill that had settled between them.

His room was a realm of its own, steeped in an ancient aura. The grandeur of the wooden four-poster bed, adorned with mysterious runes, the classic elegance of French furniture, and the ancient tapestries hanging on the walls spoke of a lineage touched by both nobility and the arcane.

With careful movements, Avery drew the curtains shut, banishing the last threads of light. She then assisted Lucien onto his bed, his form a stark contrast to the vibrant knight who had first crossed her path at the academy. Little had she imagined that their fates would intertwine so deeply.

"I'll be in the library, just a shout away. Rest now. I'll try to rustle up a sandwich later. Maybe you'll manage to eat," she offered, her voice laced with forced cheerfulness.

Lucien acknowledged her with a weary nod, his gaze averted, a silent testament to the turmoil within.

Avery hesitated beside the bed, the air thick with unspoken fears and wishes. She longed to offer words of solace, to weave a promise that all would be well, yet the truth of their situation weighed heavily on her tongue. The reality was that the fabric of their lives had been irrevocably altered. Even if they were to find salvation for Lucien, the shadow of his transformation would linger, marking him as a creature of night until a cure could be found.

CHAPTER 5

ONCE SECLUDED WITHIN THE LIBRARY'S HUSHED EMBRACE, Avery's cheeks became a canvas for the hot tears streaming down. Anger ignited within her gaze, blaming herself for their plight. If only she didn't ask him out, didn't act on her feelings, maybe he would've been safe.

Yet, wallowing in despair would serve no purpose for Lucien. Wiping away her tears, Avery resolved to avenge him and set about with renewed determination. Hours slipped by in a blur of relentless research, yielding no promising leads on the Manual of Demonic Magic or its elusive spells.

Lost in her pursuit, Avery suddenly remembered her promise of sustenance to Lucien. Hastening to the kitchen, she assembled a humble ham and cheese sandwich, a makeshift offering in their dire circumstances.

Returning to the bedroom with the meagre repast, Avery bathed the room in a soft, yellow glow. She hoped it would provide some solace to him in his weakened state.

She woke Lucien slowly from his slumber. "Hey, sleepyhead. How are you feeling?"

"Better," he responded, coughing.

Avery knew it was a lie. He looked worse than a few hours ago, but she decided not to call him out on it and instead poured him a glass of water.

"Here you go."

His trembling hands grasped the water, bringing it to his lips in a desperate gulp before turning to the plate. With a slow, deliberate motion, he sank his teeth into the sandwich, each bite seemingly an arduous task, etched with pain.

He was chewing so slowly on his food, and she worried he'd never swallow it. It was almost comical and clear that he couldn't stand the taste, yet in the weakness of his condition, he was still too polite to spit it out.

"I'm heading downstairs. Try to rest, okay? Call me if you need anything, and promise me you won't move around without my help."

He met her gaze and offered a weary sigh. "I'll do my best to behave. Don't worry."

As Avery descended the stairs back to the library, a whirlwind of emotions churned within her. She was driven by a fervent hope to save him, but beneath that hope lay a deep-seated fear. If her efforts failed, she would be left grappling with the devastating weight of his loss. It was a pain reminiscent of the void left by her mother's passing in her youth, a wound still tender despite the passage of time. Avery wasn't prepared to confront that anguish again—it felt almost selfish to redeem him for her own sake alone.

Avery's determination swelled within her, fuelled by an unwavering commitment to Lucien's well-being. An idea sparked in her mind, propelling her into action. With purposeful strides, she pushed open the door to the library and embarked on her quest.

Scanning the cluttered expanse of the room, her eyes

alighted upon Lucien's phone, nestled beneath a stack of weathered tomes. Without hesitation, she retrieved it and activated the screen, half-expecting to encounter a password prompt. To her surprise, the device yielded without resistance —apparently, Lucien was lax in safeguarding his privacy.

Fingers dancing across the screen, Avery navigated to his contacts, her heart pounding with anticipation. She located the entry for Lóthurr and pressed the call button.

After a few tense rings, the vampire's voice echoed through the receiver, a lifeline in their desperate hour.

"Hello? It's Avery."

"Ah, Avery. What brings you here unexpectedly? Is everything alright?" Lóthurr's voice, smooth and measured, resonated through.

"Not quite. We're facing a bit of a crisis. Lucien's been turned into a half-vampire, and he's refusing to drink blood."

"I see. And any progress on the manuscript?" Lóthurr enquired, his tone carrying a hint of curiosity.

"None, and we're running out of time to fix him," Avery confessed, her voice tinged with defeat. The vampire seemed their last hope for saving Lucien. She prayed he held some insight into restoring him to normalcy.

"That adds complexity. Do we have any information on who turned him?"

"No, but last night he met with a local vampire clan leader, and I suspect he's the culprit. I don't know who he is, but he'll pay for what he's done," Avery declared, her determination burning bright.

"Ah, that must be Alec. I have an idea. Meet me at the front gate in twenty minutes," he instructed.

"Understood. I'll see you then," Avery affirmed before ending the call. She hoped Lóthurr wouldn't deceive her; she knew all too well the treachery of his kind. Some vampires revelled in playing with their prey's minds, using powers that twisted reality itself.

Surveying the library, Avery sought a weapon, something to level the playing field. Her fists alone wouldn't be enough, no matter how skilled she was from her time at the academy.

Her gaze landed on a gold-clothed display, and she lifted the cover to reveal a Katana. The hilt, wrapped intricately in black, contrasted with the plain silver blade and ornate scabbard. As she touched the hilt, ancient runes glowed to life, revealing the weapon's storied past.

With the sword secured in its scabbard, Avery made her way to the property's gate, where Lóthurr awaited in a sleek Italian sports car. Though hesitant, she knew she had no choice but to trust him. After all, Lucien's life hung in the balance.

The vampire watched her with curiosity, his gaze lingering on the artefact at her side.

"Ah, hello, darling. Delighted you could join me," he greeted, his grin sending a shiver down her spine.

Avery wasted no time on niceties. "Let's cut to the chase. Where's that bastard?"

The Norseman's smile widened. "Ah, I see you've brought a companion." His eyes flicked to the artefact. "May I?" he asked, gesturing towards the weapon. "I'd like to confirm my suspicions."

Avery hesitated, uncertainty flickering in her eyes. But she sensed no malice in his request.

"You'll have it back soon. You'll need it for where we're headed," he assured her.

Slowly, she handed it over, watching as he examined the hilt with a mixture of curiosity and reverence.

"Katanas are rare treasures, but this one..." His voice trailed off, his expression turning thoughtful. "This one is different.

It's Mitsuhide's lost sword, said to house a dormant demon, waiting for its rightful wielder to awaken it. Truly remarkable."

Avery's smile was tinged with satisfaction. "Well, it definitely responded to my touch. Looks like we've got a mighty ally against Alec."

"Fascinating," the vampire murmured, handing back the weapon. "And where did you stumble upon this fortuitous find?"

"In Lucien's library, of all places," she replied, noting the intrigue in his eyes.

"Ah, fate works in mysterious ways. But enough about ancient relics. We've dallied here long enough. It's time to make our move."

With a press of a button, the engine hummed to life, and the vampire set the course. Time was of the essence, and they had a villain to confront.

"The energy of this artefact is remarkable," Lóthurr explained as they drove, his tone tinged with awe. "A mere slice from the sword releases the demon from its host, ending the possession. While some individuals may exhibit aggression, the blade absorbs their essence, gaining strength with each extraction. However, only its rightful owner can harness its complete power. Once it reached Lucien, it locked itself, rendering it inert to others."

Avery listened in silence, her mind reeling at the revelation of Lucien's latent abilities. She had underestimated him, unaware of the true extent of his abilities. Now, she carried the weight of responsibility for his fate, should they fail to reverse his vampiric transformation.

Their conversation was interrupted as the vehicle came to a stop, jolting Avery from her thoughts.

"We've arrived," Lóthurr announced.

"Finally," she breathed, relieved to leave the confines of the car.

The building in front of them seemed dilapidated, with broken windows and graffiti marring its facade. As they navigated through the deserted structure, Avery couldn't rid herself of the sense of unease.

Lóthurr guided them to the service entrance, moving with caution. "Wait here," the vampire instructed in a hushed tone. "I'll scout ahead. Stay quiet."

A tense silence filled the air as Avery waited, her nerves on edge. When Lóthurr returned, his report did little to ease her anxiety.

"There are only two guards, plus Alec," he whispered. "It seems deserted, but I can't sense dormant vampires. If they're here, we're in trouble."

Avery's resolve hardened. "Let's not waste any time, then. We need to move."

They crept through the kitchen door, their footsteps muffled by the dilapidated flooring. As they traversed the corridor towards their targets, Avery couldn't help but marvel at the building's former grandeur. What was once a majestic hotel now lay in ruins, a shadow of its former self. Antique furniture, gilded, still adorned the rooms, while brocade curtains fluttered in the drafty corridors. Beautiful paintings adorned the walls, their once-vibrant colours now faded with age, and towering East Asian vases added to the opulent ambiance.

"Before it was a hotel, this place was a lord's mansion," Lóthurr whispered, his voice barely audible.

They reached the entrance of the drawing room unnoticed. The double French doors stood open, inviting them into the heart of their enemy's lair.

"Hey, Alec! You owe me, and I came to collect," Avery said.

"Oh, hello." Alec grinned. "And what might that be?"

"Your head on a spike." Avery retorted.

"Little girl, you're deluding yourself if you think you'll get out of here alive," he said to her, then turned to his men. "Kill them! Don't let them escape."

The two vampires guarding Alec lunged at Avery and Lóthurr, their movements swift and predatory. Lóthurr's excitement was palpable, a low growl rumbling in his throat.

With a determined expression, Avery drew her Katana from its scabbard, the blade glowing with an otherworldly light. The dormant demon within the sword had awakened, pulsing with dark energy. She smirked, feeling the surge of power coursing through her veins. It was time to unleash her fury.

Spinning the weapon expertly in her hand, Avery locked eyes with Lóthurr, silently conveying her readiness for the impending battle. With a nod of approval from the vampire, she steeled herself for the confrontation ahead.

As one of the henchmen approached her, seemingly unfazed by her diminutive stature, Avery's rage boiled within her. With a swift motion, she hurled the sword towards her assailant, aiming for a lethal strike. He dodged at the last moment, narrowly avoiding the deadly blow as the blade sliced through the air with a whistle.

Undeterred, her opponent retrieved a claymore from the wall, brandishing it menacingly. Though the weapon appeared aged and worn, Avery knew better than to underestimate her adversary. With precision and skill, she prepared to face the impending clash, her resolve unyielding despite the odds stacked against her.

The clash of weapons echoed through the room as Avery

and her enemy engaged in a deadly dance of steel. Each movement was calculated, each strike met with a swift parry. Thrust, parry, thrust, parry—the rhythm of battle pulsed through the atmosphere.

Avery, with a sharp eye, identified her chance—a sofa nestled in the room's corner.

Without a moment's hesitation, she dashed towards it, leveraging the springs to propel herself into the air with a forceful leap. As her adversary prepared for the impact, she sailed over his head, landing gracefully behind him.

In one fluid motion, Avery swung her Katana with precision, severing her opponent's head from his shoulders. The head thudded to the floor, rolling ominously towards Alec, who watched in horror.

Meanwhile, Lóthurr dispatched his adversary with brutal efficiency, tearing through the soft tissue beneath the ribcage and extracting the vampire's heart with a swift motion.

With Alec now cornered, terror etched across his face, Lóthurr swiftly subdued him, pinning him to the ground with his formidable strength. Within moments, they had secured Alec to a heavy wooden chair using chains dipped in holy water—an agonising restraint for any vampire.

As they prepared to interrogate him, Avery's grip tightened on her weapon, her knuckles white with tension. The demon sword pulsated with dark energy, its presence a potent reminder of the vengeance they sought. Alec would pay for the harm he had inflicted, and Avery was determined to ensure justice was served.

"I will give you one chance to live," she stated. "One lie, and you're dead."

Avery raised her Katana, swiftly cutting the side of his cheek to demonstrate her seriousness. The blade, razor-sharp, caused blood to trickle from the wound.

The count tried to heal the injury, but it was useless. The wound wouldn't close.

Avery smirked. "Oh, I didn't tell you? This is a special sword. I can hack at you all day at my own leisure."

She sliced at him again, this time on top of his shoulder, cutting through his cartilage and making his shirt sleeve come loose.

"Bitch!" the prisoner screamed.

"Tell me. Why did you attack Lucien and try to turn him into one of you?"

"This is bigger than you think. You've got no part in the supernatural wars." He smirked.

"Say it! Who put you up to it?"

Silence.

One slash. Two slashes. These were deeper than the others. More blood oozed from the vampire. He had to give up something meaningful, or this trip ended up another dead end.

This creature needed the right amount of persuasion and pain. He didn't become a clan leader for no reason. His wounds had to be exceptional, and who was better qualified to inflict such pain than an Order of the Dragon academy trainee with a demon-possessed weapon?

"I've got all day. When I finally kill you, you'll have nightmares about me in Hell," she threatened her prisoner.

As Avery continued to interrogate Alec, she noticed Lóthurr lounging on a massive sofa nearby. His demeanour was relaxed as he observed the scene unfolding before him. His apparent enjoyment of the spectacle only fuelled her determination to extract the information they needed.

Yet, despite Avery's relentless questioning, Alec remained stubbornly silent. It was clear that more drastic measures were required. With a steely resolve, Avery drove her sword straight through Alec's chest, the blade piercing one of his lungs with a sickening thud.

Alec gasped in agony as blood began to fill his lungs, a sensation that would soon become unbearable, even for a vampire. Though they had minutes at most before the pain overwhelmed him, Avery was confident that the threat of such excruciating torment would finally break his resolve.

"Enough!" Alec gasped, struggling to talk. "I will tell you all you want. The Order wants him dead. He's too smart for his own good, too skilled in battle; they couldn't kill him on his previous assignments."

"Where's the manuscript? Speak, or I'll end you right now!" she threatened.

"In the desk behind me," he wheezed. "I have the key around my neck. But you're mistaken. There's no cure for a vampire in it. Do you think I haven't checked?" His body convulsed with pain. Avery swiftly retrieved the key from him, then swung her Katana, a smile gracing her lips as she severed his head from his body.

Lóthurr gazed at her, his surprise evident.

"What? Did you expect me to show mercy?" She wished he would provoke her further. After all, he bore some responsibility for Lucien's fate.

"Let's go. Lucien doesn't have long," she reminded the Norseman.

They hurried to the entrance of the underground parking lot, the tension thick in the air, each step echoing their silent dread. Avery's stomach churned with a sickening mix of adrenaline and regret, her body recoiling from the violent acts they'd just committed. She leaned against the cold concrete wall, trying to steady her trembling legs as the rush of combat faded away. The aftermath of the battle left a bitter taste in her mouth, a reminder of the choices they were forced to make in the name of survival.

Leaning into the shadows, Avery wrestled with the turmoil raging within her. She had never imagined herself capable of such brutality, yet the fight for Lucien's life demanded sacrifices she never thought possible. As the reality of their actions sank in, she couldn't shake the feeling of guilt gnawing at her conscience. What kind of person did it make her, to resort to violence in the name of saving a friend?

The journey back was shrouded in silence, each passing moment weighed down by the weight of their deeds. Avery couldn't help but wonder if Lucien would ever forgive her for the choices she'd made on his behalf. Would he understand the lengths she'd gone to in order to keep him alive, even if it meant condemning him to a fate he never wanted?

Upon arriving at their destination, Lóthurr broke the oppressive silence, his voice offering comfort to Avery's troubled thoughts. "I understand your concerns," he spoke, his words steeped in the wisdom of centuries. "You fear he may resent you for your actions. But in times of survival, sacrifices are inevitable. We do what is necessary to shield those we cherish, even if it means confronting choices we never imagined making."

His reassurance offered a glimmer of comfort amidst the darkness, signalling to Avery that the journey to redemption often required difficult choices and sacrifices. She nodded, grateful for the support his presence offered. In that moment, they could only press forward, trusting that their actions would eventually reveal the answers they sought.

"We've been gone for a few hours. You'll find him in a rough state," Lóthurr cautioned, his voice weighted with concern. "I wish I could be there to restrain him, but my presence might trigger him. You don't want to take that risk.

Feed him your blood and make him immortal. It'll buy him some time while we dive into the depths of that book."

Avery absorbed his words in silence, her mind already racing with the weight of their impending reunion. With a nod, she stepped out of the car, the chill of the night air wrapping around her like a cloak. "You know I'm holding onto the book until I find a solution," she stated firmly, her gaze unwavering.

"Fair enough," the vampire replied, his tone resigned. "I'll know where to find it if I need it. But for now, I'll bask in the luxury of my current state."

With a last nod, Avery turned towards the looming building before her, determination burning brightly in her eyes. As she pushed open the heavy wooden door, a sense of purpose settled over her, driving her forward into the unknown.

AVERY HURRIED TO LUCIEN'S BEDROOM, HER HEART pounding with worry, only to find it empty. Panic clawed at her chest as she raced through the halls, her footsteps echoing off the cold stone floors. Finally, she burst into the library, where her eyes fell upon the sight of Lucien collapsed on the Persian rug, his pallor ghostly against the vibrant hues of the carpet.

"Wake up!" she said as she knelt on the floor to hold him.

Lucien's eyes flickered open, the glint of a predator shining in their depths as he tightened his grip around Avery, holding her captive against his chest. She squirmed and writhed in his grasp, but his hold remained unyielding.

With a resigned acceptance, Lucien leaned in, his breath hot against Avery's skin as he tilted her head to the side, baring her delicate neck. His newly formed fangs gleamed in the dim light, their edges not yet honed to razor-sharpness. Nevertheless, with gentle pressure, he pierced her skin, drawing forth a trickle of crimson.

As the ruby-red liquid dripped down her pale skin, Lucien held Avery tighter against him, his hunger insatiable as he drank deeply from her veins. With each swallow, her life force ebbed away, her breaths growing shallow as the world around her blurred and dimmed. Despite her weakening state, she clung to consciousness, the edges of her vision fading into darkness.

"It's okay... If you get to live, everything will be fine," she whispered to him in shallow breaths.

As Avery closed her eyelids, she slipped into a dream, finding herself in the presence of her mother, ethereal and radiant in flowing white. The sight brought a flood of longing and warmth, a bittersweet reunion in the realm of dreams.

A single tear escaped her and landed upon Lucien's skin, stirring him from his consuming thirst and anchoring him in the present, pulling him back from the brink of his relentless hunger.

LUCIEN'S HEART WAS SEIZED BY PANIC, A SUDDEN RUSH OF fear and regret surging through him. With a start, he pulled away from Avery, a profound sense of horror flooding him as he comprehended the magnitude of his actions.

"Why did you come back?" he cried.

As Lucien assessed Avery's condition, a surge of guilt and desperation overwhelmed him. If he had caused her harm, he would never forgive himself. His stubborn refusal to embrace his fate as a vampire had placed her in this perilous situation.

Feeling her weak pulse, Lucien knew they couldn't afford to waste time. The hospital was too far, and Avery needed blood urgently. With a determined resolve, he bit into his wrist, allowing his blood to flow freely. It wasn't a cure, but it might buy her enough time to survive.

As her breathing began to steady, Lucien carefully lifted her limp body and carried her to his bedroom. He laid her down on the bed, tenderly tucking her in, his heart heavy with worry.

As she slept peacefully, Lucien vowed to do whatever it took to ensure her recovery. Avery was his world, along with his sister, and he couldn't bear to lose her now.

He gathered her small hand in his and knelt on the floor. He was about to do something he hadn't done in what felt like an eternity. The vampire knight was going to pray to any gods willing to listen.

CHAPTER 6

As Lucien kept a vigilant watch over Avery, his worry deepened with each passing day. He couldn't shake the fear that her condition might take a turn for the worse. Checking on her regularly became his solemn duty, a task he approached with both trepidation and determination.

Today found him once again at her bedside, kneeling in silent prayer. Though uncertain if the divine would heed his plea for a supernatural creature like himself, he couldn't help but cling to a glimmer of hope. Avery's life hung in the balance, and he would do anything to ensure her survival. For he had come to realise that she was more than just a companion—she was the very essence of his newfound existence.

Despite the whirlwind of questions and frustrations she introduced into his life, Lucien couldn't ignore the profound impact she had on him. Her vibrant spirit had infused new meaning into his world, and having experienced the sweetness of her presence, he dreaded the idea of losing her.

As Avery's eyelids fluttered open, a wave of relief swept

over Lucien. His prayers had been answered, and she was emerging from her slumber. However, beneath the surface of his joy, a lingering sense of unease persisted. Despite the miraculous turn of events, he couldn't dispel the feeling of impending dread gnawing at his soul.

"Hey, sleeping beauty. How are you feeling?" he asked, smiling.

"You're alive."

The vampire reached out and caressed her cheek. "All thanks to you, but you scared me half to death. I thought I'd lost you there when I'd finally come to my senses." He stared into her beautiful eyes. "Please don't do anything this stupid ever again."

"That was the only option. I was fresh out of humans to sacrifice." She laughed.

Lucien rolled his eyes. "Well, you've got your sense of humour, so I guess you're fine. I should stay cross with you for a few days since you turned me into a vampire without my permission, but that seems like a lot of hassle."

"There's no time for that. I'm alive; you're still here. I found the book, though. We've got so much work to do."

"How did you get it?" Lucien asked.

"I panicked when you took a turn for the worse, so I reached out to Lóthurr using your phone. Together, we paid Alec a visit at his den of darkness, and let's just say, we had a little chat with him. Well, I did most of the talking... with the help of one of your trusty swords. Lóthurr seemed to find it rather amusing. He's got a twisted sense of enjoyment, that one. Speaking of which, about that sword you had tucked away in the library..."

"The one belonging to Mitsuhide?" Lucien interjected.

"Yeah. It practically hummed with energy when I laid my hands on it. So, I figured I'd put it to good use in persuading

Alec to spill the beans. After all, he won't be needing that manuscript where he's headed. Karma caught up with him. I couldn't let him walk away after what he did to you."

"Ah, that's my girl," Lucien chuckled, a touch of pride evident in his tone. "I wouldn't have expected anything less from you."

Avery hesitated, her expression growing serious. "Before he met his end, Alec said something that's been weighing on my mind."

"What was that?" Lucien asked, his voice tight with tension.

"He said someone in the Order wants you dead. I'm thinking killing you as a vampire and saying you got out of hand would raise fewer eyebrows than murdering you as a human."

"That makes sense. I need to finish my investigation at the school and then come to an agreement with my superiors before they decide to end me. The Order has never had a vampire member. I will need your help. And possibly the help of one of my ancestors. They will need persuasion."

"You mean Prince Vlad? Is he still alive?" Avery asked, a hint of awe in her voice.

"I have a suspicion he is. Most likely pretending to be someone else somewhere in Europe. Having read so much about him, I can say with confidence that I understand his behaviour, and with that, we have a good chance of finding him."

"Do you think he will help?"

"I'd like to think so. The family stories paint him as a figure of justice. He defended Wallachia against the Turks numerous times. But in his final battle, fortune abandoned him. His army fell, and he was captured. His castle was besieged, his wife trapped inside. She chose to end her life rather than face capture, plunging into the river below. It's said that the Prince was so consumed by grief, he struck a deal with the Devil. That's how the first vampire came to be. In exchange for immortality, he sent countless Turkish souls to Hell. Once the pact was made, he vanished from the Order of the Dragon, appearing only in sporadic sightings throughout the ages."

"I would like to meet him someday. He sounds intriguing. If one can bargain with the Devil out of love..." Avery trailed off, her smile hinting at curiosity.

"That individual can bend reality to their will, and I believe the organisation fears that," Lucien responded with a knowing grin. "There's something I've been meaning to ask you."

"What is that?" the girl asked, her interest piqued.

"What about that date?" Lucien laughed.

"You're deluded if you think I'm going to..."

Lucien interrupted Avery's words with a tender kiss, a surge of magic coursing through him. When he pulled away, a smile played on his lips.

"There's no use denying it," he began, his voice soft yet resolute. "You've risked everything for me, and I'm deeply grateful. But there's more to it. I love you, Avery. I've loved you since the moment I laid eyes on you. Will you join me in hunting demons and seeking out the Prince? It may be the only way for me to survive. Once the Order learns of my transformation, they won't take it lightly."

"Well, since you put it that way, I have no choice." She smiled. "I love you too, and I have loved you since the first moment I saw you outside the office. You had this energy about you that pulled me in, and then I realised there would be no escape for me," Avery answered, drawing him in for another kiss.

"It seems destiny has been at work," Lucien mused, his tone tinged with wonder. "I stumbled upon your sword during a vampire raid. It was in the lair of a clan leader. Despite having eliminated everyone, I was drawn to his office by some inexplicable force. I grabbed the sword without understanding why, lost in a daze. Back home, I placed it in the display cabinet, and that's when clarity struck. Through research, I learned its significance—a relic tied to Nobunaga and Mitsuhide, once inseparable allies. It must carry an ancient curse."

"I like that notion of fate," Avery replied, a glimmer of determination in her eyes. "Let's honour their legacy and forge our own path. We need to uncover who ordered your demise within the Order's ranks. Such a command could only come from the highest echelons. A mere recruit wouldn't possess such insight."

CHAPTER 7

LOCATING DRACULA REQUIRED SOME EXTENSIVE RESEARCH, and the last few weeks had been gruelling. Luckily, Lucien was now a creature of the night and didn't require sleep, only the occasional feeding. Avery had been gracious to offer to help him, but it was taking a toll on her health.

Lucien felt terrible about it. He loved her and would do anything in his power to keep her out of harm's way. He had to find other sources of sustenance.

He'd found records of the Wallachian ruler in a castle's archive in Romania. It wasn't much to go on, but he was confident it would lead them closer to him. Unfortunately, the only way to inspect the documents was to travel there. The officials refused to scan the old papers and send them over.

Lucien rummaged through a drawer, retrieving a passport issued under one of his clandestine aliases, unknown to the Order. He couldn't risk travelling with an identity that might lead back to him. Precautions were essential to evade detection by his employers.

With his new identity secured, he proceeded to book his

flight online. Regrettably, he had to leave Avery behind; her condition had worsened since he first fed on her blood, a reaction that remained unexplained.

To ensure Avery's care in his absence, Lucien had arranged for a woman to tend to her. The hired help had arrived the day prior, easing his worries about leaving her alone.

After preparing for the imminent journey, Lucien made his way to check on Avery, who was currently resting in their bedroom. The notion made him blush; the room had become theirs over the past few weeks, filled with shared moments and intimate embraces. Leaving her behind tugged at his heartstrings, knowing he would miss her dearly.

He cautiously pushed the door to the chamber ajar and entered. The brocade curtains were drawn shut, their thick fabric effectively blocking out the external light. Within the chamber, only a solitary candle flickered, casting dim illumination that allowed Avery some visibility as she navigated the space.

She slept peacefully, an epitome of serenity and beauty. Lucien couldn't shake the feeling of being undeserving of her company. Avery seemed like an ethereal being sent from above to bless his life. Regardless of the challenges awaiting them, he was confident she would remain steadfast by his side, offering unwavering support.

Taking a seat on the edge of the bed, he watched over her, cherishing this quiet moment before his departure.

"Hey. I came to check on you," he whispered.

"Hey." Avery sat up slightly, propped up by her pillows. "Where are you going?"

"We talked about this yesterday, baby." The reaction was making her memory fuzzy. He hoped that she would improve in his absence. "I have to travel to follow a lead."

"Oh, I'm sorry," she added.

"It's okay. You don't have to apologise. You'll get better soon, I promise."

"I know."

Lucien stayed a moment longer, his gaze lingering on Avery's face. He wanted to imprint her image in his mind, to carry her with him wherever he went. She was his anchor, his reason for fighting, for clinging to life amidst the encroaching darkness.

Deep down, he knew that once the Order discovered his true nature, they would brand him a traitor and hunt him down without mercy. Vampires were unwelcome within their ranks, considered abominations to be eradicated.

While he had informed Avery that he needed to persuade them to allow him to retain his job, the reality was much graver.

As he reluctantly rose from the bed, whispering a silent prayer, a solitary tear trickled down his cheek, quietly acknowledging the heaviness of his burden and the fear consuming his heart.

He fought back the tears, refusing to let Avery witness his vulnerability. *Damn it!* This trip felt like stepping into a lion's den, navigating through unknown territories fraught with danger. The Order's watchful eye could be lurking around any corner, ready to pounce at the slightest misstep. But his very existence, and the prospect of a future with the woman who held his heart, hung in the balance.

CHAPTER 8

As the plane ascended into the sky, Lucien's thoughts were consumed by anticipation and uncertainty. The familiar drone of the engines provided a steady backdrop to his restless mind. Sitting by the window, he gazed out at the sprawling landscape below, gradually transitioning from the urban hustle of the United Kingdom to the serene beauty of the European countryside.

The flight was a blur of fleeting glimpses, each passing moment carrying him further from familiarity and deeper into the heart of the unknown. Through the window, he watched as the landscape transformed beneath him, from the patchwork fields of England to the majestic peaks of the Alps, their snow-capped summits glistening in the sunlight.

Hours passed in a haze of anticipation and apprehension, the monotony of the journey broken only by the occasional announcement from the flight crew. Lucien found himself lost in thought, his mind racing with questions and doubts. What would he find in Romania? Would his search for Dracula yield any answers, or would it only lead to more questions?

As the plane began its descent towards Sibiu, Lucien's heart quickened with a mix of excitement and trepidation. Below him, he caught glimpses of the rugged Carpathian Mountains, their ancient peaks shrouded in mist.

Lucien's initial destination was Bran Castle, believed to be the place where the Prince may have stayed before vanishing.

Although historians would have argued that the ruler's imprisonment was somewhere in a castle in Budapest, Hungary, the knight had a distinct thought about it. He believed he had left behind breadcrumbs as to his existence.

During the past few weeks, Lucien practised walking outside in the daytime. He hired a driver for the two-hour trip to Bran, a little town in Brasov County. On his arrival, he was happy to see the sun had set. He was making progress on keeping a straight face when the sunlight hit his skin, although still in tremendous amounts of pain. That would not go away soon.

He paid the man handsomely and walked to a hotel nearby. It was a mansion like he'd never seen before. The exterior was an architectural masterpiece of Bavarian style, with traditional details inspired by the nobles' estates that used to live in the area hundreds of years past. High walls painted in a bright white, adorned with dark wooden beams that drew geometric patterns in contrast with its roof, made up of the most beautiful red tile. The interior was of a similar style, with eighteenth-century solid wood furniture.

Lucien chose this place not because of its history, but because of its closeness to the castle. It was only five minutes away on foot, which meant he had the freedom to explore the place and its surroundings.

Upon entering his room, Lucien shed his coat and shoes before lying on the bed. Since becoming a vampire, he no longer slept, but had devised a method to rejuvenate himself through meditation. As he engaged in his calming ritual, a sudden realisation struck him. Time was of the essence, especially for Avery's sake.

A knot formed in his throat as he grappled with the weight of responsibility. The burden of guilt weighed heavily on him. Cursing the Order and everything it represented, he feared the possibility of losing the woman he loved if he failed to locate the elusive Prince, let alone maintain his own existence. Dracula's whereabouts remained a mystery, adding to his sense of urgency and frustration.

The plan was to wait until the morning to do this search legitimately, but then it came to him—he was a supernatural creature of the night. He didn't need daylight to see and didn't care about anyone's permission to get inside.

He walked out of the hotel and climbed the east side of the castle, obscured by the forest, while taking advantage of the cover of darkness. Even for a vampire, scaling up the ancient building wasn't an easy feat. The wall was crumbly and unstable; one wrong move and he would end up alarming the guards.

Lucien got into the fortification and stopped in a corner of the old courtyard to assess his situation. No sound or movement was coming from the interior; the staff all went home for the night. The knight let out a deep breath. He was in the clear.

Lucien surveyed the surroundings, detecting nothing unusual. He stuck to the shadows, moving stealthily as he explored the area. Eventually, he halted and shut his eyes, pressing his hand against the wall. Instantly, he delved into the depths of the castle's history, absorbing every detail with his heightened senses.

To his surprise, the building was talking to him, revealing

its secrets. Flashes of the past came to life behind his closed eyelids, as if by magic.

A hooded figure carrying a small candlestick opened a heavy wooden door and came out of an ancient tower. He saw a blood moon against the darkness of the sky. As the stranger turned to close the door, the faint candlelight illuminated his features. Recognition filled the knight's heart, his blood drawing him to his ancestor.

Upon glimpsing the ruler's face, he realised his depiction in the portraits was an unjust one. He finally understood those were political tools meant to strengthen the way his subjects saw him. His people weren't meant to see their king as the handsome Prince with a pale complexion and pleasant countenance, but as the cruel ruler who made their worst nightmares come true.

Vlad stopped in front of the well. He pressed on a stone, and the sound of a mechanism turning echoed through the air. Lucien noticed the stones resonate with the noise as if he was there. The masonry shifted, creating a staircase that led into an underground chamber inside the well; the Prince disappeared into the darkness of the night.

The enchantment woven into the place maintained a strong hold on the knight, keeping his palm firmly affixed to the wall. Clearly, there was more to uncover.

Vlad appeared again in the courtyard, this time shackled. He was dressed in rags, his face dirty, badly bruised, and covered in blood. He was on his knees, crying, praying, and begging for his wife to be spared, but nobody listened to his pleas. Moments later, a soldier came out of a tower and started kicking him mercilessly.

"Shut up, you damned traitor!"

The Prince fell to the ground, but that didn't stop the

stranger. He continued striking him with vigour, unmoved by the prisoner's yelps.

"Please… tell me, where is she?" he asked.

"The bitch killed herself before we seized the castle. But you don't need to worry. You'll meet her in Hell soon."

The nobleman said nothing. In his mind, he was already dead; there was only one thing he could do, and that was to avenge the love of his life.

When the guard finally got bored with kicking him and left, he ignored the excruciating pain and propped himself up on his elbow. He took some blood from his forehead and started drawing sigils, which he remembered from an ancient manuscript.

When he was satisfied with his handiwork, he started reciting an incantation he never thought he would have to use and smiled through his pain. They would soon go through his agony. The Prince was ready to make a bargain with the Devil.

The actual war was just beginning.

CHAPTER 9

When the magic that corrupted the place loosened its grip on Lucien, he collapsed on the ground, drained. Never in his life had he been able to see the past without the aid of an artefact.

When he saw Vlad reduced to a mistreated prisoner, something snapped in him. Pain struck his breast. If only those people were still alive, he would teach them what it meant to mess with his kin.

Oh, how he wished he could travel back in time and teach them a lesson!

Lucien tried to calm his mind. He had a mission, and it had nothing to do with revenge. He had to find Vlad. With him, the Order would not stand a chance. He was going to make sure of that.

He slowly got up from the ground and walked to the well. Lucien closed his eyes and recalled the memory of the Prince when he entered the secret chamber. He pressed on the same stone; the masonry split in the middle, and a small set of stairs made its appearance.

The knight made his way down, using his phone as a torch. Although his sharp vampire vision didn't extend to noticing traps, he was sure his ancestor didn't leave the place unguarded. The tunnel ended abruptly, and a heavy wooden carved door was visible.

A sculpted masonry slab was part of the centre of the door, decorated with writings, various depictions of dragons, and the sun and moon. From what the knight could remember from ancient texts, these were elements of the coats of arms of both Vlad and his father. He was in the right place.

He touched the centrepiece, hoping that he could once again see the past and a way to open this safely, triggering none of the Prince's traps. He was right; behind his closed eyelids, another scene unfolded.

The ruler took a small, round trinket from his pocket and placed it in the sculpture's middle.

To his surprise, Lucien was already in possession of the key. When he turned nineteen, his father gave him a medallion that looked precisely like Vlad's bauble and told him this was a solution against the Order, should he ever need it. He'd wondered for months what his sire's words meant and kept the piece of jewellery around his neck, out of sight, covered by his clothes.

Lucien took the necklace out and looked at it one more time. A dragon eating his own tail stared back at him. This differed slightly from the Order's badge, which included a cross above the creature. Did the lack of it mean to highlight Dracula's pact with the unholy?

The knight shook his head to dispel the silly notions. He didn't have time to ponder on philosophical questions. His own life and Avery's were at stake.

He lifted the medallion and pressed it into its circular

housing in the door. It fit perfectly, but nothing happened. Was he supposed to do anything else?

His heart brimmed with frustration as Lucien sank to the cold, unforgiving floor, burying his face in his hands. He found himself before the most crucial lead he had encountered in weeks, yet he was at a loss on how to unlock the stubborn door. Time was of the essence; daylight would soon break, and the staff would surely uncover his intrusion.

He imagined trying to tell the authorities he was in search of their long-forgotten ruler. Yeah, that wouldn't go down well, no matter how he put it.

Lucien got up and pressed his palm once again over the door and key, hoping he could conjure the visions of the past. He took a deep breath and exhaled slowly. He could do it; it was a matter of tapping into his abilities. Powerful magic already surrounded the place; he just needed to let it fill his whole being.

The images returned, and Lucien learned the next steps required to unlock the secret chamber. He traced his ancestor's actions, pressing in the correct sequence on the dragons, the moon carving, and the tile with the motto that read Veritas. Virtus. Liberta. The heavy wooden door sprang open.

The knight entered the room and stopped a few feet from the doorway to admire his surroundings. He stepped back in time five hundred years, to the time when the Prince was still a human.

There were bookshelves on every wall of the chamber, filled with what must have been thousands of manuscripts of that time. A large wooden table with a chair was placed in the corner, bearing various papers scattered across the top in such a way that it appeared like the owner could come back to retrieve his possessions.

He grabbed the vellum sheets one by one and started

reading the contents of the documents. Luckily, they were written in Latin.

After inspecting several of the papers, Lucien found they were mainly orders that dated mere weeks before the disappearance of Vlad in December 1476. It was only when he got to the last document that he found the clue he'd been waiting for.

With a smile playing on his lips, Lucien tucked the parchment into his pocket. He retraced his steps out of the secret passage, back into the courtyard, and hastened to his hotel room. Time was of the essence; his next destination had been unveiled, leaving no room for delay.

As he walked back to the mansion, a stranger started following him. The knight stopped dead in his tracks and turned around to face the unknown pursuer. He crossed his arms and crooked his head, eyeing the hooded figure from head to toe. If this was a thief, he'd chosen the wrong person to steal from.

"You've got about ten seconds to turn on your heel and run. After that, you're fair game," he threatened the figure.

CHAPTER 10

A boisterous, unmistakable laugh resonated, sending a shiver down Lucien's spine. A sense of foreboding crept over him as the laughter filled the air.

"Is that any way to greet your one and only sister?" came the voice from beneath the hood, and with a dramatic flourish, the figure revealed herself.

Lucien emitted a frustrated growl at the sight.

"Return to the academy, Alessandra," he snapped. "Are you here to put me in danger? You know if the Order discovers I'm supernatural, it's over for me. I'm too much of a liability because of what I know about their operations."

"I'm here to assist, brother. Quit exaggerating," she retorted.

"I'm aware of your version of assistance. You'll aid them in locating me. You might as well have provided them with a map to my whereabouts," Lucien accused, his frustration clear. "Here's what we'll do: You're returning to Roslyn Academy. If anyone enquires, you didn't see me."

"And here I thought you'd changed. Grow up, brother. It's

not always up to you to save the day. Sometimes the Princess can lend a hand if the hero lets her," the woman chided with a sigh. "You're doomed to spend eternity with the same backward mentality our parents had. You're not here to protect me. I can look after myself, and I am more than capable of helping you figure this out. Whatever happens, I will always have your back. We are blood, after all."

"Fine," he conceded, releasing a deep breath. "If you impede my progress, I'll send you back home. Avery and I are counting on this. This is not a game."

"Deal. I won't be a hindrance," she confirmed with a smile. "Now that's settled, can you tell me where we're headed next? Did you find what you were searching for?"

"I found a clue or two. Depends on how you're looking at it. It seems the Prince purchased some real estate abroad before his disappearance."

"So, where is the trail leading us?"

"I have an approximate location near Blois, France. The Wallachian ruler bought a piece of land under an assumed name and commissioned a residence near the town," Lucien replied, excitement resounding in his voice. "When he fled the country, he took the name Crespin Chambord, Chevalier De Lyon, to fool the authorities and get the Order off his track."

He brought the parchment out of his pocket and showed it to his sister.

"I found his secret chamber at Bran Castle, untouched since he left it centuries ago. It was quite interesting to walk in his footsteps after all these years. Maybe when we're done with this mess, I'll come back one day and step through history again. This place has been enchanted. I witnessed a real time-slip."

"You know, it has always fascinated you. When you were

little, you used to..." Alessandra's voice trailed off as the vampire stopped dead in his tracks. "What's going on?"

"There are four knights right behind us, walking in wide formation. I can feel the reverberations beneath my feet," Lucien whispered, his voice tense with alertness.

"What gave them away?" she asked.

Lucien flashed a wry smile. "A knight always recognises others of his kind. Plus, it would have been too easy otherwise. I was expecting to run into trouble at some point. Do you have any weapons?"

"I may," she replied, a mischievous glint in her eyes. "You're so silly. Do you expect a woman to wander alone in a foreign country without anything to defend herself?" With a swift movement, she produced two small blades from her sleeves. "What about you?"

"You'd think they'd allow weapons through customs?" Lucien remarked, shaking his head in disbelief. "I came to the hotel straight from the airport."

"So, what's the plan?" she asked, pulling her hood back up to conceal her features.

The vampire chuckled softly, a glimmer of mischief dancing in his eyes. "I'll dazzle them with my irresistible charm," he replied with a smirk.

Lucien motioned to Alessandra and halted, waiting for the knights to draw nearer. He harboured a faint hope that diplomacy might prove more effective than confrontation in dealing with his brothers.

"De Winter," their commander started. "You need to surrender to us if you want to leave this place unharmed."

He glanced at his sister, a sigh escaping his lips. Their pursuers had no inkling of the formidable companion by his side. She was the most adept assassin he had ever known, and if the knights weren't cautious, they would soon learn the consequences.

"There is no reason for me to surrender myself to you. You can tell your masters I will come willingly to chat with them once I find what I am looking for. No earlier," Lucien replied.

"Suit yourself. We are not your enemy. Just following orders as you used to when you were one of us. Such a shame you got turned into the creature that, until recently, you were hunting," the commander added.

"I remain part of the organisation, regardless of others' opinions."

Lucien felt a searing pain deep within his chest, a raw ache that mirrored the betrayal he felt from the Order. They were supposed to be his allies, his comrades in arms. Yet, here they were, hunting him down like a common criminal, driven by fear and prejudice.

The weight of their disloyalty bore down on him, threatening to crush his spirit. How could they turn their backs on him so easily? How could they abandon him to face the wrath of their own organisation?

"You can entertain that notion all you want, but it doesn't make it reality. Whatever trump card you're holding, I'm willing to bet it's worthless. The minds of the Order's leaders are as stubborn as stone."

"And their heads will roll on the ground once I'm through with them. Tell me, was the command to capture me alive or dead?" Lucien's voice was laced with determination.

Alessandra's demeanour shifted as she removed her hood, revealing her presence. "Well, gentlemen, are we going to exchange pleasantries or get down to business? This prelude is getting tiresome."

"Miss de Winter, always the impatient one." The leader of the knights chuckled. "Had I known you were joining us, I'd have brought more men. Your reputation precedes you."

"I hope you've heard nothing but the best," she retorted, her blade catching the moonlight as she swiftly moved in front of the man under the knight's command and sliced his throat with lethal precision.

As Lucien prepared for battle at the signal, a mix of emotions surged within him. It was a stark reminder of the harsh reality: kill or be killed. He knew that given the opportunity, the knights would not hesitate to despatch him without a second thought.

There was a time when he, too, would have acted in the same ruthless manner.

Reflecting on his past, Lucien couldn't help but feel a pang of bitterness towards the organisation that had trained him. The Order had drilled their righteousness into their recruits, instilling a sense of duty and honour that now felt tainted by betrayal.

But amidst the turmoil of conflicting emotions, there was a glimmer of resolve in Lucien's eyes. He refused to succumb to the darkness that threatened to consume him. Instead, he would fight with every ounce of strength and skill he possessed, determined to defend himself against those who sought to harm him.

As the clash of steel echoed around him, Lucien steeled himself for the combat ahead, knowing that his survival depended on his ability to outwit and outmanoeuvre his opponents. It was a battle for his life, and he was ready to face it head-on, no matter the cost.

"You're making a grave mistake," the leader warned. "By openly assaulting us, you're declaring war against the institution you vowed to defend. Our superiors will be informed, and they'll despatch more knights. Do you truly believe they'll stop at four?"

"I'm counting on it," Lucien replied with grim determination. He felt a surge of adrenaline coursing through him as he broke off a piece of the nearby fence, swiftly splitting it in half to fashion two makeshift stakes. Satisfied with the result, he launched one towards the knight positioned behind the leader. With his superhuman force and unwavering precision, he dispatched the man in an instant, impaling him through the heart.

Lucien wanted to leave one alive as a warning to the Order and all those who crossed him. He gripped the remaining stake harder and charged his victim. He would only incapacitate him to make sure he did not follow him.

He turned his head to his sister, who had the last knight on his knees, begging for mercy. He motioned for her to stop playing with him and finish it. Moments later, her opponent fell to the ground, one of her daggers stuck into the socket of his eye.

The man was still groaning in pain, but she ignored it. Instead, she took the blade out and wiped it on her victim's cloak. He should've known better before challenging them. Alessandra de Winter had no mercy in her repertoire. Being trained by their father and later by the Order, the assassin was the best at slaying unfortunates.

CHAPTER II

Looking at his elder sister's countenance, Lucien couldn't shake the wave of melancholy washing over him. The innocent sibling he once frolicked with across their family estate had vanished, replaced by a seasoned warrior sculpted by years of moulding for the Order's cause. It served as a harsh testament to the toll exacted by their family's cursed heritage.

Years of rigorous training and indoctrination had eradicated any traces of the carefree innocence they once knew, leaving behind only a mere echo of their former selves. Lucien grimly acknowledged that their family's curse had robbed them of the chance for a typical life.

With a heavy sigh, Lucien couldn't help but wonder how different things might have been if fate had been kinder to them. But dwelling on the past would serve no purpose now. All he could do was steel himself for the challenges ahead and fight to protect what little remained of their humanity in the face of darkness.

"New artefact?" He broke the looming silence.

"Yes. It was what you witnessed when the battle started. It increases the speed of my movements, making it harder for the human eye to perceive. That poor bastard didn't see it coming. It was amongst the many things our father gifted to me when I turned nineteen and took the oath to become part of the organisation."

"Father had a lot of insight. Some days, I wonder if he had the gift of clairvoyance," Lucien replied.

"Why do you think that?"

"He'd amassed a tonne of artefacts that were more than pretty baubles. He gave us things that would offer us an advantage over everything we've ever encountered. It seemed like he was aware of what we were going to come up against throughout our lives. It makes you wonder sometimes... Or maybe he had wonderful insight. It's too late now. We'll never know the truth," Lucien responded.

"So, what now? Where are we going from here?"

"We'll head to the nearest airport that can take us to France. I doubt they'll send any more goons tonight, so we need to make our way there now. My identity must have been discovered. We should go straight to my hotel to grab my stuff; it's close by. Do you have everything you need on you?"

"Yes. I didn't bother with any lodgings because I anticipated crossing paths with you. I began scoping out the castle because I had a hunch you'd head there, and before I knew it, you were scaling down its walls," his sister responded.

As they arrived at the hotel, the clerk watched Alessandra warily, as if sensing something off about the pair.

"I'll wait here for you," she said to her sibling and settled into a sofa in the lobby.

Lucien retrieved his travel bag and documents before returning to the reception desk to check out. After settling the bill for the room, he requested a taxi from the clerk, deliberately omitting to mention the destination.

As Lucien stepped into the waiting taxi, he felt a surge of urgency coursing through him. The leather seats felt cold against his skin, contrasting with the warmth of his racing thoughts. The betrayal of the knights lingered in his mind like a stubborn shadow, a reminder of the dangers that lurked within the Order.

As the car pulled away from the hotel, Lucien's gaze wandered out the window, watching the passing cityscape blur into streaks of light. His heart pounded with a mixture of determination and desperation. He prayed silently, fervently, for guidance, for strength, for a swift resolution to their quest.

Beside him, Alessandra sat in silence, her presence a comfort amidst the turmoil of his thoughts. He was grateful for her unwavering loyalty in the face of adversity. Together, they would find Vlad, save Avery, and unravel the mysteries that lay ahead.

With each passing mile, Lucien's resolve hardened. He was determined to face whatever challenges awaited them, to confront the darkness that threatened to consume them. And as the taxi sped towards their destination, he clung to the hope that their journey would lead them to the answers they sought.

Upon arriving at the airport, Lucien and Alessandra moved swiftly through the bustling terminals, their footsteps echoing against the polished floors as they navigated through the crowds of travellers. Lucien's senses were on high alert, his every move calculated to avoid drawing any undue attention.

Choosing the most travelled route into France, they blended seamlessly with the flow of passengers making their way through immigration and customs. Lucien kept a watchful eye on their surroundings, scanning the faces of those around them for any signs of suspicion or recognition.

As they passed through security checkpoints and passport control, Lucien maintained a composed demeanour, his heart pounding with anticipation and adrenaline. Every step brought them closer to their destination, yet the journey ahead was fraught with uncertainty and danger.

Despite the risks, Lucien remained focused on their objective, determined to stay one step ahead of their pursuers and protect his sister at all costs. With each passing checkpoint, their trail became increasingly obscured, their presence in France shrouded in secrecy and uncertainty.

The plane ride was enveloped in an eerie silence, broken only by the distant hum of the engines and the occasional rustle of passengers shifting in their seats. As the aircraft soared through the sky, Lucien's thoughts echoed loudly in his mind, drowning out the ambient noise around him.

Sitting in his seat, Lucien stared blankly out of the window, watching as the landscape below gradually transformed from urban sprawl to vast expanses of land dotted with patches of greenery. The rhythmic whir of the plane's engines served as a constant reminder of the distance they were covering, but it offered little comfort to Lucien, whose mind was consumed by worry and uncertainty.

Beside him, Alessandra sat in stoic silence, her expression unreadable as she gazed straight ahead. Despite the shared turmoil that weighed heavily on both their minds, neither sibling dared to break the silence, each lost in their own thoughts and fears.

As Lucien and Alessandra set foot onto the cobblestone streets of the city, Lucien couldn't shake the feeling of unease that washed over him. The towering medieval architecture loomed overhead, casting long shadows that seemed to stretch into the past. It was as if they had stepped back in time, into an era long gone yet still hauntingly present.

Despite the city's rich history as the birthplace of French royalty and the centre of intellectual pursuits, Lucien couldn't help but feel a sense of foreboding. Why would the Prince choose such a place as his hiding location? The answer eluded him, shrouded in the mists of time and secrecy.

For Lucien, this moment was monumental. After tirelessly tracking his ancestor and delving into the mysteries of his past, he had finally uncovered the missing puzzle piece. It was a bittersweet realisation, tinged with the weight of centuries-old secrets and regrets.

As he sighed, Alessandra cast a curious glance his way, her expression a mixture of concern and intrigue. Lucien knew there was no turning back now. They were on the brink of uncovering the truth, no matter the cost.

"One day, this could be me," he murmured, the words tinged with both hope and trepidation. "If we don't settle this issue with the organisation, I could see myself retiring to a place like this with Avery."

Alessandra's response was swift, her tone laced with determination. "It won't come to this, I promise you," she declared. "I will use their most powerful weapon against them if it comes to that."

Her words brought a flicker of reassurance to Lucien's heart, a glimmer of hope amidst the uncertainty of their situation. With Alessandra by his side, he felt a renewed sense of resolve. Together, they would face whatever challenges lay ahead, united in their quest for justice and redemption.

Lucien's mind churned with conflicting thoughts as he studied the map and the ancient land deed. While he appreciated his sister's unwavering support, a nagging worry gnawed at him. Could Alessandra truly turn against the very organisation that had shaped her into the formidable figure she was today?

With deliberate care, he traced their intended path on the city map, his movements precise. Unlike most modern travellers who relied on digital navigation, Lucien relied on traditional methods, wary of leaving a digital trail that could betray their movements to their enemies.

Finally, after several minutes of careful consideration, he pinpointed their destination: Château D'Auvergne, nestled twenty-five miles away from Blois. It was a strategic choice, far removed from the political machinations of the French court, yet still within reach of Vlad's influence and resources.

CHAPTER 12

As they stood before the dilapidated estate, Lucien couldn't shake the pang of guilt that pierced his heart. The crumbling structure before them was a stark reminder of the consequences of his actions. If this lead didn't pan out, if they couldn't find Vlad here, Avery's life hung in the balance. The weight of that possibility bore down on him heavily, threatening to suffocate him with its implications.

With a clenched jaw and a determined resolve, Lucien pushed aside the tendrils of doubt and focused on the task at hand. This had to be the place. They had come too far, endured too much to falter now. Gathering his courage, he stepped forward, ready to uncover the truth hidden within the walls of Château D'Auvergne.

He took a deep breath and cleared his mind, then opened the map again.

There were no other structures in the vicinity, and five hundred years was a long time for a building to be still standing.

"Maybe it was knocked down?" Alessandra asked.

"I don't think so. I've done a lot of research on him. He was a creature of habit. After being forced to leave a place once, he would do anything in his power to avoid the same situation," Lucien replied.

"What if there were other circumstances that led him to abandon his land?"

It made little sense. Vlad would never leave again. He wasn't driven out of his land in the first place; he disappeared and started again because the past was too painful. And who would've blamed him? The love of his life was dead. His people saw him as a monster. Driven by pure hatred, he became the thing of nightmares. His thirst for vengeance clouded his judgement, and the Devil took advantage of a broken man.

"No, it can't be. We haven't come this far to hit a dead end. Something is going on here; I need to find out what it is," Lucien added.

He knelt on the ground and touched the earth with his palm. There was a faint hum coming from the direction of the ruin. For a knight of the Order or a vampire alone, this would have been too hard to notice. But Lucien was both, the same as the Prince, which gave him the needed advantage.

"There's magic at play here. I don't think what we see right now is real," he muttered, then walked towards the entrance.

The heavy metal gate creaked when Lucien opened it, the sound resounding through the air. As soon as they stepped onto the grounds, the magic that glamoured the building disappeared, almost as if recognising them as guests.

As Lucien and Alessandra approached, the dilapidated ruin transformed before their eyes, giving way to a magnificent château with pointed rooftops that seemed to pierce the sky. Lucien couldn't help but smile at the sight. The moment he had been waiting for, the culmination of their journey, was finally within reach.

They strode confidently down the broad path that led to the main dwelling. The architecture, a blend of Renaissance rustic style and romantic aesthetics, spoke of grandeur and history. Despite its age, the castle stood proudly, its walls whispering tales of bygone eras.

At the heart of the estate stood the most imposing structure: a square tower flanked by two wings, which enclosed a sprawling courtyard. The tower reached towards the heavens, its presence commanding respect and awe. Lucien felt a surge of anticipation as they drew nearer, ready to uncover the secrets that lay hidden within the walls of Château D'Auvergne.

Lucien rang the doorbell and waited. Moments later, a young attendant opened the ornate wooden door. For a moment, she looked confused at the newcomers, then smiled.

"Bonjour. Nous sommes ici pour voir le seigneur. Pourriez-vous lui faire savoir de notre arrivée, s'il vous plaît?" Lucien addressed the woman.

"Anglais?" She rolled her eyes, unimpressed by his poor pronunciation.

"Oui," the vampire replied.

"You can address Monseigneur in your native language. He speaks perfect English. Follow me."

Lucien paused to observe his surroundings, seeking clues about the residents of the estate. Guided by the attendant, they traversed narrow hallways until reaching a room situated in the west wing. The interior walls of the château were adorned with panelling and painted in a variety of hues, each room boasting its own unique colour scheme.

As they entered the chamber, the attendant smiled. "Wait here. Monseigneur will be with you shortly."

The drawing room itself was not overly ornate. Several armchairs, adorned in velvet, were strategically placed. Lucien's gaze was drawn to a large tapestry hanging above a spacious sofa. It depicted a hunting scene, with a young lord on a white horse bearing a striking resemblance to the Prince.

As Lucien waited, his heart raced with anticipation. Every passing second felt like an eternity, filled with a mix of excitement and nervousness. The possibility of finally meeting the elusive Prince, his ancestor, filled him with a sense of awe and wonder.

His mind raced with questions and scenarios, wondering what the encounter would bring. Would the Prince be welcoming or hostile? Would he hold the key to unlocking the secrets of their family's past? Lucien's emotions swirled like a tempest, a whirlwind of hope, fear, and determination.

Finally, as the door swung open and Dracula strode in, Lucien's breath hitched in his throat. Before him stood the legendary figure he had tirelessly sought, now embodied in flesh and blood. It was a moment of surreal intensity, akin to a convergence of dreams fulfilled and nightmares realized.

As he prepared to speak, Lucien felt a surge of adrenaline coursing through his veins. This was it, the moment of truth. Whatever happened next, he knew that his life would never be the same.

"I see you're fascinated by the subject," the elder vampire added.

"Yes, this is almost lifelike. I beg your pardon for disturbing you at this early hour, My Lord."

Lucien was confronted by a pair of recognizable dark eyes, framed within a handsome, pallid countenance. Wavy, shoulder-length black hair caught the flickering candlelight, lending it a mesmerizing sheen. The nobleman seemed to have aged slightly, sporting a neatly trimmed beard that accentuated his enigmatic smile. Behind his deep red lips, impeccably white teeth emerged, adding to his allure.

Clad in an opulent yet refined attire, the man sported a black brocade blazer adorned with a blue paisley pattern that gleamed under the soft light. A pristine white shirt underscored his distinguished visage, complemented by tailored trousers and sleek leather shoes that rounded off the ensemble with polished finesse.

"Monsieur?" the nobleman asked.

"My apologies for my rudeness. I was so entranced by the beauty of the rendition, I forgot to introduce myself. I am Lucien de Winter, and this is my sister, Alessandra. With whom do we have the pleasure?"

"Albert Louis Chambord, Viscount D'Auvergne," the other man replied, then he walked over to Alessandra, taking her small hand in his and kissing it. "Enchanté."

Alessandra blushed.

"Exquisite," the peer uttered, never taking his eyes off her. "Mademoiselle de Winter, you are a vision. Where have you been all my life?"

Without waiting for his sister's response, Lucien cleared his throat. "My Lord, let's not get off track. We are here because of a matter of extreme urgency," he added, his tone grave.

The aristocrat raised a single eyebrow, his expression a mix of curiosity and scepticism, as if silently questioning Lucien's purpose.

"What does this French nobleman have to aid Monsieur de Winter?" The older man started walking around the room. "As you can see, I live in this secluded mansion. I haven't been outside those metal gates in years. I doubt I can be of any help."

"Power, My Lord. I came to ask for your support to deal with the Order of the Dragon," Lucien added.

"The Order of the Dragon, you say? I'm afraid I've never heard of them," the noble replied with a smile. "It seems you've made a fruitless journey, and I have other pressing matters to attend to. Mademoiselle, it was a pleasure meeting you. My assistant will escort you both out," he said, gesturing towards the door.

"My lord let's leave the pretences behind. I know who you really are, and I am confident you have realised by now what I am."

"Hmm? You must be tired from your journey," the nobleman said.

"Five hundred years ago, you came to this land pretending to be Crespin Chambord, Chevalier de Lyon. But before that, you were Prince Vlad Drakulya of Wallachia, the man who made a deal with the Devil. Correct me if I'm wrong."

The elder vampire's lips curled into a contemptuous sneer, revealing sharp fangs gleaming in the dim light.

"Why are you here, Monsieur de Winter? You stink of desperation and foolishness. You broke through my enchantment, a feat no creature could do until now, and yet you stand before me talking about my past. If you want to leave this place alive, you need a good reason."

"The same organisation your father helped found. They are hunting me down like a dog. My sister and I, we're your last living relatives, my lord. We came to seek sanctuary and plead for your aid."

"And what do they want with you two?" his kin enquired.

"I was a knight in their service when I got turned. They wish to eliminate me. There is no mystery. There hasn't been an active vampire member since, well, yourself."

The Prince took a turn about the room, seeming to ponder on the situation.

"If you're genuinely of the House of Dracul, then nothing would have hindered you from dismantling the Order on your own," Vlad chuckled. "There must be another motive driving you, but I'll await your disclosure. For now, I require evidence to confirm your identity."

"And how would we do that?" Lucien asked.

"In your world and mine, blood is sacred. I will share your memories and feelings the moment it reaches my lips. I can see the past as if it were my own. This is the price to pay if you want my help."

Lucien deliberated his choices with caution. The centuries-old vampire before him was notorious for his mistrust of others, and time was running short. Seeking guidance, he glanced at his sister, finding reassurance in her approving nod. With their options dwindling, their destiny now rested in the hands of the Prince.

"We accept," he answered promptly.

CHAPTER 13

Vlad's smile widened as he approached the knight, his senses heightened by the tantalising scent of blood.

"Perfect," he murmured, halting just inches away from his prey. With a predatory grace, he tilted his head, revealing his elongated fangs, and sank them into the other vampire's neck.

As the warm blood flowed into his mouth, Vlad's eyes widened in astonishment. A torrent of images flooded his mind, revealing his nephew's life story in vivid detail. He experienced flashes of intense training, harrowing missions, memories from the academy, and, most strikingly, the depth of the knight's love for Avery, intertwined with the ever-present fear of losing her to the Order's relentless pursuit.

In the midst of the flood of memories, Vlad experienced a surge of admiration for the knight's courage and unwavering loyalty. Despite facing overwhelming odds, he remained resolute in his commitment to safeguarding the one he held dear.

The brat didn't lie, Vlad thought, his admiration mingling with a newfound sense of camaraderie.

After finishing with Lucien, the vampire shifted his focus to his sibling, Alessandra.

In her case, he paused. He didn't need her memories, having already identified her. However, a certain unease nagged at him. Since she stepped into the room, her blood had called out to him, awakening an unforeseen desire.

As he gazed upon her, a shift occurred deep within him. Her piercing dark blue eyes seemed to penetrate his very soul, while her pale complexion beautifully contrasted with her cascading chocolate-coloured hair, which framed her face in loose ringlets.

Despite his centuries of existence and numerous lovers, no female had ever affected him in quite the same way. The intensity of his attraction to her was undeniable.

Should I indulge in her blood to quench this fleeting desire? he pondered. Countless reasons flooded his mind, warning against such a reckless act. They were descendants of his brother, and yet, half a millennium later, he found himself drawn to his own kin. However, in the end, his insatiable curiosity triumphed.

The Prince walked closer to Alessandra. "My apologies, Mademoiselle. This will hurt only a little."

He looked into her eyes as the distance between them closed. He felt like a poor, unfortunate soul under the spell of a beautiful mermaid. Vlad wrapped his left arm around her waist and pulled her closer, then used his right hand to brush the hair away from her, revealing her graceful neck.

He closed his eyes and inhaled her scent as his fangs broke through the layers of skin. The moment her blood hit his tongue, hundreds of stars exploded behind his eyelids. She tasted like life, happiness, bravery, and love, all mixed in one.

Vlad opened his gaze and kissed the area where his teeth had made the tiny wounds. Then, he pricked his index finger and smeared some of his blood on them to aid the surface in healing.

As soon as her skin was all healed, he broke from the embrace, putting on a calculated façade. He couldn't let anyone know how much Alessandra affected him. Flirting with the young woman was one thing; her spell on him was another, and a dangerous one.

Lucien cleared his throat, drawing the attention of the elder vampire.

"Now that we've established your identity, what's your plan for dealing with the Order?" Vlad enquired.

"We take the fight to them," Lucien replied.

"That may be too late. Their minions are already here." Vlad grinned at the siblings before turning to gaze out of the large windows. "Are you prepared?"

"Yes," Lucien affirmed.

"Excellent. Let's make our way to the armoury. We'll need weapons," Vlad declared.

The walk to the estate's armoury was brief. When the Prince swung open the door, the siblings were greeted by an array of artefacts displayed in cabinets and stands.

Lucien's eyes were drawn to a Katana. It felt like an extension of himself, having wielded it for so long. Alessandra, tapping into her inner assassin, selected two Italian cinquedea daggers, while Vlad, staying true to his heritage, opted for a greatsword.

As Vlad pushed open the double doors leading to the terrace, he beheld a sea of knights gathered before the estate gates, poised to strike. A smile crept onto his face. Since his departure from the Order, he had kept a low profile, avoiding attracting undue attention. But today marked a change. He finally had a reason to reveal his true capabilities.

Stepping to the edge of the terrace, Vlad leaped down to

the ground below. The organisation had made a grave mistake in coming after his kin on his own turf. Now, it was time to teach them a lesson.

"Who dares trespass on my land?" the Prince addressed the crowd.

The leader stepped forward, his armour catching the sunlight and gleaming with a polished sheen. His breastplate, etched with elaborate designs, proudly displayed the emblem of the Order—an ouroboros, symbolising infinity and renewal, woven into the metal. Steel pauldrons adorned his shoulders, extending down to shield his upper arms, while vambraces encased his forearms for added defence. Beneath his tabard, a chainmail coif offered further protection. At his side, a sturdy sword hung from his belt, and a shield bearing the same emblem leaned against him.

"You're harbouring a fugitive, my lord. The Order demands you hand him over."

"You can inform your leader that Prince Vlad Drakulya has denied complying with the demand."

"You mean to say you're Dracula? The mighty vampire everyone is afraid of?" The commander laughed.

"Don't let my appearance fool you. I can crush your little army single-handedly."

"I'd like to see you try." The man took his sword out.

With a firm grip on his greatsword, Vlad surged forward, his heart pounding with adrenaline as he charged towards his adversaries. As he closed the distance, he swung his blade, the metallic clash reverberating through the air as it met his opponent's weapon.

A swift thrust was met with an equally quick parry, followed by another thrust and parry in rapid succession. Each movement was precise and skilful, resulting in a rhythmic exchange of blows that filled the air with a symphony of clinks and clashes.

In a bold move, the enemy commander hurled his blade towards Vlad, who deftly dodged the attack. With a quick pivot, Vlad struck back, his blade hitting its target on his opponent's forearm, causing a jet of blood to spurt into the air.

Despite the intensity of the battle, Vlad couldn't help but feel a surge of exhilaration coursing through him. While he relished the thrill of combat, he knew that the time had come to bring the skirmish to an end. As much as he enjoyed the prowess of his human days, he was now a vampire, and his approach to combat had evolved accordingly.

Taking a deep breath, Vlad sensed the energy building up inside him, propelling him upward from the ground. As he ascended above the knights, his heart thumped with eager anticipation, a mighty energy flowing through his veins.

Opening his eyes, Vlad focused his gaze on his opponent below. With a determined resolve, he released his grip on his sword, watching as it soared into the sky. A whispered incantation escaped his lips, a solemn vow uttered under his breath.

"Now, always, forever and ever," he murmured, his words echoing in the air. With a swift motion, the weapon returned to him, descending with unstoppable force. In a dazzling display of power, it impaled his adversary through the heart, ending the battle in an instant.

As the dust settled, Vlad couldn't help but feel a sense of satisfaction wash over him. He had proven his might, demonstrating the full extent of his abilities to both friend and foe alike. With a knowing smile, he realised that if Lucien truly was his blood, he held the potential to single-handedly dismantle the Order.

Though the young vampire may have yet to comprehend the true magnitude of his strength, Vlad knew that his abilities were limitless, capable of commanding both humans and creatures alike with unparalleled authority.

"Observe and learn," Vlad said, turning towards Lucien, who gave a confirming nod.

With a confident stretch of his arms and a sly smirk, Vlad commanded, "As your lord, I order you to kneel!" His voice boomed across the field.

Immediately, the knights were compelled to kneel by an invisible force, their efforts to stand thwarted by excruciating resistance.

Pleased by the demonstration, the Prince pondered their next move. "What's our course of action with these knights, nephew? Should we dispatch their heads to the Order, or transform them into the very beings they've hunted? Would you grant them mercy, or let them endure the life they've sought to eliminate?"

"Death would be a kindness unwarranted. Let's turn them, have them join our cause against the Order's injustices," Lucien proposed.

"Perfectly stated. You truly are of Wallachian blood. This conflict began with me, and it will end only in their death."

Vlad returned to Alessandra, landing gracefully beside her. Her gaze met his with admiration, lighting up with a smile. Gently taking her hand, he brought it to his lips for a soft kiss. "Forgive me. What follows may be somewhat unpleasant."

THE END

THE KING OF THE UNDEAD

CHAPTER 1

The sound of hooves echoed through the air. Prince Vlad Drakulya of Wallachia, the first vampire, was travelling the English countryside with his recently found kin, atop the most beautiful white Arabian horse.

The rider looked regal, with a compelling presence. His profile spoke of power and ageless strength, while his jet-black hair was ruffled by the breeze.

Setting foot on the land of his enemy and declaring it his own stirred many memories and feelings Vlad had buried many years ago. He knew this was the right thing to do.

After claiming the Order's knights as his army, he decided to make Roslyn Academy the base of his operations. There was a lot to be done and little time. The organisation would most likely send a swift response to his betrayal, but he was prepared to deal with that. He had dreamed of their demise for centuries, and nothing would stand in his way.

"Stop!" Vlad's voice cut through the air, halting the procession of newly transformed vampire knights before the elaborate gates of Roslyn Academy.

The magical barriers around the academy prevented any further advance. Turning to Lucien with a knowing smile, Vlad enquired, "What's our next move, nephew?"

The young vampire brought him hope they would win this war when he turned up with his sister on Vlad's doorstep. He was the excuse the Prince needed to stand against the organisation and challenge their authority over the supernatural world.

"The protective spells are set along the estate's perimeter, only able to be turned off from the inside. Alternatively, a human could enter and disable the central mechanism that powers all others, situated directly within the headmaster's office at the core of the academy," Lucien explained.

"Let me," Alessandra interrupted before her sibling could utter another word.

Alessandra de Winter, famed as the Order's deadliest assassin, wielded the freedom to pursue any endeavour. Yet Vlad found himself enveloped in a protective stance towards her. Her intelligence and allure had captivated him completely, rendering him hesitant to expose her to peril.

"No, you must remain beside me, without objection. We have waged war against the Order. It goes against my principles to despatch you alone into potential danger. You are human; they might have an array of beasts prepared for an ambush," he stated, his expression grave. Vlad silently wished his evident protectiveness for the woman was perceived merely as a precaution for his newly discovered human niece, rather than the deep concern it truly was.

Revealing this vulnerability was not an option. The revelation that Alessandra was his weakness could spell disaster for both of them. Her prowess as the Order's most formidable asset was undisputed. If the organisation were ever to learn of her influence over him, they would unleash the myriad of supernatural forces they'd amassed over the years to pursue her relentlessly.

"I'll eliminate them as I have always done. They won't anticipate my approach," she declared, her voice threaded with resolve.

Vlad loved her fortitude and steadfastness. Those were some of her qualities that attracted him. But in her boldness, she forgot she was a mere human with only one life. An invaluable mortal being.

"Alessandra," Lucien whispered, shaking his head, trying to silence his sister. "It's not the time to show off."

"Brother!" she snapped, narrowing her eyes.

"Children!" Vlad chuckled. "I'll do this myself. There's no point in arguing about it. There will be plenty of time for you to prove yourselves."

The siblings exchanged looks, curious about the extent of his powers. "What's your plan?" Lucien asked.

"Find their weakest link and use it to our advantage. Now, both of you, be quiet. I have to concentrate for this to work."

Vlad briefly tuned out the world around him, focusing solely on the academy's core, blocking out all external noise. His telepathic search stretched out, seeking a soul burdened by deep sorrow. Manipulating an untainted human mind demanded immense power, especially from a distance. For his scheme to succeed, he required someone whose spirit had been shattered by grief.

Having pinpointed the perfect subject, Vlad established a psychic link, seizing control of their mind. In an instant, he materialised in the academy's kitchen, holding a knife. *Perfect*, he thought, inhabiting the chef's body. He swiftly scanned the surroundings and stealthily approached another person in the room, swiftly ending their life in a silent, unnoticed strike.

Using his host's senses as a guide, he made his way

through the corridors towards the headmaster's office. Prior to departing the kitchen, he disposed of the bulky knife, opting to conceal a smaller blade up his sleeve for safety.

Standing before the grand, intricately carved wooden door, Vlad paused to gather himself, drawing in a deep, steadying breath before firmly knocking.

"Enter!" resounded from inside the chamber.

Vlad stepped inside, pausing just past the entryway, sensing that the ease of his intrusion was unsettling.

The headmaster, engrossed in his paperwork, glanced up, slightly perplexed. "Head chef? Are you here to discuss the menu for the week?"

"Not quite," Vlad responded, his voice cold as he manipulated the chef's body to hurl the knife with lethal precision, embedding it directly into the headmaster's heart.

As he approached his shocked victim, Vlad couldn't suppress a grim smile.

"What have you done, you fool?" His foe gasped, his face draining of colour as he struggled for breath, eyes rolling back before slumping against the chair.

"I'm righting a wrong," Vlad murmured, moving closer. He grasped the knife, twisting it with calculated cruelty to ensure a fatal wound, then withdrew it, satisfaction painting his features as he watched the man's life slip away.

Vlad closed his eyes and moved methodically around the room, tuning into the unique energy of the central ward's protective spell. He was intimately familiar with this ancient enchantment; its resonance echoed the ancient magic within him, making it easily detectable. Within moments, he located its source. Walking to the bookshelf, he ran his finger over the spines of several books until one reacted. Opening it, he found a hidden compartment containing a glowing red crystal.

Taking hold of the crystal, the core of the ward, he applied force, causing it to splinter into myriad pieces. As the crystal broke apart, Vlad felt the protective energies enveloping the academy diminish, indicating the deactivation of the wards.

The assembly of knights at the academy's entrance drew a significant crowd. The courtyard swelled with hundreds of students, all eyes on the unfolding drama. Once Vlad reconnected with his own senses, a glance at his nephew conveyed his intent.

Lucien caught on immediately. "Open the gates," he commanded, and the knights complied without hesitation.

Vlad, with a hand firmly placed on the hilt of his greatsword and the bearing of a battle-hardened immortal, strode into the heart of what had long been hostile ground. His entrance was nothing short of majestic, akin to a deity of old gracing the mortal realm. A visceral thrill coursed through him, a silent prayer marking this moment as he edged ever closer to settling scores with his arch-nemesis.

May the Lord protect us. The war is finally starting.

CHAPTER 2

SEATED REGALLY ON HIS HORSE, THE PRINCE PROJECTED authority, his serious expression scanning the surroundings. The crowd of students returned his gaze, intrigued by the spectacle but also puzzled by the unfolding situation.

"Greetings," Vlad began, addressing the assembled youths. He scanned them sharply, assessing their demeanour, alert to any hint of hostility. The possibility that the Order had preempted their move and warned these students loomed in his mind, potentially complicating their mission.

"And who are you?" a young man dared to enquire, stepping out from the crowd.

Vlad offered a thin, derisive smile, amused by the boldness—or perhaps naivety—of the youth. "I hail from realms afar, here to illuminate your path through these darkened days," he declared, his tone dripping with irony. "I stand before you as a Superior Class Knight."

"No visit from the Order was announced," the young man retorted with a scoff. "Believing a total stranger? You'd have to be out of your mind."

Vlad's response was swift, his lips pressing into a thin line at the youth's boldness. "Consider this your notice," he shot back, his voice laced with an edge of mockery. "Surely, you've all heard tales of the infamous Prince Vlad Drakulya of Wallachia. It is for your benefit that I've journeyed far to grace you with my presence." His bow was overly elaborate, dripping with sarcasm.

"So, you're claiming to be Dracula?" a girl challenged, scepticism written across her face. "Forgive me, but you hardly seem the part of a vampire centuries old."

"I am precisely who I say I am, no more, no less. In time, you will come to recognise and respect me as such. I'd prefer sooner rather than later, but ultimately, it makes little difference to me."

The young man's doubt intensified, eliciting murmurs of agreement from his peers. "Dracula's a legend, a shadow of the past," he stated, eyeing the assembly with a mix of disdain and disbelief for the figure before them.

Vlad's response was to offer them a challenge, a demonstration of his proclaimed identity. "Witness then, the revelation of your mentors' true nature. Today, you stand at a crossroads; choose your allegiance wisely." His smile widened, revealing his unmistakable fangs.

Spurred by defiance, a boy conjured a bow from flames and loosed an arrow of fire straight at Vlad. With effortless grace, Vlad parried the attack with his sword, the fiery missile harmlessly dissipating.

"Who will be next to test their mettle against me?" he taunted, surveying the crowd with a predatory gaze. "Come, show me the extent of your powers."

A blonde girl, emboldened by her command over storm magic, conjured a bolt of lightning aimed straight at Vlad.

He greeted her challenge with a smirk, effortlessly

summoning a protective shield that repelled her aggressive manoeuvre. The repeated attempts to harm him only served to deepen Vlad's impatience with these youthful adversaries.

"Having demonstrated your attacks are futile against me, I now ask you to close your eyes and clear your thoughts. Witness true power," Vlad declared, a sly grin playing on his lips as he prepared to unveil the magnitude of his ancient abilities.

In an instant, Vlad's potent magic swept through the minds of all present, unveiling a vivid tableau of the Order's transgressions. The students were involuntarily immersed in scenes from his tumultuous past, their consciousness saturated with his experiences.

Vlad stood defiant before Matthias Corvinus, the King of Hungary and head of the Order, who was ensconced on a grand throne, brandishing a ceremonial sword of exquisite craftsmanship.

"Prince Vlad of the House of Dracul," the leader began, his voice echoing with authority. "Word has it you alone have resisted the purge of heretics that afflicts our land. Our Order's creed is the beacon of truth, and deviation from our path will be corrected by force if necessary."

"Your Highness," he responded, his tone measured, "to end a life is a trivial task. To extinguish a thousand lives is equally so. Yet, to win the trust of men is the greatest challenge. Let us not destroy them but instead win their loyalty. Provide for their needs, offer them shelter, and in time, they will willingly serve our purpose."

The king dismissed Vlad's proposal with a gesture. "Your perspective is clouded. Your captivity has softened you towards those we consider enemies. This is your moment of decision. The direction of your destiny is yours to command," he countered, idly twirling his substantial moustache.

Feeling the weight of his sword in his hand, Vlad offered a stiff bow and exited, his anger boiling just beneath the surface. Compliance seemed his only option, lest he become the target of the Order's wrath. It was a bitter realisation that fortune often smiled on the merciless.

Vlad then shared a more personal, poignant memory from years later, a deliberate choice meant to reveal the depth of his convictions.

Clad in his battle armour on a bitterly cold December evening, the howling wind outside the castle's stone walls, Vlad was about to join his troops when his path was intercepted by his wife.

"My lady, urgent news has arrived. The sultan's army has crossed the Danube and marches towards us. There's no time to lose if we are to emerge victorious," Vlad said urgently.

Her response came with a bitter laugh. "Years spent as the sultan's pawn, and now you're abandoned. The Order seeks your demise. No victory will satisfy Matthias Corvinus now. Your naiveté will be our undoing," she scorned.

"Are you so quick to doom your own husband?" Vlad asked, his pain clear. He had clung to the hope that their union might bloom into love, but such dreams were mere fantasies of a once hopeful heart. Now he understood the harsh truth. Her beauty could not mask the malevolence within. She was a creature of darkness, incapable of love.

"Your folly sealed our fate the moment you sided with the heretics. Should you return from this conflict, I will disown you before the Order. You will be nothing to me but a misguided soul who chose poorly and earned the enmity of his own people," she coldly declared.

"My dear, all my actions, every decision, was in pursuit of our safety, to shield you and our subjects. The tribute paid to the sultan was the price of our peace, a calm that lasted years. Had Matthias not blindly waged war against their beliefs, we might have lived without fear," Vlad elaborated, a hint of remorse in his voice.

With those final words, he turned and departed, berating himself for ever believing in a love that was never reciprocated. The pain of unrequited love lingered, a stark reminder of a marriage devoid of mutual affection. He had given her his heart completely, yet she regarded it with indifference.

As he delved into the last and most poignant memory, a solitary tear traced its way down Vlad's cheek, a silent testament to the depth of his sorrow.

Beneath the icy embrace of the winter night sky, illuminated by the glow of a full moon, Vlad's figure was a testament to his suffering. Clad in tatters, his body bore the marks of violence—bruises and wounds that spoke of brutal treatment. The verdict of death handed down by the Order's leader weighed heavily on him, yet it was the agony of loss that truly shattered his spirit. Mere hours before, he had learned of his wife's tragic end, a demise she chose under the unbearable weight of demands for atrocities committed in the name of faith. The Order had razed his world to the ground.

A deeper, more consuming pain eclipsed the physical torment of his injuries. The sting of his flesh wounds paled compared to the suffocating despair that now enveloped him. He felt utterly bereft without her presence. He found himself ensnared in a web of powerlessness, haunted by the impossibility of her return. Despite her disdain, his love for her remained unwavering—a love now unrequited and lost.

Driven by a desperate impulse, Vlad collected the blood dripping from a cut on his forehead and began to sketch ancient sigils on the ground, symbols he had discovered in a forgotten tome. As he whispered the incantations, the fabric of reality around him seemed to warp and shift.

Upon completing the ritual, a figure materialised before Vlad, regarding him with a scornful amusement. "Who has the audacity to summon Asmodeus to these desolate lands?" the figure challenged.

"Prince Vlad of the House of Dracul," Vlad declared, struggling to rise, though his battered body betrayed him, forcing him to remain prostrate.

The apparition studied him with a cold curiosity. "You are but a husk, and yet you dare to invoke the presence of the Prince of Dark-

ness. You reek of rage, bitterness, and sorrow. What is it you seek so desperately?" the entity pressed, intrigued by Vlad's audacious call.

"Time and power," Vlad managed, each word a struggle as pain seared through his lungs, yet he persevered, driven by the potential redemption this demon represented. "Offer me these, and I shall serve your will for the rest of my days."

Asmodeus's response was a booming laugh that seemed to mock Vlad's dire state. "You are merely a shattered mortal. Regardless of your past stature, your end is nigh, and you will decay as all humans do, leaving behind nothing but a skeletal remnant. What could a man on the brink of death possibly offer me?"

Vlad's reply was resolute, fuelled by the depth of his vengeance. "Grant me the means to enact my retribution, and I vow to deliver to Hell as many souls as you desire."

"Very well," Asmodeus replied, a hint of intrigue in his tone as he offered his hand to Vlad, assisting him to his feet. "Rise, for you are now my chosen. From this moment forward, you walk as my son." A smile crept across the demon's face, a mix of satisfaction and anticipation at the pact sealed between them. "Your bloodlust will be the price of my gift. Death shall be your eternal companion. As you wander the earth for aeons, nothing will quench your thirst."

As Asmodeus concluded his declaration, his thumb morphed into a sharp claw, and with a swift motion, he cut across his wrist. Dark, potent blood welled from the wound, and he positioned the bleeding cut above Vlad, allowing drops of his infernal essence to fall onto Vlad's lips.

"Drink," he commanded, a directive Vlad found himself compelled to follow. As the demonic blood touched his tongue, Asmodeus let out a chilling laugh, a sound that sent tremors of dread through Vlad. Then, with a swift, decisive movement, the demon prince conjured his sword, an ancient and fearsome blade, and plunged it directly into Vlad's heart, sealing his fate and transformation.

"I thought you promised me salvation," Vlad gasped, the words barely a whisper as he fell to the ground, life ebbing away.

"And saved you shall be, but through death's embrace. You shall rise anew, reborn as the new Prince of Darkness," Asmodeus replied, his voice a mix of solemnity and anticipation. He leaned over Vlad, placing a kiss upon the prince's forehead in a gesture that felt both benediction and farewell. "You are liberated now, my son."

Reflecting on his buried past, Vlad felt the weight of centuries bearing down on him. His promise to dismantle the Order and its dark roots had once seemed insurmountable, yet now, the chance for fulfilment lay within reach.

Observing the gathered students, Vlad noted the shift in their expressions—a blend of surprise and realisation. Despite everything, a hint of sympathy stirred within him. Their entire belief system, the values they had been taught to embrace, now lay exposed as tainted by corruption.

"We offer our apologies. Until this moment, we were unaware of the depth of their depravity." A young voice broke through his contemplation.

Vlad, looking into the eyes of the boy, recognised his sincerity.

"The organisation has been our guiding force since childhood," another girl softly contributed.

"Do not be afraid. I understand you were acting under the influence of the Order. Their crimes extend beyond stirring religious conflicts. Over the past five centuries, I have seen their relentless persecution of those who opposed their narrow beliefs. But confronting such a powerful organisation required allies and resources, which I lacked until I found my family. I remained in hiding for too long, hesitant to provoke their wrath prematurely. In hindsight, it may have been a mistake; I could have acted sooner."

Another girl took over the conversation, her tone contemplative. "We've always wondered about the purpose of hunting the supernatural. Now, the truth is obvious. The Order's self-righteousness has no limits."

"I will fault no one who stands apart from this conflict, who does not wish to swear fealty to our cause. Those who opt out may leave in peace."

Gratitude rippled through the crowd as students responded, "Thank you, Your Highness. Your kindness is beyond compare."

Upon hearing their words, Vlad was briefly contemplative. Kindness? It seemed foreign to him. Throughout his long life, he had been labelled a monster, the epitome of evil. Yet, in this crucial moment, he was seen as compassionate. Could he, who had spent centuries embodying ruthlessness, genuinely embrace kindness?

His mind suddenly went to the time when he was ruler of his country.

In the quiet solitude of his throne room, Vlad's thoughts were interrupted by the announcement of an unexpected visitor. A rich merchant from Florence, no less, had come seeking his counsel. Vlad's initial reaction was one of scepticism; experience had taught him that those with wealth often had motives obscured by greed and deceit.

"Your Majesty," the merchant began, bowing deeply in a gesture of respect that Vlad found slightly exaggerated. "I come before you wronged and seeking justice."

Vlad studied the fellow before him, noting the fine quality of his attire that spoke of his affluence, yet also sensing the desperation in his plea. His eyes narrowed as he prepared himself to sift through the words of a man who hailed from a class notorious for their cunning.

"Proceed," Vlad prompted, his voice carrying a mix of authority and an underlying caution.

"Your Grace, it was during the stillness of last night, as I lay asleep within my cart, that misfortune befell me. A thief made away with my purse, a considerable loss, compounded by the betrayal of my guard. Following a dispute earlier in the day, he abandoned his post, leaving me vulnerable, alone to safeguard my goods and my person," the merchant recounted, his voice tinged with the bitterness of betrayal and loss.

Vlad listened, his initial wariness giving way to a begrudging interest. Here was a man, stripped of his protection and robbed, not just of his wealth but of his trust in those sworn to defend him. The tale, while not uncommon, resonated with Vlad, reminding him of his own experiences with treachery and the constant challenge of discerning truth from deception.

"Understood. And the total loss?" Vlad enquired, his voice steady.

"A sum of one hundred and sixty gold coins." The merchant collapsed to his knees in despair. "Please, Your Highness, I implore you to apprehend the thief, for I am left with naught to fund my travels."

"Rest assured, justice will be served," Vlad assured him. That evening, Vlad resolved not only to return the stolen amount, but to add one more coin to the purse as a test.

Come dawn, the merchant reappeared, his demeanour now buoyant with relief. Vlad couldn't help but smile at the change.

"Sire, it appears the thief's heart was swayed by guilt, for my gold has been returned to me," the florentine announced with renewed hope.

"Is that so?" Vlad mused, his voice trailing into silence. "And the matter is resolved?"

"Indeed, yet upon counting the returned gold, I discovered an

additional coin, one not originally mine," he confessed, puzzled by the anomaly.

With this revelation, Vlad gave the order for his guards to detain the supposed repentant thief and retrieve the merchant's gold, curious to see how this unexpected turn would unfold.

"Consider yourself fortunate," Vlad intoned, a stern edge to his voice that hinted at the dire consequences that could have followed a different choice. "Had you not been forthcoming about the extra coin, your fate would have been entwined with that of the thief's."

Overcome with a mix of relief and gratitude, the merchant hastily knelt once more, pressing his lips to Vlad's hand in a gesture of deep thanks. Granted his leave, he wasted no time, practically bolting from the chamber with a speed that suggested he feared his reprieve might be revoked at any moment. His rapid departure left a momentary silence in the room, a testament to the lasting impact of Vlad's justice.

CHAPTER 3

Peering thoughtfully through the Gothic window, Vlad contemplated the expanse of the academy's grounds. Doubt lingered: had he made a mistake in selecting this location? Was the allure of Alessandra clouding his judgement?

Retreating from the glass, Vlad's reflection faded against the sunset's golden glow. With a sigh, he withdrew into the shadows of the headmaster's office.

Pouring himself a drink from an ornate cabinet, Vlad watched the amber liquid catch the dim light. Each sip stirred a whirlwind of emotions within him. Despite his efforts to rationalise, he couldn't shake the unsettling notion that drinking Alessandra's blood had awakened long-suppressed feelings.

After dispatching the knights who dared encroach upon his territory in search of his kin, he turned his attention to the Order's prized possession—Roslyn Academy.

But sentimentality had no place in his quest for retribution. With steely determination, he reminded himself of his solemn oath to avenge his wife's tragic demise. He couldn't allow himself to be swayed by fleeting desires for a woman to whom he owed nothing.

FATIGUE WEIGHED HEAVILY ON ALESSANDRA'S SHOULDERS AS she made her way to her quarters upon arriving at the academy. The journey back to England had drained her, leaving her in desperate need of rest.

Once an assassin for the Order, Alessandra had roamed Europe in pursuit of their enemies. Now aligned with them, her world had shifted dramatically. Adding to the complexity was her strikingly handsome relative, whose authoritative demeanour and impeccable features resembled a masterpiece from the Old Masters.

When Alessandra first saw Vlad at his estate in France, she felt the world tilt beneath her. It appeared fate itself had intervened, igniting her pulse and stirring butterflies in her stomach. His enduring grace, even after centuries, left her in awe, while his playful charm only heightened his appeal.

The memory of Vlad's embrace left Alessandra trembling, stirring desires she couldn't act upon. Why did he have to embody everything she longed for, and why did fate make him her kin? The forbidden nature of her feelings added to the torment.

As Vlad healed the puncture wounds on her neck, Alessandra yearned for his lips to meet hers, wishing for a moment that never came. Instead, his warm smile lingered in her thoughts, a bittersweet reminder of what could never be.

Now, his distant demeanour wounded her deeply, making their travels across Europe agonising. Each moment with him reminded her of their impossible bond. Adding to her frustration was Vlad's patronising behaviour and his attempts to protect her undermining her skills as an assassin. With determination, Alessandra resolved to confront him and reclaim her autonomy. She headed towards the headmaster's office, ready to challenge the dynamics of their relationship.

Alessandra hesitated before the intricately carved wooden door, her heart pounding with uncertainty. Part of her hoped Vlad wouldn't be there, yet she knew she couldn't avoid this confrontation. With a resigned sigh, she rapped gently on the door.

"Enter," Vlad's voice beckoned from within, sealing her fate with a single word.

Cursing under her breath, Alessandra turned the handle and stepped into the office. Vlad sat in a corner, his demeanour sombre as he nursed his drink. Despite her inner turmoil, she couldn't help but feel a pang of sympathy for him.

"Hello, Alessandra," Vlad greeted her, his eyes betraying a hint of vulnerability. "Is there anything I can help you with?"

Her resolve wavered as she drew closer to him, the urge to reach out and comfort him almost overwhelming. But she steeled herself, knowing she had to confront him.

"There is," she said, her voice steady despite the tumult of emotions swirling inside her.

"Let me know what it is, and I'll do anything I can to help," Vlad offered, his smile gentle. But Alessandra wished he would stop, for every gracious gesture only deepened the turmoil in her heart.

"What changed?" she enquired, her tone laced with a mix of curiosity and frustration.

"Hmm? I do not know what you're talking about." Vlad took another sip of his drink.

"Typical. I thought you'd be different."

"I cannot see how I deserve to be insulted in this manner," Vlad shot back, his tone defensive as he crossed his arms over his chest.

Alessandra regretted her harsh words, wondering if she had gone too far. She wished she hadn't come here at all. Dealing with monsters as an assassin was simple—kill or be killed. But confronting this enigmatic man was a whole new challenge. Despite her brother's admiration for Vlad, he remained a mystery to her.

"Surely, you can't be this clueless. Something changed after you took my blood. Don't deny it. It will only make matters worse."

"That's true. I've seen who you were," Vlad replied, his gaze unwavering as he met Alessandra's eyes.

"What about before? There was something between us. Your presence pulled at me in a way I can't explain. Don't tell me you didn't sense it. Vampires feel things on a different level, so I can only imagine what you experienced when you walked into the room."

Alessandra approached Vlad, the gap between them closing steadily. His compelling presence seemed to pull her in irresistibly. It was risky. She was now dangerously near him. One wrong move and she might regret it all.

"Tell me, Alessandra, what happened when you met me?" Vlad whispered as he leaned against the wall and drank from his glass.

She felt like he was taunting her, waiting for her to say those words. Expecting her to give into her nature. She was his prey, and they both knew it.

"I needed something I've never desired before," she replied, shifting. "I wanted you to kiss me fiercely, passionately, as I haven't experienced before."

As soon as she finished the sentence, she was right in front of him. Vlad downed the rest of his glass and dropped it to the floor. He grabbed Alessandra by the wrist and spun her around, backing her against the wall.

"You mean like this?" Both hands were on either side of Alessandra, locking her in place. There was no escaping now for either of them.

VLAD DREW NEARER, CAPTIVATED BY ALESSANDRA'S alluring fragrance. "You bewitch me," he whispered, succumbing to the irresistible attraction, and kissed her. Despite her unawareness of her impact on him, there was a certain charm in her boldness.

Why was she here? Despite his efforts to avoid complications, she had entered his office, asking for answers and daring to insult him. Her audacity both angered and fascinated him.

But now, she tasted like honey and smelled like heaven. For a sinner such as himself, he felt like redemption was closer. If only that were true. If only his sins could be expunged every time he caressed her lips.

Vlad broke the kiss, his forehead touching hers. "Is this what you came for?" he demanded, his breath heavy. Despite his inner turmoil, he managed to restrain himself. His years of self-control were the only thing preventing him from giving in completely.

"I came for answers," Alessandra replied, her own breaths ragged. Even amidst the fervour of the moment, she proved unexpectedly yielding in his embrace, prompting Vlad to ponder her motives.

"Are you satisfied?" he asked, hoping she would say yes and leave before things escalated further. "Blame it on the alcohol, and we can pretend this never happened."

"Not even close." Her arms encircled his neck as she pressed him against the wall, her lips brushing against his.

The vampire smiled against Alessandra's lips and deepened the kiss, succumbing to the forbidden temptation of the moment. In his thoughts, he accepted his inevitable damnation, allowing himself to indulge in the present pleasure. Tomorrow was a distant concern, and what lay beyond that was a matter for another time.

A sudden knock on the door shattered the intimate atmosphere, jolting them back to reality.

"Monseigneur, Monsieur de Winter requests your presence in the dining hall this evening," his aide announced.

Vlad inwardly cursed the interruption, wishing for just a few more moments with Alessandra. If only they hadn't been interrupted, he might have had her right there on his desk, lost in passion.

"Yes, Angelique. Please prepare suitable attire for the occasion," Vlad instructed.

"Is there anything else, sire?" Angelique's voice came through the door.

"No, that will be all. You may leave," Vlad replied, turning his attention back to Alessandra.

"How did she know not to enter?" she enquired, visibly flustered by the interruption.

"Angelique has been with me for a long time. We share a special bond, and she has certain privileges."

"A well-trained little maid, isn't she?" Alessandra rolled her eyes. "Is that your preference? Meek women?"

"Could it be jealousy I sense? Is the feared assassin of the

Order feeling envious of a mere maiden? The merciless femme fatale, capable of breaking any man's heart, disturbed by a servant? I've looked into your past, Alessa." He whispered her nickname like a prayer.

"I haven't given you permission to address me that way. And you still haven't addressed my inquiry," she retorted, her brow furrowing in annoyance.

"Angelique, though human, possesses sharp instincts. She detected I wasn't alone. It's her responsibility to judge when it's suitable to enter her master's privacy. Forming a connection with a human this way grants them a longer lifespan and specific abilities. They still depend on vampire blood, and if they were to slay their sire, they'd spiral into madness and meet their end."

"I've heard of the various connections vampires can forge with individuals, depending on the depth of their intimacy, but I've witnessed nothing quite like this," Alessandra remarked, her voice tinged with curiosity.

"Yes, the bond between lovers is unparalleled. It involves the exchange of blood from both parties, directly from the heart's arteries. It's a connection that transcends the boundaries of this world," Vlad explained, a smirk playing on his lips as he trailed his index finger down her neck, stopping just above her heart. "Aren't you at all afraid after what we've just shared?"

"No, not at all. Tomorrow is a new day. For now, it's just the influence of the alcohol," Alessandra replied before leaning in to engage him in another passionate kiss.

CHAPTER 4

In the dimly lit headmaster's office, Vlad stood alone, surrounded by an atmosphere heavy with the remnants of Alessandra's delicate perfume. The room felt charged with tension, every corner whispering of their recent intimate exchange.

With a heavy sigh, Vlad leaned back in the chair behind the desk. He was no stranger to danger, but Alessandra posed a distinct threat—one that stirred emotions he had long since buried.

As the weight of their shared destiny pressed down upon him, Vlad knew that he would have to tread carefully. The path ahead was fraught with uncertainty, but one thing was clear: his encounter with Alessandra had changed everything.

An hour later, Vlad entered the dining hall, his heart burdened by the evening's occurrences. Draped in a royal blue suit embellished with gold details and diamond buttons, he emanated regal grace.

Upon his arrival, he sensed the subdued mood engulfing the siblings. Alessandra, dressed in a crimson gown with a plunging neckline, appeared contemplative, while Lucien's dark attire hinted at the gravity of their discussion.

"Good evening," Vlad greeted as he approached his seat.

"Good evening," Lucien responded.

He glanced at Alessandra, but she averted her eyes, her expression unreadable. Vlad pondered whether her avoidance stemmed from their recent interaction.

"I've summoned you to discuss our next course of action. But before we proceed, I need a favour from you," Lucien added.

"I suspected there was something on your mind, but I waited for you to broach the subject." Vlad feigned innocence.

"Avery, Lord Darmon's daughter is severely ill because of me. I've brought her here tonight, hoping you can offer your expertise and maybe find a remedy."

"Let's address the part where you believe her condition is linked to you," Vlad responded, his expression growing more serious.

"This might be tied to my blood. I know the Order has been studying vampire blood and its impact on humans. From what I've learned, scientifically speaking, a vampire serves as a carrier of a virus that changes the DNA of its host. When an infected human dies, the virus affects the cellular repair system, hindering the healing process. This causes damage to the DNA's double strands, prompting a healing response with flawed genetic material."

"Yes, I've been secretly monitoring their research. Although they said they were using already-turned vampires for their experiments, I have my doubts. But focusing on the Order's recent actions won't benefit us at the moment. Please, tell me, why do you think Avery's situation is linked to you?"

"Two theories. Either Avery had a dormant pathogen resembling the original virus cells. My saliva, from when I fed on her, activated it. She'll only survive by consuming human blood. Or my blood caused her condition. Over generations, vampire blood has altered the primary pathogen. What if I can infect anyone I encounter without them needing to be dying?"

"Lucien, you can't hold yourself responsible for either possibility. De Rosier turned you, and I'm glad he's gone. He would have faced my fury for what he did to you. Regarding your theories, without thorough investigation, we're in the dark, and time isn't on our side. Let me examine Avery. Maybe there's a way I can help her, utilising my innate magic and the distinct qualities of my blood as the original vampire."

Lucien rang a bell, and a knight promptly appeared at the door. "Please bring Miss Darmon to join us," he instructed.

The aide bowed and returned shortly with a frail-looking Avery.

"Lucien, who are these people?" Avery asked, her voice tinged with apprehension as she surveyed the unfamiliar faces.

"Don't worry, my love. No one here means you harm. You're safe," Lucien reassured her, attempting to ease her discomfort.

"Why am I back at the academy? Isn't this under the control of the Order?" she pressed, growing increasingly agitated.

"We retrieved it from them. Try not to dwell on it. Your priority should be your recovery. Vlad, a member of my family, is here to examine you and determine how we can ease your illness. Please, allow him to take a blood sample."

Avery recoiled and began to tremble. “No! Please, don’t let the vampire come near me.”

Alessandra rose from her seat and approached her, with Lucien following closely behind. “She’s frightened. While it may not seem significant to you, given her current condition...”

“It’s all right, Avery. There’s no need to fear. You’re safe,” Lucien reassured her, using his abilities to soothe her distress.

Alessandra retrieved a small dagger from a concealed pocket in her dress, then leaned across the table to grasp an empty teacup. With a deft motion, she pricked Avery’s thumb, causing her to flinch at the sting, and allowed the blood to drip into the cup.

Once finished, Alessandra turned to the knight. “Escort Miss Darmon back to her room.”

After Avery's departure, Vlad picked up the teacup, dipped his index finger into it, and brought it to his lips, displaying no discernible emotion.

“What are your thoughts?” Alessandra enquired of Vlad with curiosity.

“I believe it’s time for my nephew and me to have a frank discussion. In private. Lucien, if you would please accompany me to my office,” Vlad replied, rising from his seat.

CHAPTER 5

The two vampires walked in silence towards the headmaster's office, their footsteps echoing in the corridor. Within minutes, they stood before the entrance.

Vlad turned the knob and gestured for his nephew to enter. His countenance remained stoic, his features resembling chiselled stone with no hint of emotion. However, as soon as he closed the door behind Lucien, Vlad's demeanour shifted.

With a burst of supernatural speed, he surged forward, seizing Lucien by the throat and pinning him against the wall. Centuries of existence granted him certain advantages, and tonight, if he desired to crush the younger vampire, nothing would hinder him.

"Do you take me for a fool?" he snarled, baring his fangs. "Do you believe I'm ignorant of the House of Darmon's identity? That you're requesting me to heal a descendant of those I've sworn to annihilate?" Vlad's nostrils flared with anger.

"She's nothing like them," Lucien pleaded, his voice tinged

with desperation. "You used to care about aiding the innocent from what I recall. What changed?"

"I became a vampire, and I embraced retribution against the wicked. There's no going back for me. I can never reclaim who I once was. Have you ever known a supernatural being to be caring, loving, or compassionate?"

Vlad ran his fingers through his hair, attempting to regain his composure, while Lucien shook his head in resignation.

"When you've been the monster people fear for as long as I have, all the traits that once defined your humanity vanish. I've harboured resentment against the Order for centuries. You have no right to ask me to spare her."

"I understand, but I'm pleading with you. I can't bear the thought of losing her," Lucien whispered, his defeat palpable. A tear trickled down his cheek.

"You naïve boy. For a vampire, a mortal's life holds no significance. They enter and depart your existence, and it's futile to expect them to remain unless you inflict the same curse upon them. Can your love endure the test of time? Shall we put it to the test?"

"Will you save her?" Lucien asked eagerly.

"Yes, I'll do it for you, but my mercy comes with conditions. The only chance for her survival is if she becomes a vampire. And since we don't know the cause of her illness, it must be me who turns her."

"Thank you." Lucien expressed his gratitude, a glimmer of hope shining in his eyes.

"Don't thank me just yet. There's a second condition. Once she's turned, I will control her actions. I don't trust you to handle her if she becomes like her ruthless family," Vlad continued, his tone serious.

"She won't turn into them. I know her."

"Let's hope you're right. I wouldn't want to imprison her and watch you suffer for eternity," Vlad remarked mockingly.

"At least she'll be alive," Lucien retorted as he headed for the door. "I'm going to gather some of her belongings from our old place. If my sister asks, let her know I'll return soon."

Alone in the dimly lit office, Vlad stood motionless, his back against the closed door. Shadows danced across the walls, cast by the flickering flames of the candles scattered around the room. The air was heavy with tension, thick with the weight of the decision he had just made.

His mind raced with conflicting thoughts and emotions, each vying for dominance. The soft glow of the moonlight streaming in through the window illuminated his troubled features, casting long shadows across the floor.

For centuries, Vlad had lived in the shadows, a predator in the night. But now, faced with the prospect of condemning another soul to the same fate, he couldn't help but question the path he had chosen. He knew that whatever lay ahead, the consequences would be dire. But for now, all he could do was wait and pray that he had made the right decision.

After Lucien departed, Alessandra stormed back to the headmaster's office, her heart pounding with anger and frustration. She found Vlad seated at his desk, his expression unreadable as he perused some documents.

"Your brother has left. Is that why you've come to see me?"

"How can you be so heartless?" Alessandra burst out, her voice trembling with emotion. "To suggest turning her into a vampire as the only solution? What kind of twisted reasoning is that? Did you think I wouldn't find out? I may not possess supernatural abilities, but I have artefacts that could rival any power."

"Your emotions are clouding your judgement," Vlad said.

"Is that so?" Alessandra rolled her eyes in exasperation. In that moment, she harboured a deep resentment towards him. Lucien was all she had left, her sole remaining family after their father's disappearance, and she felt compelled to defend him, even if it meant angering Vlad.

"Indeed. Your behaviour reeks of petulance," Vlad continued, his tone firm. "Pull yourself together. Such immaturity does not befit you."

"Fine, I'll compose myself. Please explain." Alessandra folded her arms across her chest.

"When I sampled Avery's blood, I discerned she is rapidly deteriorating and has only a few days left."

"Don't tell me you possess clairvoyance," Alessandra scoffed derisively. "For someone of your stature..." she trailed off, leaving the implication hanging in the air.

"I don't possess such foresight. However, her blood had a foul taste, and it's your brother's doing." Vlad sighed heavily.

"Why did you withhold the truth from him about what could have caused her condition?"

"You underestimate Lucien. Such knowledge would devastate him. To realise he brought this upon the woman he loves... imagine the toll it would take on him," Vlad explained.

"Then why confide in me? Aren't you concerned I might betray your trust and inform him?" she challenged.

"Don't be so naïve. I've observed your concern for him, albeit expressed in your own unique way."

"What gives you such certainty?" Alessandra questioned.

"Don't forget, I've tasted your blood. I've glimpsed the real you, the inner struggle with your bloodlust that you face every day. I've witnessed it firsthand. And from that, I've come to the realisation that you and I are not so different. We're both born killers, it's ingrained in our nature; we're feared and reviled as monsters. Do you think you ended up as a weapon of the Order by mere coincidence?"

Alessandra squirmed uncomfortably under his penetrating gaze.

"Your brother dwells in a realm of dreams and ideals, detached from the harsh realities of our existence. We, on the other hand, confront life's brutal truths and take decisive action. He would have pursued a cure for her, clinging to notions of romance and chivalry, only to face bitter disappointment when he realised there is no such remedy. I've witnessed this scenario unfold before. De Rosier's blood was tainted, and whoever orchestrated your brother's transformation knew it. Throughout my lifetime, I've encountered many vampires like him. Sadly, by the time I intervened, it was often too late. They spread their infection like a contagion, driving others to madness. Ultimately, they become more monstrous than rabid dogs. However, if the illness is detected early enough, I can still offer a chance at recovery," Vlad explained with a grave tone.

"Could Darmon have engineered this to distance his daughter from Lucien?" Alessandra's anger simmered at the notion of the manipulative lord's possible interference. She swore to take matters into her own hands if she ever discovered his complicity in her brother's transformation.

"I doubt he would willingly endanger his heiress in such a manner. Someone else must be pulling the strings behind the scenes, and rest assured, I'll uncover their identity and hold them accountable," Vlad assured her, his expression steely with determination.

"What about my brother? We need to find a solution for him," Alessandra pressed, concern etched on her face.

Vlad's comforting smile eased her worries. "You needn't fret about him. I've been monitoring both of you closely and knew about his state. When I took both your blood under the pretence of checking your identity, I healed him. Your brother is an idealist, always dreaming of changing the world. Did you know that's why he joined the Order? But we're family, and we'll face these trials together. Please, keep this between us."

"My lips are sealed. I appreciate what you're doing for him. I know you might attribute it to some sense of duty because we're related, but I expect nothing from you just because..." Alessandra trailed off.

"It's nothing," Vlad interjected, brushing off her thanks. "I'm simply doing what must be done. Perhaps one day, when you've lived longer, you'll understand my cryptic words. I have a knack for foreseeing the future without the gift of prophecy."

"Intriguing," Alessandra remarked, her curiosity piqued. "How so?"

"History indeed echoes its past." Vlad's voice was tinged with wisdom. "Patterns emerge, and with my long existence, I've observed the cycle of fate unfold. Everything completes its circle, making room for fresh starts. Eventually, I'll ask you to drive a stake through my heart, and though you may resist now, you'll carry out the task when the time comes."

"Why me?" Alessandra enquired, her voice imbued with both curiosity and apprehension.

"Because you're the only one who could get close enough

to do it. I'm sure you realise I can't end my existence. Lord knows I've attempted it."

"What makes you so certain that I wouldn't hesitate?" Alessandra challenged, her scepticism clear.

"Fate has intertwined our paths for a reason. We're both creatures of the night, tasked with making the tough decisions," Vlad replied, his smile enigmatic.

VLAD OBSERVED AS ALESSANDRA APPROACHED HIM, HER movements cautious yet determined.

"What if, by the end of all this, you and I are on different paths?" she enquired, her voice betraying a hint of uncertainty.

"Then I would wonder what could have led us astray. There are two possibilities for us. Either we maintain our distance, accepting it without regret or second thoughts. Or..." His voice trailed off as he closed the gap between them, pulling her into his embrace.

Alessandra closed her eyes, and Vlad felt the anticipation radiating from her. She tilted her head, offering her neck to him. Instead of yielding to the urge to sink his fangs into her skin, Vlad chose a different path. He brushed his lips against her nape, tracing a slow, torturous trail.

He sensed Alessandra shudder at the deliberate teasing of her senses, and he couldn't help but feel a surge of desire coursing through him. Despite the gravity of their situation, he found himself captivated by the intensity of their connection.

"Please," she said, her voice barely above a whisper.

Vlad tilted his head, feigning innocence, though a spark of amusement danced in his eyes. He relished the moment, drinking in the sight of Alessandra's fierce yet conflicted expression.

As she awaited his response, her breath came in shallow gasps, her chest rising and falling with anticipation. Her eyes, a tumultuous storm of emotions, locked onto his, searching for answers.

"What's the second outcome?" Her voice was barely audible, laced with a mixture of trepidation and longing.

With a small smile, Vlad closed the distance between them, his gaze unwavering. He could feel the tension crackling in the air, the palpable electricity drawing them closer.

"That's simple. You become mine," he murmured, his words a low, seductive whisper that sent a shiver down her spine.

Their lips met in a passionate kiss, igniting a firestorm of desire between them. In that moment, Vlad's mind was a whirlwind of conflicting emotions. Was it madness, or something deeper, that drew him to her so fiercely?

Could he ignore the harsh truth that she had much life left to live, being so young? A true lovers' bond endured eternally, causing him to turn her into a vampire and subject her to the same solitary destiny as his—a perpetual existence without end. Would their shared attraction carry them through the ages ahead?

As Vlad wrestled with these thoughts, memories of his unfulfilled love for his deceased wife surged through his mind. He had sworn never to expose his heart again, satisfying himself with brief affairs with willing partners over the years. He had always refrained from forming a lasting connection. Until this moment.

Alessandra's blood beckoned to him in a manner entirely

unfamiliar. Every instinct, every part of him, insisted that she was the one—the ultimate piece in his everlasting life.

"Tell me," he whispered, his voice barely above a breath. "Do you want this?"

His gaze bore into hers, searching for any sign of affirmation. I know I may be the most selfish creature to ever walk this earth. "Every time I look at you, I feel like a starved man, craving sustenance. I don't know if it's madness or love, but one thing is certain: you are the only antidote to my affliction," he confessed, his voice laced with vulnerability.

ALESSANDRA WAS SUDDENLY JOLTED BACK TO REALITY, HER heart heavy with regret. A knot formed in her stomach, and she was engulfed by a wave of uncertainty, leaving her feeling lost and overwhelmed.

In that instant, she grasped the weight of the situation—she stood on the brink of a life-changing choice. The prospect of being forever tied to Vlad filled her with dread. The notion of relinquishing her humanity for an eternity of darkness and isolation was terrifying.

Conflicting emotions surged through her mind—fear, doubt, and a profound longing for something beyond. She wondered if she was prepared to give up everything familiar for a love that felt both thrilling and overwhelming.

As Alessandra met Vlad's gaze, she felt the pull of his desire, momentarily tempted to yield to his proposition. Yet, a subtle voice within cautioned her, reminding her of the irreversible ramifications of her choice.

"I can't. You and I are from different worlds," Alessandra sighed, her voice heavy with resignation.

"You're right. You and I..." Vlad's words trailed off as he ran his fingers through his hair, his frustration palpable. "It's a mistake. Forget about it."

As he released her from his embrace and stormed off, Alessandra felt a whirlwind of emotions swirling within her. Confusion, disappointment, and a pang of longing gripped her heart, leaving her feeling adrift in a sea of uncertainty.

Once the door closed behind Vlad, Alessandra sank to the hardwood floor, the cool surface offering a stark contrast to the heat of her emotions. She wrapped her arms around herself, seeking solace in the solitude of the empty room.

So many questions plagued her mind, each one adding to the weight of her turmoil. Why did he affect her so deeply? Why did her instincts scream he was meant for her, despite the vast divide between their worlds? The enigma of Vlad only fuelled her curiosity, igniting a fierce determination to unravel the mysteries that surrounded him, even if he was reluctant to reveal them.

CHAPTER 6

Moving away from his office, Vlad traversed the academy's corridors, his footfalls resonating in the silent passages. Outside, the fragrance of summer hung thick in the air, while the night wrapped the Victorian garden in its velvety embrace. Illuminating the narrow path were elegant cast iron gas lamps, their flickering glow casting a warm ambiance, painting the winding walkway with light.

Arriving at the centre of the garden, Vlad neared the black wrought iron pavilion, its distinct hexagonal shape contrasting with the surrounding foliage. Elaborate gold embellishments adorned the pavilion, featuring fleur-de-lis, cherubs, and heraldic designs meticulously etched onto every surface. It stood as a masterpiece of artistry, reflecting the sophistication of a past era.

Nested within a serene enclave of magnolias, lilacs, and peonies, the pavilion radiated a sense of serenity and loveliness. Within its confines, a garden bench, embellished with delicate trellis and leaf patterns, beckoned guests to pause and reflect amid the verdant surroundings. Above, the ceiling was adorned with three graceful Moroccan pendant lamps, their radiant golden hues infusing the area with a captivating and exotic atmosphere.

The meeting with Alessandra had left Vlad in turmoil, his mind a turbulent storm of thoughts and feelings. Their exchanges were a rollercoaster ride, veering from intense passion to abrupt detachment. Her unpredictable behaviour was frustrating, playing havoc with his emotions. He craved solitude to regain clarity, to escape the chaotic maelstrom of emotions that followed her wherever she went.

These moments reminded him of the frustrating intricacies of modern relationships. Nothing seemed simple anymore; every interaction was tangled in layers of ambiguity and hidden motives. Vlad sat on the bench, feeling the coolness of the wrought iron against his skin amidst the warmth of the summer night. Beside him, a small table held a bronze incense burner shaped like a delicate lotus flower, emanating the sweet scent of agarwood chips smouldering within.

Breathing in the familiar scent, Vlad was transported back to his days as a captive of the monarch. It was a time he paradoxically remembered with a sense of freedom. Under Murad II's reign, he had enjoyed some autonomy, pursuing his interests without constraint. The ruler provided him with an education in warfare, horsemanship, combat, and intellectual pursuits like philosophy, history, and languages such as Turkish and Arabic.

As he grew older, young Vlad developed a genuine affection for the old sultan and his son, Prince Mehmed. Despite starting as captors, they treated him with respect and hospitality, fostering camaraderie over enmity.

Upon his eventual release, Vlad aimed to maintain peaceful relations with his former hosts, acknowledging their past kindness. However, the political landscape shifted with the rise of Matthias Corvinus. The Order launched a religious crusade, enforcing its directives with severe consequences. Faced with the threat of conflict and the safety of his wife and subjects at risk, Vlad reluctantly cut ties with the Ottoman Empire.

By refusing to pay the annual tribute that had ensured peace for many years, Vlad incited open warfare with Prince Mehmed, who now held the title of sultan. This decision played directly into the hands of the head of the Order, much to their satisfaction and advantage.

"Still brooding, I see..." a voice chuckled from behind the glass walls of the pavilion, drawing Vlad back from his introspection.

Emerging from the shadows, a young man dressed in a sleek two-piece suit stepped into view. His hair, as dark as the night sky, was styled in an artfully dishevelled manner. His eyes, the colour of the Aegean sea, twinkled mischievously, while his strikingly handsome face, with its pale complexion, seemed to glow under the moonlight.

"Father..." Vlad breathed and got off the ornate bench.

In a sacred ritual of reverence, Vlad sank to his knees before the newcomer, a sense of awe and respect washing over him. His head bowed in humility, he awaited his response. The figure mirrored Vlad's gesture, lowering himself to the ground with a grace that spoke of royal lineage.

With a tender touch that resonated with centuries of shared history, he leaned forward, pressing a gentle kiss to Vlad's forehead. In that intimate moment, a surge of warmth flooded Vlad's being, reaffirming the deep bond that connected them across time and space. It was a poignant reminder of their intertwined destinies and the weight of their shared legacy.

As they knelt facing each other, their gazes locked in

silent communion, a profound sense of camaraderie and affection enveloped them. In the moment's stillness, the air seemed to crackle with the energy of their connection, forging an unbreakable bond that transcended mere words.

"What troubles you, my son?" Asmodeus enquired with genuine concern etched in his voice. "Your anguish reached me across vast distances."

Vlad sighed heavily, experiencing both relief and vulnerability in the demon Prince's company. Asmodeus gently helped Vlad up, offering silent support and empathy. Seated together on the bench, Vlad found solace in the demon's presence, a brief reprieve from his burdens.

"I'm grateful for your unexpected visit," Vlad admitted, his voice tinged with resignation.

Asmodeus's gentle caress on Vlad's cheek offered a fleeting moment of comfort, a reminder that even in the darkest of times, there was solace to be found in the bonds of kinship.

"I am faced with tough decisions, Father," Vlad confessed, his gaze drifting into the distance.

"Address the most urgent matter," Asmodeus advised.

"My nephew implores me to spare a descendant of our enemy, and I feel torn. It feels like a betrayal of my late wife, who suffered at their hands. I swore to avenge her death by punishing all who played a part in it."

Asmodeus placed a reassuring hand on Vlad's shoulder, offering a comforting smile. "Sparring the life of an innocent should never be a dilemma. This individual wasn't involved in your betrayal. I had hoped you had evolved beyond this after all these years," he remarked, his disappointment clear.

"I have indeed changed, Father. If I were still the ruthless individual I once was, there would be no turmoil in my heart. But I will do it, even if it pains me. I shall turn her, if not for

Lucien, then for the sake of his sister," Vlad affirmed resolutely.

"The same sister for whom you foolishly harbour feelings above all else?" Asmodeus chuckled knowingly.

Vlad arched an eyebrow, uncertain of how to respond to the question.

"Of course, I know that my only son is tormented by his affections for a mortal. Our bond of blood and magic connects us, allowing me to feel your every emotion—love, happiness, sadness. It's the burden I carry as your sire. But remember, there is always a balance in this world, and it comes at a cost."

Vlad sighed heavily. "She rejected me."

"If it were any other vampire, they would have claimed her by now. But you're a gentleman, and you wouldn't subject a woman to that. Instead, you endure excruciating pain trying to suppress your nature. I wish I could ease your suffering. Since the day our paths crossed, I've never seen you in such distress. And deep down, every fibre of your being is telling you that this female is your mate."

"And what do you suggest I do?" Vlad enquired, incredulous. "I can't believe I'm seeking courting advice from a demon." He shook his head in disbelief.

"Remember, I am the Prince of lust, so have a little faith. Ungrateful brat," Asmodeus muttered in mock annoyance.

"My apologies for offending you. I didn't realise demons had feelings," Vlad countered, and they shared a moment of laughter.

Asmodeus squinted. "As an assassin, she thrives on pursuit. Now that you're the one pursuing, she's naturally cautious. But if she responded well, it means she's intrigued. Prove your commitment. When women are unsure, they need motivation. Desire can be compelling."

"After I leave, be vigilant. The Order seems poised for a significant counterattack."

"Will do, Father. Thank you for your kind words," Vlad said, as he rose from the bench.

"Anything for my son," the demon replied before vanishing into the darkness of the night.

CHAPTER 7

Vlad hesitated outside Avery's chamber, his hand hovering over the doorknob. The weight of his decision pressed heavily on his mind, but the conversation with his father had granted him a semblance of peace. With a steadying breath, he turned the handle and stepped inside.

The room was dimly lit by flickering candlelight, casting dancing shadows across the elegant furnishings. A large canopy bed dominated the space, draped with luxurious fabrics in shades of deep burgundy.

Avery lay on the bed, her delicate form barely stirring as she slept. Her once vibrant features were now pallid and drawn, evidence of the illness that threatened to claim her life. Despite the gravity of the situation, there was a serene beauty about her, an ethereal quality that seemed to transcend her mortal form.

Vlad felt a twinge of guilt constricting his chest. Yet he couldn't disregard his nephew's desperate request and the strong bond he felt with the young woman in front of him. He understood the necessity of turning her into a vampire to save her, yet the idea of subjecting her to that fate troubled his conscience deeply.

Drawing nearer, Vlad's determination solidified. He extended his hand delicately to move a strand of hair from Avery's forehead, preparing himself for the challenge ahead.

"Arise, my dear," he beckoned to her.

Avery blinked, her eyes meeting Vlad's with a blend of defiance and exhaustion. "I detect the aura of death around you, vampire. Why have you come to my chamber?"

"I am here to offer you salvation," Vlad declared, a hint of amusement in his voice.

"I would rather meet my end than succumb to your kind," Avery retorted, her words laced with defiance. Despite her fragile state, she showed no sign of backing down. The Prince found himself admiring her spirit.

"Lucien has different intentions for you. He desires your survival. I am indifferent. You are the offspring of my foe, thus making you my adversary as well."

"Lucien," Avery scoffed, shaking her head in disbelief. "Love has a way of clouding men's judgement, doesn't it? My answer remains unchanged. Leave my chamber at once, or I'll scream."

In a swift motion, Vlad used his supernatural speed to move behind Avery, silencing her protests by covering her mouth with his hand, holding her in a firm grip.

"From the moment I first saw you, a sense of foreboding has lingered. While Lucien may have protected you before, our recent conversation has only strengthened my determination. It's time I turn you into one of our kind."

With a deft movement, Vlad exposed the vulnerable nape of Avery's neck, her struggles proving futile against his superior strength. Baring his fangs, he sank them into her flesh before redirecting them to his own wrist, allowing his blood to flow into her mouth.

Avery had no choice but to consume the blood, her resistance crumbling under Vlad's relentless control. Satisfied that she had taken enough for the transformation, Vlad snapped her neck in a swift motion.

"Now, as part of our kind, I can guarantee you won't interfere with my schemes," Vlad commented, unveiling the moon through the curtains, its eerie light casting the scene in crimson hues.

Vlad gently laid Avery back on her bed, his mind heavy with the weight of his actions. With a silent call, he summoned his maid, grateful for her efficiency.

Minutes passed before a soft knock echoed through the room. "Come in," Vlad uttered, his voice betraying none of the turmoil brewing within him.

As the maid stepped in, her eyes widened in astonishment at the scene unfolding before her. Vlad occupied an armchair by the window, his posture calm and collected, concealing the intensity of the moment beneath a façade of composure.

"Monseigneur, what is your order?"

"Although I quite like to see my enemies drenched in blood, she'll need a change of clothes," Vlad informed his aide.

"Certainly, my Prince. Anything else?" Angelique enquired, her gaze searching Vlad's face for any sign of emotion.

"Yes. She will need blood when she wakes up, my dear, to complete the cycle. Would you be so kind as to let her drink from you? Fear not; I will not let you be in harm's way. I shall be here watching her the entire time."

"She can have as much as she needs if that pleases you, my

Prince," Angelique replied dutifully, though a flicker of apprehension flashed across her features.

"You're a splendid girl. Thank you," Vlad said, his gratitude tinged with a hint of remorse.

As Avery slowly awakened, Vlad observed her cautiously. With each delicate movement of her eyelids, he braced himself for her reaction, knowing well that the revelation of her transformation would likely evoke a mixture of fear and confusion.

Vlad sensed the surge of panic coursing through her veins as her gaze finally settled upon him and Angelique by her bedside. In that moment, he knew he had to act swiftly to assert control over the situation and ensure her compliance.

With a calculated move, he reached out and clasped her throat, exerting just enough pressure to keep her subdued. The weight of his grip served as a stark reminder of his authority, instilling a sense of vulnerability within her that only fuelled her fear.

Next to him, Angelique stayed composed yet attentive, her presence silently affirming the seriousness of the moment. Her steadfast loyalty reassured Vlad that he had made the correct decision.

In his grasp, Vlad could feel the tremor of Avery's heartbeat reverberating against his palm, a tangible reminder of her humanity amidst the chaos of her transformation. Despite her struggles, he remained steadfast in his resolve, knowing that her acceptance of her new reality was essential for her survival.

"What have you done to me, you bastard?" she snapped, her voice sharp with anger.

"I merely followed the desires of your beloved and given upon you the gift of life. A thank you would be appropriate," Vlad replied, a hint of amusement in his tone.

Avery struggled against his grip, her eyes blazing with fury. "You make me laugh," she spat. "I'll dance on your grave when you're dead. My father will hear of this."

"The mighty Lord Darmon, is it? Are you admitting to being under his command?" Vlad enquired, his interest piqued.

With a smirk, Avery tilted her head slightly. "Would it bother you if I said yes? Or perhaps Lucien?"

"I've made it abundantly clear. Your fate holds no weight in my concerns."

Avery giggled. "You're lying. You care about your precious nephew, and since he cares about me... well, I don't need to tell you the rest. I'm sure you can figure that out on your own, sire," she taunted, her laughter tinged with mockery.

"You've got one thing wrong. I've got a firm grip on your throat and five centuries' worth of rage in my blood against your house. Keep taunting me, and I'll show you why they call me *The Impaler*," Vlad retorted, his voice low and menacing.

"All talk and no play makes Dracula a dull master." She laughed again, but Vlad's grip tightened around her neck, causing her to gasp for air.

"I can't believe such a beautiful face conceals such a devilish creature. Tell me, why did your father send you here?" the Prince enquired.

"Who do you think I'm more afraid of? You or my father?" she replied defiantly.

"Since you persist in behaving like a monster, I'll expedite this process for you," Vlad declared, as he seized the maid's hand.

With swift precision, he sank his fangs into her wrist, allowing her blood to flow into Avery's mouth, finalising her transformation into a vampire. Satisfied with the outcome, Vlad released the maid and offered a reassuring smile.

"Remain still," he commanded, locking eyes with Avery. Unable to resist the authority of her sire, she complied without hesitation.

While Vlad tended to Angelique's wound, the maid looked dishevelled and shaken. Vlad's expression held a touch of sadness as he used his blood to heal her injury before pressing a tender kiss to her wrist, a gesture of comfort and reassurance in the midst of chaos.

"I deeply regret this, truly. I never meant for you to carry such a burden, but you're the only person here I trust completely," he whispered with remorse. As the wounds on her hand healed, leaving no trace behind, he enveloped Angelique in his arms, planting a gentle kiss on her forehead. "I'm infinitely grateful. I can only hope you'll find it in your heart to forgive me for my actions, despite my vows never to exploit you in this way."

Angelique offered him a reassuring smile, her loyalty unwavering. "There's nothing to excuse, My Lord. I am here at your service, willingly."

"You deserve far more than what I've given. Should you wish for freedom from our agreement, I would grant it immediately."

But Angelique held fast to him, her resolve clear. "No, I beseech you, do not cast me aside."

"Very well, I shall not. But I promise, from this moment forward, to shield you with all my might." With those words, Vlad gently let her go and turned his attention to Avery.

"Now, regarding our unwelcome guest," he pondered aloud, seeking Angelique's counsel.

Her suggestion came with a hint of mischief. "The dungeons have been dreadfully empty of late. Perhaps it's time we change that, My Lord."

A sly grin crossed Vlad's lips. "Your thoughts mirror mine exactly. A fitting residence for her misdeeds, indeed."

With a firm grip, he guided his captive through the hallways, navigating the shadowed paths that led to the dungeon's forgotten depths.

CHAPTER 8

After her recent meeting with Vlad, Alessandra withdrew to her room, chastising herself for yielding to the captivating spell of his kiss. His touch reignited a storm of emotions within her, prompting her to wonder why she let his charm affect her, why she couldn't just push him out of her mind and carry on as if they had never met.

Vlad possessed a disquieting power over her, a control she hesitated to admit, even to herself. His presence alone proved to be a distraction, a magnetic force that diverted her attention from her responsibilities, stirring unfamiliar emotions within her. Was this perplexing sensation merely desire, or had Vlad employed his vampiric magic to entangle her emotions?

As an assassin committed to the Order, Alessandra had never entertained such desires. Love and passion were unfamiliar notions, luxuries reserved for those not constrained by the constant demands of their mission. In a moment of self-reflection, she scorned herself for her steadfast loyalty to her duty, for being so entangled in the organisation's schemes that she overlooked the pursuit of her own happiness.

Curse him and this increasingly tense predicament. The silence from the Order was deafening, a clear sign they were biding their time, likely marshalling forces for a significant strike.

And there she stood, grappling with the prospect of succumbing to desires that clearly transcended a simple kiss. Alessandra wasn't deceived; she understood the stakes were greater than she wished to acknowledge. Yet fear lingered within her—the apprehension of emotional anguish, the kind that accompanied love and heartbreak.

Her thoughts drifted to her brother, his face etched with despair as he pleaded with Vlad for Avery's safety. His pain was palpable, a stark reminder of the emotional turmoil she had always evaded. Her own heart, tempered by years of discipline, seemed impervious to such vulnerabilities. Or so she had believed until now.

Could she establish boundaries from the outset? Perhaps framing their encounter as a one-time event, an exploration of mutual attraction with no strings attached was feasible. Alessandra trusted Vlad; he hadn't given her any reason to doubt him. She would seek his assurance about this, relying on the respectful demeanour he consistently displayed towards her, save for the moments she tested his patience.

With a solemn heart, Alessandra studied her reflection, contemplating her next moves. Determined to seize this fleeting moment of indulgence, she opted for a sheer nightgown beneath a delicate, white lace robe for their rendezvous. After styling her hair and applying a hint of makeup, she felt prepared to confront whatever the night had in store. Upon completing her preparations, she cast a last glance at her reflection, content with the transformation.

Would Vlad agree with her proposal? She fervently hoped so. The idea of his acceptance sent a thrill coursing through her, a feeling she had suppressed until now. Just the sight of him in those perfectly fitted suits ignited her imagination, sparking a desire to run her fingers over his chiselled physique. With a deep breath, she allowed herself a moment to indulge in the fantasy of his touch.

Her hand instinctively reached for the medallion around her neck, a protective charm that warned her of imminent danger. She briefly considered leaving it behind for the evening, but the sentimental value of the gift from her father held her back. Despite the temptation, she couldn't bear to part with it, not even for one night.

Alessandra made her way through the academy's cobblestone path, heading to the Victorian garden, a place she cherished, and Vlad often visited. The uncertainty of his response weighed heavily on her mind. Would he reject her? The thought of his reaction to her attire added to her anxiety. Would he scold her for her boldness, ordering her back to her room and erasing the encounter from his memory?

With a heavy heart, she pressed on, her pulse quickening and her palms damp with nervousness as their meeting drew near. The fear of his potential disapproval for tempting him was almost unbearable.

CHAPTER 9

Vlad retired to his chambers, now housed in the headmaster's suite at the academy. Despite its opulence, the room exuded the timeless charm of regency design. Dominating the space was a splendid rosewood four-poster bed, its canopy adorned with luxurious fabrics. The walls, featuring a woodland motif, added a touch of natural tranquillity.

Moving through the chamber with a graceful weariness, Vlad's mind was a whirlwind of the day's events and the choices ahead. The suite boasted spaciousness, with lofty ceilings adorned by intricate beams and tall windows offering a view of the moonlit academy grounds, now under his control.

Approaching the fireplace, Vlad contemplated the cold hearth, considering the warmth a fire would provide against the chill of the night. With a simple gesture, ancient flames sparked to life, casting a soft glow that danced across the area, illuminating his features—those of a man, or rather, a creature, caught between two worlds.

His reflection in the mirror over the mantel caught his

eye. He paused, observing the man he had become over centuries—a visage that held both the wisdom of ages and the shadows of countless regrets. The surrounding space, filled with the trappings of power and isolation, reflected his eternal journey—a prince turned predator, now a ruler in a fortress not his own.

Vlad sank into the plush chair by the hearth, allowing himself a moment of rest. The flickering light played across the myriad of ancient texts and scrolls that lay scattered on the desk. The quiet of the room enveloped him, a rare respite from the eternal night that was his curse and his crown.

The room's vastness only accentuated his solitude, as thoughts of Alessandra's kisses haunted him, turning into an obsession he couldn't shake. He longed for her presence beside him, yet chastised himself for such foolish desires. Frustration surged within him, a tempest fuelled by yearning for the woman who spurned his affections.

Driven by a desire to find respite from his inner turmoil, Vlad sought refuge in the Victorian garden, its tranquil ambiance beckoning to him. The corridors of the academy echoed with the solitary toll of midnight as he made his way, each footstep a bid to escape his turbulent thoughts. The dimly lit path offered a sanctuary in his secluded haven. However, upon reaching his destination, he discovered that his solitude was not to be, as another presence disrupted the peace of his nocturnal retreat.

"Seems I'm not the only one who finds sleep elusive tonight." Vlad interrupted the silence, his voice causing the solitary figure to startle.

"This garden is my refuge when thoughts weigh heavily upon me," Alessandra confessed.

Turning towards him, her appearance sent a tremor

through Vlad. She wore a loosely tied dressing gown that parted to reveal a long, white chemise, hinting at her curves beneath. Her hair, loosely gathered into a chignon with tendrils softly caressing her face, lent her an air of innocent disarray mingled with allure. Swallowing hard, Vlad recognised the peril he was in.

"I'm sorry. It seems my thoughts have drawn you here tonight."

"What were you hoping for?" Vlad enquired, curiosity lacing his tone.

"You," she confessed, her bare feet brushing against the cool grass as she moved closer to him. "I'm willing to offer you what you desire." Alessandra paused, her gaze locking with his as she sought the words. "But just for tonight. I ask for nothing more."

Vlad took a moment to process her words, wondering if she was playing a game with him. Could she truly be offering what he thought she was, or was this some sort of amusement for her? There was only one way to find out if she was sincere —by challenging her proposition.

He advanced towards her with measured steps, allowing her a moment to reconsider. But when he reached her, Vlad captured her lips in a fervent kiss, pulling her close, feeling the rapid beat of her heart against him. The air was filled with a palpable tension, charged with the electricity of their shared moment.

As their lips parted from their tender kiss, Vlad's gaze softened, his fingers gently tracing the contours of Alessandra's face. With a tender smile, he reached up to release her hair, his touch sending shivers down her spine.

"Beautiful," he murmured, his voice a low, intimate whisper that seemed to linger in the tranquil night air.

In that fleeting moment, surrounded by the whispering leaves and the gentle fragrance of blooming flowers, they existed in a world of their own—a world where nothing else mattered except the raw intensity of their shared passion.

"Are you sure about this?" he asked gently, searching her eyes for any hint of hesitation.

"Yes," came her breathless reply.

Gathering her in his embrace, Vlad conjured a veil of invisibility around them, shielding them from any prying eyes. They lifted off the ground together.

"We're flying," Alessandra noted, her smile wide.

"Indeed. Just hold on," he reassured, though he knew she was perfectly safe in his arms. Landing smoothly on his bedroom terrace, he pushed open the French doors and carried her inside. With a few quick strides, he placed her gently on the plush mattress, ensuring her comfort in the secluded sanctuary of his room.

A thrill of anticipation raced through him as she reclined on the bed, her hair fanning out across his pillows in a dark cascade. It seemed surreal, this moment with her. Shedding his shoes, he slid into bed beside Alessandra, turning to face her with an excitement he hadn't felt in centuries.

Gazing at her with a mix of adoration and longing, he gently caressed her cheek, noting the slight quiver of her skin under his touch. "We can simply lie here if you wish. Your presence is enough for me," he murmured softly.

"I am certain," she said, her tone steady as she positioned herself atop him. "Although there's something you should know."

He tilted his head. "What is it?"

Her voice barely above a whisper, she confessed, "I have never been with anyone before," then leaned in for a kiss. But Vlad gently halted her advance with a finger to her lips.

"You can't be serious."

"I am. It started back when I was a student here. A guy from a wealthy family asked me out, and when I said no, he started rumours about me. That was just after I started my assassin training. He was probably just jealous," she explained, her voice tinged with resignation.

"I'll make him regret it for the rest of his life," Vlad declared, anger rising within him.

"Shh." She hushed him with a gentle kiss. "Let's forget about everything else. This is about you and me." She unbuttoned her chemise with deliberate slowness. "But promise me, just tonight."

"I promise," Vlad said, though in his heart, he knew he'd do anything to have her with him again. In his mind, she was already irrevocably his.

As the fabric glided off her shoulders, unveiling her captivating figure, Vlad enveloped her in his arms, delicately guiding her beneath him. Lowering himself, he pressed their lips together fervently, stirring tremors of desire within her. Alessandra skilfully undid his shirt, discarding it swiftly. As she reached for his belt with purposeful hands, Vlad paused momentarily at this gesture.

"You're sure about this?" he asked once more, seeking affirmation.

"Yes," she breathed out, continuing with his pants.

Vlad's lips traced a path down her neck to her breast, his finger teasing the sensitive peak in slow circles. Her gown rode up, revealing the soft swell of her hips as he explored her body with eager hands.

Alessandra moaned, arching into his caress, delighting Vlad with her eagerness. He savoured the sweet torment of the woman who had upended his world, prolonging the moment. Her playful provocation warranted such sweet retaliation.

"Please," she implored, writhing beneath him, "I can't wait any longer. I want you."

"Tonight, you'll learn a lesson, my dear temptress, about the consequences of flirting with danger. Remember, I am an ancient vampire. A fierce desire burns within me, and you are the sole balm. Be still," he directed, locking eyes with her as he removed the last barrier of her clothing.

She made him want things he'd never wished for before, making his heart ache for more than anyone else could give him. Alessandra tempted him from the first moment she'd stepped on his estate. And now that he thought of it, everything she'd ever done to him was just a prelude to tonight. Her blood called to him, stronger than before, and though he had indulged in it, he still wasn't satisfied. He needed more. So much more.

Vlad leaned close to whisper in her ear, "You are mine." It was in that instant he understood he loved her. Experiencing genuine joy for the first time, Vlad knew his life was irrevocably changed after being with her.

Vlad could tell she yearned for more—a deeper bond with him. Giving in to her silent plea, he allowed her that intimacy. Deliberately, he grazed the skin above his heart, cutting just deep enough to nick the artery beneath. As a vampire, his body would heal swiftly, making this moment fleeting. He had to make it meaningful. The ruby droplets of his blood trickled down his chest.

He extended his arm toward her, the crimson streaks painting a stark contrast against his pale complexion. "Drink," he urged, his voice a blend of command and vulnerability. This act would bind them in ways words could never express. As Alessandra hesitated, her eyes wide with a combination of fear and fascination, Vlad reassured her with a nod. "Trust me," he whispered, his gaze locking with hers, conveying the depth of his commitment.

Alessandra leaned forward, her lips brushing against the wound. The moment her tongue touched his blood, a jolt of energy surged through Vlad, a sensation he hadn't felt in centuries. It was as if a part of his soul, long thought to be dormant, awakened at her touch. He watched her, a mix of awe and anticipation swirling within him. As she drank, her body relaxed, and a sigh escaped her mouth—a sign of acceptance and the forging of an unbreakable bond.

The surrounding room seemed to fade into the background. The only reality was the connection forming between them. Vlad felt a warmth spread through his chest, a warmth that had nothing to do with the physical wound but everything to do with the emotional one being healed. For the first time in his long existence, he felt truly alive, not just a creature of the night but a being capable of love and being loved in return.

As Alessandra pulled away, her eyes met his, shining with an unspoken understanding. They had crossed a threshold together, stepping into a realm where time and eternity intertwined. Vlad knew that from this moment on, their destinies were irrevocably linked. He would protect her with every fibre of his being, and in return, she had awakened a part of him he thought was lost forever.

With a gentle caress of her cheek, Vlad drew her closer, sealing their bond with a kiss that spoke of promises, of battles to be fought side by side, and of a love that would defy the ages.

"You belong to me forthwith. Completely, and utterly, mine, *iubirea mea.* You're bound to me now, forever." The Prince uttered the words and cast the spell, binding them together. The first part of the true lovers' bond was complete.

Vlad was aware Alessandra would hate him forever after this, but that was a risk he was willing to take. He was ready to spend the rest of her life begging for her forgiveness rather than suffer heartbreak, for he knew his life would never be the same after tonight.

THE NEXT MORNING, VLAD STIRRED BESIDE THE WOMAN who had captivated his heart. Her hold on him was undeniable; she had penetrated his soul, rendering his resistance futile. He tenderly kissed her lips before a soft knock interrupted their quiet moment. Rising cautiously so as not to disturb Alessandra's sleep, he donned trousers and left the room to address the intruder. Closing the door behind him, he was greeted by Angelique's anxious presence.

"I apologise for interrupting, My Lord, but we are in crisis. Monsieur de Winter has sent me with urgent news. The protective wards have weakened since dawn, allowing supernatural assailants to breach our gates. Although the main magical shield remains intact, our vulnerability has increased because of the absence of Jade Nicolay, our leading witch who disappeared a while ago, leaving us unable to reinforce it."

"Have him meet me in the armoury," Vlad instructed, pausing momentarily at the door, an additional consideration in mind. "And spare my chambers your tidying today."

"As you wish," she responded, excusing herself. Angelique's cheeks tinged with colour, her comprehension evident.

When Vlad returned, Alessandra was waking up, her eyes shining with brightness, and her hair spread like silk across the pillows—a picture of peace. He leaned in to give her a tender kiss.

"Morning. What was that at the entrance?" she enquired, curiosity in her gaze.

"Morning. It's nothing to worry about." Vlad reassured her with a small inaccuracy. "Stay here and rest a bit more; I must discuss something with your brother."

Alessandra, unconvinced, huffed lightly. "Then why is this illuminating?" She held up a medallion, its glow faint under the dim light of the room. "It's meant to warn of danger."

"You're correct. We're facing a situation, but I require you to remain here, safe, as I handle it."

"I refuse to stay idle while others might be in danger out there." With a clear display of resolve, she attempted to get up from the bed.

"Stay," Vlad commanded, his vampire swiftness allowing him to catch her mid-motion, halting her with an effortless grip. His power rendered her immobile, cradled securely in his embrace.

"What madness is this?" Alessandra's voice was a mix of bewilderment and irritation.

"I've linked us through the bond. You didn't really think our night together wouldn't change anything, did you? What kind of man would I be?"

"And you assumed I wanted more than the obvious?" Her voice held a tinge of defiance.

"We'll settle this upon my return. For now, don't loathe me too deeply." A playful smirk danced on his lips as he gently placed her back on the bed, leaving a soft kiss on her forehead.

"Make sure you come back from whatever peril you're

hurrying towards. I won't be tethered to the ghost of a reckless vampire for eternity."

"My end will only come by your hands," he assured her, brushing a tender kiss across her lips.

"Keep tempting fate and that might just be your reality," she shot back, her gaze sharp as he exited the room.

CHAPTER 10

VLAD FOUND LUCIEN IN THE ARMOURY, BUSILY PREPARING for the imminent battle. Despite the gravity of the situation, a subtle sense of satisfaction coursed through Vlad, a remnant of the night's revelations. However, he was careful to cloak this personal triumph, maintaining the stoic demeanour befitting a leader in the face of adversity.

"What delayed you? Your human didn't make the urgency clear?" Lucien's tone carried a mix of concern and frustration.

"I was informed, but I got caught up with something—or rather, someone."

"Alessandra. It's hard not to notice her fragrance lingering on you. I saw the way you two have been around each other, but I didn't expect you'd actually..."

"What happens between us is our business. We're both adults who made a choice. Nevertheless, rest assured, I've pledged my dedication to her. She is bound to me now, indefinitely," Vlad responded, his expression hardening.

"I can't decide if I should thank you or prepare your funeral," Lucien retorted with an icy edge.

"Your words might carry more weight if your beloved wasn't currently our guest in the dungeon, exposed as a spy for her father and the Order. Though I spared her life and granted her our eternal gift," Vlad disclosed, his tone laced with a hint of mockery.

"That revelation doesn't exactly warm me to your cause."

With a brotherly pat on Lucien's shoulder, Vlad attempted to lighten the mood. He then retrieved a key from his pocket, inserted it into the lock, and turned it.

As the door creaked open, revealing the treasure trove of artefacts within, a wave of relief washed over Vlad. The organisation's decision to launch a direct assault was a scenario he was equipped to handle. His life had been steeped in conflict. Direct combat was an arena he understood well. However, this attack felt minor in scale compared to the full might the Order could unleash. What was their reason for restraint?

The hope that the armoury contained something vital the organisation wished to safeguard flickered within Vlad. If the institution truly wished, they could obliterate the academy from existence, settling their scores once and for all.

"Look around for any signs of a secret door or passage. I've got a hunch about this place," Vlad instructed Lucien.

"Understood."

Activating the ancient magic within him, Vlad probed the room's depths. He discovered and pressed a concealed switch behind a glass cabinet, revealing a hidden door behind an array of weapons. This method allowed him to sense any concealed spaces in the room, and soon, his intuition proved correct.

Leading the way, Vlad entered the newly revealed passageway, navigating a dim, tight tunnel until he reached another barrier. This door yielded easily to his vampiric strength, swinging open to reveal a chamber dominated by an imposing stone sarcophagus, its age clear in its weathered surface.

With caution, they approached the sarcophagus. Vlad's mind raced with possibilities. Could it contain a being of immense power, a potential ally or weapon against the Order?

Exchanging a glance with Lucien, they silently agreed to proceed. Each grasped an edge of the stone lid, and with a concerted effort, they moved it aside. To their astonishment, inside was not a body but a magnificent gold casket adorned with elaborate engravings. The moment Vlad's fingers brushed the lettering, a shock of energy surged through him, hinting at the casket's extraordinary nature.

"Cave tibi et dragoni qui perscrutator oculos in abyssum irent." Vlad muttered the inscription that was on the lid.

"Beware of the monster whose gaze will show you the abyss," Lucien translated. "It sounds like a warning. Should we open it?"

"The abyss is my father's realm. I won't be fooled by the Order's petty tricks," Vlad scoffed with amusement.

Upon opening the casket, Lucien recoiled in astonishment, staggering backward until his back met the wall with a thud of disbelief.

Looking down at the human, Vlad realised he wasn't dead but deeply asleep. Placing his hand over the man's, Vlad channelled his magic, hoping to awaken him. The man's eyes slowly opened, revealing intense blue irises that met Vlad's gaze. In a quick movement, the stranger grabbed Vlad's wrist, and their eyes locked together.

"Father," Lucien called out, alarmed by his tumble. "Release him; he's not our enemy!"

But his warning came too late. Within moments, Vlad's strength ebbed away, and he crumpled to the ground, unconsciousness enveloping him as his head met the stone with a dull echo.

UPON DISCONNECTING VLAD'S CONSCIOUSNESS FROM HIS body, the blond man stared at Lucien blankly.

"What have you done?" Lucien's frustration was palpable, regretting the delay in searching for his father, now discovered imprisoned beneath them.

"Vampires are our enemies," the man replied, eyeing Lucien sceptically because of his vampire nature.

"Father, please, he's an ally. Can you bring him back?" Lucien pleaded, anguish evident in his eyes.

"His awareness is elsewhere. If he's truly formidable, he'll return on his own," his father stated, folding his arms and chuckling with a hint of defiance.

Lucien grappled with disbelief and dismay, lamenting the chaos caused by his father's actions against Vlad. The repercussions jeopardised the fragile unity of his recently reunited family. "We'll have to wait and see," he muttered, dreading Vlad's inevitable wrathful return.

He signalled for his knights to assist him and contemplated the daunting task of informing his sister, bracing himself for her potentially explosive reaction with a sense of foreboding he had never experienced before.

As Lucien carried Vlad's motionless body back, he was intercepted by Angelique at his chamber doors.

"What's happened to the Prince?" she asked anxiously.

"Step aside, Angelique. He's unresponsive, and I'm unsure

of what to do," Lucien replied, feeling the weight of uncertainty about Vlad's condition.

He forcefully pushed open the bedroom door and met Alessandra's alarmed gaze. Lucien gently placed Vlad beside her and released her from her frozen state with a sharp command. Then he instructed Angelique to find suitable attire for Alessandra.

"What happened to him?" Alessandra asked, caressing Vlad's face, tears in her eyes.

"He's not dead. Vlad was attempting to awaken our father with his magic, but he mistook him for a foe and displaced his consciousness. I can't explain the specifics," Lucien said.

"He's here? And he did this to Vlad?" she asked, taken aback by the revelation.

Lucien nodded. He couldn't fathom what their father had aimed to achieve with this act, but he knew there had to be a purpose.

"He challenges me in this manner. I'll make sure he remembers who he's facing."

"Shh... Not now. Let's not quarrel over this. I'll investigate his abilities and even beg him on my knees to bring Vlad back. We both know we can't stand against the Order without him. Not now, not ever."

"But he always claimed he had no powers..." Alessandra trailed off.

"He had his reasons for hiding it. Whatever he was involved in led to him being locked in a sarcophagus in the armoury. But there's more. He looked much younger, like he travelled back in time, around the same time we moved to our house in Bath."

"That's odd."

"What's even more surprising is that he mentioned Vlad would return to us if he proves himself worthy. Worthy of what? He's already proven his loyalty by taking on the organisation. If that's not proof enough, then I don't know what is," Lucien remarked.

"It's sad to see him like this," Alessandra murmured, gently stroking Vlad's cheek. "What about the situation outside?"

"The magical barrier is holding up at the moment. The Order has amassed many supernatural beings, and the problem is we lack a powerful enough spellcaster to maintain it since Jade Nicolay disappeared before we returned to the academy. Even if all the witches here combined their powers, it wouldn't be enough. So, in the interim, we have to wait. I'm optimistic that our father will reconsider when he realises how serious things are."

"I hope so too, otherwise the Order will triumph, and all our efforts will have been for nothing." Alessandra sighed, planting a kiss on Vlad's forehead. "I'll set things right for you, I promise."

Lucien noted his sister's distressed expression, saddened by her evident suffering. Though she tried to maintain composure, the scars from their past were still there.

"Meet me in the guest wing when you're ready. Guards are stationed at the room's entrance, and I've used an artefact to neutralise his powers. It's the best I can do to keep him from escaping. He'll be more receptive to you," Lucien said before leaving.

He hoped Alessandra could extract information from their father, but was Vlad deserving of her risking her soul for him? Desperate times called for desperate measures.

After dressing, Alessandra headed to the visitor wing, still reeling from shock. Memories of her childhood flooded her mind, reminding her of the monster who had betrayed her to the Order. She vowed never to forgive him.

As she approached the chamber where her father was held, Alessandra steeled herself, determined to confront him. Inside, she found him looking at least a decade younger, confirming her brother's observations.

"He's unconscious for now." Lucien broke the silence.

"Alright. Get me a chair and some rope. We're going to have a conversation," Alessandra said, her expression hinting at amusement.

"Surely, you don't intend to hurt him?"

"It all depends on our dear father. I want to assess his deservingness of my mercy. He'll receive the same kindness from me as he showed Vlad when he stripped him of his soul," Alessandra answered. Over the years, she had never challenged him, but today was different. She was resolute in reclaiming her autonomy.

"I need you to leave. This is between him and me. He hurt someone I care about."

"But..." he protested.

"I am about to commit a sin, and I don't want that burden on your conscience. He and the Order raised me as a monster. It's only fitting I become one today."

After Lucien departed, Alessandra shut the door and retrieved an artefact from her pocket. Murmuring "Da fortitudinem," she activated it, feeling a surge of power flow through her.

She then manoeuvred her father's unconscious form from the bed to the floor, securing his arms with a rope. With one end of the rope fastened to his wrists, she threw the other over an exposed beam in the room. Using her strength, Alessandra hoisted him until she was content before anchoring the rope to the four-poster bed to keep him restrained.

Seated in the chair, she observed her captive, anticipating his awakening. Mentally steeling herself for what lay ahead, she waited patiently. After a few moments, he started to regain consciousness, writhing against his bonds and emitting groans of pain.

"How does it feel to be at the mercy of the monster you unleashed?" At that moment, he transformed from father to foe.

He coughed, slowly opening his eyes.

"Ah, my dear daughter, what a pleasant surprise," he greeted with a smile.

Alessandra, blaming him for their family's woes, merely rolled her eyes. Their ties to the Order were a consequence of his lineage.

"Pleasure? Lord Jarvis de Winter, Earl of Rothbury, revels in my presence now? I recall you couldn't wait to rid yourself of me," she retorted, holding him accountable for her mother's untimely death, a casualty of his entanglement in the supernatural realm.

"You haven't changed at all. Just as feisty as your mother," he remarked.

"Don't you dare bring her into this! She was your pawn as much as I was!"

"You weren't a victim. The Order had grand designs for

you, envisioning you as the inheritor of her abilities. Liliana was the most formidable being the organisation had encountered until they turned against her and ended her life. I was helpless to intervene, but I vowed to shield you and your brother until my dying breath. I knew they wouldn't relent in their pursuit of you, no matter what measures I took, but I hoped to give you both an edge," he explained.

"So, you have all these powers, and you couldn't save her? What use are you then? You sound utterly worthless to me. Give me one good reason I shouldn't end you right here and now," Alessandra demanded.

"I know you won't kill your father. You're not that far gone." He smirked.

"You're right," she replied, then retrieved a dagger from a hidden pocket. She got off the chair and started walking, pointing the tip of the blade at him. "Maybe I'm not strong enough to kill my father. But *you* are fair game."

She had to get him to talk and fast. Vlad's life depended on it. The longer he lay unconscious, the harder it would be to bring him back.

The man suddenly smiled. "What gave me away?"

"He never called Mama by her name. To him, she was Lili. It seems he gave her that nickname after he found you," Alessandra said, crossing her arms and narrowing her eyes.

"Fair enough. You've got me. Now what? We are at an impasse."

"You're deluded. I'm about to give you a little incentive to be more forthcoming." She thrust her dagger into his abdomen and twisted it, ensuring she inflicted as much damage as she could. "Who are you?"

The man grimaced, eliciting a smile from Alessandra.

"Tell me, how do your arms feel? Can your joints withstand the weight of your body? Should I stab you more to distract your brain from the excruciating pain you must be feeling? Or how about this?" She used her blade to cut through the muscle above the elbow on both limbs. "Oh, dear me. This is going to hurt wickedly."

"You spiteful woman," he cursed. "I bear the likeness of your father, yet you treat me like a demon."

"Call it unresolved family matters. And your presence only fuels my ire. While my father has faults, yours outweigh his. You tried to take away the man I love, and now I'm here for payback. Your only hope of survival is bringing him back to me."

She plunged her blade into the opposite side of his abdomen, provoking another pained groan.

"What a waste of precious blood. Perhaps I should summon my brother for help? I've heard he had a near-fatal encounter with his lover when he fed on her. And we both know how much you despise his kind."

"Lucien wouldn't treat his father in such a manner," he spat.

"You're correct. He wouldn't. However, once I inform him you're merely a mirror image of him, Lucien will see you as prey. You see, he's susceptible to bloodlust compared to other vampires. It's a trait passed down from the House of Dracul, our lineage," Alessandra disclosed, pacing around the room.

The man remained silent, weighing his options.

"Now, shall we test my hypothesis?" she enquired, heading towards the door to summon her brother.

"No, please don't. I implore you!"

"Well?" Alessandra pressed.

"My name is Henry, and I am a doppelgänger of your father, but I can assist you. I cannot bring back Dracula. Only he can return from the realm I've banished him to. However,

I possess some of his time-travelling abilities and may help you."

Moments later, Alessandra summoned Lucien. As he stepped in, his expression changed from curiosity to shock.

"I can't believe it," he started, disbelief clear in his voice. "I never thought you'd do something like this."

Alessandra chuckled, her laughter laced with bitterness. "You've always been soft-hearted, even for a vampire," she said, shaking her head. "But he's not our father."

"How can this be?" Lucien asked, his concern evident.

"Ask him," she gestured to the doppelgänger hanging in agony.

Lucien looked at the man again, his worry growing. "How long has he been like this?"

"Not nearly long enough. He deserves worse for what he inflicted on Vlad. But he's far from off the hook yet. He claims he can aid us," Alessandra stated, then shifted her gaze to her captive. "How do you intend to prove it? If you wish to live, speak up. I have no patience for fools."

"Start from the beginning. Who are you, and what is your approach for validating your worth?" Lucien said, revealing his fangs.

"I'm not your father," Henry started, his voice wavering. "The real Jarvis de Winter is a time traveller. I had empathic abilities, but after an unknown transfer of power, I gained the ability to travel through time as well. I am unable to explain how he did it, but he's the one who imprisoned me."

"That could be why he's gone. He might be avoiding the Order," Lucien pondered, looking at Alessandra. "What puzzles me is why he brought this man here and put him in a deep sleep."

"He must have had a purpose for him. I can't understand this anymore. Was our father against the organisation, or was he working with them? He seemed to follow their orders, yet he gave us artefacts to defy them, as if he knew we would rebel against them. Maybe he travelled to the future, saw what was coming, and realised he couldn't help us alone."

"It's possible that mom's death affected him more than we knew. Maybe his grief turned into a thirst for revenge, driving him mad. She resented him for being a knight of the Order. Her death could have pushed him over the edge," Lucien suggested.

"So, what's the plan?" Alessandra asked.

"We'll go back to the day of the academy's attack. Unfortunately, I can't go further back; I'm too weak from the blood loss," Henry explained.

"Let's pray it's successful. Otherwise, you'll have a ravenous vampire and the Order's deadliest assassin on your trail. Hate to break it to you, but your odds of survival are practically nil," Alessandra warned.

CHAPTER 11

As Vlad awoke, a sense of déjà vu swept over him. He found himself back in his former bedchamber in the Princely Court of Targoviste. The surroundings felt surreal, casting an eerie familiarity on his senses. As he lay on the bed, he traced the intricate details of the sculpted headboard above him, his fingers trembling slightly. The cool texture beneath his fingertips provided reassurance amidst the bewildering circumstances, confirming that this was no dream.

Vlad breathed deeply, his eyes drifting downward to his attire—a collection of garments from a distant era. The loose cotton shirt, black waistcoat, breeches, and boots echoed the clothing he once wore. He realised he had been thrust back in time, surrounded by the familiar trappings of his past life.

As Vlad stood and paced the room, conflicting emotions surged within him. The audacity of the one who orchestrated his confinement ignited a fierce rage, eclipsing any familial bond he may have shared with Alessandra. In all his centuries as a vampire, no one had dared to challenge him in such a way.

Amidst his anger, Vlad couldn't ignore a spark of curiosity. What message did the man in the coffin intend to convey? The question persisted, demanding answers that seemed out of reach amid his tumultuous thoughts.

Taking a deep breath, Vlad tried to calm the storm within him, grappling with the unsettling uncertainty of his situation. Was he truly in the past, or was this an elaborate illusion meant to confuse him further?

Approaching the wooden door bearing his coat of arms, Vlad scrutinised its details. Yet, he noticed a subtle difference —the addition of two angels blowing trumpets, absent in his memory. Frowning, Vlad pushed aside the anomaly, focusing instead on unravelling the truth behind his mysterious journey.

Frustrated, Vlad attempted to exit the chamber, but the entrance stubbornly refused to yield. With growing irritation, he tried to push it open forcefully, but his attempts proved futile. Instead of breaching it, he phased through the door, tumbling onto the unforgiving stone floor beyond.

Cursing quietly, Vlad picked himself up, nursing his bruises from the fall. Despite being in the royal chambers, the men stationed there seemed unaware of his presence, lost in a trance-like state.

A sense of unease settled over Vlad as he considered the eerie silence and the strange behaviour of the knights. Determined to uncover the truth, he cautiously explored the palace, haunted by troubling questions. Would he starve if he couldn't escape this nightmarish situation?

In the adjacent chamber, Vlad was stunned by the surreal scene. He saw himself seated on the throne, conversing with two unfamiliar dignitaries. Recognition dawned as he realised they were envoys from the Vatican, reminding him of past encounters and stirring distant memories.

These emissaries had once pleaded with him to abandon the brutal practice of impaling in warfare. In the past, he had scorned them, mocking their faith and dismissing their pleas. This insolence had angered the Pope, leading to demands for his arrest on charges of war crimes.

Yet, the present encounter was vastly different. Instead of defiance, Vlad greeted the envoys with courtesy and gratitude. He even instructed his attendants to prepare a meal for them before they departed. As the emissaries left, Vlad, now in human form, appeared lost in thought, pondering the strange turn of events.

How had Jarvis orchestrated such a profound shift in this reality? Vlad pondered this question as he continued his search for a portal back to his own realm. He remained vigilant of the arcane forces at play in this strange world. Until he had witnessed all that Jarvis intended for him to see, he would be trapped in this surreal realm, far from the embrace of his beloved Alessandra.

Thoughts of Alessandra brought memories of his late wife to Vlad's mind, prompting him to seek her chambers. Navigating the maze-like corridors, he approached the ornate wooden door, where the sound of a woman's laughter reached him. Stepping inside, Vlad entered the bedchamber and was met with a curious sight: his human counterpart reclining on the royal bed, engaged in lively conversation with a female figure.

This scene struck Vlad as odd, as he had never recalled such vivacity between himself and his deceased wife. As he lingered, he realised that the woman's voice did not belong to his spouse. Drawing closer to the bed, he parted the curtains to reveal the figure's identity.

A surge of shock and jealousy washed over Vlad as he beheld Alessandra's familiar features—her chocolate-coloured curls and captivating eyes. She stood before him, sharing laughter and affectionate gestures with his human counterpart. The sight filled Vlad with unsettling jealousy towards the two lovers.

Vlad sighed in frustration, running his hand through his hair. This situation felt surreal. He had never known Alessandra in his past life, nor had he ever shared such intimacy with his late wife. The presence of Alessandra and the strange scene unfolding before him blurred the lines of reality.

The sound of a newborn's cry abruptly ended the laughter in the room, prompting the woman to tend to the infant. Vlad felt a pang of discomfort and quickly withdrew, stumbling out of the chamber. Whoever was behind this chaos seemed determined to torment him. The one thing vampires could never have was the experience of fatherhood in the conventional sense. The acknowledgment of his everlasting loneliness burdened Vlad, engulfing him in profound feelings of yearning and remorse.

The Prince wandered through the ancient fortress, its white walls adorned with black-painted wooden beams, each a stark reminder of his tumultuous past. The unchanging stone walls seemed to reflect his own unending existence. Descending the stairs, he entered the palace gardens.

In the warm glow of the summer sun, two dark-haired boys played with wooden swords. One stumbled and fell, prompting cries that caught the attention of their mother, Alessandra. She rushed to the fallen child, gathering her skirts as she planted a gentle kiss on his forehead.

Vlad tried to call out to her, but his voice failed him. Suddenly, day turned to night, and before him stood his former human self—bruised, battered, and bound. The mortal Vlad appeared resigned, his spirit broken as he inscribed runes to summon the demon Asmodeus.

A sense of urgency gripped the Prince as he longed to warn his mortal self of the grave mistake looming ahead. He wished to convey that embracing vampirism and seeking vengeance for eternity was not a path worth pursuing. Witnessing the potential alternate life he could have led filled him with doubt about every decision he had made since becoming ruler. Had he ever been right? Did his misguided choices inadvertently lead to the demise of his late wife and countless others? He yearned for the chance to turn back time.

Summoning all his strength, he cried out, "Stop!" His human counterpart paused, briefly glancing up from his task. Behind the mortal prince, an angel descended, majestic wings unfurled as she approached vampire Vlad.

"It is time for you to depart this world," the celestial being declared.

"But it's not my time yet. There's much left for me to do, many who rely on me," the vampire pleaded.

"You've caused enough chaos. Others can carry on the battle."

"Please, I beg you." The immortal prince sank to his knees, tears streaming down his cheeks. "I, Vlad Drakulya, admit my sins without excuse, humbling myself before the Almighty. I repent for all I've done and the pain I've caused, while seeking the Lord's forgiveness and redemption."

The angel sighed softly, offering Vlad a compassionate smile. "The Lord has heard you." With gentle reverence, she lowered herself and kissed the vampire's brow, cleansing him. "Rise, Vlad Drakulya, child of God."

VLAD'S EYES FLUTTERED OPEN, GREETED BY FAMILIAR FACES: Lucien, Alessandra, and the enigmatic figure from the coffin. Awareness returned, but beneath the relief lay a storm of emotions from his recent ordeal in the alternate realm. Alessandra, always quick to react, rose and embraced him, her lips meeting his in a tender kiss. Vlad felt conflicting sensations—gratitude for her affection yet unease from the horrors he had endured.

Despite the conflicting emotions, Vlad embraced the moment, finding solace in his companion's embrace. Yet, scars from his harrowing journey remained, casting a shadow over his reunion with reality.

"I feared I might lose you," she admitted, her smile tinged with relief.

"How long was I incapacitated?" Vlad enquired.

"A few days. I was warned you might not survive the coma, but I refused to accept such bleak predictions. And now here you are, back with us and unharmed."

"Thank you, my darling, for your faith. I am deeply grateful. But how did we thwart the impending invasion by supernatural forces?"

"We've journeyed back in time. We find ourselves precisely one day before the assault on the academy. He assisted us." Alessandra gestured towards the man resembling her father.

"Yet, the threat of the supernatural incursion still looms," Lucien interjected. "Our victory remains temporary, merely granting you time to recover your strength."

"We may have an issue," Vlad stated.

Henry quirked an eyebrow. "And what might that be?"

The Prince murmured, addressing Lord de Winter...

"He's not our father. He's Henry, a duplicate from another realm," Alessandra clarified.

"Thanks to him and his animosity towards vampires, I am no longer one. Whether to express gratitude or curse him for endangering your life is uncertain," Vlad remarked.

Henry burst into laughter. "But you have transcended into something far greater. God has bestowed His blessings upon you and thus liberated you from your constraints. You no more depend on blood to sustain yourself. Your curse has been lifted."

"I only hope that whatever I've become will suffice to safeguard the one I cherish most in this existence," Vlad said, offering Alessandra a wistful smile.

She leaned against him, resting her head on his chest. Jarvis and her brother recognised this as their cue to depart their chamber.

"Come closer," he murmured. Vlad's thoughts were in turmoil. How could he ensure her safety now? He was convinced that Henry had played a cruel trick on him. Since awakening, he sensed no remnants of his former power. He felt hollow, a sensation of fear creeping in for the first time in his immortal existence.

Alessandra lifted her head from his chest, responding to his call, her presence a balm to his turmoil. Vlad could only imagine the sorrow she must have endured during his ordeal.

"Forgive me," he murmured. "I tend to be self-centred when it concerns you. I wish I knew how to shield you from harm."

"What transpired during your absence?" Alessandra enquired.

"That man manipulated my thoughts," Vlad explained. "He dangled all my desires before me, only to snatch them away. The most distressing part is that a part of me longs to return to that illusory world. I understand it was all a fabrication, yet I still feel shattered inside." Vlad sighed, offering her a strained smile.

Alessandra extended her hand, gently caressing his face in a bid to offer solace. Overwhelmed by the urge to ease his anguish, she found herself uncertain of the right approach. She needed him to confide in her about what had transpired so she could provide the necessary support.

Sensing the weight on Vlad's heart, Alessandra realised their bond remained strong. Despite his change, she could still feel his emotions as keenly as before. This revelation puzzled her. If he was no longer a vampire, their connection should have severed. There had to be an explanation.

Breaking the touch, Alessandra met Vlad's gaze with determination. "What if..." she began, sitting upright in bed and furrowing her brow. "It can't be," she muttered, shaking her head. "I swear, I'll make that villain pay."

Vlad observed her with a mix of confusion and concern.

"I have an idea," she said at last. "Just hear me out."

Alessandra produced a small knife from her pocket, pricked her index finger, and offered it to Vlad. His gaze sharpened upon seeing her blood. Without hesitation, he grasped her hand and brought her finger to his lips.

"He may have manipulated your mind, but he couldn't

strip away your abilities. You're still a vampire," she affirmed, smiling.

"But... I don't feel like one." Vlad sighed.

"You responded to my blood," she pointed out. "He will pay for what he did to us. I don't understand his motives or why he inflicted such pain on you."

Henry needed to restore Vlad to his former self. They couldn't face tomorrow's threat with a weakened vampire. Vlad seemed disconnected from his powers. Alessandra cupped his face and leaned in to kiss his forehead.

"I need you to trust me," she whispered, undoing a few buttons on her shirt. "I believe I have a solution to help you reclaim your true self."

Using their connection, she aimed to enhance the residual magic within him. Alessandra tilted her neck. "You need to feed. And this time, don't hold back."

VLAD FOUND HIMSELF CAPTIVATED BY THE FIGURE BEFORE him, each curve of her form radiating an irresistible allure. Amidst a whirlwind of emotions, he teetered on the edge of desire and restraint, grappling with the fear of losing control.

Alessandra's urgent plea pierced through his inner turmoil, stirring a mix of longing and apprehension. Could he trust himself on this perilous path, navigating his desires without succumbing to darkness?

"Please," she urged, her voice tinged with urgency. "We require this connection. I need you close to me."

Her words pierced through Vlad's hesitation, striking a chord deep within him. Despite the looming uncertainty, he felt drawn to Alessandra's presence, unable to resist her magnetic pull.

Her proposition held a tempting appeal, promising intimacy and understanding beyond words. Vlad was both comforted and unsettled by her intuitive grasp of his desires.

Cursing her seductive power, Vlad wrestled with conflicting emotions. Yet, he couldn't deny his yearning for the connection she offered—a chance to bridge the divide between them, if only briefly.

With a low growl of frustration, Vlad tore at the fabric of Alessandra's blouse, the sound of rending fabric echoing through the chamber. His movements were rough, desperate, fuelled by an all-consuming need that threatened to consume him whole.

Pulling her close, Vlad relished the intoxicating scent of her skin, his lips tracing a fiery path down the elegant contour of her throat. Each gentle kiss expressed his yearning, a silent request for forgiveness amidst the fervour of desire. Succumbing to his hunger, Vlad sank his fangs into her flesh. The flavour of her blood sparked an unquenchable thirst, engulfing his very being.

But as he neared the pulsing rhythm of her heartbeat, Alessandra's touch brought him to a sudden halt. Her fingers, gentle yet firm, lifted his chin, forcing him to meet her gaze. Confusion flickered in his eyes, mingling with a potent mix of desire and uncertainty.

"I need this too." Alessandra's words hung between them like a whispered promise. Vlad's gaze darkened with hunger, a silent acknowledgment passing between them.

With a determined resolve, Vlad's hands moved with practised ease, deftly unfastening the buttons of Alessandra's jeans. Each button yielded to his touch, revealing tantalising glimpses of the smooth expanse of her skin beneath. As he exposed more of her, a rush of desire surged through him.

With each breath, Vlad felt the anticipation build, his senses heightened by the intoxicating scent of her arousal. And then, with a swift and decisive movement, he positioned himself above her, ready to claim what was rightfully his.

As his fangs sank into the tender flesh above her heart, Alessandra's soft moan of pleasure filled the air, a symphony of ecstasy that reverberated through the chamber. The taste of her blood, warm and intoxicating, flooded his senses, sending a heady rush of euphoria coursing through his veins.

In that moment, as their bodies melded together in a primal dance of passion and desire, Vlad felt a shift within him. It was as if a missing piece of himself had finally been found after the completion of their lovers' bond.

And as he opened his eyes, suddenly aware of the power that Alessandra was surrendering to him, he knew that their connection was stronger than ever before. With a sense of awe and reverence, Vlad gazed upon his beloved, knowing that they were now together in a way that transcended mere mortal understanding.

CHAPTER 12

As morning sunlight seeped through the curtains, Vlad woke, feeling Alessandra's presence beside him. He held her close, cherishing the intimacy of their embrace. Amidst his swirling thoughts, one stood out: his unwavering determination to be with Alessandra. With her, he felt an unbreakable bond, driving his resolve to protect her. Though Alessandra was fiercely independent, Vlad admired her strength. He vowed to stand by her side through any challenges they faced. Together, they formed an unstoppable force, bound by love and commitment.

When he drank her blood the previous night, Vlad witnessed Alessandra's resilience in the face of pain and her strength. Despite learning about his lifeless state, she didn't shed a tear. Instead, she directed her anger towards the source of her suffering, using it as fuel.

Their tranquillity was interrupted by a gentle knock, signalling Angelique's arrival to warn him of the impending threat. Vlad slid out of bed silently, careful not to disturb

Alessandra's rest. He dressed in jeans and approached the door.

Angelique bowed respectfully as he enquired about the timing. With a nod, she confirmed it was time.

Returning to the room, Vlad's gaze lingered on Alessandra's peaceful form. She appeared innocent in her slumber, prompting him to wish he could shield her from the world's dangers.

Seated on the edge of the bed, Vlad leaned in to plant a tender kiss on Alessandra's lips, whispering softly, "Wake up, my beloved wife."

With a hint of amusement, Alessandra slowly blinked her eyes open. "I don't recall marrying you last night."

Chuckling, Vlad explained, "It's a matter of perspective. In ancient times, cohabitation signified marriage to many. However, in Wallachian tradition, formal marriage is required to avoid societal repercussions."

Alessandra smirked in disbelief, pulling Vlad closer for another kiss. "How audacious," she remarked playfully. "As a Wallachian prince, can't you simply decree a new law?"

"If only it were that simple, I'd make a law to keep you by my side."

"Well, I don't mind being an outcast."

"Come here, you," he said playfully, drawing Alessandra into his embrace and settling her on his lap. "I want to proclaim to the world that you belong to me. Your objections won't deter me. 'Viscountess D'Auvergne' has a certain ring to it, doesn't it? It may be unprecedented, but I'm willing to make an exception, just for you."

Alessandra smiled at him. "I'll agree on one condition. I overheard Angelique at the door earlier. Please, be cautious today. I don't want any heroics. If you want me to marry you, then promise me you'll stay safe. I was nearly beside myself when Lucien brought you back unconscious. I can't bear the thought of a repeat."

"Your wish is my command, my lady. I'll strive to stay alive for the sake of your peace of mind," Vlad assured her, brushing his lips against hers. "I cherish you above all else, and I swear to fulfil your every desire."

"I love you too, my prince," Alessandra replied, blushing.

Vlad's heart swelled with love as Alessandra's words washed over him, her blush only adding to her radiant beauty. The endearment 'my prince' resonated deeply within him, igniting a warmth that spread through his chest.

"I like the sound of that." Holding her close, Vlad wished the looming threat would disappear, wanting more time with his Alessa. "I have to go, my love," he said regretfully, gently placing her back on the bed. "Can you assist your brother in gathering the vampire knights and supernatural students to guard the gate? There's something I must attend to before joining them outside."

"You can count on me," she responded, getting out of bed and beginning to dress.

"I'll see you shortly," Vlad said, kissing her forehead before leaving the chambers.

With each step he took, his heart grew heavier with the weight of their mission, but he drew strength from the knowledge that Alessandra was by his side, a beacon of light in the darkness that surrounded them.

CHAPTER 13

Vlad descended into the basement levels of the academy, once envisioned as the ultimate stronghold against supernatural threats. Now it stood deserted, save for Avery and another enigmatic entity.

Fuelled by Alessandra's blood and his proximity to the mysterious being, Vlad sensed its power resonating within him. With an antiquated key in hand, he approached the designated cell and unlocked it effortlessly. Inside, Vlad came face to face with a familiar figure: the Angel of Judgement, seated on the floor with a smirk.

Zerachiel addressed Vlad with a scrutinising gaze. "At last, Vlad Drakulya, we meet. I've been awaiting your appearance," she began, assessing him from head to toe.

"This can't be." Vlad staggered backward, disbelief etched on his face.

"Your experiences weren't mere dreams. They were real. For mortals, such encounters typically occur at death, as I guide their souls for examination."

"Was that what happened to me when I was unconscious?" Vlad asked.

"It's more complex, but essentially, yes," Zerachiel replied. "God has judged you and deemed you worthy. Despite your transgressions, He has granted you forgiveness and the opportunity to continue existing."

"And what might that purpose be?" Vlad enquired.

"Everything you've endured has led to this. You were chosen to lead the resistance, and I was tasked with assisting you," Zerachiel revealed.

"But why did God allow this organisation to persist?"

"There are celestial laws that prohibit interference. God has noticed the imbalance caused by the Order and tasked me with two missions," the angel explained.

"Which child did you bless?"

"There's a young lady whose blood resonates with you. A few drops of my blood on her lips triggered a reaction."

"Are you saying all this was part of God's plan for me?" Vlad asked incredulously. "That the centuries of suffering were orchestrated for a greater purpose?"

"God has a plan for every creature, human or otherwise. You're mistaken if you think you're exempt from that."

Vlad sighed, running his hand through his hair. She had a point. It was foolish of him to believe he could escape God's authority.

"Let's say I entertain your ideas. What's next? I'm facing an army of supernatural beings threatening to overrun us, and I seem to have lost touch with my vampire powers."

"I've freed you from your chains. You no longer rely on blood for survival. The demon prince's curse twisted his gift to you." She attempted to stand but stumbled. "This is the extent of my help. Years of captivity have weakened me."

"In return for your aid, you'll always have sanctuary here.

With time, you'll regain your powers and return to heaven," Vlad promised.

The angel managed a smile tinged with sorrow. "Let's go. We are needed in the battle."

OUTSIDE THE ACADEMY GATES, A FORMIDABLE ARMY OF vampires, witches, and warlocks gathered, threatening the safety of everyone at Roslyn. Lucien and Alessandra, perched atop their forces of vampire knights and supernatural students, understood one thing: despite being outnumbered, they had to make this stand count—it was their only chance at survival.

"The barrier is nearly gone. I sense the magic waning." Lucien broke the silence.

"Why is Vlad taking so long?" Alessandra asked.

"He was vague about the threat when he was alerted. Let's hope he arrives soon with a weapon that can turn the tide in our favour," Lucien replied, sharing her concerns.

Alessandra's medallion glowed brighter.

"Prepare yourselves!" she called out to the defenders at the gates. In mere moments, their protective barrier vanished before their eyes.

With the path clear, the enemy surged toward the courtyard.

"Hold your ground... wait... attack!" Lucien commanded. At his signal, the students and vampire knights surged forward to engage the foe.

The air resounded with the clash of metal and swords as

combat erupted. Meanwhile, the academy's witches countered the magical creatures with torrents of fire.

Lucien deftly faced off against two vampires with his Katana, while Alessandra wielded a pair of sai, swiftly engaging a formidable opponent. Opting for the sai's versatility, she parried and struck with precision, gaining the upper hand in the melee.

"Any sight of Vlad?" her brother asked.

"None. I'm worried about what might have happened. Whatever Henry did to him has clearly affected him. He still can't tap into his powers. If we didn't need his help, he'd be in trouble for what he did to Vlad," Alessandra said, plunging her blade into a vampire's heart, causing him to crumple to the ground.

Surveying the battlefield, Lucien noticed the academy's students holding their own against the enemy as the bodies of their adversaries piled up. Their swords gleamed menacingly as they dispatched every foe in their path.

"I hope he overcomes this. There's no shortage of supernatural creatures, and while we can handle them for now, I wonder how long we'll be able to do that."

"Not long," Alessandra said before pressing against her chest, attempting to stem the flow of blood from the dagger wound, then collapsed. The scent of her blood filled the air, causing Lucien to whirl around toward the source.

"Alessandra!" he cried out, his voice echoing.

At the sight of this, Vlad materialised beside Lucien, holding a frail-looking figure. "How did this happen?" he enquired.

"I'm not sure. She dispatched her opponent, and then I turned away for just a moment..."

"She's slipping away. Time is running out," Vlad pointed out.

Alessandra's blood formed a pool around them, attracting more enemy vampires. Within moments, they were surrounded.

"What should we do?" Lucien asked. "I can't take them all."

"Zerachiel, we need you now. Act quickly. I can fend off the vampires for a few minutes..." Vlad's voice trailed off.

"Should we turn her?" Lucien proposed.

"She can't become a vampire; her body won't make the transition. I need to complete the blessing I began years ago," Zerachiel explained.

"How will a prayer save her? Vlad, is this the weapon that will save us? Have you lost your mind?" Lucien snapped, shoving the angel to the ground. "Get out of the way and stop wasting time if you want to live, old woman." He bared his fangs, ready to confront the stranger.

"Have faith. This is no ordinary woman; she's a celestial being," Vlad assured.

Zerachiel began chanting in an unfamiliar language, fully focused on her task and ignoring the frantic vampire.

"If my sister dies today, I'll be the one to end you, right after I've drained your angel."

"I expect nothing less." Vlad smiled.

THE METALLIC WHIRRING CUT THROUGH THE AIR, triggering Alessandra's instincts to evade. Despite her efforts, the dagger seemed to follow her every move, ultimately finding its mark in her chest.

A surge of agony coursed through her, but Alessandra

pushed it aside. Pain was a familiar companion in her line of work. Yet, as she observed the crimson stain spreading across her clothes, a sinking realisation gripped her.

With each breath, Alessandra's mind raced with regret and guilt. If only she had been quicker, stronger, more vigilant. Perhaps then she wouldn't be here, wounded and vulnerable.

As Alessandra lay motionless, she overheard the heated exchange between Vlad and Lucien. Despite her efforts to reassure them, her strength waned. Darkness enveloped her senses until a distant voice called out her name.

Suddenly, a radiant figure draped in white appeared before her, casting a comforting glow in the darkness.

"Alessandra," the elderly woman whispered. "I offer my aid, but the decision rests with you."

"I'm fading," she murmured weakly. "Resurrection isn't exactly a common skill set. Who are you?"

"I am a friend of your mother," the stranger replied with a gentle smile.

"You knew Mama?" Alessandra's voice quivered with disbelief.

"I am Zerachiel, the Angel of Judgement. She's known as Raguel and served alongside me in heaven."

"You're mistakenHer name was Liliana, a skilled witch until the Order took her life." A solitary tear trickled down her cheek.

"She was a divine messenger, tasked by the Almighty to bring forth life within you—a celestial progeny endowed with the virtues of Heaven and the noble traits of humanity: honour, bravery, compassion, and self-awareness," Zerachiel explained, her expression serene.

"A child of an angel? That's quite the revelation. How does

an ethereal being give birth to someone destined to become an assassin?"

"All beings are part of God's grand design, each with a predetermined role in the tapestry of existence. Yours was to aid Vlad Drakulya in leading the resistance against the Order of the Dragon. I have glimpsed his future. Whether you live or perish, you have fulfilled your purpose. Your ordeal can now draw to a close."

"And what of Lucien?"

"He is your half-brother. Your mother passed away following your birth. Your father sought an heir and fathered him with another woman. You were too young to comprehend, and he raised you both as full siblings. There's no fault in that. Now that you know the truth, are you prepared to return to the realm of Heaven?" Zerachiel enquired solemnly.

"No, I'm not finished yet. I choose to stand by his side as we defeat our foes," Alessandra declared.

"I will mend your wounds and restore your abilities if that's your desire. But I must caution you this is your last opportunity. If you perish again, you shall return to the celestial realm. There is a delicate equilibrium in the world, and disruptions to it cannot go unchecked."

"I'm willing to accept whatever comes my way," Alessandra affirmed. "But how do I tap into my powers?"

"You must discover it within yourself," the angel said, fading into a bright light.

Lucien's grip tightened around Alessandra's hand,

his desperation clear as he urged her to awaken. "Please, Alessandra. Open your eyes."

With a slow and deliberate movement, her eyelids fluttered open, revealing eyes clouded with lingering drowsiness. As she met her brother's gaze, a spark of recognition ignited within her, accompanied by a surge of relief. The absence of the dagger's cruel presence in her chest filled her with gratitude and wonder at her survival.

Summoning her strength, Alessandra pushed herself upright, her body protesting but ultimately complying with her will. Seated upon the unforgiving concrete, she inspected her hands with a mix of awe and disbelief. The surge of energy coursing through her veins filled her with newfound vitality and purpose.

Turning to Lucien and Zerachiel, Alessandra found them watching her with concern and anticipation. The angel's gentle smile offered reassurance, but it faded as exhaustion overtook her, causing her to collapse to the ground.

A surge of determination coursed through Alessandra as she grasped the gravity of the situation. With firm resolve, she clenched her fists, embracing the potent power now pulsing within her. It was time to overcome adversity, to stand tall in its face, and to carve a path forward.

"Take cover!" Alessandra's command cut through the chaos, and Vlad and the others swiftly obeyed, dropping to the ground. As they huddled together, Alessandra's gaze turned skyward, her body effortlessly ascending, defying gravity.

In that suspended realm between earth and sky, Alessandra surrendered herself to the latent power within. With closed eyes, she embraced her divine essence, feeling it surge through every fibre of her being. When her eyes reopened, they gleamed with a radiant golden hue, an ethereal manifestation of her celestial lineage.

With a serene smile, Alessandra surrendered to the magic pulsating within her. Majestic golden wings unfurled from her back, shimmering in the sunlight like molten gold, responding to her will.

Surveying the battlefield below, Alessandra felt a wave of calm wash over her. With a flick of her wrist, she summoned the power of the heavens, conjuring a swirling vortex of wind that ensnared their assailants.

"You will show respect." Alessandra's voice echoed with authority, her words carrying the weight of her newfound divine power.

As Alessandra watched the events unfold, anticipation coursed through her veins. Vlad's authoritative presence stirred something profound within her as he called forth his ceremonial sword. Passed down through generations, the weapon held a rich history and significance, each bearer awaiting when its true purpose would be revealed. Alessandra felt the weight of centuries resting upon the blade, serving as a poignant reminder of the destiny that lay ahead.

Approaching Alessandra with solemn reverence, Vlad's demeanour reflected his deep respect for her. His bow conveyed the high regard in which he held her. Presenting the sword, Vlad seemed to channel the power emanating from the ancient weapon, its inscription a symbol of the divine justice guiding their journey.

Sed iustitia divina est non caecus. Divine justice is never blind.

With trembling hands, Alessandra accepted the sword, her touch setting off a cascade of celestial energy that crackled and swirled around her. The sky darkened above, punctuated by flashes of lightning that seemed to infuse the blade with an unearthly strength. It felt as though the heavens themselves had conspired to empower her for the battle ahead.

"Thank you, my love," she whispered to Vlad, her voice filled with gratitude and wonder. Pulling him close, she embraced him tightly, the weight of their intertwined destinies hanging heavy in the air. Their kiss was a solemn vow, a pledge to stand united against whatever challenges awaited them.

Stepping back, Alessandra fixed her gaze on the approaching adversaries, her determination unyielding. With the sword raised high, pulsating with celestial energy, she issued her ultimatum to those who dared oppose them.

"Pledge your allegiance to Vlad Drakulya, your new master, or die," she declared, her voice resounding with authority and strength. In that moment, she knew their fate was sealed, bound by a shared purpose and an unwavering commitment to justice.

THE END

THE DEMON PRINCE

CHAPTER 1

Roslyn Academy

JADE STEPPED INTO THE SILVER MISTS OF THE VEIL, THE boundary that divided the waking world from the dreamland. She had practised lucid dreaming techniques for months and now she felt ready to do this on her own, without being pulled into a dream state by someone else.

As she ventured forward cautiously, a chill swept through her, and she sensed this new realm calling out to her. The mists twirled around her, eager for her to enter. A peculiar mix of emotion and energy surged through her, causing her heart to race in response.

Jade was now standing between two worlds, the conscious world and the realm of dreams. For a moment, she paused and looked back, beholding the waking realm with a newfound appreciation. Then she turned to face the new world and walked forward, unafraid and ready for whatever was to come.

As soon as she arrived, she found herself surrounded by a blanket of snow. The fog hung low over the river and the air had taken on a mistiness that blurred her vision. While she walked the narrow path that led to the citadel, the ground treacherous beneath her feet, she noticed the river was frozen over and a tomb-like silence enveloped the land.

Jade felt an uneasiness in her chest as she realised the change in seasons meant that something had gone wrong. She picked up the pace and hoped nothing had happened to the prince who had been there to help her countless times. As she arrived at the fortress, she saw parts of it had been destroyed; the towers looked like they had been hit by missiles, and various chunks of debris lay scattered around the area.

Her hands trembled as she opened the inconspicuous little iron gate that led to the sunken garden, and there was Ashlan, facing away from her, observing the black tulips. He seemed deep in thought, his head slightly tilted to the side and his crown perched atop his wavy raven hair.

Jade exhaled a sigh of relief. He was okay. She had been expecting something terrible for a moment, her emotions running wild. Taking a deep breath, she opened her eyes and found him facing her, their gazes connecting.

Jade's expression softened to admiration as she took in the sight of Ashlan. He was the Prince of Valoraa, yet he didn't carry himself like royalty. A two-piece suit of midnight blue made him look almost commonplace. His skin was as pale as porcelain and his eyes were the colour of the sea. He had full, deep-red lips, giving him an immortal elegance. Although his royal robes were absent, his ethereal beauty beamed through, leaving no doubt about his royal status.

"I'm glad you came," he said, smiling sheepishly.

"What happened? Why did the weather change and why is the castle damaged?" Jade asked.

"My magic mirrors the chaos in my heart. I should've stayed away, but I didn't want to alarm you." He conjured a fur coat and draped it around her shoulders. "This will help you stay warm. I couldn't bear to see you shivering."

"I'm glad you're here, but you must tell me what made you so upset. I know this world was created by you, and I feel your pain deeply."

"My father is adamant that I marry soon so I can produce an heir and maintain the line of succession for the throne. After all, my sisters cannot become queens." He tsked, a slight frown appearing on his brow. "But the idea of marriage does not appeal to me. Instead, I desire to use my magical abilities to explore distant lands."

Jade stepped closer, her fingers tracing lightly through his hair while she tried to soothe him. Secretly, she wished they could travel together. Ashlan had become her confidant ever since she began visiting the dreamland. But her heart coveted more than that.

"Can't you use your abilities to escape this place?"

"It isn't as simple as one may assume. The Valoraans are cursed to remain inside their realm. It's an old spell put in place by the devil himself. I've only been able to find a dreamland loop, but I lack the strength to break free of it."

"Is there anything I can do to help? It's torture to see you in this much pain."

Ashlan shook his head, stepping away from Jade. "The evil of my world can travel through all worlds. I cannot put you in harm's way."

"I'm not worried. I'm shielded by ancient magic, and I know I'm the only one who can help you." Jade looked him in the eyes and smiled, believing he knew what must be done.

"I cannot bring about your demise. You're my only friend." He sighed.

Jade wondered if Ashlan's lack of faith in her stemmed from her mother abandoning her at the academy. That he didn't want her help because he and she were just as helpless as each other.

No. She couldn't be too hard on herself. Ashlan had come into her life when she had called to the heavens in desperation. He saved her from a dark and miserable life, and she would do anything in return to help him.

"Stop overthinking it. The academy is like a fortress. Nothing evil can get there."

"If that is your wish… I only hope that when the time comes, I will be strong enough to keep you safe. But for now, I must take some of your magic."

Ashlan unrolled a spell-infused parchment and his chants reverberated around the garden, becoming more urgent as he clamped his hand onto Jade's wrist as he drained away her life force. Agony surged through her veins like molten lava, searing her whole body and scorching her soul. She writhed and begged for mercy, but Ashlan's will was unstoppable. He gripped her tighter as he continued his incantations, his voice rising in crescendo until Jade felt like she was being ripped in two. Then suddenly, everything turned to darkness, and the torment evaporated.

Jade's eyes flew open as her consciousness returned to the human realm. She felt the softness of the bedding and the warmth of the flames. The aroma of a crackling fire and burning wood reminded her she was back at the academy. Taking a deep breath, she dabbed a corner of her sheet to her forehead, wiping away the sweat.

She attempted to return to the realm of dreams, but something restrained her. Why would he betray her like this? After all the moments they had shared, how could it conclude in such a manner? Ashlan had appeared in her dreams countless times, revealing wonders that seemed only possible in fantasies.

Her thoughts drifted back to the day their paths first crossed. Abandoned by her mother at the academy, she had felt utterly alone, turning to any deity who might lend an ear. In those initial months, loneliness and sorrow gnawed away at her, threatening to consume her entirely. Until, in a moment of desperation, she made a fateful choice. After the unthinkable, Jade found herself in a hospital bed, slipping into a coma. It was there, in the realm of dreams, that she first encountered Ashlan.

With his rosy cheeks and wavy black hair, he resembled an angel. His white robes, adorned with golden embroidery, billowed around him in the breeze as he knelt among the fragrant white roses. Despite his palpable sadness, evidenced by furrowed brows and drooping shoulders, he delicately plucked petals from the flowers.

Jade couldn't help but smile, drawn magnetically to him. She silently took a step forward and watched as he stood up, abruptly releasing the rose he had been clutching in his hands. He looked directly into her eyes in surprise, his mouth slightly agape.

"What brings you here? I thought I was alone," he asked hesitantly.

"Is this Heaven? Am I finally free of the pain?" Jade's voice quivered as she added the last sentence.

Ashlan's head drooped in disappointment. "Not Heaven, unfortunately." He sighed, his breath fogging the air.

"How did I get here, then?" She tilted her head and gave him an amused smile.

"Would you believe me if I told you I willed a beautiful lady to join me here, and you appeared?"

Jade folded her arms as she let out a laugh. "You're such a charmer. I bet you say that to all the ladies."

Ashlan chuckled, his hands going up in surrender. "Only the beau-

tiful ones," he said with a mischievous smirk. He paused, then his face grew serious as he looked away from her and up at the heavens. "I don't know what you're doing here. I like to believe that after all these years of loneliness, I have prayed for someone to keep me company and you appeared."

Jade smiled, a shy blush coming to her cheeks. "That's strange," Jade murmured, her gaze suddenly haunted. "I wished the same." She looked away from him, embarrassed at her admission. "Do you think the universe conspired to have us here?"

Ashlan cleared his throat, catching her glance with his own gentle eyes as he spoke. He extended his palm to her in invitation, and there was a silent entreaty in his gaze as well. "It's a beautiful thought, don't you think?" he said.

His tone was gentle and full of awe and wonder, as if this mysterious meeting was too beautiful for words.

Jade took that hand and never let go. Her memory unravelled like an old blanket, frayed and barely holding together. No matter how hard she attempted, she couldn't rid herself of memories of him. His smile and laughter brightened her days, and his embrace brought warmth like the sun on a snowy day. His sudden disappearance left her feeling alone and bewildered. The pain of his abandonment was excruciating, like a sharp, stabbing sensation she could not evade. Curled up in bed, she wished she could shrink away from the hurt, but it lingered. She longed for answers: Why did he leave? What had she done wrong? Why didn't he say goodbye?

As the late afternoon sun cast shadows across the room, Jade found herself drained of tears, her body swollen with grief. She felt empty inside, her heart hollow. With nothing left to do, she lay there, wishing none of it had ever happened.

CHAPTER 2

A few months later

Jade strolled barefoot down the hallways of the academy, dragging her teddy bear behind her. She was dressed in a dark silk pyjama short set, and her hair was a mass of curls. Anyone who didn't know any better upon seeing her in such a state would've thought she was a ghost.

Heading to the kitchen for a midnight snack, Jade gently turned the doorknob, hoping to catch anyone else awake off guard. Her victim had his back to her, making a sandwich on the counter. She sauntered to him and smiled, whispering, "I'm a little monster. Fear me."

Ethan chuckled and ruffled her hair as he spun around to face her. "I was expecting your antics. When will you understand you can never frighten me? You know we're the only people who roam the halls in the middle of the night. That's just how it is these days. The nights feel too brief for me to get any quality sleep." He smiled and shrugged.

"Bad dreams again?" She felt compassion for him since she had fought her own inner battles.

"You can call them that," he murmured, not taking his eyes off the sandwich in front of him.

"Is there anything in your visions that can help us with the looming danger?" Jade asked, hoping that talking about something else might boost his spirits.

"Unfortunately, no. I never know what I'm going to get when I dream. It could be days or months away." Ethan sighed heavily. "I wish I could do more, but I'm held back by this psychological block. If only I could break my mind free." He stared out the window into the darkness of the night.

"That must be annoying. Have you tried focusing on this before you go to bed?"

He nodded. "What else can I do?"

"Right before Avery left, she told me that the Order had sent Lucien to investigate potential demonic activity. She asked me to help you look into it, hoping we could figure out what's going on before he comes back."

"I'm aware of that," the boy snapped, his brows furrowed. "If they catch anyone here using dark magic and summoning demons, we're done for. They'll shut down the school, erase our memories, and that would be the end. I have no desire to go back to the mundane world."

"I don't think anyone does. They call *us* freaks of nature while they slaughter each other without mercy. That's boring and predictable."

Jade peered out of the gothic window, contemplating the place where the enhanced misfits and anyone who didn't belong in normal society were kept. That was what her mother told her once when she caught her using her powers.

Days after the incident, her dear mama sent her to this damned place. She kept telling herself that it was for her own good, but the reality was much harsher. The woman who bore her hated who she was, and thought it was best for everyone if she was out of sight.

Jade took a deep breath to soothe her turbulent emotions and urged herself to stay calm. Becoming upset risked losing control of her abilities, potentially endangering others. With an immense power coursing through her, she couldn't afford to let it slip from her control, knowing the disastrous outcomes it could lead to. Dwelling on such thoughts only invited trouble, and Jade was keenly aware of the risks.

In previous centuries, witches drew their force from nature, which made them immensely powerful. Over the years, the connection with the elements slowly eroded, meaning descendants were less and less able to use the same magic. But that wasn't the same in Jade's case. She could do whatever she wanted. And that made her very dangerous.

Jade caught a hint of pity in Ethan's gaze, a sight she resented. She didn't consider herself a lost cause; she simply required the guidance of the right mentor.

"I'm off to my dorm. Hit me up if you have any ideas about how to get out of this mess," she said, looking toward the door.

"I'd do anything to help. I am aware of how important this place is to you. To all of us." Ethan handed her a plate with a sandwich on it.

With a soft smile, Jade whispered, "Thank you for being such a good friend," before planting a kiss on his cheek. With her cherished stuffed toy following close behind, she hurried out, prepared to confront whatever challenges lay ahead.

At nearly nineteen years old, most of her peers thought it strange that Jade still held on to her teddy bear, yet it had a calming effect on her, keeping her from losing control of her emotions when things got overwhelming.

When she reached her room, Jade placed the plate on her desk and ate. Her friend was incredibly kind, and she owed everything she had to him for all he had done for her since she had to come to this cursed place.

Ethan and Avery were Jade's only friends. She was a force to be reckoned with, her reputation for destruction keeping others away. It was a bit of a blessing, as she had limited patience for the whiny lot that roamed the halls of the academy.

After finishing her meal, Jade returned to her bed and stretched out, gazing at the glowing stars she had affixed to the ceiling when she first arrived years ago. Despite the lingering sense of betrayal from her mother's actions, Jade couldn't help but smile as she envisioned a life filled with adventure, where she could explore the world under the vast night sky.

Jade tightly squeezed her eyes shut, trying to concentrate and transport herself back to the dream realm, but nothing worked. She felt her chest tighten as she remembered the moment she realised Ashlan had tricked her. He had taken a part of her magical essence, leaving her vulnerable. An irreparable damage had been done, and she was desperate to find out why and try to fix it.

Yet amidst her turmoil, she was consumed by profound anger. This wasn't merely a disagreement; it was a betrayal that had rendered her vulnerable and isolated. She harboured a desire to confront him and hold him accountable for his actions, yet a faint glimmer of hope remained, suggesting that perhaps his intentions had not been malicious.

She had been living a lie ever since she lost control of her powers, all because of him. Her hopes of restoring the balance dashed by his choices. Had she been naïve to trust him?

Jade took a deep breath and closed her eyes, desperately trying to figure out the best way to confront Ashlan and rectify the situation. She didn't know what would happen when they eventually met again, but she was determined to make sure she had all the answers.

CHAPTER 3

Upon awakening the next morning, Jade's heart quickened as she read Ethan's message summoning her to the Old Mill. Intrigued and hopeful, she wondered what revelation awaited her. Eager to find a solution to their predicament and restore normalcy to their lives at the academy, she resolved to meet him, her determination driving her forward despite the lingering sense of uncertainty.

Jade donned a sleek, sleeveless black dress adorned with ruffles, cinched snugly by a leather belt with steampunk accents. She slid into white embroidered tights and slipped on pink lace-up ankle boots with wedge heels. Completing her ensemble, she draped a pink wool overcoat over her shoulders and grabbed a lavender-coloured parasol made of Chinese oil paper.

Her dorm room nestled in the attic tower of the academy, a space most students avoided but one she cherished. Perched atop the building, it offered breathtaking views of the English countryside. Jade often retreated to her reading nook tucked into a tiny window alcove, where she'd gaze out at the picturesque landscape, lost in daydreams of the world beyond.

Descending the stairs, she navigated through the throng of students, their gazes parting as she passed. Jade's rare appearances in their midst inspired a mixture of caution and curiosity among her peers. Some whispered tales of her powers, likening her presence to a spin of the wheel of fortune—safe passage or a chance encounter with transformation. However, such rumours were merely fear-induced speculation; Jade had yet to transmute anyone into a frog.

Upon reaching the mill, Jade discovered Ethan was already waiting. His disapproving gaze swept over her attire, causing a slight tightening of his lips.

"I'm relieved you could make it, albeit late," he said in a tense tone.

Jade raised an eyebrow, surprised by Ethan's unusual demeanour. Usually steady and composed, his current attitude unsettled her, increasing her apprehension. With a subtle gesture, the boy swung open the imposing wooden door and gestured for Jade to enter.

"So, what was the news you couldn't wait to share with me?" she asked, a faint feeling of dread creeping into her heart.

Ethan directed Jade's attention to the corner of the chamber, and together they approached it with caution. As they drew nearer, Jade's breath caught in her throat at the sight before her. Dozens of candles were arranged meticulously along the floor, casting flickering shadows across the space. Surrounding a damaged brass vessel were symbols etched with black soot, their intricate designs hinting at a mysterious purpose.

"What is this place?" Jade enquired, the gravity of the situation becoming obvious.

"I took your advice and thought about it harder, and it led me to this. In my dream, I watched the ritual being performed, but I couldn't make out a face or hear anything that could lead me to a specific individual." He sighed, then pointed at the brass vessel. "Whoever did this was planning to capture the demon, but I guess they landed a powerful one. Do you see the sigils surrounding it? They're meant to keep the spirit from escaping."

"How do you know this?" she asked, her voice laced with worry.

"You mean to say you've never paid attention to Demon Studies?"

Jade shook her head in disbelief. While she had never doubted the existence of supernatural beings, encountering tangible evidence of their presence here was beyond her expectations.

"Same here. But I stumbled upon a book in the off-limits section of the library that caught my interest. I committed some passages to memory before returning it, and I believe it holds relevance to our predicament."

Jade regarded him with astonishment. "I can't believe you'd risk expulsion for this! That section is off-limits for a reason. Those manuscripts *are* kept hidden from ordinary students like us."

He shrugged casually, as if it were all part of his usual antics. "I do unexpected things sometimes; deal with it. But we have another problem. I couldn't identify the symbols. The head librarian caught wind of my snooping and put up a powerful magic seal to protect the place."

"What about the headmaster? Can we inform him about this?"

"And tell him what? That we might have a Prince of Hell

on our hands? He'll think we've lost our minds and throw us in a cell. Let's play it cool and wait for more visions. The culprit will slip up eventually, and then we can pounce. It's inevitable."

A myriad of demons prowled the world, causing caution and strategic planning before any action. It couldn't be taken lightly, as one misstep could lead to their demise.

"Sure thing, Sherlock. Let's go. This place is giving me the creeps." Jade shrugged.

As they made their way back to the academy, they passed a group of girls who seemed intrigued by the new student's presence. He seemed unfazed, smiling at the attention from his admirers.

His manner brought to mind Ashlan, someone she was fervently attempting to put out of her mind. Dreamwalkers, as dubbed by the Order, faced the peril of losing their sanity because of the excessive utilisation of their magic. This activity corroded the barriers separating reality from the realm of dreams, paving the way for potential insanity.

"I plan to find some shade and read for a while," Jade remarked.

"Sure thing. I'm going to keep digging. Maybe I can come up with an answer soon," Ethan replied before walking off in the opposite direction.

"Let me know when you uncover anything," Jade yelled after him, but it was too late—he was already out of sight. She made her way to the far corner of the garden, where she retrieved a small blanket and a weathered leather book from her handbag.

Sitting on the grass beneath the trees, a sense of tranquillity washed over her. This simple pleasure, reading amidst nature, was a cherished memory from before her time at the academy. Jade let herself relax, allowing her mind to ponder their current dilemma. They needed a solution, and they needed it soon.

As she had just opened her book and begun reading, someone suddenly appeared in front of her—it was the new student, the one who seemed to attract the swarm of female students. Jade rolled her eyes in frustration. Why had he disturbed her so abruptly? Wasn't he aware of her bad temper?

"Do you not understand the concept of politeness?" she said, her lips pressed into a tight line.

"I was simply enjoying the scenery. Is there something wrong with that, Miss...?" he replied with a smirk on his face.

"Jade, and no, you weren't just admiring the view. You were deliberately trying to get my attention away from what I was reading." She wanted him to simply say what he needed and leave. His perfectly sculpted face was an unwelcome interruption from the fictional world.

"Miss Jade, although I am glad you find me distracting, I wasn't doing it on purpose," he added.

"Just Jade." She once again gazed at him before shaking her head. "That's not true. I don't like insensitive people."

A flush rose to Jade's cheeks. She had been caught in a lie and it seemed he knew it. To divert the attention from herself, she asked the stranger, "And who might you be, causing such a disturbance with the students?"

"I'm the new transfer, As... Ashley Rex. You can call me Ash."

Jade scrutinised him closely. He was stunning—his dark hair was artfully dishevelled, and his eyes resembled the colour of the Aegean Sea. He possessed an alabaster complexion, as though he had never seen the light of day before arriving here.

Her gaze lingered on his lips—they were full and a lovely,

deep shade of pink. His mouth brought to mind memories of Ashlan, and how many times she had gazed at his handsome face.

She swallowed hard and glanced away. There was no point remembering about him. He'd left her just like her mom, with no explanation for his choice.

"Now that I know who you are, why are you bothering me? Did you not get the memo? No one messes with me," Jade chortled, drawing the attention of her classmates.

"It's interesting that you were immune to my charms," Ash remarked unemotionally. "But tell me, why would I be afraid of you? Are you some kind of royal or something?"

Jade gave a sly smile. "Look around you. Everyone keeps their distance from me. My abilities frighten other students, so they are smart enough to stay out of my way." She opened her book and pretended to read it.

"Aren't you curious about the power I possess?" Ash grinned, then conjured a ball of fire in his palm.

Jade's eyes widened. "That's really cool. So, you're an elemental witch?"

"You could say that."

"Fire witches are practically extinct now. My powers are based on the Earth element. It's hard to explain exactly, but the results are usually catastrophic." Jade felt a pang of sadness as she recalled all the times she nearly destroyed the academy's buildings.

"Earth and fire, north and south, green and red," Ash noted. "Complete contrasts, yet I am told opposites attract."

Jade considered responding with a clever comeback, but she reasoned it would only encourage his impudence. Instead, she returned to her book as if she hadn't heard him.

"We'll cross paths again before long, young Earth witch," he said cheerfully as he walked towards the academy building.

His voice carried a faint hint of familiarity to her, reminiscent of the boy from her dreams. He was the first person who hadn't been intimidated by her magic, so she valued his friendship. Quickly, she dismissed the thoughts that crept into her mind. He could never be the lad with whom she shared her midnight conversations; he was too disrespectful.

CHAPTER 4

When Ash finally departed, Jade was grateful to the heavens. He appeared as a tempting package wrapped in danger signs. Would she heed the warnings, though?

She yearned to showcase her powers, but that would only invite trouble. Several instances of accidental damage to structures because of her lack of control over her abilities had made her worry about being expelled, eventually.

After finishing her reading, Jade returned to her room. Most days, she spent her time alone, eagerly expecting the return of her beloved friend Avery—the only one who truly understood her as a witch.

Upon hearing the clock chime midnight, Jade headed to the kitchen for a late-night snack. To her surprise, Ethan wasn't there as usual. He would typically prepare food for both of them, but that night felt different.

As she opened the door, a delightful aroma greeted her. Instead of Ethan, it was Ash, cooking with his back turned to her. His humming filled the room with an unfamiliar tune. Sensing her presence, he turned around and smiled.

Jade was taken aback by his gesture but quickly recovered from the shock.

"Good, you're here. I've been expecting you." He pointed to the table with two chairs in the centre of the kitchen, which had been set with candles already lit, two wine glasses, and a bottle of red.

Jade took her seat cautiously. There was something alluring yet unsettling about this man. She wasn't sure if she could believe him, even though he said he was a witch. She had always been good at understanding other people's intentions, but with him, it was different. He was a mystery to her and, despite not knowing anything about him, he still seemed oddly familiar. This made her uneasy.

"How did you know I'd be here?" she asked, perplexed.

"I did my homework after I met you. You like to have your food alone in the kitchen and often come here at midnight once all the other students have gone to bed. Usually, it's you and your friend Ethan, but he was preoccupied tonight, so I volunteered to cook for you instead." He fluttered his eyelashes. "You'd be surprised what someone can learn with a little convincing."

Jade speculated that Ethan must have made progress in solving the problem, which explained his absence that night. She resolved to check on him the next day.

Jade couldn't help but roll her eyes, feeling exasperated. She had grown accustomed to being independent and didn't need someone putting in excessive effort to win her favour. It seemed unnecessary, yet this man persisted in his attempts to charm her. She wondered why he felt the need to do so.

With a sigh, Jade turned away from him, focusing on the ingredients still laid out on the counter.

"I promise it will be good," he whispered.

Furrowing her brow, Jade hesitated briefly before nodding

in agreement. Seeing her consent, he smiled, and they both resumed their tasks; he returned to cooking, and Jade took a seat at the table.

As he prepared the meal, Jade observed him with admiration, noting how effortlessly he navigated the kitchen. When the food was ready, she moved to express her gratitude, but he interrupted her.

"You don't need to thank me. I only did all this so I could spend more time with you," Ash remarked, a note of teasing in his voice.

He placed the cooked meal on the table—a steak with mushroom and cream sauce, accompanied by buttery baby potatoes. This arrangement of food was something that could have been seen on a restaurant menu.

"I know you're old enough to drink, so I got a bottle of wine from the headmaster's cellar." He delivered this news with a smirk.

"Are *you*?" Jade asked, lifting an eyebrow, her voice rising in pitch. Did he think he had to bribe her to stay? She didn't hate him. But did she actually want to eat in his company? No. She wasn't pleased with his methods of trying to win her over. She was used to the simplicity of being alone and the peace that it brought her. His attempts to be nice seemed wrong in her world.

"I am older than you are, but let's not worry about me. Tonight is about you. I peeked at your file. You turn nineteen in a few months, right? That's quite an accomplishment. Have you decided what you want to do after?"

Ash seemed to know that the Order gave those with powers a choice when they reached nineteen. Work for them or be banished, but Jade knew better. There was no way the organisation would let enhanced people roam the world at their leisure. There was much more to it, and one day, she planned to find out.

"Why are you doing this?" she asked.

Ash smiled, his eyes twinkling in the candlelight. "Is it a crime to want to dine with a fellow witch?"

Jade couldn't help but return the smile. "No, but people rarely do nice things for me out of the goodness of their heart," she finally confessed.

"You're hanging around with the wrong crowd. Spend more time with me, and you'll see...." His words trailed off.

Jade observed as Ash poured two glasses of the dark red liquid and handed one to her.

"Cheers," he said, lifting his glass and taking a sip.

Jade began eating, choosing to ignore him. She couldn't shake the feeling that he had ulterior motives. Was he perhaps sent by the Order? Ash didn't strike her as a seasoned knight in their employ. They underwent rigorous training for years, unlike Ash, who seemed undisciplined. She remained cautious as she continued her meal.

After finishing her plate, Jade gathered the dishes to wash them. Meanwhile, Ash watched her, his expression tinged with sadness as he sipped his wine.

"Thanks for joining me tonight."

"Thanks for the meal. It was delicious. I didn't expect it," Jade replied, attempting to pick up the remaining dishes. However, Ash caught her wrist, locking eyes with her. She pulled away instinctively, feeling the warmth of his touch.

"It's alright," he said, almost out of breath. "I'll take care of the rest."

"Goodnight," she whispered before turning on her heel and leaving the kitchen.

As she walked away, Jade couldn't shake the trembling sensation that had coursed through her hand when he touched her. It felt like electricity, an inexplicable connection that unsettled her. She shouldn't feel this way about someone she barely knew. Yet, despite her reservations, she found herself drawn to him; her gaze often lingering on his lips during the meal. Was she succumbing to some sort of enchantment, like the other female students? The thought filled her with apprehension.

CHAPTER 5

HELL WAS A DESOLATE AND MONOTONOUS PLACE. THERE was only a limited number of souls to torment, only a finite number of ways to entertain oneself at their expense. But when some foolhardy human summoned the Prince of Lust from the depths of Hell, Asmodeus answered the call. It provided a welcome respite from the endless tedium of the underworld, a chance to escape the relentless nightmare that had become his existence. Over the years, he had traversed the Earth in various guises, indulging in the freedom that the mortal realm offered.

Upon arriving in this realm, Ash, as he preferred to be called, found himself confronted by a young man in his late teens seeking to play a prank on a friend. *Typical humans, dabbling with powers far beyond their comprehension.* One glance at his infernal visage was enough to send the hapless mortal into a faint. Truly unbelievable.

Asmodeus shook his head, a laugh escaping his lips in disbelief. Were the mortals of this time so faint-hearted? Drawing closer to his victim, he noticed the emblem on the man's coat—Roslyn Academy. There was an air of difference about this person, something he couldn't quite pinpoint without further investigation. As he reached out to touch the man's cheek, a slight jolt surged through his body. Ah, this individual was a warlock.

Ash pondered his predicament. The academy was heavily warded, making escape nearly impossible. Whatever magic had been used to summon him had temporarily nullified the wards, but now he was trapped within its confines. If he wanted to blend in with the other students, he would need to alter his appearance. After a moment of consideration, he smirked and transformed into a handsome human male.

Stepping out of the shadows, Ash made his way toward the academy's main building. As he walked along the narrow path through the garden, he was immediately surrounded by a group of women who were drawn to his attractive appearance. Dressed impeccably in a form-fitting suit, he couldn't help but realise he may have gone a bit too far with his physical appearance. There was no turning back now.

Amidst the flurry of attention, one girl passed by him without so much as a glance. Her indifference piqued his interest, and he felt compelled to learn more about her. Pressing his admirers for information, Ash learned the blonde was considered dangerous, a freak of nature. Despite the warnings, he couldn't shake the feeling that he needed to meet her.

So many admonitions for someone who appeared harmless. Yet something about her reminded him of the woman who had freed him from his curse. A smile played at the corners of his lips. Meeting her seemed like a risk worth taking.

When Ash laid eyes on her, he was taken aback. It was indeed Jade, the witch who had helped him break free from the magical restraints in his latest prison. Together, their combined powers had shattered the curse placed upon him by the Fae Queen, who had accused him of exploiting one of her illegitimate daughters.

He never expected to encounter her again, yet there she was, strolling through the academy's garden. Her beauty and poise captivated him, and he sensed a strength within her that commanded respect.

Just as he was considering leaving, Jade called him out for his prolonged stare, causing his heart to race like a schoolboy on his first date. However, when their eyes met, there was no hint of recognition in her gaze. Ash knew he should depart, but he couldn't resist engaging in conversation a little while longer. He dreaded the possibility of her recalling their past interactions, knowing she might harbour resentment for how he had manipulated her and drained some of her powers.

As Ash learned more about Jade from her acquaintances, a plan formed in his mind. Knowing that the Underworld wasn't conducive to social gatherings, he decided to arrange a private meal for just the two of them.

During his many visits to the mortal realm, Ash had savoured the simple pleasures of earthly existence, such as indulging in food and wine. Upon returning to Hell, he yearned for these minor delights, yet resigned to his fate of only being able to return when summoned. He had discovered certain loopholes that allowed him to prolong his stays on Earth, and he intended to make the most of his time in Jade's presence.

As midnight approached, Ash arranged for the academy's chef to prepare a sumptuous feast and ventured into the cellar for additional supplies. When he sensed Jade's approach to the kitchen, he dismissed the cook and assumed the role of chef himself, eager to create an ambiance reminiscent of times before he had wronged her. In his desolate prison in the realm of Valoraa, she had been the sole source of solace for his suffering heart, captivating him entirely. However, despite his earnest attempts to craft a memorable evening, Ash's gestures seemed to unsettle Jade more than anything else. Had he misjudged the situation? Had societal norms changed so drastically since his last visit to Earth? Was romance truly a lost art?

Seated at the table, the prince observed Jade with keen interest, noting how she mirrored her demeanour from the dreamworld, even in the way she tucked her hair behind her ears when vexed. With newfound freedom from the confines of Valoraa, he now had ample time to acquaint himself with her. However, Jade's responses remained guarded, leaving him eager to uncover more about her and her interests. Her sudden change in attitude dampened his spirits, prompting him to push aside his plate, barely having made a dent in his dinner.

As Jade began tidying up after her meal, it became apparent to Ash that he had somehow erred. He didn't wish for her to serve him; he longed for her spiritedness. The prince reached out and caught her wrist, locking eyes with her. The contact sent a jolt of unfamiliar electricity through his body, leaving him puzzled. He pondered over what might thaw her icy demeanour. Since their encounter in the garden, she had remained distant, a stark contrast to their interactions in the other world.

Kissing her soft lips crossed his mind, but he hesitated, fearing her rejection. Instead, he released her wrist and watched as she departed. With a sigh, he tidied up, restoring order to the kitchen as if their brief encounter had never occurred.

With bottle in hand, Ash made his way to the rooftop of

the academy, relishing in the familiar ritual of moon bathing while indulging in a drink and gazing up at the stars. These were simple pleasures he sorely missed during his time in hell. As he took in the tranquil scene, he couldn't help but wish that Jade was there with him, but tonight, it was just him and his thoughts.

Though he had been the Prince of Lust for as long as he could recall, the allure of Earth's boundless possibilities beckoned to him. His journey began with a quest to break free of his curse, a journey that led him to Jade. Despite his initial intentions, he found himself inexplicably drawn to her, captivated by a connection unlike any other he had experienced.

Jade remained an enigma, a mystery he was eager to unravel.

As fatigue weighed heavily on him, Ash succumbed to sleep, his dreams filled with visions of Jade and the untold potential she held.

CHAPTER 6

JADE MADE HER WAY TO THE LIBRARY THE FOLLOWING DAY, determined to delve into the mystery of the unusual sigils from the Old Mill. Despite having messaged Ethan the previous night for an update, she hadn't received a response, which struck her as odd given his usual promptness. Resolved to seek answers, she planned to visit his dorm later that day if he continued to evade her inquiries.

Dressed in a flowing red dress, her shiny, curly blond locks cascading down her back, Jade attracted more than a few curious glances at her departure from her usual clothes.

As she pondered her choice of attire, Jade couldn't help but reflect on the origins of the dress. It was a unique piece in her wardrobe, a gift from Avery on her last birthday. Though initially hesitant because of its expense, Avery surprised her with the garment upon their return from a shopping excursion, a thoughtful gesture that lingered in her memory.

She smiled, musing over the possibility that her choice was influenced by her longing for her friend. Or perhaps there was a deeper reason behind it?

Entering the library, Jade was greeted by a breathtaking sight—a gothic masterpiece that showcased the Order's opulence. Every inch of the chamber was adorned with walnut, from the ceiling to the upper gallery and the furniture. Enormous crystal chandeliers illuminated the space, casting a dazzling glow. Stained glass windows lined the walls, each a kaleidoscope of vibrant hues. Statues of Greek gods stood sentinel throughout the room, while towering bookcases brimming with ancient tomes reached towards the lofty ceiling. The ostentatious display left Jade feeling disheartened; she couldn't help but lament the organisation's failure to utilise their vast resources to address the world's myriad problems.

As she perused the stacks, selecting a couple of books, Ash joined her, adding two more volumes to her already sizeable pile.

"What do you think you're doing?" Jade snapped. "I've no time for your nonsense today."

"Good morning to you too," he replied, the sarcasm dripping from his voice. "I'm delighted to see you." Ash grinned.

Jade rolled her eyes. She knew this was going to be a long day, and she had no patience for his playful demeanour. With people's lives hanging in the balance, she couldn't afford to waste any time.

"I bet you say that to all the girls. Now, where are your admirers hiding?" She attempted to provoke him, but he simply smiled in response.

"I've asked them to give us some space. You're the only one I want to be around," he replied, his tone earnest.

Jade gasped, taken aback by his unexpected sincerity, drawing the attention of nearby students. "No way. You're too immature for me. I prefer people who take things seriously."

Her words were sharper than she intended, but she hoped

they would discourage him from persisting. She wasn't interested in his company, especially since she and Ethan were engaged in unauthorised demon hunting.

For a moment, guilt tugged at her, but as she observed his arrogant expression, she swiftly dismissed it, convinced that he deserved her dismissal and more.

"You won't think that once you get to know me better. Just wait and see, beautiful," Ash remarked, his tone confident.

Jade sighed inwardly, feeling trapped. She briefly considered moving to another table, but the library was crowded. Why did he have to choose *her* table of all places? It seemed she would have to endure his presence for the time being.

"What are you reading, anyway?" he asked.

Jade took a calming breath, hoping to deter him with her mundane response. "Just the usual—researching demons, sigils, and such. Nothing too thrilling."

"All right, I've got two questions," Ash announced.

"Go ahead," Jade replied, suppressing her frustration.

"Why do you even care about demons? They don't really exist," Ash questioned, his tone skeptical.

Jade's disappointment was palpable as she stared at him. "So much for being more than just a pretty face," she muttered under her breath before responding more audibly. "Naturally, they exist. Look around. You're in an academy for special people. I'm a witch. My best friend is awesome at swordplay, and her boyfriend was recently turned into a vampire. All these things exist, and so do demons. They could walk amongst us."

"You're telling me the brave, bold you fears a little monster?" Ash prodded, raising an eyebrow.

"I'm dead serious, Ash. We could face a greater demon," Jade retorted firmly.

Ash considered her words before posing his second question. "Okay then. That brings me to my second question. Why do you think a demon is here?"

"Because there are loads of signs," Jade explained, leaning closer to him. "I'm not sure if you have noticed since you're new, but... the Order of the Dragon controls this place. They deal with supernatural creatures all across Europe. The wards they set up around the school went off weeks ago, so they sent someone to investigate."

THAT MADE LITTLE SENSE TO ASH. HE HAD ONLY BEEN AT the academy for a day. Unless...

"There could be multiple ones," Jade suggested. "But Lucien, the knight who was sent here, acquired a severe case of vampirism."

Ash chuckled, finding her explanation amusing. "It's almost like he caught the flu," he remarked.

"It's true," Jade insisted. "After an encounter with an ancient vampire, he was turned into one himself. There could be something else going on, but that's a story for another day. His current problem is that he can no longer be a member of the Order, let alone investigate it—according to the top members of the organisation. So he and my best friend Avery snuck out to search for an old member, Dracula. Rumour has it he's still alive somewhere," Jade concluded.

"That could work," Ash mused, considering the potential solution to the knight's troubles.

"Lucien's absence from the academy bought us some time to locate and get rid of the demon, but not forever. We need to get this done soon or the Order will send more of their men, who are far more ruthless than our vampire knight," Jade emphasised.

"I am ready to help you in any way I can," Ash affirmed. He was determined to capture the demon that had appeared before him. If he wanted to stay in that place longer, he had to banish it before they took action. Although lesser creatures weren't capable of doing any harm to him, they could sense his presence and cause complications for the prince.

"We have a deal, as long as you stop being so strange," Jade chuckled.

"You meant to say 'charming,' but you got your words mixed up," Ash retorted with a smirk. He found it amusing that she still acted as if she were uninterested in him.

The young witch rolled her eyes at him. "What am I to do with you?"

"Love me?" Ash joked, flashing his most harmless and appealing smile.

"Don't push your luck," Jade replied curtly before ignoring him for the rest of her time in the library, much to Ash's exasperation.

CHAPTER 7

In his dorm, Ash mulled over his future. He yearned to remain on Earth with the witch, but the looming presence of the knights from the Order of the Dragon cast a shadow of uncertainty. If they appeared at the academy, he might be compelled to return to hell. These knights possessed relics with enough power to banish him to the abyss, a fate he knew all too well after centuries of being cast away.

He paced back and forth in his room, wracking his brain for a solution, but no answer presented itself.

The day he was summoned, he had destroyed the sigils bearing his name. However, the members of the Order were not easily fooled. With their magical tools, they could peer into the past as if it were unfolding before their eyes.

He had never considered the organisation as an adversary until now. Yet, he also knew he couldn't linger in the human realm indefinitely. Until he encountered Jade in the dreamland. From the moment he saw her in reality, he felt a profound connection—a sensation he only experienced in her presence.

Should he disclose his true identity to her, confess that he was the one who selfishly stole part of her power?

He was a formidable demon who had disguised himself as a desolate prince from a distant realm to infiltrate her world. Exploiting her compassionate nature and trust in him, he cunningly took advantage of her. Rumours swirled around the girl, depicting her as a potent weapon. Whenever he clasped her hand, he could sense her strength pulsating beneath her skin. Should she seek vengeance, a mere touch could reduce him to dust, offering a more permanent solution than merely banishing him back to hell.

Could he appeal to her compassion? Throughout his travels, he had observed that humans were capable of empathy. But would they extend that empathy to a demon? With his options dwindling, he knew he had to act swiftly.

Suddenly, screams and tumult erupted from outside his window. Peering out, he witnessed the Old Mill engulfed in a raging inferno. There could be no doubt—the other demon was responsible for this chaos.

Jade barged into his room in a state of panic, catching him off guard. Ash wished he had more time to strategise, but his past deeds were catching up with him.

"Who are you? You have two minutes to tell the truth," the young woman demanded.

"What do you mean?" Ash replied, feigning confusion. His instinct for self-preservation told him that admitting to being a demon might not be the wisest thing to do. Ash couldn't risk her taking her anger out on him. He was still a powerful demon prince, but he wasn't sure if he could stand up to this witch's power.

"Someone set the mill on fire, and they found Ethan dead. The other students have figured out about the demons and think you're responsible. They're coming here to punish you," she said, out of breath.

"Let's pretend that I am a demon, for argument's sake. Could they do something to me?"

"Yes. The Order sends the most powerful students after greater demons to banish them back to hell. So I ask again, are you one?"

His heart was pounding in his chest as he contemplated all the probable outcomes if he spoke the truth. He could be a dead demon either way, according to what Jade had said. Taking a leap of faith, he made the most crucial gamble of his life.

"Yes." Ash sighed, finding some sense of relief in his confession. He looked at Jade, fully expecting her to deliver his fate. But then he noticed a glimmer of curiosity in her gaze.

"Which one are you?" she asked, her demeanour unaltered by his admission.

"Does it matter?" It felt strange to take comfort in that because no amount of pleading could help him if Jade killed him. But maybe there was more to his story.

He readied himself for the hate that often followed the mention of creatures of the Underworld. He really couldn't blame humans for their disdain of his kind. Demons tricked innocent people and used their souls to fill the abyss below.

"Yes. Now, please. Before it's too late," she pleaded, inching closer to him.

Despite his disbelief, Ash entertained the possibility that this dire situation might somehow benefit him. Perhaps Jade differed from the others. With no other recourse if he wished to remain on Earth, he made a decision he had never considered before: he trusted a human.

"Asmodeus," he whispered under his breath, and an icy

chill swept through the room. Anticipating Jade's reaction, he braced himself for her fury. To his astonishment, she responded with a smile.

When she finally grasped his true identity, her demeanour underwent a remarkable transformation. Without hesitation, the blonde seized his hand and closed her eyes. Just as the enraged students burst into the dormitory, Jade whisked them both away to an unfamiliar realm.

JADE SCANNED THE EXPANSIVE DESERT, FINDING NOTHING in sight. Too drained to attempt another spell, she resorted to the only other option available—trying to determine their location.

Ash observed her, then closed his eyes and let out a long breath. His smile betrayed his relief at escaping unscathed. "What made you decide to help me? I could sense you were weighing your options."

Jade sighed heavily, meeting his gaze. She had come dangerously close to letting him perish. It was a near miss that she couldn't reveal to him. When he uttered his demon name, everything clicked into place. There had been something familiar about his aura, despite his irksome demeanour. According to the ancient texts, before Asmodeus became a demon, his name was Ashlan, the Crown Prince of Valoraa. In their dream encounters, he had inadvertently revealed his true name and history to her.

"It was because of your name that I spared you," she admitted. She had often pondered how she would react if she ever came face to face with the man who had betrayed her and disrupted the balance of her powers. Yet, when the moment arrived, she felt relief rather than anger at finding him alive.

"Did you suddenly develop an affection for my name?" Ash quipped.

"No, it's not like that. I've seen you before, though not in this form."

Her mind drifted to the realm of dreams, where she had spent countless nights with him. His eyes sparkled like the clearest stars, and his smile softened the edges of her worries. He picked a wild daisy and presented it to her, and she took it with a grateful heart. He read her stories from his old homeland, each sentence like a lullaby that rocked her to sleep. Together, they watched the sun set beneath the horizon, glowing in multi-coloured hues.

The memories of their past suddenly vanished as the present beckoned her back. She turned her head to meet familiar eyes that had never failed to fill her with hope and assurance. There was his same gentle smile that never ceased to soothe her.

Jade felt a crushing weight in her chest as he continued to pry for answers. He stared into her eyes with a searching, unyielding gaze, as if he could read her thoughts and make her tell him everything. She wasn't sure if she could bring herself to talk about her darkest secrets, but she took a deep breath, determined to be honest with him.

"You've been in my dreams. At first, I thought you were an angel from above," she said, her voice trembling slightly. She paused, realising that no one else had ever heard these words. Not her closest friend, not her family.

He abruptly looked away and got up, and Jade thought he must have been too uncomfortable with her confession. But then he held out his hand to her.

"Most demons are fallen angels, yet I am a living curse that lingers forever," he said quietly, edging closer to her.

She knew she should be mad, that she had the right to yell and rant and get an answer to everything he had put her through. He was to blame for this all. Her heart wouldn't let her. Retaliation would sting her more.

But there was something precious in it all. He was still alive. That was the only silver lining of all her suffering. She could see it in his eyes when she looked at him—a flicker of hope and a glimmer of understanding that seemed to shut out all the pain and the stress of the past few months. She walked toward him and when he took her hand in his, a slight gesture that felt like a thousand words said in the same instant, it gave her relief and hope.

For a few minutes, they stood like that, their eyes locked together, his much warmer than hers. "I'm sorry," he muttered. "I am the most wretched creature in the entire world for what I have done to you."

Jade's smile widened slightly.

"You're not just Ashlan," she countered. "You're the Crown Prince of Valoraa, who became a demon after falling in love with a Fae."

"Historians often manipulate the truth to suit their own agendas. That's the Valoraan version of the tale. Have you heard of the Fae's perspective? They claim I took advantage of the Fae Queen's illegitimate daughter when they visited my kingdom. But in the end, it's irrelevant. The winners write history, and I hit the jackpot. I'm free and immortal. Whether I'm good or bad, I'll leave that judgment to you."

"But you're not bad," Jade insisted. "You came to me when I was in need. I prayed, and you answered. My mother sent me to the academy, and when I attempted to end my life, they rushed me to the hospital and put me into a coma to save me.

You've been in my dreams ever since." She hesitated, knowing there were depths of her emotions she couldn't fully express.

"So you're not angry with me or afraid of my demon nature?" Ash enquired, edging closer, his gaze searching hers.

Jade shook her head, and a wave of relief washed over the prince.

"Good. I've been wanting to do this for a while now..."

He gently brushed his lips against hers, igniting a cascade of sensations that left her breathless. His touch sent a surge of electricity coursing through her veins, and she surrendered to the irresistible allure of his kiss. In that moment, all doubts and fears faded away, replaced by a profound warmth blossoming within her. She had believed her heart to be closed off, shielded from love's embrace, yet as she melted into his arms, she realised she had never felt more alive. Time seemed to stand still as they shared a kiss that transcended the bounds of time and space, enveloping them in a timeless embrace.

As Ash cupped her face in his hands, the kiss deepened, and it felt as though a spell had been broken, revealing the hidden truth. With each tender touch of their lips, the walls he had built around his heart crumbled, allowing the past he had long concealed to surface once more. In that moment, he realised the depth of his connection to the witch from the dreamland, understanding now why he had been so inexplicably drawn to her.

For years, he had observed humans as they experienced love and hope, longing for that same connection himself. As memories of his past flooded his mind, a single tear escaped his eye, a silent testament to the emotions stirring within him. Holding Jade close, he cherished the fleeting moment, knowing that she held the power to fulfil his deepest desires.

In the quiet embrace, Ash remained silent, his heart heavy with unspoken words and unexpressed feelings. Though he feared overwhelming her or facing rejection, he vowed to protect her at any cost, even if it meant sacrificing his own life.

With unwavering resolve, he whispered softly to himself, "No matter what the future holds, you will always have a place in my heart. I will protect you, even at the cost of my life, little witch."

CHAPTER 8

As desire threatened to overwhelm her, Jade teetered on the edge of surrender. Her heart yearned to be swept away by the fervent passion of their kiss, but a voice of caution whispered in the depths of her mind, urging her to resist. Struggling against the conflicting urges pulling at her, she felt torn between the allure of ecstasy and the fear of abandonment. In that fleeting moment, she stood at a crossroads, unsure of which path to choose.

Yet, as the intoxicating temptation beckoned her closer, anger surged within her like a raging storm. With a swift motion, she stepped back, her palm connecting with his cheek in a resounding slap before she pushed him away, sending him stumbling into the soft embrace of the sand. Despite the ache in her heart and the longing that threatened to consume her, she hardened her resolve and buried the turbulent feelings stirring deep inside her.

In that moment of fierce defiance, Jade knew she could not afford to succumb to the intoxicating allure of love, not when the shadow of betrayal loomed large in her past. With every fibre of her being, she steeled herself against the tumultuous storm of emotions, determined to protect her heart from further pain and devastation.

"Ouch! What was that for?"

"Any more attempts like that and you're in for worse than a stinging cheek, got it?"

Locking lips with him was like unleashing chaos upon them. Their fates had been entwined from the start, destined for a dangerous path. What destiny awaited a witch and a demon prince? He was bound to abandon her once more, leaving Jade to grapple with the torment of her shattered heart once again.

"I wouldn't dream of making a powerful being like you angry," he replied with a smirk. "Cross my heart and hope to die."

"Oh, you impossible creature! Why don't you just leave? I'm sure I'll be fine without you."

"I'm not so sure. This might look like the human realm, but it certainly isn't. Since my abilities come from Hell, I'm as powerless here as any human. And since you're the one who stranded us here, it's your responsibility to take care of me." He smiled innocently at her. "Besides, shouldn't we talk about us? Our past together and that passionate kiss we just experienced?"

"Son of a..." Jade cursed under her breath. "I should have left you at the academy."

"Tsk, tsk." He shook his head sadly. "Is that how you treat your man?"

Jade shot him a glare that could have frozen Hell over. After she had opened up to him, he had the audacity to test her patience.

"Which I'm certain you don't," he persisted, that same

impish grin plastered across his face. “That binds me to you, and you’ve got to deal with the consequences.”

“Let’s have a chat about that, shall we? You’ve deceived me about your true identity, ingratiated yourself with me, all to steal my powers. Do you really want to see how much I care about you?” Her gaze bore into him, her fury seething beneath the surface. Jade channelled her anger, letting it surge through her veins. With a flick of her wrist, she unleashed a crackling bolt of lightning toward Ash, but he simply sidestepped it, that infuriating grin never faltering. She was furious with him for exploiting her, for manipulating her into responding to his kiss. Yet, she couldn’t deny the pull of his charm, even as she cursed herself for falling under its spell.

“I thought you were an Earth witch, so why...?” he asked.

“It’s a convoluted tale. Everyone at the academy was well aware of my Earth magic because of my penchant for destruction. But they’d be utterly astounded to discover I can wield more than one element. That’s precisely why I’ve yet to secure a mentor.” Ash’s raised eyebrow betrayed his surprise.

Most of the individuals who had offered their guidance at that accursed institution had thrown in the towel upon realising her power surpassed their own. It left her feeling inadequate, though in truth, it was they who had failed her.

“Now that you’ve ceased venting your frustrations on me, let’s find out our location. We might as well make the most of our time here and indulge in some amusement,” the prince proposed.

“Pardon?”

“You are so English, aren’t you? Always so serious. Do you sip tea while listening to the national anthem?” Ash laughed.

“You never stop talking, do you? I can’t help but wonder why nothing fazes you. You’re a demon, so of course you don’t take life too seriously.” Did he not know how dangerous she was when she got mad? And here they were, in the middle of nowhere, with no help should she lose control of her powers.

"That was a legitimate question, just so you know." Ash halted in his tracks. "I'm concerned."

"If you keep saying stuff like that, I'll have to gag you," Jade warned. She remembered the time in the dreamland when he wouldn't speak much and simply held her hand instead.

"I'm looking forward to it." He beamed.

Jade muttered something, binding Ash's lips with magic. He struggled to open his mouth but to no avail. Her mind was a jumble of thoughts, and she desperately needed to ground herself.

"Finally, some peace." She chuckled darkly. "You can squirm as much as you like. There's no reversing this until the spell runs its course. That'll be about an hour from now."

With her attention diverted from him, she surveyed her surroundings. Blast him, he was correct. This place didn't have the familiar aura of home. Was it an alternate dimension? Whatever it was, she needed to find a way back for the individuals relying on her back at the academy.

"Stay close and don't wander off. If you get lost, I'm not wasting my time trying to search for you. I'll be on my way, and you'll be stuck here," she promised.

Jade hoped the seriousness of their situation would sober Ash up. She had never faced a more dire circumstance—no shelter, no sustenance, and an endless desert with no water in sight. With her dwindling energy, Jade summoned a barrier to shield them from the scorching sun. The last thing she needed was to succumb to heatstroke.

Eventually, Ash spoke up. "What do you think we should do?"

Jade had no answer. She simply pressed on, feeling as

though they were going in circles. As her strength ebbed away, the witch succumbed to exhaustion and collapsed.

ASMODEUS GENTLY LIFTED JADE AND PLANTED A KISS ON her forehead. "It's my turn to take care of you, my little witch."

With her admission of recognising him from her dreams, everything clicked into place in his mind. She remembered him. Initially, she had been merely a means to an end, but now he grew fond of her. He had been fortunate in the dream realm that day; had he stripped away all her powers, she would have loathed him forever.

The prince released a heavy sigh. Lady Fortune seemed to toy with him, as now that he had found her, they were stranded together in this unfamiliar land.

Asmodeus held her close, refusing to let her go. He had decided. He would make the most of their time together, aiding her in growing powerful enough to confront whatever challenges awaited her. And when the timing was perfect, he would give her powers back.

In truth, Ash possessed the ability to return to the mortal realm at any moment. Yet, what stayed his hand was his longing for more time with the witch, free from any interruptions. His choice may have been self-serving, but he couldn't pass up the chance for this connection.

"Mine," he whispered into her hair before forging ahead, using his demonic energy to seek a suitable shelter for them to spend the night.

CHAPTER 9

When Jade stirred awake, she found Ash already watching her intently.

"Could you be any more awkward? How long have you been like this?" she quipped, rolling her eyes.

Ash chuckled softly. "No need to fret. We've only just arrived. I've been admiring your lovely face for a few minutes. After you fainted, I carried you around all night. Did you know you talk in your sleep?" He arched an eyebrow, a playful smirk playing on his lips.

Jade felt her cheeks flush with embarrassment.

"You were having a dream about me because you kept mentioning my lips." Ash batted his eyelashes. "Is there something you want to tell me? Maybe you long for another kiss?"

"Over my dead body," Jade exclaimed, giving him a hostile look.

She eyed him and saw the mischievous smile vanish from his face, and a new emotion replaced it. It was the same tenderness that used to surround them in the dream world, where they could be themselves and free from constraints.

"Take care of what you wish for. I can't imagine a universe without you," Ash warned.

Jade shook her head. "You know they don't care about me, only my powers. Do you think they're actively looking for us now that we've escaped? They're probably just after the demon that killed my friend. People used to despise me and now I'm gone. They're probably glad, thinking, 'good riddance, the useless witch is gone'."

"I could never think that way. You matter to me—a lot. Nothing will change that. Now, come on. Let's go. Believe it or not, I'm actually missing the academy."

"That's definitely something I wouldn't expect you to say!" She laughed.

Asmodeus gently lifted Jade to her feet, offering her a supportive hand.

"What is this place?" she enquired, surveying their surroundings.

"I had to find somewhere to shield you from the elements until you woke up again. I'm sorry; this is the best I could do," Ash explained, his tone filled with genuine concern.

Despite Ash's usual roguish demeanour, Jade couldn't help but notice the occasional sweetness in his actions, which mattered to her more than she cared to admit.

"There's no need to apologise. It's my fault we're in this mess. If I had better control over my powers or trained harder, maybe we wouldn't be stuck here." She sighed.

"You shouldn't blame yourself for having teachers who couldn't help you reach your full potential," Ash remarked.

"It's odd to think that a demon could be a better listener than my kind," Jade mused, grateful for his support during such lonely times.

"What do you say we make a deal? On our next visit to the academy, we'll show them just how much you've grown, and I will help you hone your skills."

"And what kind of payment do you expect in return?" Jade asked, her curiosity piqued.

"Nothing in particular. Just promise you won't forget me, no matter what happens." Ash squeezed her hand.

As Asmodeus finished speaking, Jade's ears pricked up at the sound of commotion echoing from outside the cavern. Channelling her remaining magical energy, she amplified the noises, rendering them louder and clearer. She discerned the shouts of men, the heavy thud of their boots, and the metallic clinking of their armour. It seemed like a vast army marching in synchronised cadence, their presence growing ever closer with each passing moment. The scent of earth, sweat, and iron permeated the air, assaulting her senses. Her heart raced as she glanced at Ash, seeking confirmation of what she already suspected. His smile and nod affirmed her fears.

"Don't panic," Ash said softly, stroking Jade's hand. "I'll take care of them."

He tried to summon a protective shield around them, but his magic felt stifled, as if an invisible force was dampening his abilities. It was a troubling revelation. Deprived of their powers, they were left vulnerable in this unfamiliar realm.

"How can you protect us?" Jade's voice quivered with fear.

"I suppose I'll have to charm their leader," Ash replied with a hint of uncertainty. "Are you willing to go along with that?"

She shook her head, her expression betraying her apprehension.

"I'm glad I have your unwavering support," he said sarcastically.

He released her hand and approached the entrance cautiously, peering out to assess the situation. Despite the anxiety bubbling within him, he maintained a facade of composure, determined not to let fear consume him, especially in front of Jade.

"Let's proceed." He beckoned to her. "Let's see what awaits us out there."

Jade clutched his hand and followed him into the light.

"We're going to be okay," he whispered, ensuring she heard him. "Trust me."

"I'm trying," she murmured in response.

As soon as they stepped outside, a sudden force overwhelmed them, plunging them both into unconsciousness.

CHAPTER 10

"DAMMIT! MY HEAD IS POUNDING," ASH GROANED, rubbing his temples as he surveyed their surroundings. The room exuded opulence, adorned with lavish decorations crafted from precious metals and gems arranged in intricate patterns. The air was filled with the sweet scent of incense and perfume, evoking an oriental ambiance that hinted at a return to the human plane, though Ash's faint powers suggested otherwise.

Two guards stood sentinel at the door, their imposing figures clad in ornate armour adorned with elaborate designs. Their helmets, shaped like the fierce visage of a dragon, added to their intimidating presence. Asmodeus remained unfazed by their attempts to instil fear; such petty tactics held little sway over a demon of his stature. Their tightly gripped swords hinted at their readiness for combat, yet they seemed to pay him little heed, much to Ash's disdain.

It was clear from their demeanour that they awaited orders from a higher authority. Had their leader noticed

Asmodeus's true nature? Ash regarded them with an icy stare, unsettled by their blatant disregard for his presence.

Ash attempted to start a conversation with them. "Where am I?"

No response. His anger grew. He was used to people obeying his every word, and their silence filled him with rage. Asmodeus had a reputation as a merciless prince who punished those who craved sin in the most atrocious ways—if he had control of his powers in this place, then he would be sure to show these people who was in charge.

Finally, the door opened, and a man dressed in dark robes stepped into the room. Ash let out a sigh at the thought of getting some answers soon. He stared at the man expectantly and waited for him to speak.

"Her Majesty has commanded your presence. Follow me to meet her."

"What have you done to the girl that was with me when we were captured? If you have harmed her, I will seek my vengeance. I guarantee it," the prince threatened.

"She is unharmed and being tended by the Queen's maids. You will see her eventually... if you cooperate," the hooded man replied.

Ash nodded silently and followed him. There was something about the messenger's voice that made him believe his words, and he didn't want to risk Jade's life. His own existence had spanned aeons of time, so if he had to die in this place, it wouldn't be a great tragedy. But of course, he wanted to spend his remaining days with the people and things he cared about.

As they moved through the chambers of the castle, they eventually reached what seemed to be the audience room. It was covered with a breath-taking stained-glass picture that depicted a familiar scene: him as a young man and the day he was imprisoned. He quickly realised he was about to come face to face with his oldest enemy—the woman who had vowed to love him but trapped him in the crumbling world of Valoraa and sealed his fate as a Prince of Hell.

Under a grandiose canopy, the ruler of the realm sat upon a magnificent glass throne, her presence commanding respect. Her piercing blue eyes bore a sharpness that hinted at her authority, while a haughty demeanour exuded from her every gesture. Adorned in an awe-inspiring attire, she wore a dusty rose one-shoulder dress adorned with countless sparkling jewels, its high slit revealing her slender legs. A matching veil concealed her nose and mouth, adding an air of mystery to her regal appearance. Delicate gold chains adorned her black ink-coloured hair, culminating in a ruby-hued headdress with intricate floral designs, lending her the aura of a goddess.

"Your Grace, the male trespasser has been brought before you," the messenger announced, bowing respectfully before his queen before turning to address the prisoner. "Kneel and show your respect to our ruler."

A heavy silence hung in the air as Ash met the woman's gaze head-on, his eyes filled with centuries' worth of resentment. Time passed differently in Valoraa, Hell, and this mysterious realm, each moment stretching into an eternity of torment for him.

Ash wondered what the Queen was up to. Thousands of thoughts swarmed his mind, but none provided the best outcome to get Jade out of this place alive. The Queen's grandeur and beauty meant nothing to him. Of course, she was no monarch when they first met, only an illegitimate princess. If he had his full powers in this world, he would have turned her to dust for the audacity to make him a prisoner once again. He, a Prince of Hell, a hostage. An amusing thought.

"Insolence!" the messenger yelled. "Who gave you permission to look at Her Majesty?"

"Kneel." The Queen repeated her command.

"I will not," Ash replied abruptly. "I do not owe you my obedience. You have abducted me and my companion. I demand you release us at once."

The sovereign's face darkened. "He speaks. Bring the other one here. Let's see if he will be more compliant."

"Right away, Your Grace." The old man bowed and left the room.

Moments later, the little witch emerged from the doorway, and relief flooded through him as he saw she was unharmed. He held her close to his chest and wished he could do more to protect her in this dangerous land.

"You're okay," he said, stroking her hair. "I thought I would never see you again."

"You can't get rid of me so easily." She smiled up at him. He wanted to say more, but he let himself feel the warmth of her body in his arms.

The Queen cleared her throat, her voice cutting through the tense atmosphere. "Now that the little lovebirds have been reunited, let's carry on," she remarked, a wicked gleam in her eyes. "Let's try this again. Kneel, or I'll make you."

Reluctantly, Ash complied, lowering himself to the floor as instructed. With Jade in the clutches of his adversary, he couldn't afford to take any unnecessary risks. Protecting her became his sole priority.

"There we go. See? We can understand each other," the Queen taunted, her smirk betraying her amusement. With a flick of her wrist, magical manacles materialised around Ash's wrists, trapping him.

"What are you doing?" Jade demanded.

"He is an intruder and a demon. I must punish him according to his crimes."

"This isn't right," Jade said, her voice trembling.

Ash glanced at her and shook his head. "It won't make a difference. She won't listen." But the witch didn't respond to him. Instead, she dropped to her knees.

"I will take both our punishments. It was my magic that took us here. Spare him. He had nothing to do with this. My power is broken, and I could not control where it brought us. Please, I beg you."

Ash wanted to roll his eyes at the woman; she never knew when to stop talking. They did indeed enter this realm without permission and were lucky not to have been killed on sight. He looked around the room for something that could interfere with his powers but came up empty-handed.

"Stop grovelling. It's beneath you. You're descended from mighty witches, and that your magic is broken is completely my fault," Ash interjected. "I take responsibility for this and offer myself as a sacrifice instead."

"You can't do this," Jade said indignantly.

"If there must be a punishment," he answered her firmly, "it should be mine."

Ash silently prayed that the woman would stop talking soon; offering himself up for her freedom was the only option available to him now. He had lived a long time and was not afraid of dying if this was how he went.

"Hush, both of you. I know what each of you is." The Queen looked at Jade. "You are human, and Asmodeus, I never expected a Prince of Hell to have any sentiment for a witch. This is certainly an unexpected development."

Ash steeled himself to prepare for whatever punishment she might inflict on them. It was a pity, as her beauty concealed a heart as black as coal.

"If you can pass the trials I set out for you, I will allow you to leave this place," she said finally.

"What tests?" Ash enquired, hopeful.

"The witch will stay by my side and be under my care, so I can see she is safe from your corruption. Through your actions, you must show me you are not the evil creature I believe you to be. Convince me, and I may spare your life."

"That won't be hard," he replied.

"We shall see. I am determined to uncover his true nature in whatever way necessary. Guards, take him to the Holy Grounds."

"It's not fair. He's a demon! He won't survive there," Jade pleaded, tears cascading down her cheeks.

"He will be weakened, but alive. That is my only kindness."

Asmodeus closed his eyes as the men dragged him away, the image of Jade on her knees weeping uncontrollably, haunting him. The sight of her anguish threatened to shatter his resolve, igniting a burning desire for vengeance against those who dared to separate them.

Silently, he vowed revenge, his mind consumed with thoughts of breaking through whatever spell or artefact was blocking his magic. Once free from his restraints, they would all face the full force of Hell's wrath, and none would be spared.

CHAPTER 11

As Jade was escorted to her chambers by a retinue of guards, she couldn't shake the feeling of unease that lingered in the air. The Queen's hostility towards Ash was palpable, unjustified given their minor transgression. There was something more at play here. Something beneath the surface that Jade couldn't quite grasp.

Once inside her room, Jade closed the heavy wooden door behind her, seeking solace in the confines of her chamber. She allowed herself a moment of respite, sinking onto the plush bedding of her four-poster bed. Exhaustion weighed heavily on her, pulling her into the depths of sleep as she contemplated the tangled web of intrigue that surrounded them. In her dreams, she searched for answers, hoping to uncover a way to navigate the treacherous waters of the Queen's court and secure their freedom.

Jade found herself in an unfamiliar dark room, and Ash was standing next to her.

"What are we doing here?" she asked.

"I came to check on you. Even though I am stuck in these

manacles, I wanted to see what you were up to. I wish I could be next to you."

"But how did you manage this? I figured magic doesn't work here." Seeing Ash restrained like an animal made Jade cry, and she reached out to touch his face with her fingertips.

"I can do things that don't require a large amount of power, like connecting with you. However, something is blocking me from doing anything else."

"Do you have any idea where we are?" she asked.

"Yes, and it's not promising. We've found ourselves in Eseron, the ancient realm of the Fae. Demons have infiltrated, and our arrival wasn't well-received. It's said that only those born of Fae blood can teleport here. But there are deceitful demons with the knack for stealing magic and wielding it for their own ends."

"Like what you did to me when we first met," Jade stated, her gaze piercing.

"About that... I'm sorry, all right? If we escape this predicament, I'll spend the rest of eternity making amends. I won't try to excuse my actions, but after enduring captivity for so long and developing feelings for you, I panicked when I finally gained my freedom. But on that regrettable day, all I intended was to borrow your abilities. If only I could return your powers now. If only my magic weren't muted by this place."

"I believe you. Anyway, we're getting off topic. Is this the reason the Queen mistrusts you? For being a trickster demon? It's not like you can change your identity."

"That's one explanation. I have heard the guards whispering about her demon lover, who hurt her tremendously. I should note that men are just as likely to engage in hearsay and rumour-mongering as women are to indulge in some juicy gossip. But that would be typical behaviour of my kind, considering our track record for questionable conduct."

"You're a Prince of Hell. Can't you use your charm and get her to let us go? You've made the female students at the academy fall for you before. What happened? Have you lost your touch?" Jade asked, her interest piqued.

"Fae have a special magic which only they can use. She glimpsed into my heart and knows I'm not my own person anymore." Ash sighed.

"Out of all the times when I actually need your help, you're unable to spin a lie to get us out of this mess," Jade remarked, rolling her eyes in annoyance. "And what about me? I was the one who got us into this predicament. Any idea why that might be?"

"No clue, but it seems the Queen has taken a liking to you more than to me, so there's that. Just do nothing reckless that'll put you in danger," Ash warned.

"I won't, I promise," Jade assured, though she knew she'd do whatever it took to ensure their safety. She hoped her magic would recharge soon.

"I'm sorry. There's no way I can rely on my powers to pass her tests. If it weren't a matter of life or death for me, this would be amusing. Instead, I have to pretend to be human and face the challenge at a tremendous disadvantage."

"I hope you can overcome this and we can escape this wretched place. Remember to stay composed," Jade advised.

"Do not fret. I will win this by any means necessary. I won't let a little queen from a strange land outwit me," Ash promised.

Once Ash regained consciousness, he surveyed his surroundings and locked eyes with the Queen, who was gazing at him.

"Ah, hello, my love," she greeted him with a smirk. "It's been a while."

He had expected how long it would take her to recognise him, and the answer came immediately. As soon as he stepped into the audience chamber, he saw through her façade. The stories she spun for her people were built on lies, and he wasn't pleased to see her.

"Let's get the facts straight since there's no one else around. You never had feelings for me, only for my status." Ash grinned and gave her a once-over. "So, you spun a tale to your mommy that I, the Crown Prince, took your innocence." Of course, the aging Fae Queen believed her daughter's story. She was illegitimate and cared little for politics. But the truth was different.

"Your Highness," the Queen said sarcastically. "Can I still call you that? Ah, what does it matter? You always had a flair for the dramatic. All you had to do was marry me, and your soul and your kingdom would have remained intact."

She'd approached him for marriage, and he'd agreed hesitantly, growing to like her. But eventually, he saw through her façade and broke off the arrangement.

"Not only did you destroy my life, but you also hastened my father's death."

The Queen stared at him in shock. "He knows my deception. What am I to do?"

"Nothing can be done now. I've lost my kingdom and my people are long gone. And I have become the most skilled punisher in Hell." Ash chuckled darkly.

Ashlan found himself imprisoned within the confines of his own kingdom, devoid of an heir to reclaim the throne. As the relentless years of captivity wore on, his humanity waned, and he sank deeper into his demonic nature. When he utilised Jade to break free from his chains, what emerged was nothing more than a wretched trickster demon.

"Is that supposed to impress me or instil fear in my heart? You may call yourself a Prince of Hell, but you're still just a demon."

"That's where you're wrong again. As time passes differently in Hell, I have evolved into a leader of the abyss, with thousands of years of experience. Surprisingly, my newfound strength only caused the anguish of the past to be felt more intensively; every wrong done to me was as vivid as if it just happened. I tried to bury these feelings and move forward, but now so close to the very source of my suffering, I know that no amount of time can keep me contained."

The Queen laughed mockingly. "Are you stupid enough to believe I will free you? The tests are just a spectacle for my people to amuse themselves with. Your carcass will remain in the Holy Grounds eternally and only then will I be appeased for you breaking off the engagement."

"We shall see about that. Time has always been my ally. I am, unlike you, eternal." Ash closed his eyes, waiting for the woman to leave.

The Queen leaned forward enough to almost brush the tip of her nose against Ash's. Snaking a hand around his back, her long nails scratched his flesh, a caress and a threat all in one. Then she kissed Ash's lips, whispering, "For old times' sake."

A chill ran down Ash's spine as he jerked away from her touch, the ethereal manacles constricting around his wrists. He took a deep breath and met her gaze, his heart pounding in his chest.

"Never do that again," he said through gritted teeth, his voice barely a whisper.

The Queen smiled, a devious twinkle in her eye, "I look forward to having you here with me for eternity, my pet."

"Foolish woman, don't you know by now? I am death." Ash sneered.

"You don't frighten me, Ashlan. I am always one step ahead of you. No matter how much time passes between us."

"You will pay for your arrogance!" Ash bellowed. "I will have my revenge and put an end to this once and for all."

"Until then, Ashlan, pray you receive a swift ending." The Queen laughed wickedly as she walked towards her palace, leaving Ash alone with his thoughts.

CHAPTER 12

The following day, the Queen's chambermaids arrived to rouse Jade and provide her with a bath and a set of clothes. Despite her situation, she feigned politeness and made small talk. Her mind wondered about the way the Queen had been treating Ash during his imprisonment. She felt guilty for how she had treated Ash when he'd arrived at the academy. He had a tendency to joke around and not take much seriously, but she couldn't hold that against him; after all, he was a creature of the Underworld.

Once prepared, Jade dismissed her attendants and went to inspect the bath. It was fashioned much like what she would expect from a medieval world—wooden, similar to oak, and clouded with a homemade mixture of Epsom salts. The room was filled with a subtle, flowery scent.

Jade undressed and stepped into the tub, desperately needing a bath after being lost in the desert for so long. What a treat it was to let the scented water wash away the strain of walking for hours on end. Maybe this pampering would restore her magical powers. Her breathing slowed as she closed her eyes and was transported back to the dreamworld.

"You look like you're enjoying yourself," Ash whispered.

Startled, Jade attempted to cover herself with her arms and noticed that her clothes and towels were gone.

"So you can still use some of your magic, huh? You took away any kind of covering I had! As perverted as you are, I was actually worrying about how you were doing in the Holy Grounds."

Ash chuckled. "I'm sorry, but I can't see a thing from this spot. Though, I guess if I got closer, I could enjoy the view."

"If you do that, I'll go down to where the Queen holds you and torture you to death myself," Jade said sternly.

"Oh, really? Maybe one day I'll test that theory, just for kicks."

"Then why did you dare risk the Queen's wrath by speaking with me? She'd be livid if she caught wind of it."

"I merely wanted to see how you were faring. Is that not reason enough? Can't we acknowledge our concern for each other?"

Jade rolled her eyes. "Can we please stay focused on the task at hand?"

"You're no fun, you know that? Fine, back to business. I've been informed that the first trial will take place today, but they didn't provide any further details."

"I shudder to think what the Queen has planned for you."

Ash sighed. "Your guess is as good as mine. I have to go now. Someone's approaching my location. If these trials end up being the end of me, at least I got to see you naked."

"You're such a pervert! And didn't you just say you couldn't see anything, anyway?"

"Hey, it's a demon's prerogative to lie... especially when

they're rather fond of someone." Ash chuckled before disappearing.

WHEN ASH WOKE UP FROM DREAM WALKING, HE FOUND one of the Queen's aides watching him.

"Breakfast is served, m'lord," the guard said sarcastically, presenting a tray of food.

"Do you give all your prisoners this treatment or is it just for me?" he asked, poking at his meal.

"Nah. That's especially prepared for you. Miss Jade will eat with Her Majesty while you get the leftovers from the Queen's dinner table." The man turned to leave but half-heartedly threw a bottle of water at Ash's feet.

"What, no wine? I am really disappointed by your queen's hospitality."

"I thought that too until I remembered the death sentence hanging over your head. There's no point in being too nice to you when you're going to die, anyway. Count yourself lucky that you get to breathe your last in our mighty land."

"I wouldn't be so sure about that," Ash replied confidently. "You can go back and tell your queen that I won't give up without a fight."

"If you say so, m'lord." The man bowed again mockingly before leaving.

Ash felt a deep ambivalence toward the visitor. On one hand, he had eaten nothing since his imprisonment and was grateful for the scraps of food they had brought. But he couldn't let go of his suspicions. After all, the Fae were notoriously untrustworthy, and he wasn't certain that the Queen wasn't plotting some new scheme to keep him captive.

He found the world of the fairies utterly strange. He had never experienced hunger before, and he couldn't comprehend why it had such a profound effect on him.

Shuddering at the thought of what else this place had in store for him, he savoured the meagre meal, gulping down the water that accompanied it. He knew it wasn't as satisfying as the food from the human realm, but he was determined to survive.

Ash clung to life, even amid an unfamiliar and uncomfortable situation. He finally understood why humans were so reluctant to leave the world of the living and enter the Underworld.

His body felt heavy as he slumped against the ancient tree on the Holy Grounds, his magical shackles sapping his energy away. He knew he had to break free from the Queen's hold, but exhaustion weighed him down, making it difficult to even open his eyes. Despite his weariness, Ash tried to reach out to his adoptive son, Vlad, through their connection, praying that somehow his call would reach him across realms.

As he heard a faint sound drawing closer, Ash's hopes rose, only to be dashed when he saw it was Jade approaching. She gasped in shock at the sight of his aged face and fell to her knees, tears streaming down her cheeks. Jade reached out to him, gently caressing his cheek. How could he feel so powerless in front of the woman he loved?

Jade's touch was as delicate as a butterfly's wings as she gently wrapped her hand around Ash's scarred wrist, offering comfort during his suffering. Ash's heart skipped a beat, his breath catching in his throat. Her touch was like a soothing balm, tender, easing the ache in his muscles and the burden on his soul. But even as he revelled in her touch, he couldn't shake the feeling of unworthiness that gnawed at him.

"It's not your fault," Jade cried, her voice choked with tears. "I'm sorry for what's happened to you."

"Don't waste your tears on me," Ash replied, his voice barely above a whisper as exhaustion washed over him. "I brought this upon myself. I am not worthy of your sympathy."

"I've begged Her Majesty countless times to forgive you, but she keeps refusing. We must do everything we can to escape this place if either of us is to survive," Jade said desperately.

"But I'm so tired. I feel my life slipping away from me. You should go alone. I cannot be a burden to you," Ash said weakly. Did they poison his food? He had been feeling fine before he ate and now his health was declining.

"What kind of nonsense are you speaking? We'll leave here together. Don't give up on me now!" Jade shouted, the anger in her voice mixing with the pain.

"We never truly began," Ash whispered, his voice heavy with remorse. "I was a fool to think I could ever win your heart after all I've done. Remember your dreams? I shamelessly used you. I wanted you to harness your power so I could manipulate you into breaking the curse that bound me. And I did. I stole your magic to save myself, and then I abandoned you without a second thought. I don't deserve to stand beside you."

"You may not have wanted us, but I do. I'll never regret the day I fell in love with you, no matter how much you try to push me away. You're trying to shield me from the truth of why the Queen despises you, but I am not concerned about that. All that matters is what I feel for you. I love you now and I'll love you for the next million years, and every million after. Whatever happens, no matter what you do, I will always cherish you."

Ash took in the sight of Jade's tear-streaked face, illuminated with love's tears that caused her emerald eyes to sparkle. Her blonde hair partially hid her expression, but he could still make out her quivering lips as they curved into a watery smile. Her gaze was foggy, fighting the tears that threatened to spill over, and her slim hands trembled in his. The shimmer of her teal dress cascaded around her, spilling onto the ground like a waterfall in its beauty.

Jade summoned her magic to save Ash, despite knowing his dark past.

"You foolish girl. You mustn't waste your power on me," he pleaded, his heart heavy with the weight of all his wrongdoings.

"Shh. Enough of that," she interjected, her attention fixed on the cursed chains ensnaring him. With a flick of her wrist, the manacles dissolved into nothingness.

"All right, that's better," she panted, struggling to lift him from the ground. "You're definitely heavier than you appear."

When his feet finally made contact with the earth, he smiled faintly at her before an arrow buzzed through the air towards her chest. In a flash of motion, Ash used his remaining strength and leapt in front of her. He encased her in a protective embrace and shielded her from the projectile with his own body.

Jade let out a maniacal laugh. "You should have known better. I begged you to run away with me so I could manipulate you into being killed, but you simply couldn't understand. So I had to resort to my theatrics, making it seem like I needed to be 'saved' in order to make you succumb to your destiny."

As soon as the intruder spoke again, a chill ran down his

spine. Ash knew in an instant this wasn't his beloved Jade. "Who are you? What have you done with my little witch?" he bellowed, his mouth twisted in rage.

"I am the weaver of your fate, sent by none other than the Queen," came the bitter reply. "She sends her regards. You're as good as dead now." The woman chuckled darkly. He could feel the chill of death creeping over him as the malicious words echoed in the air.

CHAPTER 13

After Jade had dressed, she heard a knock at her door.

"Come in," she said, awaiting the Queen's attendant.

A petite woman wearing an off-shoulder dress with a high slit and veil entered the room. She looked like a miniature version of the Queen, only less glamorous. Was this traditional attire for this realm? It certainly seemed so.

"Her Majesty requests you join her for breakfast," the young maid informed her.

"That sounds great," Jade replied and followed her around.

She was surprised to see that these people lived much like humans did—in a medieval era. The castle was constructed of stone, lit by braziers, and attendants used oil lamps to navigate during darker hours. Meanwhile, beeswax candles lit up the Queen's chambers.

Besides these light sources, large mirrors adorned the walls, used to cast light and make the place appear brighter without excessive use of candles. Jade noticed there were no paintings in the rooms she'd seen; she wondered why this was so—usually kings and queens were fond of displaying their ancestry and wealth in such ways.

As they stepped into the dining room, Jade was taken aback by its resemblance to the others. Gilded mirrors decorated the walls, while a grand mechanical clock depicting a serene forest scene embellished the opposite wall. The ceiling shimmered with a mosaic of mirrors, and the space was bathed in the warm glow of countless candles.

Seated at the head of the table, the Queen was already being served by her attendants, her regal presence commanding the room.

"I'm glad you joined me," she said with an inviting smile.

If Ash wasn't a captive, Jade would have thought the woman before her was a friend. But that was far from true.

"I have no other option. You have a tight grip on Ash. One word from you could send him straight to his death," Jade reminded her.

"There's no need to be so hostile. Demons are known deceivers. I learned this lesson through experience. I am giving you a chance to see Ash for who he really is. Nothing more and nothing less."

"Why do you care what happens to me? You're just a stranger from a distant land," Jade responded, her words heavy with exasperation. She was not thrilled by the Queen's tests. Ash had been by Jade's side for a long time, though he had been pretending to be someone else.

"Let's just say I've been fascinated with you since we first met, and I'm invested in your future. Three tests from the Fae realm are nothing for a Prince of the Underworld. Don't think of me as an adversary. Consider me your fairy godmother. Though I may appear young, I have accumulated vast wisdom over many years," the Queen said with a smile. "I am merely striving to show you the true nature of the demon kind. I had nobody to warn me as I fell prey to a vicious one in my past."

"I have no choice but to believe you for now, but don't assume I trust you just because you are trying to 'look out' for me. Trust is earned, and that is something you haven't done yet," Jade replied, pushing her food around her plate.

"Well, let us start from the beginning. It is forbidden to mention a ruler's name in my culture. However, I will make an exception for you. My name is Ayanna and I come from the House of Navaar. It is a pleasure to make your acquaintance."

"I can't say it's been a pleasure being a captive, but I'll let that slide for now," Jade remarked, her voice tinged with curiosity. "It's said that you can see into a person's soul. So, you know more about me than even I do. Tell me, why do you care about me?"

The Queen regarded Jade with a measured gaze before responding. "You are inexperienced with dark magic, and you don't fully comprehend the implications of travelling with a being from the Underworld. Yet, you treat him as more than just an acquaintance. There's a desire for romantic involvement."

"Help me understand him, then," Jade retorted, frustration clear in her voice, "but don't expect me to let him go. Start with the truth. Why was I able to come here?"

"That's an interesting question. What element is your magic?" Queen Ayanna enquired.

"All of them," she answered, and the Queen's eyes widened in shock.

"Well, you said you want to earn my trust. What's wrong?" Jade asked.

"It's hard to say without testing your abilities, but it's

possible that someone in your family was one of us. Maybe in the past, before I became queen, someone escaped the realm alive. It's not impossible," Queen Ayanna speculated.

Jade weighed her options and fabricated a story, hoping she would buy into it. "I... feel some sort of familiarity since I've seen you. I want to believe you, I do, but I need something more to go on," she replied, her tone carefully chosen to evoke empathy.

The Queen regarded her with a contemplative gaze, waiting for further explanation. Jade seized the opportunity to steer the conversation towards her primary aim—ensuring Ash's safety.

"I need to see Ash for myself. My heart won't rest until I know he's okay," she asserted, her eyes shimmering with unshed tears.

Slowly, the Queen waved her hand, and one mirror began showing Ash's location. "His trials have started today. This is the best I can do," Queen Ayanna said softly.

He looked haggard, like hundreds of years had passed, still chained with the magical manacles, sitting under the shade of a tree. Ash was resting while humming a song Jade was sure she'd heard once before. His eyes were closed as a figure approached him.

She was shocked to find that the woman bore an exact resemblance to her. The Queen sneered from her throne but remained silent, providing no explanation.

Jade strained to catch the conversation between the imposter and Ash, her heart pounding with anxiety as she sensed the danger lurking in the air. The imposter's coaxing words sent a shiver down her spine, and she couldn't shake the feeling that something sinister was afoot. Was the wicked woman manipulating Ash into a trap, luring him away from the safety of the palace grounds, only to meet a deadly fate?

When Jade witnessed Ash being wounded by an arrow, a surge of rage and dread consumed her. She cursed herself for ever believing the Queen's deceitful promises that the tests would be harmless to a Prince of Hell. As she watched Ash falter, she knew in her gut that the arrow wasn't ordinary. It was likely infused with dark magic, posing a grave threat to his already weakened state. Panic gripped her heart as she realised that Ash's life hung in the balance, and she feared the worst.

Wild electricity raced through Jade's veins as sparks crackled at her fingers and the ground trembled beneath her feet. Power surged through her body, and she knew she was ready to avenge Ash and destroy the castle if that was what it took.

With a fierce flick of her wrist, Jade overturned the dinner table and sent the crockery shattering around the chamber. Suspending the cutlery in mid-air, Jade pointed them at Queen Ayanna, who was standing just inches away from her.

"Take me to him or you die. Your choice."

"You won't leave this place unharmed if anything happens to me." The Queen sneered.

With determination burning in her eyes, Jade growled defiantly, her voice unwavering. Despite the frustrations and annoyances Ash often caused her, the mere thought of him meeting his end sent a chilling wave of dread coursing through her veins, causing her stomach to knot with fear. As she approached closer, brandishing the weapons with purpose, she drew blood from the ruler's skin, a silent warning of the dire consequences should any harm befall Ash under her watch.

"Now!"

The ruler let out an amused laugh. "Fine, let's see him." She opened a portal to Ash's location.

Jade animated the curtain tiebacks, making them snake around the Queen's neck and wrists. They squeezed tight until her eyes bulged with terror.

"What's this?" Queen Ayanna's voice tremored.

"Insurance, in case you decide to cross me. Now, walk, or I swear I'll take your life today."

"Love makes people do foolish things."

The Monarch's harsh laughter sent a chill down Jade's spine, but it only fuelled her determination further. Ash wasn't just a friend; he was her saviour, her confidant, and someone she owed her life to. She would stop at nothing to ensure his safety.

As they approached the Holy Grounds, a surge of powerful energy coursed through Jade as if the very place recognised her heritage. The Queen had gravely underestimated the strength and resolve of a descendant of the Fae. With each step closer to the impending confrontation, Jade's resolve solidified, her determination unwavering.

Jade's rage boiled over as she summoned a powerful wave of air, hurling the imposter away from Ash. The doppelgänger crashed against a tree and slumped unconscious.

Rushing to Ash's side, tears streamed down Jade's face as she frantically pressed her hands against the arrow protruding from his chest. Her heart pounded with fear and desperation, but she refused to let despair take hold.

"I'm here, my love. You'll be okay," she sobbed, trying to heal him despite the Queen's words.

"You're still half human, little fledgling. The Holy Grounds may have given you a power boost, but you can't heal anyone, so stop fooling yourself. Soon, he'll be a dead demon and you've only got yourself to thank for that. You should've spared him and cast him away when you had the chance."

Jade cruelly tightened the cord around the Queen's neck until she struggled against the binds, gasping for air.

"That's fine. I will make sure you go to hell where you belong. Save him or you're next."

The woman collapsed to the ground, and Jade relaxed her grip, turning her gaze back to Ash. The pool of blood around him grew larger as each second passed.

"There's a poison called Living Silver which is fatal in the right circumstances. I ordered my assistant to put it in his food. Without an open wound, the thing is harmless, but once the arrow pierced his skin, it became deadly to him."

"How can we save him?" Jade demanded, her voice holding a ragged edge of desperation.

"Maybe you can. But the question is, how far are you willing to go for a demon?"

"I will do anything for him," Jade replied without giving it a second thought.

"Very well, then. There is no danger of death from the presence of Living Silver in the bloodstream if it is sufficiently diluted. Since you're a half-Fae, I do not know what will happen to you, but if you're willing to take that risk, then he has a chance."

"I don't care! Let me help him!" she cried out, her courage pushing forward.

The Fae gave a single nod of agreement. "Take a sharp object and cut your skin, then press it against his chest."

Without hesitation, Jade looked around and found a small rock nearby. Using it as a blade, she sliced her palm deep enough to draw blood and placed her hand protectively over his heart.

"Whatever happens to me, you need to let him go. He's not your subject, and you've already punished him for trespassing."

"His fate is sealed," the Queen sneered in delight.

Jade's complexion paled as the toxins flooded her veins. With trembling hands, she tenderly pressed her lips against Ash's forehead for a last farewell before she crumpled to the ground, unconscious.

CHAPTER 14

As Ash's senses returned, he felt a surge of panic when he saw Jade lying unconscious beside him. His mind raced, trying to recall the events leading up to this moment. They had discussed escape, but then darkness had enveloped him.

Frantically, he reached out to shake Jade gently, hoping to rouse her from her slumber. "Jade, wake up," he pleaded, his voice tinged with urgency and fear. But she remained unresponsive, her form still and silent. Ash's heart pounded in his chest as he grappled with the uncertainty of their situation and the desperate need to ensure Jade's safety.

He glanced over and saw the Queen perched on a boulder nearby.

"What did you do to her? Is she..." He couldn't finish the question, the mere thought of her being gone too unbearable to face. Ash felt for Jade's pulse, barely registering the faint beat in his fingertips.

"These were my tests and you've both passed. She used her life to save yours. Most commendable, if you ask me."

The Queen's voice was calm, cold. Her lack of emotion ignited Ash's rage even more. He wanted nothing more than to make sure she paid for nearly taking Jade away from him.

He closed his eyes to calm his mind, and when he opened them again, a ring of Hellfire had engulfed him and Jade. His powers roared back to life. The blue flames burned brighter than the sun, casting a soothing warmth over his body. The Queen would pay for her transgressions this time. He would not be merciful. Ash's eyes narrowed and his lips curled into a sinister smirk as he stepped away from the protection of the flames.

"It's time you paid for your crimes against my woman," he hissed. "I'm going to make you scream as I tear through your skin like paper. Your suffering will be legendary."

"Empty threats don't work on me, demon," the Queen retorted.

Asmodeus's grin widened, relishing in the fear he saw in her eyes. "I am Asmodai Wrath," he declared, his voice dripping with malice, "the evil spirit known throughout the ages for my immense power and brutality. It is my pleasure to introduce myself to you properly. This is what you made me."

He took a step closer, looming over her with a menacing presence. "I suppose I must thank you. Without your treachery, I would still be the naïve Crown Prince of Valoraa. Enjoy your last moments, for soon I will take what is rightfully mine —vengeance!" His words echoed through the chamber, filled with the promise of retribution.

Ash unleashed a torrent of Hellfire, filling the air with an infernal heat. The woman swiftly put up an ethereal barrier, her gaze icy as she stared at him.

"A demon is still a demon, no matter what it's called," she spat, her defiance unwavering. "It's the duty of the Fae to exterminate such vermin and cleanse the world. Is that all you've got?" Her eyes flashed with determination as she braced herself for whatever onslaught he had prepared.

The Prince's laughter echoed through the chamber, sending shivers down her spine. "Oh, no. I'm just getting started!" he declared with a sinister grin. With a flick of his wrist, he summoned thousands of blades, each one gleaming with dark intent. They sliced through the protective barrier with ease, and some even drew blood, staining her once flawless skin with crimson droplets.

The Queen was already making her next move as hundreds of archers appeared on the edge of the sacred grounds, their arrows poised to pierce Jade's skin.

Ash knew he needed Jade's power to escape this place, but he had to distract Queen Ayanna long enough to allow Jade to regain consciousness. He had to act fast.

"Attack!" The Queen's voice thundered through the air and an onslaught of arrows ripped through the sky towards the little witch.

Without hesitation, Asmodeus unfurled his leathery, demonic wings, shielding Jade from the onslaught of magical projectiles with his own body. His wings, dark and formidable, absorbed the brunt of the attack, each blade ricocheting harmlessly off his armoured form. He stood tall and resolute, a guardian in the face of danger, determined to protect her at any cost.

In that moment, he vowed to repay the debt he owed her, a debt he could never fully settle—preying on her naivety, taking her powers, and leaving her without an explanation. This was his opportunity to make amends, to prove that he was more than just a demon, to show her he was willing to sacrifice everything for her sake.

Jade had given him a chance to get his magic back by mixing her blood with his, and for that, Ash was extremely grateful. He had been freed from the grasp of the Holy Grounds, and now he was prepared to use every ounce of strength he had left to protect her. Pain shot through him as each arrow pierced his wings like a bolt of lightning, but he refused to yield. His gaze remained on her beautiful face and he smiled, knowing that if this was to be his end, then at least they would perish together. A single hot tear cascaded down his cheek, trickling onto her warm skin. Jade's eyelids fluttered as she opened them and gazed up at him.

Asmodeus gazed into Jade's eyes, his heart heavy with the weight of their impending fate. "I am sorry, my love. The Queen's power is too great to overcome now that she has reinforcements. But if this is our end, I will make sure we leave this world together," he declared, sealing his vow with a passionate kiss.

Jade pulled away from his embrace and smiled, extending her arm towards him. "You're such a silly demon," she said affectionately. Ash took her hand, understanding her unspoken desire. Without hesitation, he channelled his remaining power and magic, transferring back the abilities he had borrowed and more, infusing her with newfound resilience.

Jade turned away from him, a malicious smirk filling her features. "You shouldn't have underestimated us, bitch."

With a menacing glint in her eye, Jade lifted off the ground, her gaze settling on the Queen and her minions. "You should have known that our bond would be your downfall," she declared, her voice ringing with power. "Our connection is now your death sentence."

Snap! Jade's fingers cracked with deafening intensity, and in an instant, the entire regiment of the Queen's reinforcements dissolved into nothing but ash.

The Queen gaped in horror, visibly stunned by the spectacular display of power before her. Jade clarified that she had no intention of sparing her own kin.

Jade's eyes blazed with immense rage as she summoned Ash's eternal sword—the flaming symbol of Hell's authority that each Prince wielded upon transformation—now bound to her will. With a fierce grip, she clasped the hilt, and memories of Ash's near-death experience flooded her mind, igniting an unquenchable thirst for revenge.

With an almost otherworldly determination, she turned her focus to the Queen, her enemy. With a wave of her hand, she froze the woman into a living sculpture of ice. Then, fuelled by raw emotion, Jade unleashed the power of the eternal sword with a flick of her wrist, shattering the icy statue into a million glittering pieces.

Jade felt a sense of relief when she emerged victorious. But was gaining the upper hand worth adding cruelty to her character? She wasn't satisfied with her actions. Taking a life was no cause for celebration. She was only pleased that she could protect the man she loved.

Her affections for Ash, whether he went by Ashlan, Asmodeus, or something else, were unyielding. It wasn't until he appeared in the mirror, bathed in a pool of blood as he fought for his life, that she fully understood the depth of her love for him. In an instant, she was determined to do whatever it took to reach him and save him.

She stared into his eyes with an expression of adoration. It was as if she was seeing him for the first time and never wanted to let him go.

"I can't thank you enough for fighting so hard to stay alive. I don't know what I'd do without you."

Ash beamed, stroking her hair. "You're such a foolish little witch. I'll always be here for you. I'm immortal, after all."

Jade tried to respond, only for Ash to quiet her with a kiss.

"Let's go home," he said in a hushed tone, drawing her into a hug. "I swear I will never let you go."

Jade took a deep breath and concentrated on her destination and the people in it. She had little experience with travelling between realms, but she knew that magic came from within. She just had to believe she could do it and she would succeed. Then she opened her eyes and counted to three. Much to her surprise, they had made it.

CHAPTER 15

"We're here!" Jade exclaimed, glancing at Ash, who smiled back. "I can't believe we've made it."

"I knew you could do it," Ash replied, leaning in for a tender kiss.

Their happiness was interrupted by the sight of supernatural beings taking over the academy's courtyard.

"That doesn't look good," Jade whispered.

They had landed on the roof of the main building and Ash's magic was hiding them from view, cloaked in a protective bubble.

"We need to help them," she pointed out. She noticed students were being led by the siblings Alessandra and Lucien de Winter, who were putting up a fight against the invaders.

"Look at me," Ash pleaded. "No heroic stunts today. You must swear it to me. I don't want to lose you."

She gazed at him lovingly and stroked his cheek.

"I have to. My friends need me."

Jade flew towards the middle of the courtyard as a horde of creatures began encircling the de Winter siblings.

Suddenly, Alessandra fell to the ground, a blade plunged deep into her chest.

Fear filled her heart. The assassin was the academy's strongest warrior. Years of training had taught her how to handle this type of situation, and Jade's thoughts turned to Ash's words. After what he went through in the realm of the Fae, he was too weak to fight. Humans were fragile beings. No matter how much they trained, it didn't change that.

Jade spun around to cast a protective spell on Ash, freezing him in place before turning her attention to the two strangers who were heading towards Alessandra. One was attempting to heal her, and the other was keeping her brother from completely falling apart. Jade held off the creatures while these newcomers helped the fallen assassin; she knew her own powers would be better used against the monsters instead of trying to heal anyone since she was drained from using too much magic already. Travelling to another realm had taken more out of her than expected.

Alessandra stirred as the healer who had been tending to her suddenly collapsed. She rose from the ground, her body surrounded by a magical light, and a pair of golden wings manifested from her back.

The second stranger flew over with a sword in hand and gave it to Alessandra. As she took hold of the weapon, storm clouds filled the sky and lightning struck the blade. After thanking the man with a kiss, she spoke aloud to all those gathered.

"Swear allegiance to Vlad Drakulya, your new master, or die!"

Alessandra's voice sliced through the air like a sharp dagger, her words cutting deep into the very souls of those who stood before her. She stood in all her divine glory, her heavenly sword held confidently aloft, her wings flapping powerfully behind her and her face illuminated by the eerie lightning circulating through her blade. Jade felt a chill run down her spine as she heard the menacing words from Alessandra's lips. She had encountered the powerful assassin before, but she had not expected the sheer force of authority radiating from her being.

Jade couldn't help but grin when she saw Alessandra in her angelic form. She looked divine. It was ironic that she was both half angel and a deadly assassin. Quite a paradox indeed.

Suddenly, the light of an explosion momentarily blinded the students, and a wave of heat swept across the courtyard. An unnatural silence descended upon the scene, and when the smoke settled, the monsters lay in charred piles, wisps of smoke rising from their corpses.

Jade watched as Alessandra descended from the sky like a divine being, her wings fanning out majestically. When she addressed them, her words were so powerful they seemed to reverberate through the air. "You have all shown great courage and strength in the face of danger," she said. "I am proud of you."

An admiration for the assassin blossomed in Jade's heart. Suddenly, it occurred to her that the second newcomer's body had vanished, and questions raced through her mind. Could this healer have unleashed an explosion powerful enough to exterminate these creatures? Was such a feat even possible?

Jade's pulse raced as she thought about Ash. She faced him, dreading the conversation ahead, but was relieved to see him present—he hadn't disappeared like the rest of the creatures. The protective spell had worked, though he didn't look too pleased with her.

She reversed the enchantment and journeyed to him, attempting to appease him. She was sure he wouldn't let her hear the end of it for a while.

"I can't believe you did that," Ash growled, narrowing his gaze.

"I'm sorry. I just didn't want to see you in danger after you fought so bravely in the Fae realm."

"Flattery won't get you out of the doghouse, little witch."

"How about this? Will it do the trick?" She drew him into a kiss and felt Ash smiling against her lips.

"Maybe. We'll revisit this conversation later. For now, those people need us," Ash replied, his tone firm but contemplative.

Ash's hand enveloped hers, his touch gentle yet resolute. Drawing her close, she felt the comforting warmth radiating from his body and sensed the unfurling of his leathery wings behind her. As they ascended into the sky, the air hummed with anticipation, and distant murmurs of conversation drifted up from the courtyard below.

Jade glimpsed the awe-struck expressions of those below before they gently touched down on the cobblestones.

Releasing her hand, Ash and Jade were greeted with smiles from their siblings.

"Glad to see you," Alessandra said, her smile radiant.

"Happy to be here," Jade replied, returning the smile.

"I am thankful for your aid earlier," the dark-haired stranger added in his velvety rumble of a voice. "It seems you have already met my father."

Jade glanced at Ash, puzzled. He smiled in return. "I know I look too young to be a father, but this is my adopted son, Vlad Drakulya, Prince of Wallachia. Vlad, allow me to introduce the love of my life, Miss Jade Nicolay."

Jade took Vlad's hand and shook it warmly. It was strong and soft like his father's.

"I can't believe that you have a father so young, my love," Alessandra said to Vlad, who chuckled in return.

"Hey, don't judge a man by his looks. I may appear your age, but I am full of surprises. I guess that's one of us," Ash teased Alessandra with a playful grin, his eyes glinting mischievously.

"It is a pleasure to meet you, Miss Nicolay. Your display of magic was nothing short of extraordinary. We are lucky to have you on our side," Vlad declared with genuine admiration.

"Oh, it was trivial, Mr Drakulya," Jade replied modestly.

"Rubbish! Please call me Vlad. Anything more formal and I may start thinking that I'm as old as this one here!" Vlad said with a chuckle, gesturing towards Ash. "Speaking of which, what do you prefer to be called these days, Father?"

"Ashley Rex, but everyone can refer to me as Ash. Titles really aren't important when you've been alive this long. What's a thousand years when surrounded by all this beauty?" Ash smiled at the group.

"Couldn't agree more!" Vlad laughed heartily. "This is Alessandra, the love of my life, and her brother, Lucien. They travelled from France to recruit me in their fight against the Order. It was hard not to join in their cause since they've always been a nuisance to me."

"Now that we have some help, I think is necessary we come up with a plan," Lucien added, his tone serious.

"We must make her talk by any means necessary. I am sorry, brother, but there's no other way," Alessandra stated firmly.

"You're right," Lucien replied, his expression grave. "Our lives are on the line, and it's crucial that we take control."

"Well said, nephew. We can't wait for them to make another move. We must identify their vulnerabilities, and Avery must comply one way or another. I just hope she can come to her senses in time."

"Me too," Lucien added, sighing. "We need to act fast. We have an opportunity to create an impact, but we must be quick. Let's go get Avery and get this done."

"Speaking of which, where is Avery?" Jade enquired.

"It's a long story," Lucien said, sighing. "It's all my fault. Once she fed me her blood to save me from dying, she contracted a virus that ended up killing her slowly. Vlad had to turn her into a vampire to stop that process, but ended up discovering that she had been plotting with her father from the beginning."

"Poor Avery. It sounds like she went through a lot. Lord Darmon is really a piece of work. I wonder what his endgame was," she said.

"There's really only one way out of this. We must take out their leader and the whole organisation will crumble. I just hope we can make it in time," Vlad replied, his voice resolute.

Jade and her four companions pressed forward toward the dungeon. The air grew thick with an eerie scent, sending shivers down Jade's spine. As they ventured deeper into the darkness, a gripping sense of fear permeated Jade's senses, warning her of the lurking danger.

The group came to a stop in front of a solid stone door secured with a large iron lock. Dreadful shadows seemed to assail them from every angle as they advanced closer to Avery's location.

Jade stepped forward and laid her hand on the iron lock, feeling its icy surface. With a sudden burst of strength, she forced the lock to click, and the door creaked open.

Gripping their weapons tightly, the group crossed the threshold into Avery's prison. As the heavy door slammed shut behind them, a chill ran down Jade's spine, signalling the ominous atmosphere that surrounded them.

The air within was thick with smoke and the stench of

acrid sulphur, obscuring any glimpse of the ceiling that loomed ominously above. Twisted, unintelligible symbols covered every inch of the walls, casting an eerie pall over the room. Soot and ash stained the surfaces and floors, as if marking Avery's departure and taking whatever solace she had found with her.

Amidst the darkness, a small wooden box caught Jade's eye near the entrance. Avery must have left it there before her departure, accompanied by a key.

With caution, Jade opened the box. Inside lay a delicate map revealing the Order's secret locations, meticulously hand-drawn and painted by Avery. As Jade surveyed the room with resignation, she knew their mission had just become even more perilous.

"She's gone," Jade muttered. "I don't think she's coming back this time."

Ash stood in the centre of the chamber, taking in the damage that had been done. The walls were cracked, the furniture overturned, and the floor littered with shards of broken glass. This was the scene of struggle, and the telltale stench of evil lingered in the air. "It's clear that demons did this," he mumbled.

Jade nodded, her eyes still wide with shock. "The place had been warded. Do you think they came during the fight while we were distracted?"

Ash shook his head. "It's hard to say. They could well have been the demons that came through when the Order sent Lucien to investigate," he said.

"Yes," Jade agreed, her voice little more than a whisper. "There's a good chance that they lay low and waited for a good time to strike and make the most impact."

There was a moment of silence as they all tried to come to

terms with what had happened. Finally, Jade broke the silence. "What can we do now?" she asked.

"Nothing. She was our only hope," Vlad chimed in. "We have to find her before the Order gets a hold of her."

"I just hope she's okay. All this time, I was looking forward to having my best friend back."

Alessandra tried to reassure them, but her voice wavered when she spoke. "We'll find her. Don't worry... we have a time traveller on our side."

Lucien asked fearfully, "Do you think he will help?"

Ash growled in response. "He'd better, or else he'll find out the hard way what happens when you mess with us."

The reality of their situation weighed heavily on Jade's heart. She had no way of knowing if her friend would still be alive by the time they found her. She steeled herself, refusing to rely on any stranger to save them. Opening her hands, she began to chant an ancient spell. A spell she didn't even know she knew.

The darkness of the dungeon was suddenly replaced by a brilliant light that nearly blinded them all. But for all its brightness and power, it could not conceal the fear and anxiety over the unknown that lingered in the air.

THE END

THE ASSASSIN HEIRESS

CHAPTER 1

Roslyn Academy

Alessandra squinted against the darkness, her eyes slowly adjusting to the faint reddish glow glinting off the walls. Shards of glass crunched beneath her feet as she took a tentative step forward. She saw Avery in the corner, tucked into a foetal position on the hard iron bed, motionless and unaware of their presence.

She looked up at Jade with wide eyes, her heart pounding in her chest. "Did you send us back in time?"

Jade shook her head. "No. I tapped into the magic lingering from Avery's last few moments here. We'll need to act quickly before they fade."

Vlad voiced his curiosity from behind them. "What's the plan?"

"I didn't have one," Jade said, her hands shaking and her eyes blazing with determination. "I saw an opportunity and seized it. With any luck, this will give us some answers about who kidnapped her."

Jade was trembling, but she stood firm beside Ash as the two huge demons appeared in the cell. They had an ominous air about them that seemed to fill the room like a physical weight, and Ash let out a furious roar. "Amon and Shax! How dare you enter here!" But the monsters ignored him, their attention fixed on Avery.

Jade's voice wavered but remained steady as she whispered, "They can't hear you, my love."

The demons eyed Avery menacingly, their yellow eyes glinting in the dim light. One of them stepped forward and snarled, "Your father sent us to take you back home, sweetheart. If you don't cooperate, the only thing he will get is your rotting corpse."

Avery's lips twitched into a bitter smile as she replied, her voice dripping with venomous rage. "Ah, so the old man is calling his creation home? Let's see how he likes it when I'm done with him." The other demon let out a guttural chuckle and produced a leather sack filled with dark powder. With precise movements, they began tracing symbols onto the walls and floor. Avery watched with curiosity as the patterns revealed themselves in black dust.

Avery shifted her gaze from the golden box to Jade and then away again, her eyes glassy with resignation. Her mouth opened, though no sound emerged. Finally, her quiet words were emitted with a hint of desperation. "Do not look for me."

The demons encircled Avery, their malevolent grins widening as they chanted in a demonic tongue that reverberated off the walls. She thrashed against their iron grip and screamed until her voice went hoarse, but it was futile. In the blink of an eye, they vanished in a puff of sulphuric smoke that floated up to the ceiling, leaving only the scent of brimstone behind.

Alessandra's eyes were ablaze with fury as she glared at Ash. She was shaking, her heart pounding as if it would break out of her chest. Her voice quivered when she spoke. "Tell me everything you know before I send you to the abyss to join them!"

Jade stepped in between them, one hand raised like a shield. Her voice was cautious but firm. "Alessandra, be careful. He may know who they are, but that doesn't mean he's responsible for what happened."

Alessandra allowed herself one fleeting glance at Lucien, who was supported by Vlad on one side, his whole body trembling and his shoulders slumped. Despite her anger, her heart broke for him. Lucien loved Avery with all his being. Seeing her being taken must have been devastating for him too.

Ash snarled back at her, "Those guys are Marquis of Hell. Mercenaries and nothing more, but they're ruthless. Wait until I get my hands on them."

Lucien shifted his weight, bringing attention to himself. "They mentioned Avery's father. Do you think he could be behind all this demonic activity?"

Vlad rubbed the back of his neck, deep in thought. After a few moments, he nodded. "It looks that way. I remember Avery was terrified of him."

Alessandra crossed her arms, lips pursed. "He's probably well-hidden and heavily guarded. Any chance these symbols can point us to him?"

Ash bent down, examining the intricate shapes carved into the stone floor. He ran his fingers along each glyph and muttered something under his breath. After a few minutes, he shook his head. "No. It seems to be some type of spell for locating and travelling to their master. Lord Darmon, I assume. But it requires blood to activate, so I doubt we could replicate it."

Lucien's words were barely audible as he enquired, "Are you implying that she might be beyond my reach?"

Vlad responded, "When I last spoke to her, she appeared to have accepted her fate as her father's minion and was aware that she would see him again, despite me confining her here. It's almost as if she saw it coming."

Lucien's voice trembled. "Uncle, you share a blood connection with her. Can't we use demonic magic to bring her back?"

Ash's response was firm. "That's not how our magic operates. My son would need to be a demonic being for that to be possible, and I don't condone sacrificing one life to save another. It never ends well."

Lucien's brows furrowed, his frustration simmering just beneath the surface. He clenched his fists, his knuckles turning white as he struggled to contain his mounting anger. His eyes bore into the figure before him. The room grew tense, filled with an uncomfortable silence, until Lucien could no longer hold back.

With a sudden burst of emotion, his voice crackled with anger as he blurted out, "Then what's the point of you even being here, demon? You have done nothing to assist me in retrieving Avery."

The words hung heavily in the air, each syllable infused with his frustration and disappointment. His voice wavered with disbelief and defiance, his body language mirroring his internal turmoil. The room seemed to vibrate with the intensity of his outburst, and the weight of his words resonated with his genuine confusion and a touch of desperation.

Vlad intervened to calm the tense atmosphere between the two. "Let's not let this turn into a battle of words. We're all equally frustrated, searching for clues and trying to comprehend this situation. I don't think my father is to blame. Jade, what are your thoughts? Avery seemed to gaze in your direction."

"I don't believe she saw me. Rather, I think she knew I would come to this cell and that its memory would preserve her last moments here. She glanced at the box, then back at us, showing that she wants us to continue the fight against the Order. My intuition tells me that this map could be the key to finding her."

The group found themselves suddenly released from the memory spell as a soft light enveloped them.

"Let's rest and start again tomorrow," Alessandra said, taking Vlad's arm as they made their way towards the exit.

"Agreed," Ash chimed in, supporting Jade in assisting the still-traumatised Lucien.

As they settled into their chamber, Alessandra turned to Vlad, her expression questioning. "You're keeping something from the others, aren't you?" she probed.

"You'll have to be more specific. I keep many things from people," Vlad responded, his attention shifting towards Alessandra. He helped her out of her clothes before escorting her to the bathroom, where he filled the tub with steaming water for them both.

Alessandra turned to find Vlad in the doorway, his gaze locked onto her.

"Don't play games. You know what I'm referring to," Alessandra pressed.

She held Vlad's gaze as he disrobed and slipped into the water beside her. The latent desire between them charged the air, though neither made a move.

"Do I?" he murmured, his voice low and heated.

She splayed her fingers across his bare chest, conflicting emotions churning within. Grief and confusion over Avery still gripped her heart, yet Vlad's proximity intoxicated her senses. She tingled with temptation, aching to give in, but hesitation held her back. His nearness was a bittersweet torture, pleasure and anguish intertwined.

"You noticed my slight hesitation," he continued. "You and Ash know me better than anyone else. I didn't want Lucien to run off in that state after her. When I saw her being taken away, I tried to use our blood connection. She's being held in another realm, or worse, dead."

"Thank you for protecting my brother, my love." She gazed at him through hooded eyes and whispered, "My prince."

"Anything for you, Alessa." He pulled her closer and kissed her soft lips, the water splashing around them. After a few moments, Alessandra pulled away.

"It's unlikely that Lord Darmon killed his own daughter," she continued. "It's more likely that she's his puppet, following his orders like his other minions."

"But what if she's in a different realm? Can our powerful witch track people in other realms?" Vlad asked.

"No." She shook her head. "But I know someone who can move between them with relative ease. My father."

"Then we shall find your father," Vlad declared, his eyes smouldering with unspoken intensity. He drew nearer, radiating heat, and seized her waist to pull her firmly against him. His kiss was feverish, fervent, belying his stoic restraint.

When he finally broke away, his hands trembled as they

cradled her face. “God, I thought I’d lost you today,” he rasped. Before she could respond, his mouth claimed hers once more, desperate to convey what words could not.

She yielded to his fervour, letting his passion sweep away the residual fear that had gripped them both. Enveloped in his arms, the terrors of the day melted away. There was only this—the warmth of his skin, the hammering of his heart matching her own. No more words were needed. For now, after coming so close to losing everything, this was enough.

CHAPTER 2

The tranquil Victorian garden provided a refuge for Alessandra. She sat on a rustic wooden bench that had been carved from a single piece of dark-stained wood. The gentle sounds of the fountain's cascading waters and the sweet floral scents that wafted through the air enveloped her in a soothing embrace, easing her troubled mind.

As she inhaled deeply, the delicate fragrance of the blooming flowers carried her away to a place of peace and tranquillity. Gazing into the shimmering depths of the fountain, she watched as a solitary leaf floated by the calm waters. A small frog leaped from one lily pad to another, its nimble movements barely making a ripple on the serene surface.

Looking up to the starry sky, Alessandra basked in the comforting hug of the cool breeze that gently brushed against her skin. With closed eyes, she let her mind wander, losing herself in the moment until her thoughts faded, bringing clarity and calm. Alessandra felt confident that she could take on any challenge that her future held for her.

Suddenly, a new presence interrupted her peaceful

daydream, causing Alessandra to startle. "It's you," she uttered, recognising the familiar figure.

Ash appeared before her with a playful chuckle. "Did you put my son to sleep and go wandering around the academy?"

Alessandra's gaze softened as she thought of the vampire who was slumbering in their chamber, a behaviour that astonished her. "Maybe. He's been sleeping much more recently. I wouldn't have thought it was possible for his kind."

Ash's mouth curled into a knowing smile. "Your blood is special and makes him more human," he said, his deep voice calm. She nodded in agreement and Ash continued, "Plus, there's this thing called love. Worries seem to fade away when you're close to someone you love. He's more content than I've seen him in centuries."

Alessandra sighed. "He will not be too happy tomorrow." She grimaced, understanding the reality of the situation despite how hard it was to accept it.

"You're leaving," Ash stated.

Again, she nodded her head in confirmation. Her mind reeled with all the ways things could go wrong if he joined her on her quest to find her father—a path filled with danger from members of the Order who wanted to use her against Vlad.

"I have to go look for my father, and taking the Order's most sought-after vampire away from the academy is not a wise choice. He'll want to come, but I can't risk his life. I'm the chink in his armour now. The Order will use me as bait."

"Take me instead. I may not have my full strength yet, but I'll do what I can to help you out," Ash offered.

Jade interjected with a wide grin as she appeared behind them. "A road trip? Count me in!"

Alessandra jumped and let out a breathy chuckle. "You scared me!" She gestured her open hands towards the two of them. "Both of you are welcome to come along if you don't give me a heart attack."

Ash rolled his eyes and lightly teased, "I thought assassins weren't supposed to be scaredy-cats. I'm not so impressed."

Alessandra bowed mockingly with her palms pressed together as if begging for mercy. "My deepest apologies, Your Highness. Must have forgotten my assassin hat from your son's chamber."

Jade snickered while Ash gave her an unamused side glance.

Moments later, Ash clapped his hands together and exclaimed, "It looks like we're going to get along famously! Let's not wait around until your overprotective boyfriend wakes up and impedes our fun."

They all shared a laugh at the thought of Vlad sending them to their own rooms.

"That is the cost of me going out with the headmaster, I suppose." Alessandra smiled at the thought of Vlad. She cherished him too much to risk any harm coming to him, so the best decision for them both was for her to leave him at the academy.

"To find out where my father is now, we must return to Bath. It holds special meaning for him and is where we shared many of our happiest moments."

"Do you want me to leave a message for when Vlad wakes up?" Jade enquired. "Think of a message you'd like to leave for him, and it will be visible when he wakes up."

Alessandra's heart pounded as she tried to decide how to tell Vlad the news. She was certain he would be furious, but she felt it was her responsibility to keep him safe from the Order, who were notorious for their merciless behaviour towards supernatural creatures. Though Alessandra had never considered herself brave, the thought of not being with

Vlad brought tears to her eyes, and she courageously spoke up.

"All set. I just hope he will forgive me. What should I do now?" she asked Jade.

"Concentrate on that image while I cast a spell," Jade replied.

Alessandra obeyed and watched as the witch worked her magic. Once done, Jade flashed a smile at Alessandra.

"Vlad will someday forgive you. He holds an old-fashioned belief that he should be the one to rescue the damsel in distress. However, I'm confident that with your guidance, he'll move past this mindset. You're a total badass, and you don't need anyone else to overcome obstacles."

"All right, let's get this started. Everyone, join hands," Jade instructed. "Since I've already been to Bath, I can teleport us there with my spell. But I'll need your help, Alessandra, for the rest of the way."

"Got it," she replied, nodding.

"This is such a lovely feeling," Ash remarked. "We're already holding hands like best friends."

"Does he always talk nonsense?" Alessandra laughed.

"Quiet, Ash," Jade scolded him. "I need to focus on the spell." Turning to Alessandra, she added, "You have no idea."

Ash jumped in, protesting, "Hey, I'm still here, ladies." His eyebrows furrowed in annoyance.

With a hushed incantation, Jade enveloped them in magic. In a blink, the scene shifted to a shadowy Bath alley, cramped between looming buildings. The narrow path twisted ahead like a maze, illuminated only by the weak flicker of the street lamps. Their pallid light cast the uneven cobblestones in odd, disorienting shadows.

As Alessandra looked around, she noticed the walls were made of weathered brick, and in some places, ivy grew up the sides, clinging to the rough, uneven surfaces. The air was thick with a faint mist, which added to the surreal and otherworldly atmosphere of the alleyway. It was as though someone had transported them to a different time and place. The only sound that could be heard was the distant mewling of a cat, lending an air of ominous stillness to the surroundings.

As they stood there, Alessandra felt a sense of uneasiness creeping over her. It was as though the alleyway held a secret. Something they were not meant to discover.

"Hey, if this doesn't pan out, remind me to take you monster hunting so we can make some money as mercenaries," Alessandra said, trying to break the looming silence.

"Ha, don't worry! With us together, no beast will be safe." Jade chuckled.

"Don't forget about me either." Ash fluttered his eyelashes.

"I thought you'd want to do something with the boys?" Jade smiled.

"I'm all about adventure, not like the other two," Ash joked.

"Let's get back to business. We still have to figure out where we are and how we can get to my old home without being spotted by the Order," Alessandra commanded.

"Before that, tell us which magical place from your childhood we're going to visit," Ash demanded with a raised eyebrow.

"Ah, sorry about that. It's called Prior Park Mansion. It's been in my family's possession for quite some time, although it had to be rebuilt twice due to it burning down."

"Wow, I didn't know your family was so well-off," Jade exclaimed in surprise.

"We don't talk about it."

Jade's excitement was palpable as she spoke. "I can't believe you had a butler. I'm getting Sebastian vibes."

Ash raised an eyebrow at Jade's enthusiasm. "What's the big deal about a butler?" he enquired. "And who's this Sebastian guy? Is he some playboy you've been seeing before me?"

Alessandra rolled her eyes at Ash's assumption. "No, Ash. He's not a real person. Jade is just excited because the butler reminds her of a character from an anime she loves."

Jade nodded. "Yeah, he's like my childhood crush come to life."

After Jade's admission, Ash pulled out his phone and scrolled through a few images before speaking. "Hm, you have good taste." He paused for a moment before speaking again. "You know I can change into any form, right? I can make all your fantasies come to life," he added with a mischievous grin.

"I don't think I want to hear this," Alessandra replied, her voice tight with unease. She couldn't shake off the feeling that something was watching them.

"Are you sure they're watching your house, or are you taking your role as an assassin too seriously?" Ash asked.

Alessandra felt a tinge of anger at his remark. She had worked hard to become who she was today, and it wasn't just a game to her. But she pushed it down and reminded herself that he was just trying to lighten the mood.

With a deep breath, she forced a smile and responded confidently, "I'm certain. But that won't stop us from getting the job done."

"I've dealt with their kind before, but I never thought they'd be so vicious," Ash confessed.

Alessandra's heart pounded as Ash spoke. Memories of gruelling, cruel training flooded her mind, but she refused to let fear show on her face. She straightened her back and summoned bravery.

"Same here. I feel like I've been burying my head in the sand when it comes to them. I feel bad for you, Alessandra," Jade sympathised.

"No need to pity me," she replied, her voice steady. "I was born into this, so I knew what I was getting myself into. It's all new to you guys, and that's the hard part."

As she spoke, her mind raced with images of countless battles fought, lives taken. But instead of crumbling, she pushed emotions aside and focused on the task at hand. The night air hung heavy, silent as they walked, but she stayed grateful for the darkness that hid threatening tears.

A wrought-iron gate, which creaked ominously in the gentle breeze, marked the entrance to the neighbouring cemetery. The group stepped inside, their footsteps echoing through the graveyard. Headstones were scattered haphazardly, some of them centuries old.

"We have to be quiet here," Alessandra murmured. "They train the knights to recognise unusual sounds, so no sudden noises."

"I may have a solution for that, unless they have a witch of their own," Jade replied, then gestured with her hands. An enormous bubble enveloped the trio, muffling all sound.

The night fog had descended upon them like a heavy silken blanket. They strolled down the lane from the main entrance of the old, forgotten chapel. Mist only added to the eerie atmosphere, making it increasingly terrifying with every step. Bare trees surrounded the cemetery, twisted branches reaching like skeletal fingers. An owl's occasional hoot was the only sound they could hear.

As the group walked along the path, the shadows appeared to follow them, creating a haunting orchestra of dark shapes in the air. Now and then, they observed the weathered gravestones that lined the way, seeking solace in the hush. However, the chapel ahead was even more daunting.

Moss encrusted the aged walls of the building, and its stained-glass windows depicted tales of death and hopelessness. They could feel the weight of time upon them, as if the fog was concealing more sinister things lurking nearby.

Alessandra's keen ears perked up, and her senses tingled with an inexplicable awareness. The faint sound that emanated from the chapel was unlike anything she had heard before—an ethereal melody that seemed to transcend the boundaries of reality.

As she listened, the world around her seemed to blur, the bustling city fading into the background as if they had been transported to a different realm. Time lost its grip, and seconds stretched into moments that held no significance. It was as though they were suspended in a realm of magic and enchantment. Alessandra's heart quickened, and she exchanged a bewildered glance with her companions. None of them desired to enter, but it was the only way to the mansion undetected by the Order.

The group hesitantly pushed open the door and the surrounding fog dissipated like smoke. Inside the chapel, the air was still and heavy, as if it held the secrets of the past. The walls were adorned with dark paintings, and candles flickered, casting eerie shadows on the ground. As they walked down the aisle, Alessandra couldn't help but feel as if she was trespassing into a forbidden world. However, their mission was too important to back down now. They had to get to the mansion without raising suspicions.

From the shadows of the chapel, a voice resounded, "Welcome." Jade ceased her spell to muffle sounds since their presence was already exposed. Alessandra had no clue who the speaker could be, as it wasn't her father or any known Order member.

With growing frustration, Alessandra raised her voice, "Reveal yourself. I am not here to play games. Are you an ally or an enemy?"

The voice responded with an eerie laugh that sent shivers down her spine. The group shared a glance, confirming their need to prepare for a fight. Ash summoned his sapphire-coloured flames, setting the stone floor ablaze to illuminate the area.

The Hellfire burned with a fierce intensity, casting an ominous blue glow over the chapel. The light revealed every detail of the ornate architecture, from the towering stone arches to the intricate gold inlays, giving the room an otherworldly ambiance.

From a shadowed corner a cloaked figure emerged, its movements slow and deliberate. The heavy fabric of the cloak rustled like restless spirits as it approached the fire, pausing for a moment as if contemplating a weighty decision. Leaning forward, the mysterious individual whispered something into the flames, the words so low and faint that no one else could hear them.

Silently, the enigmatic presence stepped away from the fire and vanished into the darkness, leaving the mystery of its whispered secret to be kept by the flames. For a fleeting moment, the air hung still with an unsettling silence until the flames flickered and vanished, shrouding the chapel in darkness, with only the faint glow of the moon outside providing any light.

The passage of time seemed suspended in that instant, leaving those who bore witness with a profound sense of awe and unease. It was as if the chapel itself had held its breath, patiently awaiting the figure to reveal its secret before exhaling and withdrawing into the shadows once more.

As they stood in the aftermath of the encounter, each individual grappled with their own thoughts and emotions, struggling to make sense of the inexplicable events that had transpired.

And as the last echoes of the mysterious figure's departure faded into the darkness, the chapel remained cloaked in silence, its secrets hidden away, waiting to be discovered by those brave enough to seek them out.

CHAPTER 3

ALESSANDRA REGARDED ASH'S EVIDENT DISAPPOINTMENT with a mix of empathy and amusement. She knew he had been itching for combat, and the standoff with the mysterious cloaked man had only whetted his appetite for action. Though Ash now seemed frustrated at the anticlimactic outcome, Alessandra felt a swell of relief that the encounter hadn't turned violent.

Her musings were broken off by Ash's voice. "That was strange," he grumbled. "I was hungry for a fight."

She couldn't help but giggle at his eagerness. "The night still has plenty in store," she stated. "Whoever, or whatever that was, it put out your fire. I didn't think that could be done."

Ash's aspect grew more serious as he replied, "You're correct. My Hellfire is special; it comes from my soul so no other prince of Hell can control it. Yet a duke of Hell has the power to snuff it out with no effort at all. It wasn't wise for us to face him directly."

Alessandra contemplated Ash's explanation, trying to

comprehend the magnitude of this stranger's abilities. She could not ignore the feeling that there was more to this enigmatic figure than they imagined.

"Just so I understand this correctly," Jade chimed in. "Are princes lower ranked than dukes down in Hell?"

Alessandra couldn't help but roll her eyes at Jade's query. "Yes, princes are lower ranked than dukes," she verified. "It's basic demonology."

Ash responded, "Hell isn't 'down there'. It is on a different plane, parallel to all the others."

The assassin grinned. "I'll keep that in mind for my next demonology quiz."

Their humorous exchange came to an abrupt end when Alessandra's instincts kicked in. "Hold up," she announced, raising her hand to pause them. "I have a bad feeling about this."

Just then, a voice echoed through the chapel, causing them to startle. "You should listen to your gut instinct, Alessandra," the voice uttered. It was the same creepy voice from before, now coming from inside their heads.

Jade stepped forward and lit the strategically placed braziers around the area. When the chapel glowed brightly, the figure reappeared, but this time it kept changing its form.

"Who are you?" Alessandra demanded.

"I am Azaroth, the demon with a thousand faces. It is a pleasure to meet you at last," he replied in a soothing voice.

"What do you desire from us?" she enquired, her heart pounding in her chest.

Azaroth laughed before his form shifted again. "I ask for nothing from you, my dear. I only wish to watch and see what the great assassin of the Order can do."

Alessandra gritted her teeth together as she heard this. Azaroth was trying to manipulate them, but she didn't know how to fight back against an entity with so many forms and powers.

The demon changed shape again, taking on the image of Alessandra's father. She gasped and stepped away from him in surprise.

"Come join me, my daughter," Azaroth spoke in her father's voice. "Together we can rule over the Order, all of Hell, and more."

Alessandra's eyes narrowed as she realised what was happening. The demon was trying to use her love for her father against her. She dropped to the floor, her hands trembling as she pulled out a dagger hidden in the top of her right boot. Her assassin training had taught her not to hesitate, but when she saw the demon with her father's face, it was like a stillness descended on her. She shook off the shock and swung at the creature with all her might.

Moonlight flashed off her dagger as she hurled it, spinning, at the demon. She ducked under raking claws, their fiery heat scalding the air above her. Lunging in, she stabbed at its chest but the creature skittered back, evading the blow. She circled, seeking an opening, but its speed matched her own. Again and again they collided, blade glancing off scales, claws narrowly missing flesh - a deadly dance with neither able to strike true.

Jade and Ash advanced with purposeful strides. Yet, as they neared the menacing demon, an unseen and formidable force propelled them backward. Their bodies staggered, their momentum abruptly halted. The proximity to Alessandra, locked in a fierce battle with the demonic entity, felt insurmountable. A pulsating wall of impenetrable energy materialised, creating a dividing barrier.

Frustration and anguish etched their faces as Jade and Ash relentlessly pounded their fists against the barrier. Their actions conveyed a profound message, a visual portrayal of their desperate desire to aid their friend. Each blow reverberated, echoing their steadfast tenacity to surmount the obstacle and reach Alessandra's side. The demon's laughter echoed throughout the chamber as if it were mocking their attempts. Alessandra looked over at them and shook her head, signalling that they should stay back. Defeated, the couple backed away from the barrier.

"Your tricks won't work on me, demon," Alessandra yelled as she parried a ferocious attack.

The demon's laugh turned silken as his form morphed again, adopting the guise of a striking man. Silver hair cascaded over broad shoulders, framing a sculpted face. But it was the eyes that gave Alessandra pause—brilliant emerald pools belying ancient cunning. She steadied her grip, wary of the predatory intelligence watching her every move.

"Is this more to your liking, my dear assassin? I hear you have a thing for pretty monsters."

As she recalled her demand for answers, her eyes bore into him with an icy intensity. The edges of her lips curved downward, and her hands were clenched into tight fists. "I asked you a question. Is there a reason you're toying with us? Ash told me who you are. We could all be dead by now if you wanted. So, tell me, what's your game?"

The demon roared with fury and pushed Alessandra to the ground with a single shove. He then advanced towards the illuminated barrier that was sectioning the room, his eyes blazing a trail of fire towards Ash.

"Asmodeus," he snarled. "I see you are running around with an assassin from the Order and a mighty witch. Quite curious indeed. Why have you forsaken your post in the abyss?"

Ash, better known as Asmodeus in Hell, took a step

forward, his gaze unwavering from the demon. He looked at Alessandra, silently instructing her to stay down. "I didn't forsake my post." He spoke calmly, despite the rage emanating from the other demon. "I merely took a detour."

Azaroth, still in his handsome form, threw his head back in laughter. "A detour, you say?" His laughter subsided as he took a step closer towards the barrier. "I've been waiting for you to slip up, Asmodeus. You were always quite the thorn in my side in Hell."

"What do you mean?"

Azaroth laughed. "You are Lucifer's little obedient soldier, wouldn't you agree? Why do you think you've been summoned out of Hell so often? It's all been down to a little help from me. And when you return—and trust me, you will—your followers will notice that stench on you. The stench of human feelings, love, etc. You're a changed demon now, Asmodeus. You're not worthy of ever returning to the pit."

Ash's features hardened at Azaroth's taunting words. His eyes, full of mischief, now radiated a deadly seriousness. He clenched his fists, the air around him buzzing with latent power. "I am no one's soldier," he retorted, "And my worthiness is not for you to judge."

"And as for my 'stench'..." His lips twisted into a snarl. "At least I'm not a coward hiding behind illusions."

Azaroth's lips curled in icy amusement. "Such harsh words, Asmodeus," he purred, tone laden with false affability. "I'd hoped we could chat cordially, like old friends. But it seems you've forgotten your place."

"I have forgotten nothing," Ash shot back. "Especially not your penchant for deceit."

The room's atmosphere was a powder keg ready to detonate. Alessandra and Jade observed the standoff with bated breath, neither daring to speak. This was a viper's nest, and any sudden moves could mean disaster.

Just as it seemed the tension could not get any higher, Azaroth broke into a fit of laughter, the sound echoing off the chapel walls. "Oh, Asmodeus." He cackled. "You've always been too serious for your own good. I am nothing more than a spectator enjoying the minor war between some tiny creatures and the Order. Do you think the organisation has got where they are by being a force of good?"

"So, what do you want from us? What's your play? Are you here to help or hinder?" Alessandra asked.

Azaroth's laughter faded as he turned his gaze to Alessandra. "Help or hinder? Such binary thinking, dear assassin," he chided. "The world isn't divided into black and white, good and evil."

Alessandra gripped her dagger tighter, her knuckles turning white. "You're avoiding the question," she countered, her voice steady.

Azaroth let out a nonchalant shrug. "What I want is immaterial. It's what you want that matters, Alessandra," he said, his voice dropping low. "What are you willing to do to protect your friends? To ensure their survival against the Order? Are you ready to spill blood, even if it's your own?"

Alessandra fought to keep her composure as she swallowed hard. In all her years as an assassin, she had never crossed paths with a foe like Azaroth before. His every word was deliberately chosen and laced with menace. Though icy fear churned within her, Alessandra stood tall and did not retreat. She had confronted countless threats in the past and survived. She would not let this demon, dire as he was, shake her resolve. Gathering her courage, she met his serpentine gaze directly.

"What I want is for you to leave. To stop interfering in

matters that don't concern you," she shot back, her gaze unwavering.

Azaroth let out a slow, appreciative clap. "Bravo, Alessandra. So much spirit." His gaze hardened as he looked back at Asmodeus. "As for you, old friend, it seems your brief detour has changed you more than you think. You're no longer the demon I knew. Your time among humans has... softened you."

Ash, who had been observing the exchange, stepped forward, his eyes glowing with an inner fire. "And you're just as manipulative and deceitful as always, Azaroth. Your games end here."

Ash's gaze connected with Jade's, who had abruptly materialised by his side, prompting him to grasp her hand firmly. United in their powers, they held onto a glimmer of hope.

"Indeed," Jade confirmed, her grip on Ash's hand growing tighter. The atmosphere crackled with electric anticipation as they intertwined their abilities. Their fused magic crafted an intricate tapestry of vibrant power, casting a radiant glow throughout the chapel's sombre interior.

Jade and Ash raised their unoccupied hands, their fingertips aglow with amassed strength. Bound by unending willpower, they unleashed a surge of energy, colliding it head-on with Azaroth. The rush of mystical force surged through the air, causing braziers to flicker and the stones of the chapel to quiver under its sheer might.

Azaroth hissed, his form rippling as he sought to evade the incoming assault. Yet the merged prowess of Jade and Ash persisted relentlessly and swiftly. The blast struck Azaroth with unrelenting vigour, evoking a shrill cry of agony that reverberated through the chapel.

Alessandra sprinted forward, her dagger held high. Azaroth was recoiling from Jade and Ash's attack, his attention on them. He didn't see Alessandra until it was too late. With a battle cry, she plunged her dagger into Azaroth.

Silence gripped the room as Azaroth hovered, wavering on the brink. Then, with an anguished howl, the demon erupted in a blast of power, his body bursting apart and dissipating like mist.

Alessandra reeled back, chest heaving, her fingers numb around the hilt of her fallen dagger. Beside her, Jade and Ash slumped breathless to their knees, utterly depleted.

For a long moment, none of them moved, their minds struggling to process the magnitude of what had just transpired. The air was heavy with a palpable sense of disbelief and exhaustion, each of them grappling with the surreal reality of their victory over the ancient demon.

CHAPTER 4

Gasping for breath, Alessandra lay collapsed as her mind spun wildly. Azaroth's cryptic words lingered, their implications obscure yet demanding. Had the demon's verbal snares held any truth, or were they only more deception?

His layered taunts needled her thoughts. The allusions to the Order, Asmodeus, herself—they formed a puzzle with missing pieces. One she struggled to assemble into meaning.

With ruthless skill, Azaroth had scattered partial facts and veiled threats, delighting in misdirection. But Alessandra sensed some greater strategy underpinning it all. She strained to discern the larger picture, to unravel the demon's designs.

"What did he mean, Ash?" Alessandra enquired, turning her gaze to the demon, who was trying to recover his strength. "Why did he say that you were 'a changed demon'?"

Ash's eyes flickered open. He looked at Alessandra, his gaze heavy. "He was just trying to get under my skin," he dismissed, his voice raspy. "It's what he does best. We shouldn't read too much into his words."

Alessandra remained unconvinced. She knew Ash was

trying to brush it off to avoid the topic. But Azaroth had been too interested in their affairs for it to be just random talk. There was something more. Alessandra had a sinking feeling that they were only scratching the surface of a much larger problem.

"Are you sure about that?" she pressed. "You knew him before, didn't you? What if there's some truth in what he said? What if there is a bigger threat to the Order?"

The silence that followed was heavy. They had won the battle, but a sense of unease lingered. As the adrenaline of the fight drained away, they were left knowing that their struggle was far from over. Azaroth might be gone, but his shadow still loomed over them, a reminder that dangers still lurked in the darkness.

Alessandra got up from the floor, then pulled the other two up. "Let's not dwell on it. For all I know, he could've been the Order's dog, placed at the entrance to the secret tunnel. We're here to find clues to my father's whereabouts, so let's do just that."

Guiding orb aloft, Ash led them further within. Ancient air hung heavy, their footfalls rousing dust motes to dance in the pale light. Though eerie, a sense of stillness pervaded the chapel's heart, untouched by their battle. There was something hallowed here, eternal. Shadows could not mar the steadfast sanctity of this place.

Scanning the room, Alessandra found various symbols etched into the stone walls, faded but still discernible. Some were emblems she recognised from her training with the Order, others were unfamiliar, belonging perhaps to ancient sects or old magic.

Alessandra's breath caught as her gaze fell upon a familiar sigil - one intricately linked to her father. An eminent dragon formed the emblem's centrepiece, scales gleaming in deep emerald and crimson, wings spread in a display of formidable power. Sharp talons clutched an ornate sword, grasping the hilt with undeniable authority.

Surrounding the dragon, elaborate runic patterns and arcane symbols adorned the edges like an ancient tapestry. Each intricate curve seemed to thrum with energy, resonating within Alessandra's spirit. The sigil evoked her father's tales of mythic battles and forgotten realms now lost to time.

Significance was attached to the colours of the emblem too. The vibrant green symbolised growth, renewal, and the ever-present connection to nature. The fiery red evoked passion, courage, and the unyielding spirit that ran through her bloodline.

As she stared at the image, a mix of emotions washed over her—pride, longing, and a burning desire to uncover the truth behind her father's legacy. It served as a reminder of the weight of responsibility that came with it.

Now, with the emblem before her, she felt a surge of determination. Alessandra took a deep breath, ready to step into the unknown and embrace the challenges that awaited her.

"We're on the right path," she said, her voice a whisper, her gaze intense.

A radiant light beckoned from the passage's depths, flowing from an ornately carved altar nestled in the chamber beyond. Intricate symbols and arcane script adorned the walls, their significance gradually revealing itself. As she drew nearer, Alessandra traced the elegant engravings, once shrouded in shadow now limned in luminescence.

With bated breath, Alessandra, Jade, and Ash shared a knowing glance. They had come too far to turn back now. Together, they stepped further into the altar room. Their eyes were immediately drawn to a stunning painting that hung on the wall. The vibrant colours and elaborate details captured their attention, but it was the subject of the painting that left Alessandra breathless.

It was her mother, lovingly rendered in exquisite detail. The artist had truly captured her gentle spirit, reflecting the warmth and compassion Alessandra cherished in her fading memories.

She approached with trembling steps, overcome with a flood of emotion. This painting was more than a mere image —it radiated her mother's very essence. Alessandra reached out a quivering hand, fingers gently tracing the brushstrokes. In that fleeting contact, she felt profoundly connected, as if her mother was right there, watchful eyes brimming with affection.

Bittersweet longing pierced Alessandra's heart. Here was the one she had lost yet loved so dearly, preserved in timeless splendour. The beauty of the portrait stirred joy at this glimpse of her mother's graceful soul. Yet it also brought deep sorrow at the permanence of her absence. Tears blurred Alessandra's vision as she beheld the painting. It answered none of her questions, only deepening the hollow ache of missing her family. But in rediscovering her mother's comforting presence, she found unexpected solace tinged with pain.

In front of the painting, Alessandra broke down, her tears cascading down her cheeks as she mourned the loss of her mother once again.

Jade and Ash stood by her side, their own eyes filled with empathy and understanding. They offered a comforting presence, allowing Alessandra the space she needed to release her grief. A tender silence filled the room, only interrupted by the sound of Alessandra's soft sobs.

As the weight of her emotions eased, Alessandra wiped

away her tears and took a deep breath. Though her heart ached, she drew strength from the love she shared with her mother and the memory of her presence. She rose to her feet, a renewed fortitude shining in her eyes.

"I'm so sorry, guys. I didn't mean to break down like that."

Jade placed a comforting hand on Alessandra's shoulder. "Hey, there's no need to apologise. We understand. Finding this place, it's a deeply emotional moment for you."

"Absolutely, Alessandra," Ash chipped in. "And if you want to talk about it, I'm a superb listener. Thousands of years in Hell listening to all those souls whine about how their death was unfair gives a demon a lot of perspective."

Jade rolled her eyes. "You had to ruin it, didn't you?"

Alessandra couldn't help but chuckle through her lingering tears. "You two are something else. Even amid my breakdown, you make me laugh."

Jade shook her head, a small smile playing on her lips. "Well, what are friends for if not to bring a little humour into the mix, even in the toughest of times?"

Ash dramatically placed a hand over his heart, feigning a wounded expression. "Ah, my tragic existence. Misunderstood by all, except for my dear friend Alessandra."

Alessandra playfully rolled her eyes. "Oh, please. Don't get too carried away now, Ash. Let's focus on the task at hand."

Jade nodded in agreement. "He's right, though. We're here for you, Alessandra. Through the laughter and the tears, we've got your back."

Alessandra's gratitude overflowed. She squeezed Jade's hand and smiled at Ash's theatrical display. "Thank you both. I'm lucky to have friends like you. Now, let's take a deep breath, wipe away these tears, and continue on our journey. We have mysteries to unravel and a destiny to fulfil."

Ash straightened his posture. "Indeed, my lady. Onward

we shall march, facing danger and adventure with style and charm."

Jade rolled her eyes once again but couldn't hide her amusement. "Oh, Ash, always the showman. But you're right, Alessandra. Together, we're a formidable trio. We'll face whatever comes our way and come out stronger on the other side."

Alessandra's heart swelled with gratitude. She knew she was not alone in her quest. With Jade and Ash by her side, she felt invincible. Their friendship was a beacon of light in the darkness that surrounded them.

As Alessandra, Jade, and Ash entered the next room, a chilling draft filled the air, sending a shiver down their spines. The chamber was engulfed in an eerie darkness, illuminated by flickering torches that cast dancing shadows on the ancient walls.

The door behind them slammed shut, sealing them inside. Panic surged within Alessandra, but she remained resolute, knowing that she had to face whatever lay ahead.

As their eyes adjusted to the dim light, they noticed a series of detailed carvings etched into the walls, depicting menacing creatures of legend. The air grew heavier, and an ominous presence filled the room, as if unseen eyes were watching their every move.

A deep rumbling sound reverberated through the chamber, causing the floor beneath their feet to tremble. The carvings on the walls came alive, transforming into ethereal manifestations of the creatures they depicted. The once motionless figures now moved with eerie fluidity, their eyes glowing with an unsettling light.

Alessandra's heart raced as she realised they were facing the guardians of the chamber. The mystical entities, trapped for centuries, woke up because of their presence and intended to test their worthiness.

With a bone-chilling howl that reverberated through the chamber, the first guardian lunged forward, propelled by an otherworldly force, its monstrous claws extended and poised for a devastating strike. Alessandra's heart raced in her chest as she, Jade, and Ash moved in perfect synchrony, their actions a testament to their shared determination and honed abilities. She braced herself, ready to confront the imminent threat.

In a display of agility and speed, they gracefully evaded the razor-sharp claws, countering with calculated precision. Their movements flowed seamlessly, a well-practiced choreography that showcased their tenacity. Every swing of her weapon, every nimble dodge, ignited a fire within Alessandra, reinforcing her belief that they were capable of facing any challenge.

However, the guardians' embodiments of darkness and malevolence proved to be more than mere opponents. The very room seemed to pulse with their nefarious power, magnifying their strength. Shadows writhed and contorted, giving birth to insidious tendrils that slithered across the floor, ensnaring their limbs in a vice-like grip. Each constriction threatened to immobilise them, testing their resilience and fortitude.

Despite the encroaching darkness, Alessandra refused to succumb. Alongside Jade and Ash, she fought back, their spirits unyielding. She summoned every ounce of strength, pushing beyond her limits, determined to break free from the suffocating grasp of the shadowy restraints. With each struggle, every defiant motion, they defied the insidious influence seeking to bind them.

This was another sign that they were getting closer to finding the whereabouts of her father. Only he would think to protect his legacy with dark magic.

As oppressive darkness smothered the chamber, Alessandra's steadfastness blazed defiantly. She now grasped that these shadow guardians were more than just physical foes—they embodied her father's mystical might.

Drawing upon her inner strength, Alessandra tapped into the latent power that had always been a part of her. She focused her mind and summoned a brilliant aura of light that radiated from her core, pushing back the encroaching gloom.

Jade and Ash, sensing her unwavering resolve, followed suit, channelling their own unique abilities. Jade's agility and precision became a whirlwind of energy, cutting through the shadowy tendrils that threatened to ensnare them. Ash, with his affinity for manipulating fire, conjured blazing flames that licked at the shadows, driving them back.

Together, they fought against the guardians, their unity a beacon of light in the face of darkness. Alessandra couldn't help but feel a bittersweet mix of emotions. On one hand, she resented her father for the challenges he had left in his wake. But she couldn't deny the connection that drew her closer to him with each passing trial.

As they continued their relentless assault, the guardians grew weaker, their dark energy waning. The room trembled, and cracks formed on the walls, releasing a blinding light that shattered the remaining shadows.

In the battle's aftermath, Alessandra's heart swelled with emotions. She had come one step closer to uncovering the truth about her father, his motives, and his role in the mysterious events that had shaped her life.

With each victory, they grew stronger, their bond forged in the crucible of battle. And as they stood amidst the wreckage of their foes, Alessandra knew that no matter what trials awaited them in the future, they would face them together, united in purpose and resolve.

CHAPTER 5

EMERGING FROM THE CHAPEL'S TWISTING PASSAGES, THE trio found themselves in an expansive chamber awash in the moonlight's otherworldly glow. Alessandra's pulse quickened as recognition dawned—this was the fabled place her father's tales had conjured. Its splendour stole the breath from her lungs.

The expansive chamber revealed a celestial wonder above—a ceiling crafted entirely of toughened glass, allowing the soft lunar glow to cascade into the room. The shimmering beams danced across the chamber's walls, creating an ambiance that ignited a sense of wonder within their hearts.

Alessandra couldn't help but smile, her gaze fixated on the door standing proudly at the end of the hall. It was the very door her father had described—the entrance that would lead them into the long-awaited embrace of the mansion itself.

She felt a pang of nostalgia as she stepped into Prior Park mansion, her childhood home that had once been filled with warmth and laughter. Now it lay in decay, a haunting reminder of her father's mysterious disappearance.

The air inside was heavy with memories and neglect. Dust danced in the sunbeams that filtered through the cracked windows, casting an ethereal glow upon the worn wooden floors. Cobwebs clung to the corners, veiling the once elegant décor with a shroud of abandonment.

Every room she entered carried echoes of her past, triggering bittersweet emotions within her. The grand staircase, where she used to play and imagine glorious adventures, now sagged under the weight of time. The once vibrant wallpaper peeled from the walls, revealing faded remnants of a life she had long left behind.

In the old drawing room, Alessandra's gaze fell upon a portrait of her family, its frame tarnished and cracked. Her father's absence left an empty space in the composition, a painful reminder of the unanswered questions that plagued her.

As she ventured further, the mansion seemed to whisper its secrets. The creaking floorboards and the howling wind through the broken windows whispered of forgotten tales and unspoken truths. It was as if the very walls held the answers she sought, waiting for her to unravel the mysteries that lingered in every shadow.

With each step, she felt the weight of responsibility, the duty to reclaim the lost legacy of her family and uncover the truth behind her father's disappearance. The mansion became not only a physical labyrinth but also a representation of her own journey of self-discovery.

Alessandra's heart raced with anticipation as she explored the dilapidated corridors of the old mansion. The air was thick with dust and the musty scent of neglect, as if time itself had forgotten this place.

As she moved deeper into the labyrinthine maze of forgotten rooms, a faint glimmer of hope ignited within her.

She had heard whispers of her father's secret study, a sanctuary where he would immerse himself in ancient texts and delve into the mysteries that consumed him. It was said to hold the key to his knowledge, and perhaps it also had the answers she sought.

Her footsteps echoed through the abandoned halls, the sound a poignant reminder of the solitude she felt. The grandeur of the mansion had faded over the years, its once opulent decor now reduced to faded wallpaper and cracked marble. Yet, within these decaying walls, Alessandra sensed the lingering presence of her father, guiding her toward his hidden sanctuary.

With each step, her excitement grew, mingled with a tinge of trepidation. What secrets would she uncover in her father's study? What truths lay hidden among the ancient tomes and artefacts that adorned the room? Her mind whirled with possibilities as she moved closer to her destination.

Alessandra's steps halted at an aged oak door, its wood greyed and splintered from years untouched. The very air seemed alive with anticipation, as if the portal held its breath, poised on the cusp of revelation. She raised an unsteady hand, fingertips hovering above the tarnished brass knob. Her pulse thundered—a heady blend of eagerness and apprehension.

With a gentle twist, the door creaked open, revealing a dimly lit room bathed in a soft, golden glow. The air was heavy with the scent of aged parchment and the faint aroma of incense. As she stepped across the threshold, her eyes widened with wonder.

The chamber bore testament to her father's insatiable hunger for lost wisdom. Shelves stretched across the walls, bowed under the weight of leather-bound tomes, unrolled scrolls curling with age, and curios from faraway lands. Gold-leafed spines glinted in the sparse light, etched with glyphs from tongues long dead. Strange instruments of metal and glass cluttered tabletops, their arcane purposes veiled by dust and time.

Jade trailed closely behind, her presence a comforting reassurance. With a graceful flick of her wrist, she ignited the candles adorning the room. The warm glow of the flames illuminated the surroundings, casting mesmerising shadows that danced along the rows of books. The interplay of light and shadow seemed to breathe life into the stillness, as if the secrets within those ancient tomes yearned to be whispered into existence.

Upon entering, Alessandra's eyes were drawn to a large wooden desk cluttered with parchments and leather-bound volumes. The surface bore the marks of countless hours of meticulous study, ink stains and worn edges testifying to her father's tireless pursuit of understanding.

She approached the desk, running her fingers lightly over the worn wood, tracing the intricate carvings that adorned its surface. Emotions welled up within her—nostalgia, longing, and a deep sense of connection to her father. She could almost hear his voice, guiding her through the pages of knowledge that lay before her.

As she surveyed the room, Alessandra's eyes landed on a hidden alcove tucked away in the corner. It was a smaller space concealed behind an intricately woven tapestry that depicted scenes of mythical creatures and celestial beings. Something inside her urged her to investigate further.

With cautious steps, she approached the alcove and gently pushed aside the tapestry, revealing a hidden door. Its surface bore markings and symbols she recognised from her father's notes, confirming that this was the entrance to his most guarded sanctuary.

Her heart swelled with excitement and trepidation. She knew that beyond that door awaited the culmination of her father's knowledge, the secrets that could hold the key to understanding his disappearance and the mysteries that had plagued her. Taking a deep breath, she steeled herself for what lay ahead.

Alessandra reached out, her hand grasping the doorknob. She turned it. The door swung open, revealing a room bathed in an otherworldly glow. The walls were adorned with various symbols, and the air crackled with a sense of ancient power.

As she crossed the threshold into her father's hidden part of the study, a wave of emotions engulfed Alessandra—awe, wonder, and a profound sense of purpose. The room, steeped in an air of reverence, held the promise of unveiling the ambiguous truth that had eluded her for far too long. The arduous journey she had embarked upon had led her to this pivotal juncture, where she stood poised to embrace the profound knowledge that awaited her.

Alessandra, Jade, and Ash found themselves standing in her father's abandoned chamber, surrounded by a sea of forgotten books and dusty relics. Their eyes widened with curiosity as they surveyed the room, unsure of what peculiar surprises awaited them.

Alessandra's voice rang out with a touch of apprehension. "Ash, just a friendly reminder. Try to resist the urge to touch anything. We wouldn't want any ancient curses or angry spirits coming after us."

Ash flashed a mischievous grin, his eyes gleaming. "Oh, don't worry, Alessandra. I've been known to charm angry spirits with my irresistible wit. They can't resist a good joke!"

Jade rolled her eyes, trying to stifle a laugh. "Let's not tempt fate. Remember, we're here to solve mysteries, not become them."

Ash dramatically feigned offence, placing a hand over his heart. "Jade, you wound me! Here I am, just trying to add a little levity to this dusty situation."

Alessandra couldn't help but chuckle. "All right, Ash. Just remember that if you accidentally summon a ghost, you're in charge of making friends with it."

The trio shared a light-hearted laugh, momentarily forgetting the eerie atmosphere around them.

Alessandra knew that by delving into the depths of his research, she would not only uncover his legacy, but also find the answers she sought. She took a deep breath, her eyes fixed on the vast expanse of knowledge that lay before her, ready to embark on a journey that would forever shape her destiny.

Hidden within the forgotten corners of the mansion, Alessandra's heart quickened as she stumbled upon remnants of her father's research. Scattered notes and weathered parchment hinted at his deep involvement in ancient mysteries and arcane knowledge, fuelling her curiosity and igniting a newfound sense of purpose.

The notes, written in her father's distinct handwriting, unveiled tantalising fragments of his journey. They spoke of his tireless pursuit of forbidden knowledge, and his relentless quest to uncover the secrets that lay beyond the veil of reality. Alessandra traced her fingers over the faded ink, absorbing the words as if they were a lifeline connecting her to her father's legacy.

As she pieced together the scattered puzzle, a tapestry of her father's discoveries emerged. Within the pages of ancient texts and forgotten lore, a wealth of knowledge awaited, unlocking insights into unseen realms, mystical artefacts brimming with untapped potential, and the existence of enigmatic beings that defied human comprehension.

Each note unravelled a layer of her father's obsession,

painting a picture of a man driven by a desire to protect and preserve the delicate balance between worlds. His involvement in ancient mysteries extended far beyond mere curiosity—it was a calling, a sacred duty he had willingly embraced.

Alessandra's mind raced with questions and possibilities. She found diagrams detailing intricate rituals, sketches of enchanted artefacts, and references to ancient prophecies that foretold the coming of a great upheaval. Her father's research hinted at a world teetering on the brink of chaos, where dark forces conspired to disrupt the fragile harmony that held existence together.

These vestiges of her father's research were more than just remnants from a forgotten past; they were the breadcrumbs leading her closer to the truth. They fuelled her mission to continue his work, to understand the significance of his findings, and to carry the torch he had ignited.

With every page turned, Alessandra delved deeper into the enigmatic world her father had inhabited. She immersed herself in the complex tapestry of ancient myths and forbidden knowledge, determined to unravel the secrets that had driven her father's actions and, ultimately, shaped her own destiny.

Jade broke the silence. "Wow, I knew Lord de Winter was astute, but I've never imagined this."

"Yeah, my father's obsession was something else," Alessandra replied. "I wish I knew what to do with all this. Nothing in my training prepared me for this moment. But I know one thing for sure, his disappearance is linked to this. Any ideas, Ash?"

Ash leaned against a nearby bookshelf, his eyes scanning the scattered notes and relics with intrigue and contemplation. "Well, from what I've learned over the years, knowledge is power. And it seems like your father was searching for something powerful. Something that could tip the scales in favour of either light or darkness."

He paused for a moment, his fingers tracing the edges of an ancient talisman. "Perhaps your father's disappearance is connected to the very thing he was searching for. It's possible that he delved too deeply into forbidden realms."

Jade nodded in agreement, her expression thoughtful. "If that's the case, then we must tread carefully. Whatever your father was involved in, it attracted powerful forces. And they won't hesitate to eliminate anyone who poses a threat to their agenda."

Alessandra's eyes sparkled with determination and uncertainty. "I won't let fear paralyse us. My father dedicated his life to protecting the realms, and I will honour his legacy by continuing his work. We have to find out what he was searching for and uncover the truth behind his disappearance."

Ash offered a reassuring smile. "You're right, Alessandra. We may not have all the answers now, but together, we'll navigate this intricate web of mysteries and secrets. We'll follow the clues, consult the notes, and seek any allies who can shed light on your father's path."

Jade stepped forward, placing a hand on Alessandra's shoulder. "We're with you every step of the way. Whatever challenges lie ahead, we'll face them together, as a team. We won't let anything or anyone stand in our way."

Alessandra's firmness solidified, her gaze reflecting a newfound strength. "Thank you both. Your support means everything to me. Together, we'll uncover the truth, protect our world, and bring my father back."

With a smile gracing her lips, Alessandra shifted her attention back to the desk. Her hand extended, fingers delicately brushing against the weathered leather of the journal's cover. A subtle shiver coursed down her spine, as though the touch itself had summoned her father's spirit, infusing the pages with his soul.

As she lifted the journal from its resting place and cradled it in her hands, she noticed it bore the marks of a well-loved companion. The weight of the journal was reassuring—could it hold the answers she had long sought?

Alessandra carefully opened the notebook, revealing handwritten script adorning the pages. Each pen stroke spoke of her father's meticulous nature, his dedication to documenting thoughts and discoveries. The scent of aged paper mingling with faint ink filled her senses - a heady mix of nostalgia and purpose.

As she turned the pages, her eyes fell upon a particular entry, its title drawing her attention. There, in the elegant cursive script, was the letter she had been searching for—the words penned by her father, preserved within the confines of the journal.

My Dearest Lucien and Alessandra.

If this letter has reached your hands, it signifies that the time has arrived for you to unravel the final pieces of the intricate puzzle I've left in my wake. As your father, it pains me to communicate with you from the realms beyond, yet I must emphasise the gravity of the mission at hand.

Even before embarking on this expedition, I possessed foresight regarding my own destiny. I understood that my path would culminate in an untimely conclusion, but I willingly embraced this sacrifice for the greater good. Now, it is my solemn responsibility to disclose the whereabouts of my resting place, a tomb of profound significance and the crucial key to locating the weapon capable of shifting the tides against the Order.

Beneath the very foundations of our ancestral estate lies a concealed labyrinth of catacombs. A sacred realm untouched by the passage of time. It is within these forgotten depths that my final abode resides. The catacombs house the enigmas of our family's heritage, and within their ancient walls, you shall unveil the clues that shall steer you towards the true might of the weapon.

I implore you, my dear offspring, to exercise caution as you traverse the catacombs. The serpentine corridors and dilapidated passageways teem with perils, while the ethereal beings dwelling within serve as both guardians and gatekeepers of our family's secrets. Show reverence in their presence, and they shall serve as your guiding light towards the heart of the tomb.

Once you reach the inner sanctum, an altar bathed in other-worldly luminescence shall greet your sight. It is there that the ultimate key awaits you—a symbol of our shared purpose and the culmination of my life's labour. Concealed within these sanctified walls lies the weapon you seek. An inexhaustible source of power capable of shattering the Order's dominion over our realm.

Yet, remember, my cherished children, that the weapon is not solely an instrument of annihilation; it represents hope—a beacon that shines even amidst the darkest of hours. Wield it with compassion, and a dedication to justice. Allow our family's legacy to guide your actions, and let love and unity be your guiding principles.

As you embark upon this arduous voyage, know that my ethereal presence shall walk alongside you. Draw strength from our unbreakable bond, from the love coursing through our veins. Allow it to be your shield against the tribulations that lie ahead, for your hearts are pure and your determination resolute.

Lucien, my son, your unwavering loyalty and unyielding grit, shall serve you admirably. Alessandra, my daughter, your resilience and indomitable spirit have forever been a wellspring of inspiration.

Together, you form a formidable force, destined to affect the transformation our world so desperately craves.

Unravel the secrets concealed within the catacombs, embrace the power of the weapon, and allow justice to illuminate your path. Fulfil our family's legacy and reclaim the equilibrium that the Order's malevolence has disrupted.

With eternal love and belief in your strength,
Your father

Her heart quickened as she read the familiar words, the emotions welling up within her, threatening to spill over. It was a bittersweet moment, a convergence of past and present, of memories and longing.

Alessandra marvelled at her father's profound love, his foresight to leave this cherished message. The letter was a shining beacon, illuminating their path forward. A tribute to his faith in their potential to uphold his legacy.

With trembling hands, she clutched the journal to her chest, feeling the weight of her father's presence within its pages. She knew that within those written words lay the key to their future. A path that would lead them closer to the truth, closer to the weapon that could change the course of their world.

In that moment, Alessandra made a silent vow—to honour her father's memory, to unlock the secrets contained within the journal, and to embark on the journey that lay ahead.

As Alessandra tightly clutched her father's worn journal to her chest, an ominous laughter filled the air. The sound, like nails on a chalkboard, sent shivers down her spine, and her heart skipped a beat as she immediately recognised the distinctive cackle. It could only belong to one creature—Azaroth. He wasn't dead after all.

"So you're alive," Alessandra muttered, her voice laced with surprise.

Azaroth grinned mischievously, his eyes gleaming with amusement. "Yes, Alessandra. Death has a way of being quite temporary when it suits my purposes," he replied, his tone dripping with sarcasm.

Ash rolled his eyes, unimpressed. "You're not funny," he interjected, his annoyance palpable.

Jade crossed her arms, a stern expression on her face. "We're not here to entertain you, Azaroth. What do you want?" she demanded, her voice filled with defiance and impatience.

Azaroth's grin widened, his gaze shifting between the three of them. "Oh, but you are, my dear friends. I will let you in on a little secret. You have been captured by the Order, and this is nothing but a dream."

CHAPTER 6

Vlad's arm remained outstretched, the bed beside him vacant and cold. His eyes fluttered open, greeted by the sight of dishevelled sheets and tangled blankets, reminders of the night he had shared with Alessandra. He reached out, fingers grazing the pillow that still held the faint impression of her head, a bittersweet reminder of their intimacy.

Closing his eyes, Vlad replayed the sound of her voice, the weight of her words settling in his heart. "I'm sorry. I have to find my father. Please understand." He knew someone must have helped her plant that image in his dream, but he admired Alessandra's courage. She possessed a strength, a fierce need to confront her family's secrets head-on. It both captivated and worried him.

Yet, as his mind traversed the labyrinth of possibilities, a knot of anxiety tightened within Vlad's chest. The dangers posed by the Order and their relentless pursuit loomed large in his thoughts. He believed in Alessandra's resilience, her ability to face whatever challenges awaited her, but the uncertainty of their future cast a shadow over his heart.

With a heavy sigh, Vlad rose from the empty bed, a mix of hope and apprehension swirling within him. His trust in Alessandra's capabilities warred with the ever-present fear of the unknown. He vowed to support her from a distance, to be her silent guardian, while steeling himself for the battles yet to be fought.

The Prince, now dressed, made his way to the headmaster's office, a place that had become his own. In his mind, he silently summoned Angelique, who stood dutifully by the door, awaiting his arrival.

"Your Highness," Angelique said, her voice filled with reverence as she bowed her head, then opened the door and gestured for the Prince to enter.

"Would you be so kind as to summon my nephew, Lucien, and enquire about the whereabouts of my father and Miss Nicolay?" Vlad requested with a sense of urgency.

"I apologise, Your Excellency," Angelique replied, her voice tinged with regret. "Only Monsieur de Winter is present at the estate today."

A surge of restrained anger coursed through Vlad's veins as he heard the news. "What has happened to the other two?" he enquired, his voice carrying a mix of concern and frustration.

"It seems they left the estate last night, along with Miss de Winter," Angelique responded, her tone holding a tinge of sorrow.

A heavy silence enveloped the room, the weight of the revelation sinking in.

"And you allowed them to leave?" Vlad's voice thundered, reverberating through the hallways. The maid stood before him, head hung in shame, unable to offer a response.

"My apologies, Angelique," Vlad said, his voice mellowing, realising that the blame did not lie with her.

"You could have done nothing to prevent their departure."

Overwhelmed with guilt, Angelique dropped to her knees, tears streaming down her face. She dared to look up at him, her gaze filled with remorse and a plea for forgiveness. "You don't have to apologise, Master," she whispered, her voice laden with regret. "I should have awakened you the moment I realised what was happening, but... you were sleeping so peacefully. I couldn't bear to disturb you."

Vlad's expression softened, and he offered the maid a compassionate smile. "Do not burden yourself with guilt, Angelique. Your intentions were pure, and you acted out of concern for my well-being."

Tears continued to flow down Angelique's cheeks as she looked towards him, her gaze brimming with sorrow. "I am sorry, Your Highness. Please forgive me," she pleaded, her voice trembling.

Vlad's heart softened further, and he extended a forgiving hand. "There is nothing to forgive, Angelique. You have been devoted to me. Now, please fetch Lucien."

With relief and gratitude, Angelique rose from her knees, wiping away her tears. "Thank you, Your Highness," she muttered before leaving the room to carry out his request, a renewed strength in her steps.

Lucien entered the office shortly after, his expression stoic and filled with a sense of responsibility. Vlad's gaze met his nephew's, and they both knew they were now faced with a dire situation.

"Uncle... you've heard, I suppose," Lucien began, his voice tinged with disappointment and concern.

"Yes," Vlad replied, his voice reflecting a touch of sadness. "Alessa has proven herself to be quite the independent spirit. Enlisting the help of my father and Miss Nicolay, she has embarked on a daring journey. Although I'm relieved she had the foresight not to go alone, I can't help but feel disappointed she left without a word in the dead of night."

Lucien's face grew darker as he spoke. "That's just the beginning of our troubles, Uncle. Lóthurr, the leader of the Shadowcrest clan, has sent word that the Order has captured them. His spies relayed this information a few minutes ago."

A sinking feeling settled in Vlad's heart as he realised the gravity of the situation. How had the Order captured Alessa, despite having a demon prince and a powerful witch by her side? It spoke volumes about the growing strength and cunning of their adversaries.

Vlad's voice trembled with desperation and determination. "We must bring her back, Lucien, no matter the cost. Have the Order made any demands or communicated their intentions?"

Lucien shook his head. His expression hardened. "Not yet. It seems they want to keep us in the dark. But we can't afford to wait. We must act swiftly to rescue Alessa before they carry out whatever sinister plans they have in store."

Vlad's eyes narrowed, his mind racing with thoughts of strategising and gathering allies. "We will find her, Lucien. I swear it. We will assemble a team, reach out to our contacts, and leave no stone unturned until Alessa is back safely by our side."

With a renewed sense of purpose, Vlad and Lucien locked eyes, their willpower mirrored in their gazes.

"What are you thinking?" Vlad asked, his voice filled with concern and a touch of apprehension.

Lucien paused for a moment, gathering his thoughts before responding with a resolute tone. "I have seen firsthand how the Order can manipulate their knights and turn them against their own. It wouldn't be impossible for them to do the same with Alessandra."

Vlad's brows furrowed, his mind grappling with the gravity of the situation. "Do you believe they would go to such lengths?"

Lucien's gaze hardened, his conviction unwavering. "I believe so. We have amassed a formidable alliance of supernatural beings, and Alessandra has discovered and unlocked her true powers. It appears we may have gained an advantage. Perhaps the Order fears losing control."

A feeling of disquiet came over Vlad as he considered the possibility of the Order resorting to such extreme measures. The thought of the love of his life enduring torture and manipulation sent a chill down his spine.

"Breaking someone through torture is a horrific task," Vlad murmured, his voice laden worry and anger.

Lucien nodded, his expression solemn. "Indeed, it is. I know this personally. When an assassin went rogue in the past, they sent me to apprehend him. I brought him back, but the transformation he underwent in the dungeon was so severe that he became unrecognisable."

Vlad took a deep breath, exhaling slowly as he tried to steady his racing thoughts. "Thank you, Lucien, for keeping a level head in this tumultuous situation. I know it's difficult, but we must stay strong for Alessandra. I believe she possesses bravery that will sustain her until we bring her back. And as for Avery, something deep within me tells me we will find her soon enough."

They stood wordlessly, the silence heavy with their unified resolution and shared anticipation. Despite the risks and uncertainties that lay ahead, Vlad made a tough decision. He knew that Alessandra's life hung in the balance, and he couldn't bear the thought of her suffering at the hands of the

Order any longer. Fortitude burned in his eyes as he turned to Lucien.

"Lucien, I can't stand idly by while your sister remains captive. I will go after her and bring her back, no matter the cost," Vlad declared boldly.

Lucien's brows furrowed, worry etched on his face. "But Uncle, it's far too dangerous to go alone. We need a plan."

Vlad's hand tightened on Lucien's shoulder, gratitude and concern flickering in his eyes. "Lucien, I need you to stay here at the academy while I embark on the journey to rescue Alessandra. You must remain vigilant, for news of Avery may come at any moment."

Lucien nodded, his expression serious and resolute. "I won't fail you. I'll keep a watchful eye and gather every bit of information that comes our way. We won't let the Order slip through our fingers."

A glint of reliance and tenacity flashed between them—brothers-in-arms conferring without words.

"I have faith in you, Lucien," Vlad avowed, his tone laden with certainty. "You're a capable leader. The academy and our allies will stand strong under your steadfast guard." He gripped Lucien's shoulder, his words steeled. "And together, we will see Alessandra and Avery safely returned. Of this I am sure."

As Vlad observed Lucien's resolute demeanour, a sense of pride swelled within him. The weight of responsibility settled upon his nephew's shoulders, yet Lucien stood tall, ready to face the challenges that lay ahead. Vlad couldn't help but marvel at the transformation he had witnessed in him, from a young and uncertain recruit to a formidable man, and soon to be a leader.

A flicker of worry passed through Vlad's mind as he contemplated the dangers that awaited him on his solitary journey. He couldn't shake the gnawing fear of the unknown, the lurking shadows that threatened to consume him.

Bracing himself for the treacherous road ahead, Vlad fortified his resolve. Thoughts of Alessandra's courage and resilience echoed in his mind, bolstering his determination. He pledged to himself that he would not rest until he had rescued her from the clutches of the Order.

As Vlad turned to leave, he uttered a silent prayer, a plea to the fates to keep Lucien safe and guide him through the trials that awaited. He knew their destinies were intertwined, and that each played a vital role in the grand tapestry of their mission.

CHAPTER 7

Vlad contemplated the idea of bringing his loyal knights along on his journey to the Order's current stronghold, Corvin Castle. However, after careful consideration, he dismissed the notion. Travelling with a horde of vampires was a sure way to attract attention, and discretion was of utmost importance in his mission. After all, the element of surprise could be a powerful weapon against their nefarious enemies.

Within the hallowed halls of Roslyn Academy, nestled in a forgotten corner, lay the Sanctum of Sylnor Relics—a chamber steeped in mystery and brimming with the remnants of ages long past. Stepping into the chamber illuminated by flickering torchlight, Vlad's eyes surveyed the meticulously organised shelves, each cradling a relic of untold power and ancient significance. The air crackled with a tangible energy, as if the artefacts themselves held dormant magic.

Amidst the display, Vlad's attention was drawn to an amulet, its craftsmanship unparalleled. Embedded within its intricate design were sigils of protection and wards against supernatural forces. Legends spoke of its origins, tracing back to a long-lost civilisation renowned for their mastery of enchantments. As Vlad clasped the amulet around his neck, he felt a subtle hum resonating through his being. The item shrouded him in a shield, making him invisible.

Venturing deeper into the chamber, his gaze settled on a tome resting upon an ornate pedestal. The pages contained cryptic incantations and forbidden knowledge, which ancient scribes had laboriously transcribed. The tome exuded an aura of forbidden power, a tantalising glimpse into the secrets of prohibited magics. Vlad traced his fingers over the text and absorbed the arcane wisdom that ancient scribes had carefully preserved across the ages.

And then, his eyes fell upon the Blade of Mystoria, a weapon of extraordinary craftsmanship and mystical properties. Crafted from a rare alloy infused with magical essence, the sword shimmered with an ethereal radiance. Its edge was honed to perfection, capable of slicing through enchantments with surgical precision. Etched along the blade were sigils of binding, channelling the raw elemental forces into a potent strike against supernatural adversaries.

As Vlad grasped the hilt, power surged up his arm, intertwining with his very essence. The blade seemed to resonate with his presence and was attuned to his command. It was not just a weapon; it was an extension of his will, a conduit for his magical prowess.

Vlad's thoughts were consumed by Alessandra, filled with an inflexible desire to rescue her, regardless of the price he had to pay. The connection they had formed during their treacherous quest had evolved into something profound, a bond that surpassed the dangers they faced.

With his heart ablaze and his mind focused, Vlad embarked on a relentless pursuit to rescue the woman who had captured his soul. The journey would be perilous, but he knew that the power of their connection would carry him through. For Alessandra, he would face any danger, defy any obstacle, and prove that their love was unbreakable.

For three consecutive nights, Vlad embarked on a harrowing odyssey to the forbidding gates of Corvin Castle in Romania. Beneath the ethereal radiance of the moonlit sky, he traversed hazardous terrains, every step a testament to his purpose. The path that stretched before him was riddled with uncertainty, shrouded in an ominous aura that would have deterred lesser souls. Yet Vlad pressed on, unflinchingly forging ahead, undeterred by the perils that awaited.

As the darkness descended, cloaking the world in an inky veil, Vlad tapped into the depths of his vampiric prowess. His supernatural abilities endowed him with preternatural speed and agility, enabling him to navigate the shadows with uncanny swiftness. To mortal eyes, his movements were a mere blur, an ethereal phantom leaping over obstacles and hurtling through the night. The wind whispered tales of his passage, carrying the echo of his determination across the land.

Throughout those long and gruelling nights, Vlad's senses remained heightened, tuned to the faintest tremors of peril lurking in the abyss of darkness. His keen vampire vision pierced through the veil of night, granting him the ability to detect hidden threats and discern the treacherous paths that led to his destination. Beady eyes watched him from the shadows. Unseen creatures prowled the underbrush, their presence betrayed only by the rustling of leaves and the faintest of growls. Vlad remained undeterred, unshaken by the ominous forces that sought to impede his progress.

With each passing night, Vlad's anticipation swelled, his heart pulsating with a fierce intensity that matched the rhythm of his steps. The moon seemed to watch over him with a benevolent gaze, its gentle light lending him a modicum of solace in the face of the arduous journey that lay ahead.

As he ventured deeper into the heartland of Romania, the supernatural forces that governed the region became more pronounced. The occult realm seemed to converge with the mortal plane, blurring the boundaries between the living and the undead. Ancient curses and spells lay dormant, waiting for unsuspecting souls to awaken them with their presence.

Vlad's vampiric nature drew attention, like a beacon calling out to creatures that hungered for a taste of his immortality. Vicious werewolves prowled through dense forests, their eyes glowing with feral intensity as they tracked his every move. Cunning witches harnessing dark magic laid crafty traps and wove intricate spells to ensnare any who dared to trespass upon their domain.

As he delved further into the Romanian countryside, Vlad encountered more treacherous adversaries. Vengeful spirits, restless from centuries of torment, materialised with ethereal whispers and bone-chilling moans, seeking to bind him to their tragic fate. Ancient vampires, powerful and malevolent, rose from their slumber, their thirst for blood insatiable and their strength unmatched.

The very landscape itself seemed to shift, transforming into a labyrinth of ominous caves and passages. The earth beneath his feet quivered with latent power, concealing ancient tombs and forgotten crypts, each one harbouring its own guardians and secrets. Danger was imminent, and it carried its scent in the charged energy of the air.

Despite the mounting perils that beset him, Vlad's resolve remained steadfast. He navigated through treacherous terrain, his vampiric abilities his only advantage. The shadows became his ally, granting him temporary sanctuary as he evaded the gaze of his adversaries. His heightened senses detected danger from miles away, allowing him to expect and counter the threats that lurked in the darkness.

As the nights blended together, fatigue threatened to cloud his mind, but Vlad pushed through, drawing strength from the thought of Alessandra's presence at the end of his journey. Her memory sustained him, giving him renewed energy and a resolute purpose that propelled him forward.

Finally, on the third night, as the first rays of dawn painted the horizon with hues of gold and pink, Vlad arrived at his destination. He stood before the imposing gates of Corvin Castle, his heart pounding with relief and anticipation. The long and arduous journey had led him there, and he knew the true test awaited within those ancient walls.

The castle stood proudly against the backdrop of the Romanian countryside, a majestic fortress that exuded both grandeur and an air of mystery. Its towering walls, crafted from ancient stone, reached toward the heavens, casting a formidable shadow upon the land below.

Its architecture bore the marks of centuries past, blending Gothic and Renaissance elements in a harmonious union. Turrets and battlements adorned its perimeter, standing as sentinels of protection and fortitude. Each stone, weathered by the passage of time, whispered tales of a bygone era of knights and noble aspirations.

As Vlad's eyes lingered on the majestic Corvin Castle, a bitter irony filled his thoughts. The Order chose this remarkable fortress as their seat of power, which marred the grandeur and historical significance of the castle. It was a cruel twist of fate that such a symbol of heritage and nobility had fallen into the hands of those who sought to wield darkness and control. The castle's grounds, once graced by the footsteps of noble rulers and brave knights, now echoed with the whispers of the Order's nefarious plans. It was a desecration of the castle's true legacy, a stain on its storied history.

Vlad couldn't help but feel a surge of indignation. The Order's presence within the castle walls tainted the memories of valour and chivalry that once thrived there. The clash between the castle's noble past and the sinister machinations of the Order created a dissonance that echoed through Vlad's soul.

Yet it was precisely because of the Order's stronghold within Corvin Castle that Vlad's resolve burned brighter. He saw it as a challenge, an opportunity to reclaim the castle's genuine spirit and restore its rightful purpose. It was a personal quest to liberate not only Alessandra but also the castle itself from the clutches of darkness.

Vlad knew that within those walls lay the key to unravelling the Order's plans, the knowledge that would aid him in rescuing Alessandra and thwarting their malevolent agenda. It was a daunting task to confront the very heart of the enemy's power, but Vlad was undeterred. He would face the Order head-on, reclaiming Corvin Castle as a bastion of light and justice.

With his determination steeled, Vlad took a step forward, ready to infiltrate the castle's walls and confront the Order's grip on power. Corvin Castle, despite its current tainted state, held the promise of redemption. Vlad promised to resolve the clash between the castle's noble heritage and the Order's sinister presence, ensuring that honour and righteousness prevailed within its hallowed halls once more.

The ancient weathered wooden gates groaned in protest as Vlad approached, as if reluctant to grant him passage. The sound echoed through the surrounding silence, serving as a sombre reminder of the fortress's age and the secrets it held within.

As the gates swung open, the faint scent of damp stone and aged timber wafted towards Vlad, a tangible invitation to step into the realm of mystery and intrigue that lay beyond. The threshold between the outside world and the enigmatic corridors of Corvin Castle beckoned him forward like a portal into a realm untouched by time.

As Vlad stepped through the solemn gates, an overwhelming wave of memories washed over him, transporting him back to the darkest chapter of his human existence. The image of his tattered form, dressed in rags, with a face battered, dirty, and drenched in his own blood, resurfaced in his mind. It was the day when his life had shattered. The day Bran Castle had fallen to his enemies.

On that fateful day, he had found himself on his knees, tears streaming down his face. A desperate plea had escaped his lips, begging for his beloved wife's life to be spared. But the cruel hands of fate had dealt him a devastating shock. The news had come, a crushing blow to his shattered heart, that she had taken her own life. In that moment, something inside Vlad had broken beyond repair.

The memory of a heartless soldier, fuelled by sadistic pleasure, relentlessly delivering kicks upon kicks, flashed before his eyes. He could never forget the pain and humiliation the heartless man had caused him. But it was the crushing weight of learning of his wife's tragic fate that had driven him to the edge of despair.

In the depths of his anguish, Vlad had made a dangerous pact. His own blood, mingling with his tears, had become a macabre offering, a plea to the infernal realm. With a trembling hand, he had summoned Asmodeus, the Dark Prince himself, and laid his own life on the line. He had offered himself as a weapon, a vessel for vengeance, in exchange for the chance to punish his enemies and keep his flickering flame of life burning.

Love, he realised, was a bitter and blind mistress. Despite his wife's cruelty, he had loved her with an intensity that defied reason. The heart could be a foolish moron, blindly grasping at love even in the face of suffering.

The memory of that pivotal moment lingered, a haunting reminder of the price he had paid, of the darkness that now coursed through his veins. As Vlad stepped further into the depths of Corvin Castle, the weight of his past and the promises he had made bore down upon him. It was time to settle the score, to make his enemies pay for the unspeakable horrors they had unleashed upon him.

Every step he took echoed with purpose, resonating with the weight of his past sufferings. No longer would he be the helpless victim at the mercy of his tormentors. This was the turning point. He would rise from the ashes of his past and unleash a storm of retribution upon those who had shattered his life.

The castle's shadows whispered his name as if beckoning him to embrace the darkness that had consumed him. Vlad, now a creature of the night, wielded a newfound power, honed by the trials he had endured.

As if sensing his presence, the sun-drenched courtyard suddenly came alive with a legion of knights, their polished armour gleaming under the radiant rays. Their swords were drawn, their eyes filled with steel and confusion as they confronted the enigmatic figure before them. Vlad's lips curled into a smirk, his eyes glinting with an eerie intensity.

With a swift motion, Vlad extended his arm, palm facing the sunlit sky, and closed his fist. A surge of dark energy crackled through the air, casting an ominous shadow upon the once-bathed courtyard. In an instant, the knights' legs buckled beneath them, their bodies collapsing to the sun-kissed ground with bone-shattering thuds.

It was a paradoxical sight, the clash of sunlight and darkness, as the fallen knights writhed in pain, their voices echoing with cries of anguish and confusion. Vlad's gaze softened, a flicker of remorse passing through his eyes. They were unwitting victims, entrapped by the false promises and manipulation of the Order they so faithfully served.

Yet, Vlad knew that to rescue Alessandra and exact his long-awaited retribution, he had to confront these obstacles head-on. The bonds of knighthood still held sway over his own heart, but his allegiance to justice burned brighter than the midday sun. He saw himself as a renegade knight, a warrior of truth, standing against the corruption that permeated the very organisation these knights represented.

Drawing upon his own experiences and the depths of his power, Vlad approached the fallen knights with a mixture of caution and compassion. In that moment, he yearned for these men to awaken from their slumber, to see through the veil of deception that had ensnared them. With unwavering firmness, he whispered words of redemption, hoping that someday they would break free from the chains that bound them and join him in his quest for justice.

As the courtyard fell silent, save for the gentle rustle of the wind through the sunlit leaves, Vlad took a moment to gather his thoughts. The battle had only just begun, and the weight of his mission rested heavily upon his shoulders.

CHAPTER 8

Consciousness crept back as Alessandra's eyes flickered open, her mind fogged with disorientation. As the blurred forms around her coalesced into sinister clarity, icy dread seized her heart. She was suspended in an iron cage, hanging lifeless in a vast chamber lit by guttering torches. Rusty shackles gnawed her wrists, sending spikes of agony through her rigid body.

Nausea roiled within as recognition dawned—she was a prisoner in this macabre dungeon. A lamb brought to slaughter. Shadows danced around her, warped into leering faces by the erratic firelight. Rusted implements of torture glinted on the walls, awaiting her flesh and screams. The sadistic hunger in this room was palpable, like a predator toying with helpless prey.

The fetid air assaulted her nostrils, thick with the stench of mildew and crumbling stone. The relentless drip of water reverberated through the chamber, each echo a taunting laugh at her predicament. She was alone. Jade and Ash had disappeared without a trace, leaving her to fend for herself in this nightmare prison.

In the darkness, she could hear the skittering of rats, their claws scraping the cold stone floor as they scavenged for food. She shuddered at the thought of their beady black eyes watching her, just waiting for her to drop her guard.

Fear gnawed at her insides, tightening its grip as she strained against the merciless chains holding her captive. The frigid metal links seemed to taunt her futile struggles for freedom. The burden of isolation weighed down upon her, amplifying her vulnerability and helplessness.

A nagging ache of concern took root within her, tinted with a haunting sense of loss. Had they endured the same fate? The uncertainty plagued her thoughts, feeding her escalating disquiet. Their faces flashed in her mind, their absence a hollow void in her spirit.

"Is anyone here?" Alessandra's voice trembled with apprehension. The heavy door groaned open, revealing Vlad's imposing figure. The flickering torches cast dancing shadows on the cold stone walls, heightening the tension in the air.

Vlad's eyes met Alessandra's, a glimmer of regret briefly crossing his face before he lowered the cage and swung open its door. As he encircled her in his arms, Alessandra's heart skipped a beat, feeling a mix of relief and confusion. She was briefly tricked into feeling safe by the warmth of his hug.

The metallic sound of a dagger being unsheathed echoed, signalling an impending threat. The hushed gasp that escaped Alessandra's lips mingled with the tense stillness as if the chamber itself held its breath, bracing for the irreversible shift in their fates. He thrust the blade into her abdomen while looking her in the eye.

"Why?" Alessandra's voice rose above a whisper, filled

with disbelief. Her eyes searched his face, longing for answers that seemed to elude her grasp.

Vlad's grip tightened on the dagger, his voice now laced with a chilling edge. "You've ruined me more than the Order did, and I will make you pay for it," he declared, his words slicing through her heart more than the sharp blade.

It was a moment frozen in time, brimming with a storm of emotions. The lingering echoes of their voices, haunted and tinged with anguish, hung in the air, blending with the suffocating atmosphere of the chamber. Alessandra stared into Vlad's eyes, the truth of his intentions etched upon his face.

She closed her eyes, summoning her inner strength amidst the chaos of the chamber. Her voice, a mere whisper, carried a resolute tone as she spoke. "You're not him. Nice try, Azaroth."

A knowing smile played at the corners of her lips, defying the darkness that surrounded her. In that moment, she pierced through the facade, unravelling the illusion that had been crafted to deceive her with her resilience and spirit.

Azaroth's confident demeanour faltered for a fleeting moment, a flicker of surprise crossing his face. The power of her revelation reverberated through the air, shattering the illusion he had woven around them. Despite his malevolent intentions, Alessandra remained steadfast in her knowledge, refusing to succumb to his deception.

The demon's smile widened, a sinister glimmer in his eyes as he responded to Alessandra's defiance. His voice dripped with dark amusement. "Ah, my dear Alessandra. How delightful it is to witness your tenacity. I wonder, how many times can you endure this torment without losing your precious mind? Let's put that to the test, shall we?"

Alessandra's gaze remained steady, unyielding in the face of his taunting words. She knew the magnitude of the trials that awaited her, the depths of darkness he would unleash upon her. But she refused to let fear consume her.

Days blurred into nights, and Alessandra found herself lost in a perpetual haze of uncertainty. Azaroth's relentless torment had eroded her sense of time, leaving her trapped in a disorienting void. The dungeon walls seemed to close in on her, whispering eerie secrets and echoing with haunting cries.

Unable to distinguish reality from illusion, Alessandra's mind teetered on the precipice of sanity. She paced the confines of her cell, her steps faltering, her fingers trailing along the cold, damp stone. Shadows danced along the walls, their shifting forms mocking her fragile grasp on reality.

A cacophony of voices echoed through the chamber. Whispered taunts and haunting laughter reverberated within her mind. Alessandra clutched her head, trying to drown out the tormenting echoes, but they only grew louder and more insistent. Time had become an elusive spectre, slipping through her fingers like grains of sand.

In her disoriented state, Azaroth took advantage of Alessandra's vulnerability, appearing before her in the guise of Vlad as many times before. His voice, laced with deceit, cut through the suffocating silence. "My dear Alessandra, can you no longer discern truth from fiction? Is your mind unravelling like a fragile tapestry?"

Alessandra's eyes darted around the chamber, searching for a glimmer of reality amidst the swirling chaos. "You won't break me," she whispered, her voice resolute. "I will not surrender to your twisted games."

Azaroth's laughter filled the air, bouncing off the walls and invading her senses. "But I already have. I have ensnared your mind, twisted your perception. There is no escape from the labyrinth of illusions I have spun around you."

Fear clawed at Alessandra's heart, threatening to consume

her. She struggled to find a semblance of truth, to cling to the memories that anchored her to her identity. But with each passing moment, the line between reality and illusion blurred, slipping through her grasp like smoke.

She closed her eyes, desperately seeking solace in the depths of her own mind. Slowly, a fragment of clarity emerged. Alessandra mustered her strength and silenced the voices that assailed her.

"I am not alone," she whispered, her voice filled with defiance. "I will find my way back. Your illusions cannot extinguish the fire within me."

Azaroth's facade wavered for an instant, a flicker of frustration crossing his face. He swiftly regained his composed demeanour, his eyes gleaming with wicked delight. "My dear Alessandra, how amusing it is to witness your struggle! But mark my words, the darkness will consume you. I am patient."

As Azaroth dissolved into the ethereal mists, Alessandra clung to the fragment of clarity, vowing to reclaim her sanity and pierce through the veil of deception. Though trapped within the labyrinth of her own mind, she resolved to emerge stronger, defying the darkness that sought to devour her.

Alessandra sank to her knees, overwhelmed by the weight of her torment. The walls of the dungeon seemed to close in around her, their suffocating presence stifling her every breath. Hot tears streamed down her face, mingling with the dirt and grime that coated her skin.

"I can't do this anymore," she choked out, her voice raw with anguish. The relentless onslaught of illusions had worn her down, chipping away at her resilience, and now her spirit crumbled beneath the weight of despair.

Amid her breakdown, the demon materialised once more, his visage a cruel mockery of Vlad's. He circled her like a predator, his eyes gleaming with sadistic pleasure. "Ah, Alessandra, look at you. Broken and defeated. How easily the mighty fall."

Alessandra lifted her gaze, her eyes red and puffy from her tears. "Why? Why do you take such delight in tormenting me? What have I done to deserve this?"

Azaroth's lips curled into a malevolent smile. "Deserve? Oh, it's not about deserving. It is about power. I relish in the power I hold over you. In the control I exert over your very sanity."

She trembled, her voice quivering with a mix of fear and anger. "You're a monster. A heartless creature who thrives on the suffering of others."

Azaroth laughed, the sound grating on her already frayed nerves. "Yes, my dear, that is precisely what I am. And you, Alessandra, are my prized possession. A delicate toy I can manipulate at my whim."

Alessandra's anguish turned into a burning rage. Through tear-filled eyes, she glared at Azaroth. "I will not allow you to break me. I will find the strength to defy you, no matter the cost."

Azaroth's expression shifted, a flicker of annoyance crossing his face. Yet, he maintained his composed facade, relishing in the emotional turmoil he had wrought. "How amusing it is to watch your futile resistance. But mark my words, Alessandra, your spirit will crumble. There is no escape from the darkness that surrounds you."

With a final mocking smile, Azaroth vanished, leaving Alessandra alone in the desolate dungeon. She remained on the cold, damp floor, her body wracked with sobs. Her spirit was battered but not yet broken. Through the depths of her despair, a tiny ember of hope glimmered, a spark that refused to be extinguished.

Torment and despair consumed Alessandra's mind as she stood in the chamber, and a profound darkness enveloped her. As if a veil had been lifted, Alessandra felt a side of her that had long been suppressed. The weight of her past traumas, the pain of betrayal, and the relentless manipulation she had endured unleashed a torrent of emotions within her.

The ember of resilience and hope that once burned bright within her now wavered, threatened by the encroaching darkness. She felt a sinister presence whispering in her ear, coaxing her to embrace the shadows, to let go of her inhibitions and surrender to the seductive allure of power.

Alessandra's eyes, once filled with determination and kindness, now gleamed with a haunting emptiness. Her laughter echoed through the chamber, a chilling sound that sent shivers down the spines of even the most hardened souls. Her every movement became erratic, as if she danced to the rhythm of her fractured psyche.

She was no longer her old self. In her place stood a twisted embodiment of her deepest fears and darkest desires. The world around her warped and distorted, mirroring the chaos within her mind. Reality became a splintered tapestry, where nightmares and memories merged into an indistinguishable haze.

With each passing moment, Alessandra sank deeper into the abyss, her grip on sanity slipping away like grains of sand through her fingers. The lines between right and wrong blurred, morality lost its hold, and the desire for vengeance and retribution consumed her every thought. The wounds inflicted by the Order, who recruited her into this awful world, seared through her being, fuelling the flames of her fury.

The pain she endured became the catalyst for her descent into darkness. Betrayal and anguish intertwined, gnawing at her soul and eroding the foundations of her once noble spirit. The torment she suffered at their hands, both physical and emotional, ignited a fierce fire within her, demanding justice and retribution.

As the memory of their cruel acts played on an endless loop in her mind, Alessandra's thoughts became consumed by a singular purpose—bring down the Order and make them pay for their transgressions. The intoxicating allure of vengeance called to her, promising an end to her suffering and a restoration of balance.

Yet, with each step she took down this dark path, Alessandra felt herself slipping further away from her former self. The tendrils of anger and hatred wrapped around her heart, constricting it with a vengeful grip. The clarity she once possessed wavered, eclipsed by a thirst for revenge that threatened to drown out her reason and compassion.

Amid her internal turmoil, doubts crept in like insidious whispers in the shadows. Was her pursuit of vengeance blinding her to the consequences? Was she losing sight of the very ideals she held dear? The weight of these questions bore down upon her, causing her resolve to waver.

But even in the face of uncertainty, Alessandra remained resolute. The pain inflicted upon her had stoked a fire that could not be extinguished. It burned with a ferocity that fuelled her every thought, urging her forward on this perilous journey.

As she continued to descend into the depths of her own darkness, Alessandra knew that the path she walked was fraught with danger. The wounds inflicted by her enemies were deep and raw, festering with rage and sorrow. But she refused to be defined by their cruelty. Instead, she would wield her pain as a weapon, channelling it into a relentless pursuit of justice and vengeance.

With each passing moment, as she sank deeper into the abyss, Alessandra's transformation became more pronounced. The girl she once was faded, replaced by a force to be reckoned with, driven by a thirst for retribution. The lines between right and wrong continued to blur, but during the chaos, she held fast to her singular purpose—to make them pay.

CHAPTER 9

As Vlad stood in the courtyard, the world around him seemed to fade away, his focus narrowing. He attuned his senses to the subtle rhythms of the castle, searching for that familiar echo, that steady cadence that belonged to Alessandra's heart.

His eyes closed, shutting out the surrounding distractions. With each beat of his own heart, he reached out with his consciousness, seeking the elusive connection that tethered him to Alessandra's existence.

As the minutes ticked by, Vlad's focus intensified, his concentration unyielding. He could almost taste the anticipation, the yearning to find her and be united once more. The bond between them pulsed with primal energy, an unbreakable thread that transcended the physical realm and bound their spirits together.

And then, amidst the cacophony of sounds, Vlad's ears caught a faint but unmistakable rhythm. The heartbeat was like the gentle and steady flapping of a butterfly's wings. It was Alessandra.

A surge of hope coursed through Vlad's veins, his heart quickening in response. He opened his eyes, a renewed determination shining in their depths. He had found her, not merely with his senses, but with the depths of his very soul.

With each step, Vlad ventured deeper into the heart of the castle, guided by a combination of his own intuition and the faint echoes of his beloved Alessandra's presence. The corridors, dimly lit by flickering torches, seemed to stretch endlessly, an intricate maze of stone and mystery.

As he navigated the winding path, Vlad encountered ornate tapestries adorning the walls, depicting scenes of battles fought and heroes celebrated. The vibrant colours and elaborate details seemed to come alive, whispering stories of valour and sacrifice. It was as if the castle itself sought to inspire and embolden Vlad on his mission.

After what felt like an eternity of twists and turns, Vlad stood before the entrance to the Knight's Hall. The massive doors loomed before him, imposing and adorned with intricate carvings of knights in fierce battle. He could almost hear the echoes of clashing swords and the resounding cheers that once filled this hallowed space.

With a deep breath, Vlad pushed open the doors, revealing the grandeur of the ancient space. The hall stretched out before him, bathed in soft candlelight that flickered upon the polished stone floor. Long tables lined the hall, draped in rich tapestries and adorned with silverware and goblets; remnants of a time when chivalry and honour reigned supreme.

The air was heavy with a sense of anticipation, as if the very walls held their breath in foresight of Vlad's arrival. Rays of sunlight filtered through stained glass windows, casting vibrant hues upon the walls.

Sat at the largest table in the middle of the room, on a

chair that resembled a throne, was Vlad's younger brother, Radu. The sight of Radu sent a surge of conflicting emotions coursing through Vlad's veins. Memories of their shared childhood filled with laughter and camaraderie were in contrast to the bitter resentment that had grown between them over the years.

Radu's countenance held a mix of authority and weariness, his eyes reflecting the weight of his responsibilities as the head of the Order. Dressed in regal attire, he exuded an air of calculated power, his presence commanding the attention of all those in the hall. The siblings locked eyes, their gazes a silent battleground where years of pent-up emotions waged war.

The knights of the Order, loyal to Radu, stood guard around the hall, their armour gleaming in the flickering candlelight. Their presence served as a constant reminder of the division that had driven a wedge between the brothers.

Vlad's footsteps echoed through the hall as he approached the table, his face a mask of determination. He knew that this confrontation with Radu would be a defining moment, one that would either lead to reconciliation or deepen the rift that had torn them apart.

The silence was only disturbed by the far-off crackling of the hearth and the soft murmurs of the knights as they looked back and forth between the siblings, unsure of what was going to happen.

"Welcome." Radu broke the silence, his voice carrying a hint of arrogance.

"Where are Alessandra and her companions?" Vlad countered, his tone laced with annoyance that simmered beneath the surface. The years of tension between them had carved deep furrows of resentment, and Vlad's patience with his younger brother was wearing thin.

Vlad's piercing gaze bore into Radu, his eyes narrowing in frustration and disbelief. He had come to Corvin Castle to rescue Alessandra and free her from the clutches of the Order. And now, faced with Radu's presence and his seemingly nonchalant demeanour, Vlad's irritation threatened to boil over. He clenched his jaw, the subtle tensing of his muscles visible as he fought to maintain composure.

The Prince's grip tightened around the hilt of his weapon, his knuckles turning white. The subtle movement didn't go unnoticed by Radu, who responded with a condescending smile.

"So you're alive." Vlad's voice dripped with surprise and disdain. He could hardly contain his curiosity, although he dared not show it openly. "I dare not ask what devil plucked you from Hell and placed you at the helm of the Order."

Radu's lips curled into a sly smile. His eyes glimmered with a hint of mischief, knowing full well the impact of his actions. "Ah, dear brother, one's survival often hinges on alliances and a touch of cunning," Radu replied, his voice laced with calculated confidence.

Vlad's annoyance deepened at Radu's cryptic response, his frustration fuelling his desire to uncover the truth behind his brother's newfound position of power.

"You've chosen a treacherous path, Radu." Vlad's words carried a weight of disappointment. "To think you would align yourself with those who have caused so much suffering. It is a betrayal beyond measure."

Radu's eyes hardened momentarily, a fleeting crack in his composed facade. "Betrayal is a matter of perspective, brother," he retorted, his voice taking on an icy edge. "I have chosen the side that guarantees power and control, a path you seem to have forsaken."

"I shall not ask again. Where is she? I hope..." Vlad trailed off.

"You hope?" Radu echoed, a note of curiosity lacing his words. "Ah, your hope may prove to be both your salvation and your undoing."

Vlad's patience reached its limits. His emotions churned within him like a tempest ready to break loose. His grip on his weapon tightened once again.

"I will find her, Radu." Vlad's voice resonated with determination. "And if any harm has befallen her, no force in this world or the next will protect you from my wrath."

"No need to threaten me," Radu retorted with a smirk. "You shall have the pleasure of reuniting with your friends." His words held a veiled promise, leaving Vlad to wonder about his brother's true intentions.

Vlad's mind raced. He knew Radu was cunning and unpredictable, capable of weaving intricate schemes and manipulations. The thought of being reunited with his friends stirred a mix of hope and caution within Vlad. Was this a trap, or did Radu have a change of heart?

"What game are you playing?" Vlad's voice carried a sharp edge, betraying his wariness. "You speak in riddles, but I will not dance to your tune."

"You underestimate me." Radu chuckled, his voice dripping with smugness. "But the truth shall be revealed in due time. Prepare yourself for the reunion you so desperately seek. The stage is set, and the game is afoot."

As the brothers locked eyes, the battle of wits and wills intensified.

Radu's eyes gleamed with anticipation as he motioned to one of his knights, a loyal servant who had pledged his allegiance to the Order. The knight, recognising his master's call, approached the table with a sense of duty etched upon his face.

Radu's voice resonated authority and excitement as he addressed the knight, his words dripping with intrigue. "Is it ready?" he enquired, his gaze fixed upon the knight's attentive countenance.

The knight bowed respectfully before his master, his demeanour displaying a blend of loyalty and eagerness. "Yes, my lord," he replied with conviction. "The preparations have been made, as you commanded. The stage is set. We are waiting for your order."

Vlad's gaze narrowed, suspicion still lingering in his eyes as he observed the exchange between Radu and the knight. The air crackled with tension, each passing moment adding another layer of intrigue to the unfolding events.

"Very well," Radu replied, his voice carrying a hint of satisfaction. "Bring forth our honoured guest and let the grand performance begin. The time for revelations is upon us."

"If you'd like to follow me, my lord." The knight beckoned, his voice laced with respect and a hint of urgency. Vlad's gaze locked with the knight's, a silent understanding passing between them. With a curt nod, Vlad acknowledged the man's command, ready to confront whatever awaited him beyond the confines of the Knight's Hall.

Radu, his eyes gleaming with anticipation and intrigue, rose from his chair. His movements were fluid and confident. He trailed behind Vlad, a calculated distance maintained between them as they made their way toward the threshold of the hall. The cool air outside greeted them, though the sun cast long shadows across the castle courtyard.

As Vlad's gaze swept across the courtyard, his eyes widened in disbelief and fury. Before him stood a grand stage, a macabre spectacle designed to taunt and torment. The centre of attention were two colossal bird cages suspended in mid-air, their iron bars casting long shadows upon the ground below.

Inside the first cage, his heart sank at the sight of his father. Once a proud prince, his spirit was crushed under the weight of captivity. The flicker of hope that had ignited within Vlad's heart was instantly extinguished, replaced by a seething rage that burned like wildfire.

In the adjacent cage, his eyes locked with Jade's. Her usually vibrant and defiant gaze was now filled with fear and uncertainty.

The cages swayed gently in the breeze, their occupants trapped and vulnerable, subject to the whims of their captor.

Anguish flooded his veins, blending with a volatile mix of fury and resolve. His fists clenched, knuckles blanching as he struggled to rein in the tempest inside. This was a targeted blow to all he cherished, a ruthless gambit devised to crush his soul and probe the depths of his tenacity.

His gaze darted between the cages, capturing his father's weary eyes pleading for salvation, and Jade's blend of desperation and trust, imploring him to rescue them from torment.

"Wait, wait! Before you say anything, let's not forget about the pièce de résistance," Radu exclaimed, a wicked gleam in his eyes.

Alessandra emerged from the depths of the dungeon, her presence transformed. Clad in a tight-fitting leather ensemble that accentuated her lithe form, she exuded an aura of both danger and allure. Her dark hair cascaded in waves down her back, framing her face like a mysterious veil. Her eyes, once filled with innocence, now gleamed with a fierce determination, like smouldering embers ready to ignite.

In her hand, she wielded a large whip, its coiled leather an emblem of the power she held. With each step, the echo of her boots against the cobblestones resonated through the courtyard, a rhythmic beat that echoed her newfound confidence. Her movements were purposeful, every sway of her hips and arch of her back hinting at a hidden strength.

She carried herself with the commanding presence of a ringmaster at a circus, a master of ceremonies in this twisted game. Her whip cracked through the air, creating an electric anticipation, the sound slicing through the silence like a sharp command.

Vlad's muscles tensed as he felt Radu's hand firmly gripping his shoulder, restraining him from rushing to Alessandra's side. With a glimmer of defiance in his eyes, Vlad turned to face his brother, his voice laced with anger and desperation. "Enough games, Radu! She's suffered enough at your hands. Release them now!"

Radu's grip tightened, his fingers digging into Vlad's flesh. It was a silent warning that resistance would only bring further consequences. A sinister smile curled on his lips, a twisted pleasure derived from the suffering he inflicted upon others. "But brother, the show has only just begun. We can't disappoint our audience, can we?"

Vlad's jaw clenched. His gaze fixed on Alessandra as she commanded the focus of the onlookers. Her whip cracked through the air with a resounding echo. He knew Radu basked in this sadistic performance, revelling in the chaos he had orchestrated. But Vlad couldn't bear to see Alessandra subjected to further torment, her spirit manipulated for the amusement of their twisted brotherhood.

"You can save one. Maybe... Choose wisely before your lover tears them to shreds," Radu uttered.

Vlad's muscles tensed as he turned to face his treacherous brother, his voice laced with anger and desperation. "You expect me to choose? You think I can condemn any of them to such a fate?"

Radu's laughter echoed through the courtyard, chilling Vlad to the bone. "Choices must be made, sacrifices must be offered. Such is the price of power." His eyes gleamed with malicious delight.

"Then I choose them all," Vlad uttered, his voice filled with a newfound doggedness.

CHAPTER 10

As Vlad summoned a surge of his power and directed it towards Radu, he predicted the impact of his attack. However, to his surprise, an invisible barrier materialised in front of Radu, intercepting the blast and preventing any harm from reaching him. The barrier shimmered with an otherworldly energy, revealing the intricate web of dark magic that protected Radu.

Azaroth's voice resonated with a chilling undertone as he addressed Vlad, his words laced with a sinister allure. "Ah, Vlad, my dear brother, it seems time has clouded your perception. Allow me to reintroduce myself. I am Azaroth, a being born from darkness, the harbinger of chaos, and the embodiment of your shattered brother, Radu."

Vlad's eyes widened with shock and dread as the truth of Azaroth's identity unfolded before him. The realisation that his twisted adversary was an amalgamation of his own flesh and blood sent a shiver down his spine.

Azaroth's sinister smile widened, his gaze filled with perverse satisfaction. "Yes, dear Vlad, I hold the memories of your betrayal, the abandonment you inflicted upon your kin. You brought me into his existence through your ambition."

Vlad's features contorted with anguish and remorse as he confronted the consequences of his past choices. The weight of guilt pressed upon him, threatening to suffocate his spirit. He had once believed his decisions were justified, but now he faced the embodiment of his forsaken brother, a stark reminder of the pain he had caused.

"It is fitting that we stand here, facing one another in this twisted dance of destiny," Azaroth continued, his voice a venomous hiss. "Our intertwined paths converge at this moment, and the echoes of our shared past reverberate through the present."

Vlad's resolve hardened, his gaze meeting Azaroth's. "I may carry the burden of my mistakes, the consequences of my actions, but I will not let them define me. I will face you, Azaroth, and put an end to this cycle of darkness that ensnares us both."

Azaroth's voice dripped with venomous mockery as he taunted Vlad, his words cutting through the air like icy shards. "Do you remember the Sultan's court? The place where we both suffered, where we were both prisoners of war. Tell me, brother, do you recall who escaped that wretched fate? It was you, Vlad, who left me behind to face the horrors that awaited."

Vlad's heart sank as the weight of his betrayal settled upon him, mingling with guilt and regret. The memories of that fateful day at the Sultan's court flooded his mind, haunting him like spectres from the past. He could still see Radu's pleading eyes, the desperation etched upon his face as Vlad made his escape.

"I thought of nothing but survival," Vlad murmured, his voice heavy with remorse. "I believed that if I could break free, I could save us both. But I was wrong. So very wrong. I never knew the extent of the horrors that awaited you and the torment you had to endure."

Azaroth's laughter cut through the air, a chilling symphony that echoed with cruel satisfaction. "Survival, dear brother, comes at a steep price. The Turks, in their insidious pursuit of power, subjected me to unspeakable experiments. Each one more sadistic than the last, stripping away my humanity until all that remained was a vessel for darkness."

Vlad's eyes glistened with unshed tears, his heart aching with the weight of his brother's suffering. He reached out a hand, trembling with longing and regret. "Radu, forgive me. I never wanted this for you. I never intended to leave you behind."

Azaroth's smirk twisted into a malevolent grin, his eyes gleaming with malice. "Your words of remorse hold no weight, Vlad. The past cannot be undone, and the torment I endured has moulded me into what I am now. I embraced the darkness to survive, to cling to a semblance of existence."

Tears welled up in Vlad's eyes, a mixture of grief and desperation. "I will find a way to free you, Radu. I will undo the sins of our past and bring you back from this abyss."

Azaroth's laughter reverberated, seeming to mock Vlad's hope. "Foolish, naïve brother. Redemption is an elusive dream, and the path to salvation is paved with blood and sacrifice. The darkness that consumes me now is the legacy of our shared pain."

Vlad's heart shattered, burdened by the weight of his brother's suffering and the realisation that their fates were forever intertwined. Determination flared within him, fuelled by a desperate need for redemption. "I will confront your darkness, Azaroth. I will fight for my brother's freedom and reclaim the bond we lost."

The demon's grin widened, his eyes burning with malevolence. "Fight if you must, dear brother." As Azaroth's wicked laughter echoed through the air, a cloud of darkness surged forth, engulfing Vlad in its suffocating grip. The inky blackness swirled around him, obscuring his vision and sapping his strength. The air turned heavy with malevolence, as if the very essence of evil had taken form.

Vlad's heart pounded in his chest, his senses heightened as he braced himself for the battle that lay ahead. With a primal roar, he summoned his inner power, a surge of energy that radiated from his core. His eyes glowed with an intense determination, piercing through the darkness like fiery beacons.

Amid the swirling abyss, Azaroth materialised, his form wreathed in shadows. His eyes glinted with a feral hunger, his lips curled into a sadistic grin. With a swift motion of his hand, tendrils of darkness shot forth, lashing towards Vlad like venomous serpents.

Vlad's reflexes kicked into overdrive as he dodged and weaved, his movements a symphony of agility and precision. His body moved with a dancer's grace, his muscles coiling and releasing as he evaded each assault. But the darkness was relentless, a ferocious adversary that sought to consume him.

Summoning his own powers, Vlad unleashed bolts of searing light from his fingertips, aiming to disperse the encroaching darkness. The beams of radiance sliced through the shadowy tendrils, momentarily pushing back the encroaching abyss. But Azaroth merely laughed, his voice carrying a chilling edge.

"You think your feeble light can overcome the depths of darkness?" the demon taunted, his voice dripping with disdain. "I am the embodiment of shadows, born from the very despair that festers within human souls."

Ignoring the taunts, Vlad clenched his sword, revelling in

the surging power that pulsed within him. He closed his eyes, focusing his energy, and channelled it into his blade. As his concentration peaked, the very essence of his weapon transformed.

The single blade multiplied before his eyes, splitting into thousands of shimmering projections that filled the surrounding air. The courtyard became awash with an ethereal sea of deadly projectiles, each one a glimmering testament to Vlad's newfound strength.

With a flick of his hands, Vlad unleashed the onslaught of shimmering blades, propelling them towards Azaroth. The missiles sliced through the oppressive darkness, piercing the veil of shadows that surrounded his enemy.

The sea of projectiles closed in on Azaroth, their relentless assault tearing through the fabric of darkness. They collided with Azaroth's defences, their radiant light clashing with the malevolent shadows that shielded him.

But Azaroth was no ordinary foe. Like a dancer embracing chaos, he gracefully weaved between the glimmering projectiles, his motions fluid and precise.

Yet Vlad's willpower did not waver. He adjusted his strategy, his mind sharp and focused. With a surge of power, he sent forth a concentrated beam of energy, cutting through the remaining darkness and converging upon Azaroth. The beam bore down upon him, searing through the shadows with its fiery brilliance.

The demon, surprised by the intensified assault, staggered momentarily, his facade of invincibility cracking. The beam pierced through his defences, grazing his form and leaving a burning mark upon his flesh. An enraged hiss escaped his lips as he recoiled from the burning pain.

Vlad seized the opportunity, capitalising on Azaroth's momentary vulnerability. He pressed forward, closing the distance between them with resolute purpose. His sword, still pulsating with the remains of his power, found its mark, slashing through the surviving barriers and striking true.

Azaroth's voice resonated with a commanding tone, cutting through the tension. "Alessandra, heed my call and come to my side. Show everyone where your loyalty stands."

Alessandra's eyes glazed over as the spell took hold, eroding her will. She stepped forward, taking out a dagger from her boot, her voice devoid of emotion. "As you command, Master. I will fulfil my duty."

Vlad's heart sank, a mix of anguish and desperation filling his voice. "Alessandra, please, snap out of it! Fight against his control. Remember our love."

Alessandra's gaze remained fixed on Azaroth, her movements cold and mechanical. "Love is a weakness."

Azaroth grinned wickedly, revelling in the discord he had sown. "Vlad, your pleas fall on deaf ears. Alessandra belongs to me now. Prepare to face her wrath."

Vlad's eyes burned with determination as he readied himself for the inevitable clash. "If I must face her, then I will do so, hoping our love will prevail. Even in darkness, there is light."

The battle began, each strike punctuated by the clash of weapons and the sounds of swirling energy. Alessandra, under Azaroth's influence, attacked with calculated precision, her blows fuelled by his dark power.

Vlad skilfully evaded her attacks, his movements driven by a mix of self-preservation and a desperate desire to break the spell. "Alessandra, please listen to me! Remember the moments we shared, the bond we forged!"

Alessandra's voice remained detached, devoid of emotion. "You talk too much. Stop playing and fight me!"

With every parry and dodge, Vlad sought to reach the

depths of Alessandra's heart, hoping to rekindle the spark of their connection. "Alessandra, remember who you truly are. You are not a pawn of darkness. You are a warrior of light, my love."

As the clash between Vlad and Alessandra intensified, a spark of realisation ignited within Vlad's mind. He knew he had to break the hold Azaroth had over her. With a quick calculation, he feigned a momentary stumble, allowing Alessandra to close in on him.

Seizing the opportunity, Vlad swiftly closed the distance between them, his hands reaching out to cradle her face. In that fleeting moment, their eyes locked, and he poured every ounce of his love, every cherished memory, into that gaze. For a split second, her eyes softened, a hint of recognition flickering within them.

As their lips touched in a desperate, bittersweet kiss, time seemed to pause momentarily. Vlad's heart ached with a blend of trust and sorrow, hoping against all odds that this act of love would break through the shadows and bring Alessandra back to him.

But even as their lips met, Alessandra's hand, still under the influence of Azaroth, remained firm. In a cruel twist of fate, she thrust her dagger forward, piercing Vlad's heart.

Pain seared through Vlad's body as the blade found its mark. He gasped in agony. The taste of blood mingled with the ghost of their kiss as he stumbled backward, his gaze locked with Alessandra's.

Tears welled up in his eyes, a mixture of anguish and love. "Alessa..."

A SUDDEN JOLT COURSED THROUGH ALESSANDRA'S BEING, shattering the hold Azaroth had over her. Panic gripped her heart as the realisation of what she had done washed over her. She stumbled back, her eyes widening in horror at the sight of Vlad's wounded form.

"No..." Alessandra gasped, her voice trembling with disbelief and regret. She clutched her shaking hands to her chest, her body shuddering with the weight of her actions. The darkness that had clouded her mind for far too long dissipated, and the genuine horror of the situation unfolded before her.

Vlad's brows furrowed, his features contorting with pain as he locked eyes with Alessandra. In that moment of intense connection, a tumultuous storm of emotions surged within him. Anguish clouded his gaze, etching lines of sorrow upon his face as if a weight had settled upon his soul. Yet, amidst the agony, a flicker of understanding danced in his eyes, a glimpse of recognition that spoke of the intricate web of experiences they had shared. The unspoken words in their gaze conveyed a depth of emotion and a profound sense of the complex journey that had brought them to this moment.

Tears welled up in Alessandra's eyes as she fell to her knees, her strength draining from her body. "Vlad... I... I'm so sorry," she choked out, her voice tinged with regret. She reached out a trembling hand toward him, but the weight of guilt kept her from closing the distance.

Vlad's voice, strained and filled with both sorrow and a flicker of forgiveness, reached her ears. "Alessandra, it's not too late," he whispered, his words carrying a faint glimmer of hope. "Fight the darkness that has consumed you. Remember who you are."

Alessandra's heart wavered between despair and the small spark of hope Vlad's words ignited within her. She realised that her true self had been trapped beneath the veil of Azaroth's influence, and the moment of clarity she now experienced was a precious gift.

Alessandra's voice, laced with newfound strength, echoed through the chaos of the battlefield. Her golden eyes blazed with a radiant light, an emblem of the angelic powers that surged within her. With each passing moment, her steadfastness grew, fuelled by the love she held for Vlad and the desire to free him from the clutches of darkness.

With a wave of her hand, a shimmering golden barrier materialised around Vlad, cocooning him in a protective embrace. The barrier sparkled with divine energy, warding off any harm that threatened to reach him. Alessandra's touch upon Vlad's face was gentle, her fingers tracing a path of reassurance.

"Hang in there, Vlad," she whispered, her voice filled with tenderness and determination. "You're safe now. I won't let anyone harm you."

Turning her gaze towards Azaroth, Alessandra's countenance shifted from fear to resolve. The weight of her past dances with darkness had transformed into a steely desire to break free from his influence once and for all.

"I have danced to your tune for far too long," she declared, her voice ringing out with a strength that belied her previous vulnerability. "But today, the music changes. It's time for you to face the consequences of your actions."

Alessandra unleashed her angelic powers, gathering the pure energy within her being. Golden light radiated from her, casting a brilliant glow upon the battlefield. Wings of light unfurled from her back, their ethereal beauty contrasting with the darkness that had threatened to consume her.

With a swift movement, she lunged at Azaroth, her movements fluid and graceful. Her whip crackled with celestial energy as it whirled through the air, lashing with precision. With every strike, the burden of liberation and justice resonated, showcasing her newfound strength and need to break free from the shackles of control.

The battlefield was a symphony of chaos and fury, the clash of powers resounding through the air. Alessandra, now fully unleashed in her angelic form, stood tall and resolute, her eyes ablaze with a righteous fire. The weight of her past struggles and the battles fought echoed in her heart, fuelling her determination to bring an end to the darkness that had plagued her.

Azaroth, his once confident demeanour now tinged with uncertainty, met Alessandra's gaze. His dark eyes flickered with a blend of desperation and defiance. "You think you can defeat me, little angel?" he sneered, his voice laced with arrogance. "You're just a mere puppet, a vessel for powers you cannot fully comprehend."

Alessandra's response came swift and unwavering, her voice resonating with a clarity that cut through the chaos. "I may have been your puppet once, but no longer. I am guided by love, by the strength of my heart, and the light within me. And that is a force you can never extinguish."

As their powers clashed, Alessandra could feel the weight of her journey, the sacrifices made, and the resilience that had carried her through. She pushed forward, her heart resolute and her will unyielding. The battle was not only a physical one but a battle for her very soul, a testament to her ability to rise above the darkness that had sought to claim her.

"You cannot defeat me!" Azaroth spat, his voice laced with desperation, as he attempted to rally himself. "I am eternal! Darkness will always prevail!"

Alessandra's voice cut through the chaos, filled with a conviction that resonated with the very fabric of her being. "Darkness may linger, but light endures. Love and hope will always triumph over the darkest of shadows."

With a last surge of energy, Alessandra unleashed a torrent of celestial power, a dazzling display of radiant light that enveloped Azaroth. The darkness recoiled and dissipated, replaced by the brilliance of the light she emanated. Azaroth's form exploded and turned to dust.

As the last echoes of the battle faded, Alessandra stood amidst the aftermath, her chest heaving with the exertion of her fight. She surveyed the battlefield and the defeated demon who lay in a pile of ash before her.

Alessandra's heart swelled with both relief and concern as she released Ash and Jade from their captivity. She ensured their safety before turning her attention back to Vlad, who lay still beneath the protective embrace of her magic barrier.

Approaching him with gentle steps, Alessandra knelt beside Vlad, her hands trembling slightly as she reached out to touch his face. His features, once filled with determination, now wore the weariness of the battle and the weight of their shared ordeal.

"Vlad," she whispered, her voice laced with tenderness and worry. "You're safe now. We're safe."

Alessandra's panic surged through her veins like a torrential wave as she watched Vlad lying still, unresponsive to her words. Fear clutched at her heart, threatening to drown her in a sea of despair.

"No," she pleaded, her voice trembling with desperation. "Vlad, please. Don't leave me." Her voice cracked, betraying her anguish as she gently shook his shoulder, hoping for any sign of life.

Alessandra's heart pounded against her chest, its rhythm matching the frantic beat of her thoughts. The weight of the moment bore down upon her, pressing against her chest with an unbearable force. Each passing second without a response from Vlad felt like an eternity, amplifying her anguish to unimaginable heights.

The courtyard seemed to close in around her, the air thick with tension and unspoken fears. Her breaths came in shallow gasps, barely providing the oxygen her trembling body demanded.

Tears streamed freely down Alessandra's face, their salty trails marking her cheeks with glistening despair. The ache in her chest intensified, a visceral pain that tore through her being. Her voice, strained and fragile, echoed in the air, pleading for a sign, any sign, that the man she loved still clung to the thread of life.

The weight of his fate, their shared destiny, settled upon her shoulders like an unbearable burden, threatening to crush her spirit.

With every passing moment, her panic transformed into a desperate resolve. She refused to accept defeat, refused to let the darkness claim the one person who had become her beacon of light in a world that had grown increasingly dim. Her trembling hands pressed harder against Vlad's unmoving form, as if willing her own life force into him, urging his dormant spirit to awaken.

Time seemed to warp and distort, its passage becoming indistinguishable as her hope teetered on the precipice of despair. But just as the darkness threatened to engulf her, a flicker of movement, almost imperceptible, stirred within

Vlad. It was a faint pulse of life, a whispered promise that rekindled the dying flame within her.

Alessandra's tear-filled eyes widened, hope flooding her features as she watched Vlad's eyelids flutter. The slightest sign of consciousness sparked a renewed surge of determination within her. She clasped his hand tighter, as if anchoring him to the world they shared, refusing to let him slip away.

"Vlad," she whispered, her voice both a plea and a prayer. "Come back to me. Fight, my love. Fight."

As if in response to her impassioned plea, Vlad's eyes slowly opened, revealing a glimpse of the vibrant soul that lived within. The heaviness that had weighed upon Alessandra's heart lifted, replaced by a surge of relief so powerful it brought her to her knees beside him.

A single tear slipped down Vlad's cheek, mirroring the mix of emotions that flooded their shared space. His voice, weak yet resolute, pierced the stillness, echoing with the strength of their unbreakable bond.

"Alessandra," he croaked, his voice a fragile melody in the air. "I'm here."

Overwhelmed by a cascade of emotions, Alessandra's tears mingled with a smile that bloomed upon her lips. She caressed Vlad's face, tracing the contours of his features with trembling fingertips, grateful for the flicker of life that remained within him.

"I thought I lost you," she confessed, her voice a tender whisper. "But you're here. You're with me."

Vlad mustered his strength, his gaze meeting hers with a fierce steel that mirrored her own. His hand found hers, intertwining their fingers, bridging the divide that had threatened to consume them. In that sacred moment, time stood still, allowing them to savour the depth of their love and the triumph over the trials that had tested their very essence.

"Alessa," he whispered, his words infused with a blend of gratitude and determination. "We've endured the darkest of storms, but we've emerged together, stronger than ever. Our love has defied all odds, and it will guide us as we rebuild and reclaim what was lost."

Tears glistened in Alessandra's eyes as she held tightly onto Vlad's hand, her touch a lifeline that transcended the physical realm. Their intertwined fingers became a symbol of unity and unwavering support, proof that their bond could withstand even the harshest tribulations. They had faced down their demons and emerged victorious, their hearts beating as one in the face of uncertainty.

As they stood together, their gaze locked in a silent understanding, Alessandra knew that no matter what challenges lay ahead, they would face them together, hand in hand, their love a beacon of light in the darkness that surrounded them.

THE END

THE VEILED HUNTRESS

CHAPTER 1

As acrid smoke surrounded her, Avery felt a sharp sting in her eyes, blurring her vision into a hazy mist. Amid the crackling flames, her pulse seemed to echo in her ears, a foreboding feeling weighing heavily in her stomach.

The commanding figure, whose memory had haunted Avery's restless dreams, remained seated on his ominous obsidian throne. The emotions flooded over her, especially the burning anger at how her childhood had been twisted and stolen for his benefit.

Avery felt a chilling shiver as her father's cold voice echoed in the chamber. "Welcome back, daughter," it purred, as sleek and lethal as a dagger concealed in silk.

Avery tightly clenched her hands, desperately searching for courage. "I won't be your puppet any longer," she declared, praying her voice did not tremble and betray her.

Darmon observed her, his pale eyes devoid of life just like a midwinter moon. A slow, predatory smile stretched across his face. "You can never escape your destiny. It is carved into your very bones. You will always be my aide and serve my ambitions."

Unwanted memories flooded Avery's mind; excruciating experiments that melted flesh from bone and the endless trials where a single failure meant death. The soul-crushing moments where her heart had shattered, along with her trust in her father. She shook under the immense weight of the past, wondering if she had the strength to keep its sinister grasp from stealing her future.

Avery took a steeling breath, desperately willing strength into her trembling limbs. "I decide my fate now," she asserted. "I won't let you manipulate me again."

Darmon's condescending click of the tongue struck Avery like a heart-wrenching whip, fuelling her anger and humiliation.

His icy stare sliced through her, as sharp and invasive as a blade splitting flesh from bone. She fought the urge to recoil, to shield her vulnerability from his ruthless gaze, which seemed to dissect the very secrets of her soul.

"You truly believed you could escape me, daughter?" Darmon purred, a predator toying with helpless prey. He rose from his imposing obsidian throne, darkness swirling about him like a vengeful spectre.

A hurricane of conflicted emotions thrashed inside her. Defiant anger warred with lingering grief for the loving father she had always longed for him to be. Her heart seemed on the verge of bursting from the pressure.

"It is your destiny to serve my ambitions," Darmon pronounced, his tone invoking images of unmarked graves and forgotten victims. "With your powers harnessed, we shall conquer the supernatural world and seize control of the realm."

Unwanted tears pricked hotly at Avery's eyes, but she

refused to shed them, to show even that small weakness. "I won't allow you to twist me into a weapon," she insisted, nails carving crescents into her fists. "My life belongs with Lucien now."

A cruel smile split Darmon's stony face. His pale eyes stared through her, devoid of the faintest spark of empathy or mercy. "That vampire has filled your head with frivolous fantasies, but it is far too late to fight fate's design."

In a sudden burst of preternatural speed, his claws clamped her throat in an iron grip. Skin sizzled under the unnatural heat of his grasp. Agony erupted within Avery, but she clung desperately to her love for Lucien—an escape keeping her tethered as she drifted toward unrelenting darkness.

Through the bleak haze smothering her mind, she gritted out her vow. "You won't succeed..."

Oblivion slowly consumed Avery's vision. Darmon's voice rolled out like a chilling bell in the still night air. "When you wake, we will have started anew," it purred.

As darkness enveloped Avery's dwindling consciousness, her thoughts instinctively sought Lucien with an unwavering, desperate yearning.

"Lucien... don't lose hope," she whispered weakly, clutching at the lifeline of their bond as her strength seeped away. "I will find my way back to you again."

Though the world fell away around her into endless shadow, Avery focused every ounce of her unwavering determination on their connection, mentally screaming his name.

Lucien... listen. My father is coming...

In a tranquil instant, she experienced the reassuring warmth of Lucien's presence, akin to an unseen, radiant hand softly entwining with hers. A tiny flame of faith kindled within her heart. She could almost feel the comforting pressure of Lucien clasping her hand, his voice echoing distantly but edged with worry.

Avery! What happened? Where are you?

Before she could respond, intense pain erupted through her body, originating from Darmon's ruthless efforts to sever their bond. Agony wracked through her as she involuntarily cried out. Lucien's desperate voice grew fainter as darkness dragged Avery backwards.

No! Avery, don't go! I will find you, I swear it... Just hang on...

Avery drifted aimlessly in that vast, impenetrable night, her thoughts sluggish and disjointed. Unwanted memories assaulted her—the agony of endless experiments, being forced to betray Lucien. It would be dangerously easy to surrender hope here, to let exhaustion overpower her.

But Avery clung fiercely to one unshakeable truth: she would never again be Darmon's puppet. She was a fighter who carved her own destiny. If only she could break free of this smothering darkness, she would stand against him once more. *Wake up!* she commanded her leaden body. But she felt terrifyingly frail, drained of all power and will.

"You are mine now, daughter." Her father's bone-chilling voice echoed through her mind. "Resign yourself to your fate."

The battle within Avery still burned. "No..." she murmured, her whisper dripping with defiance. Though physically subdued, her spirit remained indomitable. Her resolve to defy him remained staunch.

She wandered through the vast emptiness, her eyes scouring for a glimmer in the engulfing shadows that menaced to swallow her essence. The conviction that guiding stars endured in this abyss held onto her, akin to Lucien's steadfast love—a constant beacon in her heart.

Avery plunged relentlessly into the void, feeling a sense of self fraying at the edges with each heartbeat. But she clung to the last burning shreds of courage, fanning their fire with memories of stolen hours with Lucien—secret meetings at the Old Church, the electric thrill of their first kiss, the rare smiles that transformed him. She wrapped these precious moments around her like shields against despair.

As endless darkness pressed down on her, smothering like a physical weight, Avery felt hopelessness's insidious poison seeping through the cracks in her resolve. "Please," she whispered into the void, "give me a fighting chance. I cannot endure this alone."

With the last dregs of her strength, Avery hurled her plea into the lightless abyss, praying some benevolent force lingered within these shadows. "Lucien, I need you now more than ever. Please, you must find me..."

Suddenly, a vision pierced the gloom; Lucien standing defiantly before Darmon's shadowy throne, his features etched with rage.

"You will not claim her," he pronounced, his voice heavy with power and shaking the very air. Quick as light, his Katana slashed through the clinging darkness. Blinding radiance erupted from the silver blade, banishing the oppressive shadows.

The vision vanished as suddenly as it had appeared, leaving longing and renewed belief tangled within Avery like threads pulling her in opposite directions. Had she merely conjured a fantasy from desperation? Or had Lucien truly discovered some way to bridge the unfathomable divide separating them?

She had no notion whether their bond could transcend this cursed oblivion. Still, she poured every ounce of her waning spirit into that fragile lifeline of belief.

Suddenly, Avery felt a subtle shift in the darkness,

followed by the faintest sliver of a beloved voice whispering her name, impossibly distant but achingly familiar.

"Avery..."

Elation surged wildly within her. "Lucien!" she cried with raw desperation, willing her voice to breach the gap. "Save me, I beg you."

Through their tenuous link, Avery felt the full force of Lucien's emotions collide into her—bottomless love entwined with rage and determination. She focused every fibre of her being on strengthening their connection, pushing against the abyss with all her might until she could feel the brush of his spirit against hers.

The shadows shuddered, seeming to recoil from the brilliance of their bond.

His voice resonated through her mind with conviction, each word a glowing promise. *"I am coming for you."*

Avery clung to the fragile spark of confidence now kindling within her. Together, their love could illuminate even the blackest night.

CHAPTER 2

Lucien paced the moonlit courtyard, a tempest of dread and frustration churning within him. Each minute that crawled by in silence felt like another merciless cut across his already ravaged heart. The quiet itself seemed alive, a stifling veil weighing down upon him.

Sinister thoughts haunted Lucien's mind, painted in indelible shades of blood and anguish. Had Darmon already extinguished the fiery light in Avery's defiant eyes? Subjected her to unimaginable agony simply because he could? Lucien dug his nails ruthlessly into his palms until crimson welled up, channelling waves of rage at his own helplessness to protect her.

At last, his comrades shuffled into view, their hollow expressions mirroring the bleak pain roiling inside Lucien. Haunted shadows lingered in their downcast eyes, echoes of whatever fresh trauma the Order had so callously inflicted. Lucien's soul cried out in anguish at the visible evidence of their suffering. He yearned to erase the vivid pain marking their features, to restore even a glimmer of hope's light back into their weary hearts. But Lucien feared they had lost such innocence now, just one more casualty in this endless conflict shadowed by his old employer's cruelty.

As the battered group hobbled inside, Lucien's gaze raked their bodies, taking stock of each visible wound his comrades had been forced to endure. "What new torments did the Order inflict?" he bit out through clenched teeth as he gently treated a vicious gash marring Jade's arm.

She offered a faint, hollow laugh, barely disguising bone-deep exhaustion. "Nothing we have not survived before." But her flickering eyes betrayed the truth: Darmon was slowly extinguishing even their formidable endurance.

After settling the group as comfortably as their ravaged forms would allow, Lucien joined Vlad, where he broodingly watched the hearth's dying embers decay to sullen ash.

Vlad's lip curled in disgust. "We should raze the Order's strongholds for this. Make them truly suffer as we have endured." His knuckles whitened as if already wrapped around his tormentors' throats.

But Lucien just gazed sightlessly into the faint glow, all light leached from his blue eyes by fear and anguish. "More violence will only breed darker shadows. We need light." His voice dropped to a tortured whisper. "Or I fear we shall lose hers forever."

The words seemed to drain the feverish rage from Vlad. Grim understanding softened his expression. They had won the battle with Azaroth, but this larger war still threatened to snuff all fragile confidence, starting with the bright flame of Avery's spirit if they could not reach her in time...

ALESSANDRA'S CRIES, RAW WITH ANGUISH, SLICED THROUGH the stillness of the night. Her mind, ensnared in torment's unyielding grip, shivered under the onslaught of vivid nightmares. In this maelstrom of despair, Vlad's murmurs drifted like a calming balm, his words weaving a sanctuary around her. Gently, he held her quivering form, anchoring her to safety, and drawing her away from the precipice of her fears.

From the doorway, Lucien observed them, a deep ache hollowing his chest. Silently, he sent up a fervent prayer into the shadows, smothering his soul. "Avery, wherever you are, I swear I will save you." He clung to this vow like an ember kindling against despair's frigid gusts. "Our love must be the beacon to guide you home and banish the darkness haunting you..."

He started his tireless pacing in the moon-washed courtyard as if sheer momentum could somehow close the unfathomable distance still separating him from Avery. Each restless step marked his doggedness. He was determined to search through every hidden crevice of existence if it meant holding his love safely in his arms again. Until then, only love and faith could accompany him in the small hours of this interminable night.

At last, Vlad emerged, his grim features softening with empathy as he met Lucien's hollow gaze. In that shared moment bloomed an unspoken camaraderie. No matter what fresh hells awaited them on the path ahead, they would confront the flames together to shield their loved ones. Without the persistent glow of Avery and Alessandra's spirits, only a void would remain, and they were firmly committed to not letting endless darkness claim their victory.

"How's Alessandra doing?" Lucien finally whispered, loathe to further disturb the fraught stillness.

Vlad exhaled heavily. "Ill at ease still. The memory of my blood on her hands haunts her. She woke screaming, begging my forgiveness for nearly taking my life while enthralled." His tortured gaze met Lucien's. "I fear I will lose her to remorse," Vlad confessed, his voice dropping lower. Beneath the weight of Alessandra's agony, his formerly proud shoulders sagged.

Lucien gripped Vlad's arm, willing his own conviction into the gesture. "You know she was the Order's helpless puppet then. The guilt belongs to her tormentors alone."

Vlad grimaced. "I know, yet she cannot absolve herself. She flinches from my touch, fearing she will cause me harm again." Raw anguish carved new lines across his weary features.

Lucien swallowed against the ache in his own throat, grasping for words of solace. "Give her time," he urged gently. "Keep showing Alessandra that your love remains unshaken."

At last, Vlad summoned a small but grateful smile. "As ever, your counsel provides needed perspective, nephew. My bond with Alessandra will mend, I am certain, however long the process may take."

Lucien's chest constricted, the journey ahead seeming endless and shrouded in gloom. "I, too, must keep my trust in Avery," he whispered. "And hope that she can find her way back through whatever darkness imprisons her now."

Vlad's weathered features softened with solemn empathy. He cradled Lucien's cheek in one battle-scarred hand as if the gesture could help shoulder his torment.

"Have courage," the older vampire urged gently. "No force can eternally separate what destiny has firmly linked. Either we shall reclaim the women we hold dear from this darkness, or we shall spend eternity combing every obscure realm in our relentless pursuit of their light."

Their gazes locked, pouring waves of conviction and a shared purpose that words could never adequately capture.

"For now, try to rest," Vlad implored. "The nights to come will demand every ounce of resilience and valour we can muster."

Lucien shut his eyes in the face of a wave of sorrow. How did one rest when cruel oblivion threatened to consume his other half? When the soul cried out constantly for its missing piece, its vital orbit thrown disastrously off balance?

Still, he forced a brusque nod of acquiescence to Vlad's wisdom. Too many relied on him holding the fraying threads of composure and leadership together to allow himself to unravel now. Somehow, he must distil all his volcanic grief into steely, enduring patience and fortitude. Anything less could mean surrendering his guiding star—his beloved Avery—to inescapable darkness forever.

With Vlad's departure, silence once more claimed dominion over the moonlit courtyard. Lucien resumed his ceaseless pacing, each weighted step echoing with the agonising beat of uncertainty throbbing sickeningly inside him.

Amidst the stillness surrounding him, an odd sensation sparked along the periphery of his consciousness—subtle yet oddly magnetic, like the phantom tug of a muted heartbeat straining toward connection.

Lucien froze in his tracks, every finely honed sense focusing to razor sharpness. Could it be...? Reaching desperately along the slender filament of psychic connection binding his soul to Avery's, he poured every mote of concentration and yearning into that fragile lifeline.

And then, scarcely daring to breathe in the stillness, he felt it. The faintest brush of Avery's beloved essence against his. Fragmented and impossibly distant, yet undeniably her. A maelstrom of elation and terror crashed through Lucien. She lived, struggling across some unfathomable gulf to reach him from whatever malign prison Darmon had devised.

Not wasting a heartbeat more, Lucien hurled his own devotion back to her along with their tenuous thread of connection.

"Avery! What happened? Where are you?"

Silence.

"I will find you, I swear it... Just hang on..."

The stillness absorbed his ardent vow. Somewhere, somehow, perhaps she had caught his whispered promise between one faltering breath and the next.

Drawing a shaky breath, Lucien tilted his head toward the soft moonlight above in silent supplication. *"I am coming for you."*

The connection dimmed as swiftly as a guttering candle, leaving Lucien stranded in crushing silence and doubt. Yet even that fleeting, fragile lifeline had reignited the smouldering embers of conviction buried deep within his embattled spirit.

He clung to that tenacious light desperately, letting it guide him like a lone star scintillating against the endless night. No matter how lost Avery herself seemed in some vast, dark abyss, Lucien silently vowed he would follow that flame's beckoning promise anywhere. He'd traverse straight through the darkest hellscape and guarded perils imaginable just to shelter his beloved safely in his arms once more.

With siege-hardened resolve reinforcing his every fibre, Lucien turned on his heel to abandon the empty, moonwashed courtyard, his boots echoing with fierce purpose. His thoughts galvanised now around assembling the forces and strategic counsel needed for the battle looming ominously ahead. The time they so desperately required to save Avery was swiftly bleeding away.

As he rushed to phone Lóthurr, his heart pounded with anxiety, hope, and a simmering fury barely held in check. "Have you heard anything about Avery?" he demanded urgently.

Sympathy filled Lóthurr's tone, though it carried a heavy weight of gravity. "I'm afraid Darmon has taken the girl deeper underground. But don't lose faith—help is on the way."

Lucien's grip on the phone tightened, and he willed himself to remain steady. "Who's going to help us out?"

"A gypsy witch. A valued ally and friend to our cause," Lóthurr explained. "Her magic is formidable. If your bond with Avery remains, she might be able to trace her."

Lucien closed his eyes for a moment, releasing a shaky breath. Relief washed over him like a soothing wave. "Thanks, buddy. With the witch on our side, we can get through these never-ending shadows."

"Stay strong, Lucien. We will bring her back safely," Lóthurr promised.

After ending the call, Lucien's resolve grew stronger, preparing him for the upcoming challenges. He had spent too much time hiding, watching evil grow unchecked. That was about to change. Now, with courageous friends bound together by loyalty, they were ready to fight back and restore what was right. They would either lift the darkness covering the land, or Lucien would break through it himself to save what he cherished most.

At the sound of approaching footsteps, Lucien turned sharply, a predator sensing vulnerable prey. But it was only

Vlad who stepped from the gloom, face carved with solemn purpose.

"Any developments on Avery?" Lucien enquired through gritted teeth, his gaze drilling into the other man in search of any revealing information.

Vlad responded with a solemn shake of his head. "None as yet. However, there are murmurs of peculiar demonic activity near the old cathedral. It might provide a slender lead."

Lucien's fists clenched, resisting the rage surging within him. Although patience was not his strong suit, he promised himself to persevere, for Avery's sake.

Vlad placed a firm and supportive grip on his shoulder. "Stay strong for her. We will find her and exact vengeance on those who took her."

Lucien gave a tight nod, a silent pledge to contain his burning anger until Avery was secure. Yet, if any misfortune had touched her at Darmon's hands, nothing on this earthly realm could shield him from the tempest of Lucien's impending fury.

For the love of his life, Lucien was prepared to walk the fine line between brutality and self-control. Until they were together again, the inner beast would constantly cry out for justice. She was his beacon, his essence of humanity; without her, there was nothing but a deep, dark void.

After parting ways with Vlad, Lucien secluded himself in his chamber, enduring the excruciating passage of hours until the arrival of the gypsy witch. He once again reached out along with the psychic bond shared with Avery, whispering words of solace.

Even though the connection was muted, he could sense her essence, flickering weakly like a candle bravely resisting the engulfing darkness. "Hold on, my love," he silently urged. "I'm coming for you."

The next day, news reached the academy of the Romani envoy nearing its gates. Lucien rushed downstairs, his caution swept away by the currents of desperate hope.

The massive doors creaked open, revealing two imposing figures adorned with their unmistakable clan tattoos. In their midst walked a petite woman, her features hidden beneath a hooded shawl.

Lucien's gaze locked onto the scene, his intensity unfaltering. "Are you here to help us?"

The female advanced, throwing back her hood to unveil her face. "I am Madame Leana of the Crescent clan," she affirmed, her voice possessing a melodic yet resolute cadence. Sharp eyes peered into Lucien's soul with a penetrating gaze.

Lucien nodded, resolution etched across his features. "Let's get started. There's a life at stake."

The witch's lips curved into a knowing smile. "Darkness will not triumph today. Shall we?"

With Madame Leana's arrival, Lucien swiftly guided her to the academy's ritual chamber. Every fibre of his being urged him to act immediately in locating Avery, yet he clung to the fragile threads of his patience.

"Before we dive in, just a heads up," Lucien warned, "Lord Darmon's no joke. He's got some serious dark magic up his sleeve. Not many have gone up against him and come back to talk about it."

Madame Leana nodded gravely. "Your apprehension is justified. But trust in this. I've harnessed magics just as ancient. The shadows will not triumph."

Her words, resounding with confidence, reignited hope within Lucien. Finally, with the witch's aid, they would have what was needed to unravel the mystery shrouding Avery's whereabouts. This was more than a mere breakthrough; it was as if a beacon had been lit in the darkest night, guiding them towards reuniting with Avery and mending the torn fabric of their fate.

In the centre of the chamber, Madame Leana gathered arcane tools of candles, crystals, and elixirs. She turned to Lucien. "Focus on your connection to the girl. I will handle the rest."

Lucien closed his eyes, immersing himself in the ethereal link that bound him to Avery. Madame Leana's once melodious voice adopted an eerie rhythm as she commenced the ritual.

The chamber became laden with oppressive power, yet Lucien shut it all out, focusing solely on the delicate lifeline connecting their souls. *Avery... guide me to you...*

Madame Leana's voice rose, reaching a mesmerising crescendo. The flames of nearby candles seemed to stretch towards her as if drawn by the swirling energy enveloping the gypsy witch.

White-knuckled, Lucien gripped the edges of the carved table. His entire being was entrenched in the psychic tether to Avery, urging the witch's spell to penetrate the shadowy shroud that concealed her.

The chanting reached a breathtaking climax. The chamber quivered, ancient artefacts rattling on their shelves. Lucien squeezed his eyes shut against the blinding light emanating from Madame Leana's ritual tools.

When he dared to open them again, the room had stilled. Yet Madame Leana stood before him, her gaze ablaze with purpose.

"It is done," she said. "I know where the girl is being held."

A surge of relief mingled with an undercurrent of fury within Lucien. Finally, after endless nights of waiting, he could take decisive action.

"Tell me," he commanded, his veins pulsing with blood-lust. He would tear Lord Darmon's stronghold stone from stone to reclaim Avery if need be.

Madame Leana's melodic voice echoed with gravity. "Patience, vampire. Recklessness jeopardises all. We must strategise our attack and gather allies."

Lucien, though consumed by the desire to rescue Avery, mastered his savage instincts. He knew she spoke with wisdom. The time had come for judicious action, not mind-less chaos.

CHAPTER 3

In the depths of blackness, Avery clung to her lifeline—the cherished memories of Lucien's love. Pain gradually pierced the void, pulling her into consciousness.

Reluctantly, she opened her eyes, though her vision remained blurred. A hulking demon hovered over her, and a darker figure observed from the shadows. Her father.

"... admirable resilience..." the creature rumbled. "Time for another dose..."

Agony erupted through Avery's veins as the demon injected her. Straining against her bonds, her back arched.

This was his bidding, Avery realised. Yet, she would not break. Especially not when her last thoughts were of Lucien.

Despite the demon's injections causing fresh agony, Avery refused to cry out. She wouldn't give her father the satisfaction.

She comprehended his twisted purpose for this torture—he aimed to mould her into the perfect assassin for the Order. Not entirely vampire nor demon, but a hybrid amalgamation, endowed with the powers of both races.

Revulsion simmered within Avery. Her sire cared nothing for her humanity or free will; she was merely a vessel for his vile ambitions.

Even in the present moment, he watched with clinical indifference as the demon pierced her flesh repeatedly, infusing her veins with its cursed blood. Avery could feel the foul substance seeping through her, warping her spirit.

She clenched her teeth, determined to resist and aid Lucien in thwarting her father's nefarious plans. In her mind, she repeated Lucien's name like a mantra, clinging to memories of his love to preserve her sense of self.

Her inner light dimmed, dwarfed by hellish shadows. Yet, as long as she clung to Lucien, hope endured. Each injection of demonic blood felt like liquid fire coursing through Avery's veins. Despite thrashing against her bonds until the leather cut into her skin, she couldn't escape the relentless agony.

Throughout the ordeal, her father observed dispassionately, jotting notes on a clipboard. To him, she was a mere experiment, a subject to be tested and disposed of if necessary.

Avery gazed at him, pleading for mercy. "Father... please..." she croaked, her voice brittle and weak. She desperately wanted to find any trace of compassion, anything to end this torture.

However, Lord Darmon's stony expression remained unchanged. "Progress requires sacrifice, daughter. You should feel honoured to further the Order's great work." His indifferent response extinguished Avery's last fluttering belief of awakening any humanity within him. Here, there was only ambition, devoid of mercy or love.

Drawing from the deepest well of her strength, Avery breathed out Lucien's name, each syllable a fervent, silent prayer. In the encroaching shadows nibbling at her vision's edge, she conjured the memory of his gentle smile, a solitary beacon in the engulfing darkness. As the tendrils of unconsciousness started to wrap around her, teetering on the verge of surrender, she could nearly make out the faint echo of Lucien's voice—a soothing whisper in the recesses of her dimming awareness.

Avery clung to that faint sound with all the fibres of her being. It was the escape connecting her to the world outside this nightmarish chamber, the only thread binding her to Lucien and the love they shared. Every whisper of his voice, even through the darkness, felt like an embrace, a promise that they would be together again.

With every infusion of demonic blood, Avery's animosity toward her father burned like a smouldering ember within her. The once-conflicted resentment of an abandoned daughter had transmuted into fiery contempt for the man who could mercilessly subject his own flesh and blood to such torment.

With sudden clarity, Avery realised Lucien was her genuine family now. For him, she would fight with every remaining ounce of her humanity. It was his love that anchored her, gave her strength to resist her father's wicked designs, and would guide her back to the light.

Despite the agonising injections, Avery's abhorrence for her father festered like an infected wound, poisoning her heart and spirit. She was aware of the destructive nature of harbouring hatred, knowing well its ability to corrode the soul. Yet, confronted with such torment, she found herself unable to suppress the surge of anger within her.

To her, there was no justification for the insatiable ambition that had utterly consumed her father. The man who had once been her parent now stood as a monstrous figure, lost in the darkness of his own desires.

There had been a time when she dared to dream that he might love her if only she proved herself worthy, achieving the impossible feat of making him proud. She had tried desperately to earn his affection. Through the trials she endured, Avery came to see the futility of her efforts. Her father was incapable of such emotion; incapable of love.

As the poison of demonic blood coursed through her veins, Avery's resolve solidified. She swore to herself that even if she emerged from this ordeal as a monster, she would never be her father's obedient puppet. She would sooner embrace death than kill for the Order and become a pawn in his malevolent games.

Avery clung to that defiant spark within her. She would show mercy where Darmon showed none. She would hold on to the memory of her humanity, refusing to let the darkness engulf her.

Gathering her determination amidst the relentless agony, Avery shifted her focus to meet the gaze of the man who had formerly held the role of her father, the figure standing above her. Her voice, barely more than a croak, betrayed her desperation. "Why?" she implored. "What has led you down this path?"

For a fleeting moment, something crossed Lord Darmon's face. Uncertainty, perhaps? Remorse? But it was quickly replaced by an impenetrable mask of indifference.

"You seek understanding where none exists," he replied coldly. "I act under reason. My duty is to further the Order's power and secure what is rightfully ours."

Avery shook her head bitterly. "No... there must have been a time when you were still human inside, before..." Her voice trailed off as she searched for any glimmer of humanity in him, a thread that could be tugged to bring her father back from the abyss.

However, Lord Darmon simply signalled to the demon, instructing it to continue the brutal infusions. As fresh waves of agony washed over her, Avery confronted a painful truth—whatever traces of humanity had once dwelled within him were long dead, devoured and decayed by the darkness that now shrouded him. He stood as the elder monster in the room, and that was something she couldn't alter.

CHAPTER 4

Lucien's mind teemed with determination as he considered the forces they could rally for the impending battle. The urge to charge blindly for Avery's rescue warred with the need for a well-constructed strategy. He knew that a headlong rush into the Order's stronghold could spell doom for all of them.

Madame Leana's words brought him back to the present. Her gaze focused on some distant point as if foreseeing the events to come. "The witch Jade and the demon Ash will play pivotal roles. And, of course, your army of vampire knights, sired by both you and Vlad."

He felt a glimmer of hope. The knights, bound by loyalty to him and Vlad, were a formidable force. Their combined might could tip the scales in their favour.

With a determined nod, Lucien agreed. "I'll get them set for the attack as soon as it gets dark. With Jade, Ash, and your magic on our side, we can take down the Order's stronghold."

Madame Leana acknowledged him with a nod. "The pieces are aligning. Have faith."

Icy purpose surged through Lucien, quelling the turmoil of emotions that had roiled within him. He would leave no stone unturned, no plan unexecuted, to breach the stronghold, reunite with Avery, and vanquish the darkness that held her.

Departing from the ritual chamber, he wasted no time and made his way to the academy's training quarters. The atmosphere was charged with energy as his vampire knights diligently honed their weapons and clad themselves in armour etched with symbols of power. Every instance of metal scraping against metal, every glimpse of a blade meeting the whetstone, signified their commitment to the upcoming battle.

Lucien, embodying his commanding presence, scrutinised his army with a discerning eye. In the impending assault, every detail held significance. As he moved among them, he discerned unshakable obedience in their eyes and a fierce resolve to defeat the enemy. These vampires had been tempered in the crucible of loyalty, bound to their masters, and were prepared to instil fear in the hearts of those who dared to oppose them.

His knights responded with a collective thump of fists against their chests, a growl of acknowledgment reverberating through the training quarters.

Content with their preparations, Lucien left them to their tasks and entered the serene embrace of the Victorian garden nestled within the academy's grounds. Dappled sunshine filtered through the foliage. The melodic chirping of birds, and the overall tranquillity of the garden, sharply contrasted with the storm of turmoil awaiting him.

As he traversed the sunlit garden, Lucien sensed the world

holding its breath, bracing for the impending chaos and conflict. He endeavoured to reflect outward composure, though an inner tempest raged relentlessly.

Behind the veneer of measured calmness, fears clawed at him. What if their arrival proved too late? What if Avery's suffering had surpassed redemption? These dire concerns, too heavy to vocalise, lay buried beneath the weighty mantle of duty.

Kneeling amidst the blossoms, Lucien closed his eyes, conjuring an image of Avery's cherished countenance. His whispered prayer resonated with fervour, a silent plea to any deities that might be listening.

"Hold on, my love. When the sky turns crimson in the sunset, I shall come for you. I swear this, even if the forces of hell stand in my way."

Rising to his feet, he gazed upward, allowing the sun's warm rays to infuse him with steadfastness. The hour of destiny loomed, and faith and resolution became their celestial guides.

As he departed the tranquillity of the garden, Lucien sought Jade and Ash. In Jade's candlelit chambers, they awaited him with expectation, determination etched on their faces. Lucien approached them, speaking solemnly. "It's almost time. Are you ready?"

Jade met his gaze, her resolve unswerving. "We are prepared." Ash nodded.

Lucien retreated to his quarters, a sanctuary of solitude before the storm of battle. There, he dressed himself in his combat gear, each piece an indication of his readiness for the looming conflict. The black armour, adorned with intricate symbols of power and protection, embraced him familiarly, a reminder of the strength and resilience within. Each piece had been a gift from Vlad, bestowed with the promise of safeguarding the future.

In the quiet of his room, with the last rays of sunlight dancing through the windows, Lucien donned his helmet. His words, a soft but fervent prayer, filled the space. "Guide our forces swiftly, lend strength to my sword arm, and keep Avery from harm." His voice bore the burden of determination.

Emerging from his chambers, Lucien radiated an aura of hope and steadfast resistance. With every stride, his commitment to the mission solidified—the rescue of Avery from the shadowy depths that held her. It wasn't just a battle against foes; it was a quest to reclaim love and light from the jaws of darkness.

CHAPTER 5

At dusk, Lucien was mounted atop his majestic white stallion, with Jade and Ash by his side. The gathered rescue forces stretched out before him, an army of vampire knights, armoured and vigilant.

Madame Leana, her presence imposing, sat on her own steed at the rear. As the sun dipped below the horizon, she began her incantations, tracing arcane symbols that shimmered with mystic power.

A portal to the forest outside Garmarth Castle tore open before them, reality itself bending to their will. Lucien raised his mithril sword, projecting his commanding voice to the waiting knights.

"This night we ride for justice! Onward!" With the forceful battle cries of his knights, they charged, crossing the supernatural threshold.

The quest to save Avery had begun. Failure was not an option. Lucien's focus was squarely on the path ahead and the reckoning that awaited those who had dared to take his love from him.

Lucien rode through the swirling portal, the vampire legion following him with resolute loyalty. Ash, Jade, and Madame Leana flanked him on their steeds, their presence lending an air of ominous power to the scene.

Upon passing through the gateway, they emerged into the serene surroundings of a forest bathed in moonlight. Ancient trees stood around them, their leaves rustling in the gentle night breeze, whispering stories of battles and legends long past. The moon's glow filtered through the canopy, casting a serene, otherworldly light on their surroundings.

In the distance, Garmarth Castle towered imposingly. Its massive walls, built from colossal stones that bore the scars of weather and war, stood defiant against the night sky. Each stone was a witness to the castle's storied past, etched with the wear of time and the echoes of ancient conflicts. In the moonbeam, these rugged boulders took on a ghostly pallor, giving the fortress an awe-inspiring yet sombre character.

Before this grand, historical backdrop, Lucien, his figure cloaked in the silvery sheen, signalled a halt with a raised gauntleted hand. His commanding presence was as steadfast as the castle itself, as his forces gathered in the shadow of its timeless walls.

"Heads up. The fortress is right in front of us," he declared. "Stick to the plan. Take down any opposition, but keep in mind, Darmon is our main target. I'll deal with him myself."

The vampire knights disappeared into the woods like shadows, each group heading to their assigned positions. Lucien turned to Jade and Ash, his eyes alight with fierce tenacity. "We shall draw their attention to the castle's gate. Let the assault begin."

Their steeds thundered forward as they approached the citadel's entrance. The sounds of clashing steel and battle cries already filling the night air as the first wave of knights engaged the bewildered guards. Lucien's doggedness was unshakable. They had reached the culmination of their relentless pursuit.

But as they neared the entrance, an unsettling feeling crept over Lucien. The guards seemed too few, and the fortifications around the Order's headquarters appeared strangely lax. An uneasy suspicion churned within him, like a shadow hinting at a hidden threat.

Before a warning could escape his lips, the massive gates of Garmarth Castle exploded open, and an army of undead warriors surged forth, their malevolent eyes gleaming with hate. In their shadow, a monstrous demon, unlike any Lucien had ever seen, emerged from the keep's depths.

"Ambush!" Lucien's voice thundered, his sword flashing into his grip as the undead horde swiftly encircled them. Faced with this sudden onslaught, Jade and Ash conjured blistering arcs of magic and hellfire, while Madame Leana countered with her own arcane incantations.

But the demonic general leading this unholy army only laughed, its voice grating like iron. "Little fools, did you think we wouldn't be prepared for your intrusion?"

As Lucien battled, his heart pounded with an icy dread. The sight before him revealed a grave miscalculation; the Order's forces were far more formidable than anticipated. Yet, driven by the burning need to save Avery, he refused to let despair take hold. With his fangs bared in fierce determination, he plunged into the fray, charging at the demon general with a reckless courage that disregarded the lurking dangers.

In the thick of battle, Lucien's sword clashed against the demon's jagged blades, sparks flying with each bone-jarring impact. His movements were a blend of attack and defence, a dance of desperate survival against overwhelming odds. Surrounding him, the battleground was a whirlwind of disorder and sorcery.

Jade, wielding her white magic with precision and grace, became a beacon of hope. Her spells illuminated the battlefield, turning advancing undead soldiers into piles of ashes, each burst of her power a testament to her strength.

Meanwhile, Ash was an unstoppable force, his form blurring into a whirlwind of destruction. He moved with a fierce intensity, his actions a fiery tempest that left nothing but scorched earth in his wake. His relentless assault ensured that any enemy daring enough to come near was swiftly met with a fiery end.

Amidst this chaos, Lucien fought on, each swing of his sword fuelled by the singular goal of reaching Avery, refusing to let anything stand in his way.

As Lucien battled fiercely on the ground, his attention was intermittently drawn to the aerial spectacle above. Madame Leana, a master of her craft, was a whirlwind of concentration and power amidst the chaos. Her hands moved with deft precision, tracing intricate patterns in the air as she cast potent counter-spells. These shimmering barriers of magic rose like protective domes above them, repelling and dissipating the dark spells hurled by the Order's sorcerers. Energy crackled in the atmosphere as her counter-magic clashed with the enemy's curses, producing bursts of light that illuminated the battleground.

On the ground, Lucien was a force to be reckoned with, his sword cutting a relentless swath through the legion of undead. Each swing of his blade sent enemies stumbling backward, their numbers momentarily thinning before him. The undead, with their lifeless eyes and gnashing teeth, surged towards him like a relentless wave, but Lucien met them with an unyielding determination.

As he fought, he moved ever closer to where Madame Leana was concentrating her efforts. Her presence shone as a ray of hope, pivotal in shifting the momentum of the battle. With each step, Lucien pushed through the horde, his mind singularly focused on breaking through to join forces with her, knowing that together, their combined strength could shift the balance in this perilous fight.

With a fierce thrust, Lucien impaled his sword into the demon's chest, causing the monstrous creature to stagger back, howling in agony. But there was no time to savour this momentary victory—the ambush still raged around them.

"We keep fighting!" Lucien roared, his voice cutting through the clamour. "For Avery!" Renewed by desperation, he sliced through the demon's legs before twirling to decapitate more opponents, his sword arm unfaltering.

Jade sent a pack of undead foes into fiery oblivion. "We'll never back down!" she declared defiantly. Madame Leana nodded silently, her eyes blazing as she summoned radiant bolts of heavenly fire.

Lucien barked out commands to his allies, resolute in his judgement to press forward. Somewhere within the castle, Avery awaited rescue, and he would fight, no matter what obstacles or terrors lay ahead.

He carved a path through the relentless forces that sought to block their advance, his sword a gleaming blur of deadly purpose. Despite the crushing burden of fatigue and injury, he refused to stop.

Madame Leana, not far from Lucien, unleashed a cataclysmic shockwave. The air trembled as her power surged forth, obliterating an entire battalion of undead warriors in a blinding explosion of energy. Despite this display of might,

Lucien couldn't help but notice the grim truth; the enemy seemed endless. As quickly as one foe fell, another took its place, an unceasing tide of darkness.

Nearby, Jade and Ash stood back-to-back, an island in the storm of chaos. Their voices intertwined in a symphony of incantations, weaving protective wards to fend off the ceaseless onslaught of dark magic. Each spell cast was a battle in itself, a struggle to maintain their ground under the relentless assault. Lucien could see the strain on their faces, and the sheer effort it took to hold the line.

Amidst the clashing and spell casting, a daring plan began to crystallise in Lucien's mind. The battle was hanging by a thread, and desperate times called for desperate measures. What if he pushed his stallion to its limits, leaping over the spiked gates to infiltrate the fortress alone? The idea was fraught with peril, yet it beckoned to him with the allure of turning the tide.

With this thought, Lucien urged his white stallion forward. The horse responded with fervent energy, its hooves thundering against the ground. His hands clenched the reins tightly, his entire being focused on the daunting gates that loomed ahead. In that moment, the chaos of battle seemed to blur into the background. His heart raced, fuelled not only by apprehension of the unknown ahead but also by a fervent desire to reach Avery. Every fibre of his being was aligned towards that singular goal, driving him towards what could be the most perilous, yet decisive action of the battle.

The spiked gates approached with dizzying speed. With reckless abandon, Lucien shouted for his noble steed to leap. For one suspended, heart-pounding moment, they soared through the air. Then, the world exploded in a deafening cacophony as horse and rider crashed through the reinforced wood gates, sending a shower of splinters and debris flying.

Lucien was dashed from the saddle as his mount collapsed lifelessly to the ground. Every inch of his body throbbed with pain; every bone screamed in protest. But it was nothing compared to his burning need to reach Avery. His mithril armour was battered and blood oozed from multiple wounds, but he clutched his sword steadfastly.

Lucien, dishevelled and slightly disoriented, paused to take in his new, eerily quiet surroundings. The once familiar clamour of battle was conspicuously absent, replaced by an ominous silence that blanketed the castle's empty courtyard. He found himself at the core of the enemy's domain, yet an uncanny stillness prevailed, like the deceptive lull before a tempest. His heart raced with the anticipation of hidden dangers, the certainty of a trap lurking in the shadows.

Turning cautiously, his heightened senses strained to detect the slightest hint of movement or threat. "Show yourselves!" he demanded, his voice echoing defiantly against the ancient walls. Blood seeped from a cut on his forehead, but it did little to dampen his spirit. He marched forward, each stride a fusion of courage and unease, guiding him closer to the imposing entrance of the stronghold.

When he reached the massive oak and iron doors, Lucien summoned his remaining strength and heaved them open. The tortured screech of metal grated on his ears. As he stepped into the cavernous hall beyond, torchlight flickered, revealing a labyrinth of vacant corridors branching off in all directions. Where were the keep's forces? The ominous stillness sent shivers down his spine.

Lucien inhaled deeply, recognising a faint yet unmistakable scent—the sweet fragrance of Avery's skin. His preternatural senses came alive, guiding him toward her elusive trail. Though he knew it was likely a trap, he had no choice but to follow it.

His grip on his sword tightened as he stalked through the stone passages, guided solely by Avery's lingering fragrance. With each step, torchlight gradually gave way to consuming shadow. Yet he pressed on, relentless in his pursuit.

Finally, he arrived before a nondescript wooden door. It was here that the scent was strongest. Without hesitation, Lucien knocked it open and charged into the impenetrable darkness beyond, prepared to face any obstacle, any adversary who dared stand between him and his love.

"Avery!" he shouted, his voice ringing through the oppressive darkness. He braced himself for a confrontation, ready to battle any enemy that lurked. But what he heard in response was not the clash of swords or the hiss of dark magic. Instead, a weak cry pierced the shadows—Avery's voice, calling out from below.

Lucien froze, torn between relief and a mounting sense of dread as Avery's weak cry echoed. He spotted a cramped, spiral staircase that led downward, presumably into the foreboding castle dungeons. Without a second thought, he took the slippery steps two at a time, his heart pounding with urgency.

"Avery! Hold on!" Lucien called out as he descended into the clammy, oppressive darkness of the dungeon. Her voice led him through the serpentine passages, the rusty iron bars lining the way only increasing his determination.

Lucien's heart pounded as he raced through the shadowed corridors, finally halting before a massive wooden door. It was old and imposing, its surface etched with arcane symbols that seemed to pulse ominously in the dim light. Faint, muffled sobs seeped through the cracks, igniting a fierce determination in his chest. With a roar that echoed his inner turmoil, he channelled his dwindling strength and rammed the door off its hinges.

The room beyond was a dim cell, its air heavy with despair. In the gloom, Avery was a broken figure against the filthy wall, her wrists cruelly chained. Her face, once vibrant, was now drawn and pale, a stark testament to her suffering. But at the sight of Lucien, a flicker of life reignited in her eyes, a fragile flame of hope amidst her anguish. She attempted to stand, her words a hoarse murmur, "You came..."

Lucien's heart ached as he rushed to her, his arms enveloping her trembling form. His sword, an extension of his resolve, swiftly broke the chains that imprisoned her. "I swore I would find you," he whispered back, his voice a tender caress as he gently brushed her matted hair away from her face. Despite her frailty, Avery managed a weak smile, her spirit unbroken. "I never gave up hope."

Lifting her with utmost care, Lucien's emotions swirled with relief and joy. They moved through the castle, a labyrinth of shadows and silence, remarkably unimpeded. Holding Avery close, he navigated the deserted halls, her safety his only focus. Yet, the lack of resistance was unsettling, casting a pall of suspicion over their escape. The eerie absence of foes, the quiet ease of their departure, seemed too simple, too unchallenged. Lucien's senses remained on high alert, his mind racing with the possibility of unseen dangers lurking in the quietude of their escape.

CHAPTER 6

As they emerged into the imposing hall, a vast expanse illuminated by flickering torches, an unsettling sound shattered the silence. A slow, deliberate clapping resonated, each echo weaving a haunting melody through the air. The hall, with its high ceilings and grandeur, suddenly felt oppressive, the shadows cast by the torches seeming to dance menacingly around them.

Lucien's heart sank as he scanned the room, his grip on Avery tightening protectively. Then, materialising atop the majestic staircase like a phantom from the darkest of nightmares, stood Lord Darmon. His aura was icy and foreboding, standing in sharp relief against the comforting warmth of the torchlight. His smile, wide and contemptuous, was a mocking sneer that sent a shiver down Lucien's spine.

Lucien's mind raced, his thoughts a tumult of anger, fear, and determination. Darmon's appearance was not just a physical threat but a psychological one, his clapping a sinister symphony that seemed to mock their efforts and undermine their hope. His towering presence in the grand hall heightened the seriousness of the moment, casting an ominous aura over them. Lucien felt a surge of protective instinct, his resolve hardening against the looming confrontation, even as his heart pounded with the uncertainty of what was to come.

"Well done," he sneered, his voice dripping with malevolence. "You've found my precious daughter. But did you honestly believe I'd allow you to take her so easily?"

Lucien clutched Avery tighter and raised his sword, determination etched across his face. "Your hold on her is broken, Darmon. You've lost."

Darmon's smile grew wider, like a grotesque parody of glee. "Lost? My dear Lucien, the game has only just begun..." With a sinister gesture, he twisted his hand through the air and started chanting, his intentions chillingly clear.

Avery let out a piercing cry of anguish as her body transformed. Her once-pale skin turned a sickly shade of red. Grotesque horns erupted from her head, and demonic wings tore through her back. The insidious twist of Darmon's magic had turned her from a vampire into a fully manifested demon.

Her voice, now guttural and inhuman, hissed menacingly, "You will not have me..."

Lucien staggered back, horror etched across his face as Avery completed her transformation. The familiar contours of her once-beloved form were now twisted by demonic fury. She hovered in the air on ominous crimson wings, hissing with a frightening and otherworldly cadence.

Darmon's malevolent laughter echoed through the hall as he addressed the demonic incarnation of Lucien's love. "Come, fulfil your purpose! Kill the fool who dared to steal you away!"

Lucien felt tension building inside him as he prepared to confront the sinister power that had taken hold of Avery. However, as she dived towards him, there was no glimmer of recognition in her obsidian eyes. The woman he had loved so dearly was no more.

With savage speed, Avery seized Lucien by the throat, effortlessly lifting him off the ground. He gasped for breath, his sword tumbling from his grasp. This abomination wore Avery's face, but it was devoid of her essence.

"Finish him!" Darmon's command rang out from atop the stairs. Lucien did not struggle or plead.

Lucien was gasping, the demonic claws around his throat squeezing tighter, each breath a battle against the encroaching darkness. Darmon's eyes gleamed with malicious satisfaction from afar, savouring the imminent defeat of the once indomitable vampire. Lucien's heart pounded with despair, his mind a whirlwind of regret and unfulfilled promises.

In this dire moment, the castle's doors burst inward, shattering the tense air with their explosive entry. Ash, a figure of wrathful vengeance, stood framed in the doorway, his body wreathed in dancing flames, his eyes burning with an intensity that matched the inferno surrounding him.

The hall reverberated with Ash's thunderous shout. "Avery, no!" His arm swept forward, unleashing a fearsome wave of hellfire magic. Avery, caught in its path, was flung across the room, away from Lucien. The sea of flames that followed appeared to engulf everything in its wake.

Lucien crumpled to the ground, air finally rushing back into his lungs. Ash was at his side in an instant, lifting him up. "Come on. We must fall back. The battle is slipping from our grasp!" he shouted, his words almost drowned by the deafening roar of the flames consuming the hall.

Lucien's gaze was fixed on Avery, his heart wrenching in his chest. "I won't. I have to get her back." His voice was a desperate whisper, a plea to a fate that seemed already sealed.

But the relentless fire, a barrier as solid as any wall, had already ensnared them in its deadly embrace, separating him from Avery.

Ash's words were a harsh dose of reality amidst the chaos. "There's nothing to be done right now. Last time I checked, fire kills vampires, and I don't have enough power left to hold him off, protect you from the flames, and keep Avery from killing you while you try to rescue her."

Lucien's heart sank, torn between the instinct to save Avery and the need to survive. The realisation that he was powerless to change the course of events was a bitter pill to swallow. As he allowed Ash to lead him away, his last glance back was filled with a tumult of emotions—despair, love, and an unwavering vow to return.

Leaning heavily on Ash, Lucien staggered toward the exit, each step an effort against his crushing despair. The echoes of Darmon's enraged roars behind them served as a haunting echo of the turmoil they were escaping. The roar of the inferno and the demonic Avery, now just echoes as the doors swung shut, sealing the fiery turmoil inside.

They had made it out alive, but the victory was hollow, the cost immeasurable in Lucien's heart. The haunting vision of Avery, consumed by darkness and engulfed in flames, replayed relentlessly in his mind, feeding a profound sense of despair. He was tormented by the thought of her succumbing to that malevolent transformation, her fate now an agonising mystery.

Yet, in this bleak moment, Lucien couldn't ignore the fact that Ash's intervention had been their salvation. It had given them a fleeting opportunity to escape, to regroup and perhaps to continue their struggle against the Order's relentless evil. The battle, indeed, was far from finished, but the uncertainty of Avery's fate cast a long, dark shadow over any sense of purpose.

Once at a safe distance from the now-blazing castle, Ash allowed them a moment to pause. Lucien rested against a tree, its cool bark sharply contrasting with the intense heat and chaos they had just fled. His thoughts were a tempest of feelings—sorrow, remorse, and a resolute feeling of inadequacy. The burden of the night's occurrences weighed heavily on him, each breath feeling like a battle against the overwhelming tide of despair that threatened to consume him. The distant, dancing flames of the burning castle served as a sombre reminder of the fierce battle they had recently faced and the unclear journey that still awaited them.

The uncertain path ahead seemed to stretch endlessly into darkness as Ash broke the heavy silence. "What happened at the gates?" His voice was urgent, laced with concern. "One minute we were fighting, then you just disappeared!"

Lucien's response was a shake of the head, his eyes mirroring the depth of his despair. "It was a trap," he murmured, defeated. "Darmon... he turned Avery into something she's not. She didn't even recognise me." His words trailed off, lost in the haunting image of Avery, now a stranger under Darmon's dark influence.

Ash's hand tightened on Lucien's shoulder, a gesture of solidarity in their shared anguish. "We'll get her back, don't worry. I can open a portal back to the academy. We'll regroup with the others, then..."

His words were abruptly cut off by a thunderous explosion that shook the very ground beneath them. The night sky was illuminated as the entire fortress succumbed to the flames, sending a rain of debris cascading around them. Yet, amidst this chaos, Lucien's gaze was resolute, fixed on the hellish scene where the castle once stood. His thoughts were entirely fixated on Avery, ensnared within the raging inferno. A profound sense of failure engulfed him, more suffocating than the smoke that rose in billowing clouds.

At that moment, Lucien's entire world seemed to contract to the blazing inferno before him, where every flicker and flame symbolised his inability to save the one he held dear. The realisation that Avery, the person he had braved so much to rescue, was still in the clutches of darkness, was a torment that no physical wound could match. The path ahead was not just uncertain; it was a labyrinth of guilt, fear, and unresolved desperation.

BACK WITHIN THE SOMBRE WALLS OF THE ACADEMY, Lucien found himself in the imposing presence of the council. The room, usually a place of wisdom and strategy, felt oppressively heavy, its air thick with anticipation and unspoken questions. He stood there, a solitary figure at the centre, his posture reflecting the immense burden he carried.

As he recounted the events of the disastrous assault, his voice was steady, but the underlying tremor of emotion was unmistakable. Every word he uttered reverberated throughout the chamber, underscoring the significance of their unsuccessful mission. The council members, their brows furrowed and expressions sombre, paid rapt attention, their silence casting a weighty pall over the room.

The suffocating cloak of failure bore down on Lucien, its weight constricting his chest with each breath. Every council member's gaze seemed to pierce through him, searching for answers or perhaps laying blame. The air was thick with disappointment and the bitter tang of defeat.

Lucien's recounting was more than just a report; it was an admission of his deepest fears and regrets. He spoke of the fierce battle, the unexpected strength of the enemy, and the heart-wrenching moment of Avery's transformation—a moment that replayed in his mind with painful clarity. As he spoke, his hands clenched and unclenched at his sides, a physical manifestation of his inner turmoil.

In that room, under the inquisitive eyes of the council, Lucien felt the full magnitude of what they had lost. It wasn't just a battle; it was a blow to their cause, to their hope, and to his heart. With each uttered word, the atmosphere chilled, and it felt as though the walls were tightening, echoing the squeeze within his soul.

"You never should've charged in alone," Ash said, his anger cutting through the air like a blade.

Lucien bristled, a defensive fire igniting within him as Jade chimed in. "Ash is right; that was too reckless."

Clenching his fists, Lucien retorted, "I did what I had to! I won't abandon Avery."

Vlad raised his hands diplomatically, but Lucien saw the clear divide among them. They thought he had jeopardised everything. They couldn't comprehend his need to reach Avery, no matter the peril.

Madame Leana watched pensively, her eyes reflecting the deep contemplation of a strategist. Lucien hoped desperately that she understood his motivations when no one else seemed to.

Alessandra's voice, sharp and decisive, cut through the tension. "Enough arguing! It wastes time and focus. We reformulate the strategy and strike back."

Ash and Jade had the grace to look ashamed, acknowledging the wisdom in Alessandra's words. Lucien knew she was right—unity was crucial, regardless of their internal disagreements. Yet doubt gnawed at him relentlessly. Had he doomed their mission?

Self-doubt twisted in Lucien's gut. Ash and Jade's accusations were a constant echo. If only he had adhered to the plan, Avery might be safe now. Instead, his impulsiveness could have condemned her. Lucien silently begged Avery's forgiveness, desperately praying it was not too late to reclaim her. But doubt tore at his confidence like a wolf toying with wounded prey.

The council room buzzed with uncertainty. Alessandra, though still recovering, suggested, "What if we hit them from multiple sides? It might overwhelm them."

Vlad gently intervened. "My love, let us handle the planning for now. You need more time to heal."

Alessandra objected, but Lucien observed the subtle trembling of her hands, a stark reminder of the recent pain. The ordeal was still too fresh.

Reluctantly, Alessandra eased back into her chair, acquiescing to Vlad's wisdom. Lucien's admiration for her willpower to contribute despite recent trials deepened.

Shaking off his doubts and getting his head back in the game, Lucien was determined. "We've got to save Avery. I'm not giving up on her—it's not too late to change things. No way I'm letting the shadows take her without one heck of a battle."

Amidst the ongoing discussions, Lucien couldn't shake a despairing thought. *Can any of us fully recover from the scars this evil left? Even if we defeat the dark minions ruling the Order, these haunting memories and trauma seem destined to linger, casting shadows over our lives forever.*

As Lucien tried to focus on strategising their next steps,

his thoughts kept returning obsessively to the unsettling image of Avery's transformation into a demon. The grotesque details were etched into his memory—the guttural voice, the obsidian eyes, and the leathery wings emerging from her back.

A wave of nausea swept over Lucien as he recalled the moment she had seized him by the throat with supernatural strength, poised to end his life at her father's command. His fingers instinctively went to his neck, vividly remembering her crushing grip.

Was the woman he loved truly lost to him now? Was there a sliver of hope that the real Avery remained buried deep within the hellish shell Darmon had forced upon her?

These lingering uncertainties threatened to shatter Lucien's determination. Yet, he desperately clung to one fragile lifeline—the memory of Avery briefly emerging from the castle flames returned to her vampire form. In that fleeting moment, he had glimpsed recognition in her eyes once more.

That fragment of belief was all Lucien needed—the faintest glimmer that he could reach the real Avery again. He vowed to traverse the fires of hell a thousand times if it meant saving her.

CHAPTER 7

In the oppressive gloom of her cell, Avery existed in a limbo of nightmares and fractured memories. The concept of time had dissolved into a meaningless haze, her only anchor the flickering recollections of Lucien's love. It seemed like countless lifetimes had passed since the day she was cruelly torn away under Darmon's dark command.

The cell, with its chilling, solid stone walls, had become a world of endless night. Her spirit, though battered, clung to the faintest glimmers of hope, like a drowning person clinging to a life raft in a stormy sea. Every moment was a struggle against the encroaching despair, against the shadows that sought to erase the warmth of her past.

Suddenly, the distant, muffled sounds of combat pierced her numb consciousness. The clangs and cries, the symphony of a battle raging beyond her prison, sparked a dim, flickering curiosity. But then, cutting through the cacophony like a ray of light through darkness, came Lucien's voice. It was a sound she feared she'd never hear again, a powerful, familiar call that resonated with all the love and desperation of their bond. His voice acted as a soothing salve for her wounded soul, assuring her that she remained in his thoughts, never abandoned or isolated.

Disoriented, Avery struggled to lift her head, the effort monumental after endless hours of desolation. Her eyes, heavy with despair and weakness, slowly focused on the doorway. And there he was—Lucien, his presence a beacon in the endless night of her captivity. His features, etched with concern, love, and pure determination, were the most beautiful sight she could have ever imagined.

Witnessing him and catching her name on his lips ignited a spark of hope that ran deep within her. It was a fragile, trembling flame in the overwhelming darkness, yet it was enough to stir a reminder of life beyond these stone walls, of love waiting to be reclaimed.

"You came..." Avery's voice barely reached a whisper, a fragile utterance that appeared to bear the burden of all her suffering. As Lucien moved swiftly to her side, his every action spoke of urgency and care. With deft movements, he shattered the chains that had bound her, the sound of breaking metal ringing like a clarion call of freedom in the dismal cell.

As soon as the shackles released her, a wave of relief swept through Avery. It was a mild, calming wave that appeared to infuse vitality into her weary body. The cold, hard reality of her imprisonment seemed to momentarily fade as the warmth of hope and deliverance enveloped her.

In Lucien's presence, Avery felt a flicker of strength returning to her. His familiar face, etched with worry and fierce determination, was a sight that she had replayed in her mind countless times during her darkest moments. Just as he had vowed, he had located her, standing as a symbol of love and resilience amidst the depths of despair.

Lucien's eyes, filled with an emotion that spoke volumes, locked with hers. In that gaze, Avery saw not just the man she loved, but her saviour, her anchor in a storm that had threatened to swallow her whole. The awareness that he had braved uncharted perils to find her stirred appreciation and wonder in her heart.

In the safety of his presence, the horrors of her captivity seemed to recede, if only for a moment. Avery, though weak and worn, felt a resurgence of hope and an indomitable will to survive, to return to the world she knew, the world where Lucien's love was her guiding star.

Their reunion, a fleeting sanctuary in the abyss, was abruptly shattered. Avery's blood turned to ice when she beheld Darmon's sinister emergence, grinning malevolently like a puppet master revelling in his twisted play. She tried to warn Lucien, her voice a desperate plea, but then agony, an inferno of torment, seized her.

It was as if molten lava, searing and relentless, was coursing through her veins, reshaping her from the inside out. The last thing she saw through eyes blurred with tears was Lucien's distraught face etched with helplessness at witnessing her transformation.

Then, as though dragged into a tempest of anguish, Avery's consciousness seemed to retreat behind a wall of fire and rage. A demonic force, an insidious puppeteer, took control. The comforting embrace of nightmares replaced the fleeting solace of Lucien's presence, and she tumbled back into the abyss of her tortured dreams.

Trapped in the demonic form her father had cruelly forced her into, Avery experienced the overwhelming sensation of her consciousness being suppressed. It was like sinking helplessly in deep water, painfully aware of her surroundings yet completely powerless, as some dark force manipulated her body against her will.

Lucien's anguished countenance emerged like a spectre through the haze of rage clouding her mind. His silent plea seemed to reach out to her, a desperate call for the Avery he once knew. Instead of responding, alien words spilled from her lips, forming threats in a guttural distortion of her own voice.

Horror seized Avery as she sensed her monstrous new form, a vile extension of her own being, lifting Lucien into the air by his throat. Her talons dug into his vulnerable flesh, and though she screamed internally for the malevolent force controlling her to cease, it only tightened its grip.

Mercy arrived as a sudden blast of flames knocked her away from Lucien. She collided with the unforgiving stone, momentarily stunned. The iron grip on her mind and body relinquished its hold, but only slightly.

In that fleeting moment of respite, Avery clung desperately to the sliver of free will that remained. She struggled to wrest back dominance, determined to show Lucien that the true essence of her being still lived under this hellish exterior.

Unable to articulate externally, she concentrated all her energy on their psychic bond, mentally projecting her desperate cry: *Lucien! I'm still here, trapped inside this thing! Please, don't leave me...*

The hope that he somehow heard her agonised internal plea was the sole lifeline preventing Avery from succumbing entirely. She knew that if she allowed this malevolent force to seize complete control, the last flicker of her true self would be extinguished.

Avery persisted in her futile struggle, attempting to push back against the encroaching darkness that whispered insidious promises in her mind.

The tenuous connection with Lucien's mind snapped abruptly, leaving her in a disorienting whirl as she soared through the blazing corridors of the castle. When the demonic force that now controlled her body crashed into them outside, a sinking realisation accompanied the horror—Lucien was gone.

Deep within the murky confines of her besieged mind, Avery faintly perceived Ash hauling a bruised and weary Lucien to his feet. His urgent shouts were like distant echoes, struggling to penetrate the dense fog of her altered consciousness. A sense of desperation gripped her heart as she helplessly watched her potential saviours step through a glimmering portal, their figures dissolving into nothingness.

Inside, Avery's soul screamed, "Come back!" Her internal cries of anguish echoed through the desolation of her mind, but they were unheard, lost in the void that her existence had become. The portal sealed shut, trapping her in a distorted reality, a captive within her own twisted existence.

Around her, the remains of the battlefield lay in smouldering ruin, a haunting landscape that mirrored the chaos within her. The sensation of abandonment was overwhelming, a crushing blow to her already fragile state. Lucien, her beacon of hope, had disappeared, leaving her stranded in a monstrous existence, tormented by the remnants of her humanity.

In that desolate moment, Avery felt the true depth of her transformation—an existence trapped between two worlds, unable to reach out or be heard. The realisation that she was now alone, a lone figure amidst the ashes of destruction, was a haunting and inescapable truth. Engulfed in a tumult of confusion and despair, her mind desperately held onto the diminishing memories of Lucien and her past life, a vivid contrast to the grim and monstrous existence she was currently enduring.

In the aftermath, Darmon approached her corrupted figure, still kneeling in the dirt. Through the eyes of the monstrous creature she had become, Avery beheld his smug smile.

"It seems your dear hero has abandoned you," Darmon gloated, his icy voice dripping with satisfaction. "Now, let us leave this worthless place behind. I have grand plans for utilising your new talents..."

If Avery had control of her grotesque features, tears of abject misery would have streamed down her face. However, all she could do was watch helplessly as Darmon opened a portal, spiriting them away to some ominous, unknown destination.

Avery drifted into the depths of desperation as Darmon seized her mutated form, propelling them through the portal. They emerged in a crumbling, overgrown courtyard surrounded by broken walls adorned with dead vines.

Ominous clouds veiled any trace of sunlight, casting the ruined castle grounds in muted grey hues. Avery discerned a crooked, partially collapsed tower, its top rotunda conspicuously absent in the desolate landscape.

"Welcome to Château de Draven, my dear," Darmon declared, his voice oozing with sinister delight. "A jewel of French nobility, now a forsaken relic. Quite fitting, don't you think?"

Avery shivered inwardly at his words. The desolate ruin

mirrored her own inner emptiness. Imprisoned in her demonic form, she was helpless as Darmon led her towards the castle's main structure.

The remnants of the once-grand chateau loomed around them, its silence haunting. The damp, musty air clung to them, heavy with the ghosts of its splendid past. Despite her monstrous shell, Avery recoiled from the eerie aura of decay.

"A bit of training before we begin," he mused, leading them into a spacious overgrown courtyard. Nature, relentless in its reclamation, had woven a tapestry of moss and ivy over the once-proud stones, a sharp difference from the demonic presence that now defiled the historic grounds.

Therein waited a dozen hulking, red-skinned demons armed with jagged spears—a personal guard summoned from some hellish domain. At Darmon's approach, they eagerly stomped hoofed feet, awaiting his command. The courtyard, once a backdrop for refined gatherings, now played host to a sinister spectacle.

Darmon smiled coldly. "Now, let us see a demonstration of what my creation can do."

At those chilling words, Avery felt the demonic persona controlling her raise up to its full, imposing height. Massive wings unfurled, and vicious talons were bared, a murderous look crossing its stolen features. The grotesque transformation sent shivers down Avery's spine, her own consciousness trapped within the monstrous shell.

The enthralled demons surrounding them brandished their weapons with brutal delight at the sight of their target. Avery could only scream soundlessly, her silent cries echoing her despair at the horrors about to be unleashed.

Unable to control the mutated flesh forced under Darmon's sway, Avery watched her demonic shell tear through the guards with feral bloodlust. Every pleading thought for restraint went unanswered, and the courtyard became a gruesome theatre of violence. The stench of blood and the grotesque tableau of ragged corpses lingered in the air.

Darmon watched from the sidelines, a fascinated spectator as the last demon fell. His smile, a twisted enjoyment of the violence he orchestrated, sent chills down Avery's spine.

Clutching the amulet that commanded her, Darmon's actions filled her with terror, knowing the monstrous power she possessed was only the beginning of a greater wave of suffering to come.

In the slaughter's aftermath, Avery numbly watched Darmon seize control of her once more. As he pulled them deeper into the shadowy ruins of Château de Draven, her thoughts turned anxiously towards Lucien.

She knew he would try to find and somehow save her, driven by love and guilt to redeem his failure. Part of her desperately hoped for that miraculous rescue, yet the practical part of her mind feared what wrath her warped body might unleash if he confronted her again.

She existed now as neither vampire nor demon, but an abominable hybrid, a monstrous convergence of both species. Within her, the apex abilities of vampires and demons intertwined creating a volatile mix. Her blood pulsed not only with vampiric impulses but also with deeper, primal, demonic desires for violence and devastation.

The thought of Lucien facing her under Darmon's influence haunted her. The insatiable lust for brutality within her would overwhelm the remaining traces of mercy. In this new shell, restraint was non-existent, replaced only by a feral hunger to destroy everything in its path. Dread consumed her as she contemplated the possibility of Lucien becoming another casualty in the wake of her horrific rampage.

Avery blinked back helpless tears, the physical manifestation denied by her transformed state. She wished desperately that Lucien would let her go, to forget the grisly entity his love had become. Death, she believed, would surely be kinder than the twisted ruin Darmon had made of her.

Avery sensed the monstrous strength granted by her warped hybrid bloodline, far exceeding the capabilities of either parent race alone. The vulgar display against Darmon's demon guards had only scratched the surface of the savagery these newfound talents could unleash.

Avery was deeply terrified by this realisation—the knowledge that beneath her usurped flesh lay a destructive force, dormant yet ready to be unleashed for whatever wicked intentions Darmon had planned.

When Darmon deemed her 'training complete,' Avery feared for wherever he might unleash her as his weapon. She knew no defences would hold against the embodiment of terror he envisioned–an unchained beast of hellfire, chaos, and retribution incarnate.

Avery desperately hoped that Lucien would not attempt to face that nightmare creature, despite his yearning to reclaim the lover cruelly taken from him. The thought of her mutated hands rending his heart from his noble chest, her demonic blood revelling in his grisly end, was a vision too agonising for her to bear.

CHAPTER 8

Avery's steps were heavy with despondence as Darmon guided her through the dilapidated corridors of the castle. Her eyes, once vibrant, now reflected a deep, unspoken sorrow. Each command from Darmon was like a physical burden, pressing down on her with the grim awareness of her own helplessness. Stepping into an empty, unsettling chamber, the weight of his ambitious schemes appeared to grow, enveloping her in a tangible cloak of desolation.

In the midst of this bleak march, something unexpected stirred within Avery. A subtle shift, a momentary loosening of the invisible shackles that bound her will to Darmon's. Her eyes widened slightly, a spark of hope igniting in their depths. Tentatively, she tested this newfound slack in her mental bonds, pushing against the limits of Darmon's faltering control.

Darmon, absorbed in his own thoughts, was caught off guard as Avery's monstrous form jerked violently, her talons scraping against the ancient wall, leaving deep scars in the stone. His eyes widened in shock and anger. "You dare resist?"

he spat out, his hand scrambling for the amulet, seeking to tighten his grip on her once more.

The moment was brief, but it was a crack in the fortress of Darmon's control, a glimmer of rebellion that shone through the darkness of Avery's captivity. It was a silent battle of wills, her newfound resistance clashing against his hurried attempts to reassert dominance.

Avery's movements towards the door were frantic and uncoordinated, her wings flailing wildly, knocking over fixtures in her path. There was no plan in her mind, no strategy—only the primal urge to escape, to seize this fleeting opportunity for freedom.

But as she lurched desperately across the chamber, a sudden, excruciating pain shot through her. Darmon's magic, like invisible chains, snapped back with a vengeance, snatching away her brief glimpse of liberty. Her body froze mid-step, the freedom she had just begun to taste cruelly snatched away.

She crumpled to her knees, the agony rendering her helpless. The brief illusion of escape shattered, leaving her once again ensnared in her monstrous form, a puppet to Darmon's whims.

Darmon approached, his voice dripping with scorn. "Did you truly think you could escape me?" He stood above her, his gaze cold and contemptuous as Avery trembled under his stare, a victim of his unrelenting dominance.

"Perhaps I have been too lenient," he mused, his eyes flashing dangerously. "Allowed you to cling to some futile hope of defiance." He leaned closer, his presence menacing. "But no more. Now, you will learn what it means to be truly obedient." His words were a chilling promise of the tighter grip and harsher dominion that awaited her.

Darmon reached into the depths of his robes, his fingers

wrapping around the handle of a ceremonial dagger. As he pulled it out, the strange glyphs etched into the blade seemed to come alive, twisting and turning in a sinister dance. "Pain has been a useful teacher," he said, his voice cold and calculated. "Let's resume our lessons."

With a wave of his hand, Darmon's magic forced Avery's monstrous arm to extend, bending her will with ruthless efficiency. Avery watched in horror as he positioned the dagger above her outstretched hand. Then, with deliberate slowness, he pressed the blade into her flesh, carving through skin and sinew. The precision of the cut was terrifying, the pain indescribable.

A silent scream tore through Avery as her body convulsed in agony. The torture she was enduring was unimaginable, beyond any physical pain she had previously known. Darmon loomed over her, his eyes gleaming with cruel satisfaction. The sight of her suffering seemed to bring him a perverse joy.

Avery shook uncontrollably, trapped in her monstrous form and at the mercy of her captor. She was powerless to stop him as he meticulously peeled back the skin of her palm, each movement calculated to inflict maximum pain. Mute and agonised, she could do nothing but endure the relentless cascade of injuries, each one a brutal lesson in 'obedience.'

Eventually tiring of focusing on just her warped hand, Darmon circled Avery's hunched demon form. "I think the wings could use some of our attention..." he purred, placing one hand almost gently between the leathery appendages extending from her spine.

Without warning, scorching pain shot through Avery's entire back. The razor-edged dagger carved mercilessly into the sensitive flesh and thin bones, flaying wings from the body in excruciating degrees.

She would have wailed to the heavens if her jaw were her

own. But Avery could only suffer in silence as the torture seemed to last for eternity. Finally, she teetered at the edge of her endurance, ready to plunge into that black oblivion.

Relief, however, remained elusive. Darmon applied just enough healing to keep her conscious, only to continue inflicting atrocious new pains on her mutilated form. In those moments, Avery couldn't help but think that death would have been a far more merciful fate.

As Darmon's relentless torment continued, Avery found herself paralyzed, unable to escape the physical agony he wrought upon her. In these unbearable moments, her only solace was to withdraw into the deepest recesses of her mind, seeking shelter in the sanctuary of her memories.

There, in the quietude of her psyche, she conjured images of Lucien, each memory a precious balm to her ravaged spirit. In her mind's eye, she pictured the strength and solace of his embrace, its warmth a vivid contrast to the harsh, cold reality she was currently enduring. Lucien's gentle touch soothed her pain, his whispered words of love and reassurance echoing like a sweet melody amidst the cacophony of her suffering.

This mental refuge, built from cherished moments and tender recollections, became Avery's fortress against the onslaught of Darmon's sadistic magic. Clinging to these fragments of happier times, she found the strength to endure, to resist being completely consumed by despair. Within this sanctuary of her mind, Lucien stood as a shining pillar of hope, symbolising a love that continued to glow vibrantly, undimmed even by the darkest moments.

As the torment stretched on endlessly, Avery's newfound resilience seemed to silently defy her captor. Darmon scowled, intensifying his attacks, but was met only with passive stoicism.

"What manner of sorcery is this?" he eventually snarled,

confusion mixing with frustration as Avery endured silently. "You dare withstand me so insolently?"

Darmon, enraged by Avery's lack of response, raised his hand in a furious gesture, signalling an even harsher punishment. But fate intervened; his magic, unstable and erratic, suddenly recoiled. The walls trembled, and with a thunderous crash, debris rained down, trapping him beneath. Half-buried in rubble, his plan had dramatically backfired.

Pinned beneath the rubble, Darmon's initial fury quickly transformed into a barrage of threats and vulgar outbursts. Yet, as his predicament became more dire, his furious outbursts gradually turned into desperate bargaining and pleading, laying bare his true state of helplessness amidst this unforeseen turn of events.

Avery's eyes widened in disbelief, struggling to process this unexpected turn. Despite her scars and pain, felt a glimmer of hope flickering within her. Maybe, just maybe, the tide was turning.

"Come now, release me... we shall let bygones be bygones." He appealed to Avery's motionless form under his control. "Did I not gift you your magnificent power? Together, no one could oppose us!"

If she could have spat at his feet, Avery would have. But outwardly she could only observe his humiliation silently. Inside, her mind raced. Was there a chance now for escape?

Avery gathered her willpower, concentrating on coaxing any movement from her transformed, unwilling body. Darmon's iron grip had weakened, a crack in his control now evident. This was her chance, and she knew she had to take it, no matter the cost.

Summoning all her strength, she managed to lift a heavy clawed limb. Each movement was an arduous battle, but inch by painstaking inch, she dragged herself towards the possibility of escape. Darmon's voice echoed behind her, a cacophony of threats that eventually faded into hoarse, desperate pleas.

Away from Darmon's gaze, Avery suffered intense pain with every motion. Her wings were tattered, her bones broken and twisted from relentless torture, yet she persisted. Her progress was slow, driven by a primal instinct for survival, like a wounded animal seeking the sun's comforting warmth.

At last, her bloodied palm felt the touch of grass, offering a striking contrast to the cold stone she had just left behind. Sunlight enveloped her battered form, a gentle caress against her wounds. In this moment of fragile peace, a flicker of hope ignited within her. Maybe, just maybe, she had reclaimed a part of her soul in this desperate flight for freedom.

But a chorus of guttural shouts shattered that dream. A pack of Darmon's demon sentries bounded over, roughly seizing Avery's prone form. Helpless once more, she retreated into her mind as they hauled her back down the stone steps into darkness.

Avery lay broken at the feet of her captor, his enraged voice filling the air. His fury was palpable, berating her for her daring but doomed attempt to escape his dominion. He mocked her hope, scoffing at the idea that light could ever penetrate the perpetual darkness of his reign.

The sound of chains rattled through the gloom as they were mercilessly tightened around her, forcing her battered body to stand upright against the cold, damp wall of the castle's depths. The room was a tomb-like void, save for the two of them—captor and captive, creator and unwilling creation.

In this desolate place, Avery's spirit remained her only

unbroken attribute. Her body might have been chained, but her defiant gaze remained unbending, a silent testament to her indomitable will.

Darmon's smug laughter reverberated off the uncaring stone walls, pleased with his restoration of order from chaos. He turned to Avery, his voice dripping with venomous smoothness, a predator relishing his control over his trapped prey.

"Now then, my dear... where were we?" Darmon's talons traced a path down Avery's scarred cheeks, each touch sending a wave of revulsion through her. His gesture was a chilling reminder of the never-ending torment that awaited her.

"Did you really think a fleeting moment in the sun could save you?" he taunted. "There's no escape. You're mine, in life and death."

His words, dripping with malice, ignited a defiant flame within Avery. Though weak, she lifted her bloodshot eyes to meet his, her gaze attempting to convey the contempt she couldn't voice.

Darmon's grin only grew at her silent challenge. "Ah, there's still some fight in you. Good!" he said with perverse delight. "It will be all the more satisfying to extinguish." His hand moved lower, his touch igniting a fresh wave of revulsion in Avery, a stark reminder of her helplessness in his vile presence.

"My lord!" came a sudden shout as a demon underling burst into the dungeon chamber uninvited. Darmon's claws tightened angrily around Avery's throat.

"What is it, fool?" he snapped, impatience etched across his face at the interruption.

The lackey trembled slightly under Darmon's baleful glare.

"Surface forces requesting reinforcements. We are under attack!"

Darmon hesitated, then smiled slowly with sinister delight. "Well, now... it seems we have guests."

CHAPTER 9

LUCIEN'S FOOTSTEPS ECHOED IN THE COUNCIL CHAMBER, each step a measure of his growing desperation. His mind was a whirlpool, circling tirelessly around one goal. Rescuing Avery. Days had passed since their failed attempt, but the image of her twisted into some demonic puppet was seared into his memory, replaying over and over.

Vlad, standing with his arms firmly crossed, broke the tense silence. "We need to find out where Darmon has hidden her," he said firmly. "Only then can we plan a new attack."

Seated at the table, Madame Leana nodded, her expression pensive. "My visions are clouded... fragments of old castle ruins, deep in a vast forest," she murmured, her fingers massaging her temples as if trying to dispel the fog of her elusive foresight.

Lucien halted, his frustration boiling over. "We can't just sit around!" he exploded, his voice a sharp crack in the tense atmosphere. "Avery could be suffering unimaginable things right now. We have to go after Darmon immediately!" His shout reverberated off the walls, his eyes, fraught with anguish, beseeching them to feel the urgency that was eating him alive.

In the midst of this charged air, Ash chimed in, his tone curious yet uneasy. "But how did Darmon even turn Avery into a demon? Is that something his magic can do?"

Vlad, pondering, stroked his chin thoughtfully. "To transmute someone so profoundly... it would require tremendous power and is likely irreversible." His words, which carried subtle implications, hung in the air, adding to the weight of the challenging mission ahead.

"That kind of magic can scramble things, right? Make creatures violent, mindless," Ash pressed.

Lucien's body went rigid, a sharp pain clenching his chest as the stark reality of Avery's condition, so long pushed to the back of his mind, was laid bare in Vlad's words.

"Is there a way to control the demon Avery has become?" Vlad's voice was hesitant as he turned to Madame Leana.

The witch, her face etched with grave concern, slowly shook her head. "Tampering with such magic risks shattering her mind completely. We must focus on restoring Avery's soul, not further binding her to this cursed form."

Lucien's nod was bitter, his resolve tinged with pain. No matter how Avery had been transformed, he knew he owed it to her to fight for her freedom, for the return of her will.

As plans began to take shape around the table, a sudden spark of inspiration hit Lucien. "The manuscript!" he exclaimed, striding swiftly to a locked cabinet. With a sense of urgency, he retrieved an ancient text on demonology, its pages worn and tattered, a relic from the Old Church he had brought to the academy.

"This book," he said, holding it out, "is full of ancient spells for bending dark forces." The possibility hung in the air, a thread of hope. “Maybe it holds the key to undoing Darmon’s work on Avery.”

Ash leaned closer, his eyes gleaming with enthusiasm. “Holy hell! If I can ambush Darmon with some of these spells,” he said, almost breathless with the prospect, “we might be able to free Avery from whatever he’s using to control her.”

Madame Leana traced a weathered demon sigil on the manuscript experimentally. “Unleashing such unstable magic will surely draw Darmon’s full wrath. You must strike precisely while we occupy his attending forces.”

Vlad crossed his arms. “Darmon has always coveted the power bound within these pages. By wielding it freely before him, we issue a brazen challenge none can ignore.”

Lucien felt renewed conviction flow through the group, driving out despair. The manuscript imparted genuine hope. With it, Ash could be the wild card turning fortunes in their favour at long last.

As they studied their options, Jade spoke up pensively. “What about the arcane map taken from Avery’s cell? It could hold clues.”

Lucien’s expression grew intense, his brow creased with concentration. “I’ve had our top mystics go over it thoroughly,” he said. “But Darmon’s magic is elusive, leaving no discernible trail. We’ve already scoured the locations. They turned up nothing.”

Jade leaned forward, her voice insistent. “But what about the physical contact Avery’s demon form made? Couldn’t there be some magical residue we can use for a location spell?”

Madame Leana, deep in thought, nodded slowly. “Possibly. Ash’s connection to her might help us trace the faintest traces of her aura.”

Ash flexed his hands, a determined glint in his eyes. "I'm ready to break through any magical shields that might be hiding her."

A flicker of hope ignited in Lucien's heart. With their combined strengths and the intricate web of magic they wielded, perhaps they could indeed penetrate the darkness shrouding Avery's whereabouts.

"Then we need to act fast," Lucien said decisively, a newfound determination in his voice. "The longer we wait, the deeper Darmon could bury her."

They gathered quickly in the ritual chamber, driven by a palpable sense of urgency. The enigmatic map was spread out while Madame Leana began setting up the focal point of their spell, each movement precise and calculated. The air was thick with anticipation, the group united in their singular goal to unearth Avery from Darmon's clutches.

"Clouded forces obstruct my sight still around those castle ruins," she muttered.

Ash cracked his knuckles, unfazed. "We're getting Avery back."

Madame Leana passed him an engraved silver bowl. "Focus your power. Amplify Avery's essence to guide my vision."

Brow furrowing, Ash manifested swirling energy, the runic bowl glowing in his palms. Madame Leana worked swiftly, movements synchronising with the rising occult forces.

The very air thrummed with impending revelation. Lucien observed intently, hardly daring to breathe. Then Madame Leana gasped. The obscuring fog lifted at last.

"I see now! The western tower concealed below the broken ruins... shadowed dungeons where Avery lies captive."

Lucien gripped the table's edge at the news. "Can you open a gateway there directly?"

Madame Leana nodded, resolute. “The path is clear.”

“Ready the knights. We embark at once!” Lucien added.

Madame Leana’s divination triumph electrified the room with a new purpose. Finally, after tension-wracked days, they had pierced the veil to uncover Avery’s location.

Lucien swiftly departed to rally the vampire knights for immediate mobilisation, his preternatural speed fuelled by single-minded urgency. Too much time had already been sacrificed while Avery endured torment and madness in the merciless dark.

Returning to the council chambers, Lucien found the rescue party gathered, faces set with solemn determination. Madame Leana stood ready beside a shimmering gateway and Jade gripped the Manual of Demonic Magic tightly with anticipatory focus.

Ash stepped forward, buckling on his engraved battle armour. “The legion is arrayed in full martial force, ready at your command.” His steady voice left no doubt that failure could not be abided this time.

Lucien gave a sharp nod of acknowledgment. The hour for preparation had passed. Destiny called them to action. To cross the gateway into the belly of evil, retrieve their lost light, and salt the cursed earth that had defiled her.

Hand tightening on the pommel of his mythic blade, Lucien addressed them all. “We end this nightmare now!” Their answering cry shook the hall’s rafters as, one by one, they stepped into the swirling portal that promised justice... or oblivion.

CHAPTER 10

As soon as they emerged from the portal, the rescuers found themselves in an eerie, overgrown courtyard surrounded by crumbly walls. Foreboding clouds obscured the sun, draping the castle grounds in subdued shades of grey. Broken walls covered in dead vines stood as silent witnesses to the citadel's former grandeur.

The air was heavy with the scent of decay, and the sounds of rustling leaves mixed with distant creaks and groans from the dilapidated structure. The courtyard, once a place of nobility and beauty, now lay in ruins, a forsaken remnant of a bygone era.

Lucien's heart tightened at the sight, the sombre atmosphere amplifying his sense of urgency. Guided by Madame Leana's divination, they had a purpose here—to rescue Avery from the depths of this run-down fortress.

Without exchanging words, the group moved forward with cautious steps. The uneven cobblestones beneath their feet echoed with the ghosts of a time long past. The castle seemed to come alive with whispers of the secrets it held, as if the stones themselves remembered the tales of joy and tragedy.

The grand entrance loomed ahead, a dark portal into the heart of their mission. Lucien inhaled deeply, sensing the heavy burden of responsibility resting on his shoulders. The time for deliberation had passed; now, they ventured forth into the haunted corridors, hoping to bring light to the shadows that clung to the castle.

As the group advanced through the dilapidated corridors, eerie echoes accompanied their every step. The air grew thick with an otherworldly tension, signalling an imminent confrontation. Rounding a corner, they found themselves face to face with an ominous line of demonic guards, red-skinned and armed with jagged spears.

The demons stomped their hoofed feet in unison, their malevolent eyes fixed on the intruders. Lucien tightened his grip on his weapon, determination and apprehension etched on his face. Beside him, Ash stepped forward, his eyes aflame with magical energy.

With a swift motion, Ash raised his hands, and an intense burst of hellfire magic enveloped the demonic guards. The creatures writhed and roared as the flames consumed them, their forms disintegrating into smoke and ash. The corridor, once crowded with ominous figures, now stood empty, the echoes of the demons' demise lingering in the air.

Lucien spared a glance at Ash, who wore a steely expression. The infernal sentinels had been vanquished quickly, yet the aftermath of the confrontation hung heavily in the castle's shadowy corners.

As the group pressed on, the oppressive atmosphere of the fortification seemed to intensify. The shadows clung to the ancient stones, whispering of forgotten secrets and malevolent deeds. Lucien led the way, his senses attuned to any sign of Avery's presence.

The corridor widened into a grand hall with a crumbling ceiling, revealing a night sky strewn with spectral constellations. Moonlight cast an ethereal glow on the worn tapestries that lined the walls. The group moved forward, guided by Madame Leana's divination.

Suddenly, they reached a set of ornate double doors adorned with symbols that seemed to writhe and pulse. Lucien exchanged a wary glance with Ash, who nodded, acknowledging the magical wards that protected whatever lay beyond.

Madame Leana's voice, soft yet resonant, filled the space, harmonising with the old magic around them. The symbols etched on the doors briefly shimmered with light, then faded away like vanishing fog. Accompanied by a creaking groan, the doors slowly opened, unveiling a vast chamber beyond.

As the group entered, the air thickened with a palpable malevolence. The chamber was dominated by a large, obsidian throne, upon which sat a figure shrouded in shadows. Darmon, the orchestrator of Avery's torment, regarded them with cold amusement.

"You've come a long way to meet your demise," Darmon sneered, his voice echoing through the room. Lucien's jaw clenched, but he remained resolute. The time for confrontation had come.

Yet, as Darmon prepared to unleash his dark powers, Ash stepped forward once again. With a sweeping gesture, he conjured a vortex of hellish might, and the shadows recoiled. The sinister aura permeating the chamber appeared to tremble under the might of Ash's powerful magic.

The group prepared themselves for the looming clash between illumination and darkness, a pivotal struggle that would determine the destiny of Avery and the age-old fortress that had witnessed centuries of triumph and despair.

"Your dark games end here," Ash declared.

Ash's celestial vortex collided with the menacing forces that emanated from Darmon, creating a dazzling display of light and shadow. The clash echoed through the chamber, shaking the very foundations of the ancient fortress.

Lucien's gaze remained fixed on Darmon, his heart pounding with anxiety and anticipation. Avery's fate hung in the balance, and he could sense the ebb and flow of magical energies as the confrontation intensified.

The obsidian throne seemed to capture the swirling forces, magnifying Darmon's wickedness. Around him, shadows converged, morphing into tendrils that slithered out like ghostly serpents. The air hummed with a palpable charge of unfathomable power as the clash between Ash and Darmon reached its climactic point.

Amidst the whirling magical tempest, Darmon's voice cut through, dripping with arrogance. "Your feeble attempts to defy me are futile. Avery belongs to the darkness now, and you shall witness her transformation into a force beyond your comprehension."

Lucien gritted his teeth, determined not to be swayed by Darmon's taunts. The stakes were too high. He drew strength from the memory of Avery's true self, buried somewhere within the demonic shell.

Suddenly, the room trembled, and an otherworldly howl filled the air. The shadows recoiled as if repelled by an unseen force. Lucien squinted through the magical maelstrom, trying to discern the source of this disturbance.

Jade stood at the forefront, her eyes ablaze with a mystic

light. She chanted incantations that seemed to resonate with the very essence of the stronghold. The ancient stones responded to her call, pulsating with a purifying energy.

As the dark tendrils entwining the throne began to unravel, a subtle shift occurred in Darmon's previously unshakable demeanour. His mask of confidence faltered, replaced by a fleeting glimpse of uncertainty. Sensing his moment, Ash intensified the power coursing through him, his hands swirling with an inferno of hellish energy. The vortex he conjured pushed against the looming shadows, lighting up the room with its fierce glow.

The moment Lucien stepped forward, the air in the chamber charged with anticipation. His sword, reflecting the chaotic light of the room, was more than just a weapon—it was an extension of his tenacity. He moved with fluid grace, each step measured and deliberate.

Darmon, recovering from his momentary lapse, responded with a sinister speed. He conjured a blade of pure shadow, its form flickering and unstable, yet deadly. The clash of their swords rang out, a discordant symphony of light and darkness.

Lucien's movements were a dance of precision and skill, honed from years of combat. He parried and thrust, his blade cutting through the air with a sharp hiss. Darmon countered with equal ferocity, his shadow blade a blur of motion, leaving trails of darkness in its wake.

Their swords met in a flurry of strikes and blocks, sparks flying with each contact. Lucien's arm muscles tensed with each swing, his focus absolute. Darmon, for his part, fought with wild, untamed energy, his attacks unpredictable and ruthless.

The sound of metal against shadow filled the chamber, echoing off the ancient walls. It was a battle not just of physical might, but of wills. The determined heart of a warrior against the corrupt power of a sorcerer. Each strike, each manoeuvre, was a testament to their opposing causes, a struggle that was as much about saving Avery as it was about defeating the darkness.

CHAPTER 11

The chamber became an arena where light clashed against darkness, an explosive dance of opposing forces. Darmon, now visibly frustrated, watched his meticulously laid plans begin to crumble. The foundation of his control over Avery wavered under the assault.

"Bring her to me!" Darmon's voice echoed through the cavernous halls of the castle.

In response to his orders, a horde of demonic guards emerged from the shadows. Their grotesque forms, twisted by dark magic, moved with unnatural speed as they converged on Avery's location. The air crackled with malevolent force as the minions closed in.

Jade redoubled her efforts to dispel the lingering darkness. Her incantations echoed through the chamber, entwining with Ash's celestial magic. The very fabric of the castle seemed to resist the encroaching demonic forces. As the first of the guards lunged forward, Ash unleashed a surge of radiant energy. The hellfire struck the minions, causing them to writhe in agony. Some dissipated into shadowy remnants, while others recoiled from the sheer force of the onslaught.

Jade's magic intertwined with Ash's, forming a barrier that momentarily held the demonic minions at bay. Darmon's influence, however, was persistent, and the minions pressed on with unnatural tenacity.

"Lucien, be ready!" Ash called out over the tumult, his eyes blazing with celestial power.

With a swift and practised motion, Lucien swung his sword, fending off the advancing demons. He fought not only to protect himself and his allies but to create a barrier between Avery and the encroaching darkness.

Amidst the chaos, a haunting scream echoed through the chamber. It was Avery's voice, though distorted by the demonic influence. The minions, driven by Darmon's commands, were dragging her towards the throne where Darmon sat, still struggling against the combined forces of light arrayed against him.

Hearing the anguished scream, Lucien's determination deepened. He couldn't let Avery fall into Darmon's hands. Letting out a fierce battle cry, he launched himself into the fray, his sword slicing through the air, striking the demonic guards with lethal precision. Ash and the others were quick to follow, each tapping into their distinct powers to combat the advancing darkness.

The arcane energies clashed with the malicious forces, creating a chaotic spectacle of lights and shadows. Avery's struggles against the minions became more desperate as they tried to force her towards Darmon's throne. But Lucien fought with the strength of a man fuelled by love and desperation.

Madame Leana's eyes glowed with concentration and resolve. She chanted ancient incantations, seeking to sever the dark connection that bound Avery to Darmon's will. The very air seemed to ripple with the intensity of the magical battle.

As the minions closed in, Ash summoned a hellfire barrier, creating a protective circle around Avery. The demonic entities recoiled, their twisted forms writhing in pain as they encountered the hellish might.

"Stay back!" Ash asserted, his voice resonating with a commanding presence.

But Darmon, sensing the turning tide, unleashed a surge of dark energy. The minions, empowered by their master's malevolence, redoubled their efforts. The battle reached a fever pitch, the crash of opposing forces echoing through the chamber.

Lucien fought his way through the demonic horde. His sword cleaved through the shadows, each strike aimed at protecting Avery. She continued to resist with every ounce of her being.

Madame Leana's incantations reached a crescendo, and a surge of mystical power enveloped Avery. As Darmon's hold faltered, Avery's resistance against the minions grew more forceful and noticeable.

With a final, resolute incantation, Madame Leana severed the dark link entirely. Avery, liberated from Darmon's control, collapsed to the ground, panting and disoriented. The demonic guards dissipated into shadows, leaving only echoes of their malevolence.

Silence descended upon the chamber, a stark contrast to the chaos that had just ensued. It was a haunting stillness, punctuated only by the laboured breathing of the weary rescuers and the faint hiss of dark magic fading into the ether. Lucien, his face a canvas of relief and worry, quickly moved to Avery's side. Gently, he gathered her into his arms, cradling her with a tenderness that belied the ferocity of the battle just fought.

As the oppressive shadows retreated, it became clear that this victory was more than a physical triumph. It was a fight for Avery's very soul, a fight against the consuming blackness that had threatened to claim her. In the wake of this hard-won battle, Darmon's presence loomed from his throne, his simmering rage palpable. His eyes, filled with malevolent fury, watched as his carefully laid plans came undone.

Blinded by a surge of protective fury, Lucien's gaze fixated on the cuts that marred Avery's delicate skin. The wounds inflicted during her struggles against Darmon's minions fuelled the fire of rage within him. With a speed that blurred the line between mortal and supernatural, Lucien darted toward Darmon.

In a single, fluid motion, Lucien closed the distance, his hand seizing Darmon's neck with an iron grip. The atmosphere crackled with tension as time seemed to freeze. Avery, still disoriented from the recent ordeal, looked on with a mix of surprise and concern.

With a swift and decisive movement, Lucien snapped Darmon's neck, the sickening sound echoing in the chamber. Darmon, once a puppet master revelling in cruelty, now slumped lifelessly, his malevolent gaze extinguished. The vampire's eyes glowed with a fierce, possessive protectiveness as he cast aside the vile orchestrator of Avery's torment.

In the aftermath of the battle, a profound silence enveloped the chamber. Lucien stood, his posture rigid, beside Darmon's still body. Each breath he took seemed to echo in the hushed air, a testament to the intense, vengeful struggle that had just concluded. The atmosphere hung heavy with the solemnity of their deeds, serving as a palpable reminder of the sacrifices undertaken for the sake of love and the quest for justice.

Avery, her own emotions a whirlwind, stepped toward Lucien with hesitant steps. The scars on her arms and back spoke volumes of her suffering, yet there was a subtle shift in her demeanour. As she looked at Darmon's fallen form, a faint sense of relief replaced the shadow of torment in her eyes.

The rest of the rescue team moved closer, their faces a complex tapestry of shock, relief, and quiet respect. Madame Leana observed them, her gaze mirroring a profound comprehension of the sacrifices and victories of their voyage.

Though the battle had left its scars, the chamber now thrummed with the undercurrent of a hard-fought victory. Lucien, a portrait of determination mixed with exhaustion, turned to face Avery. In his eyes, the fire of a man who had moved heaven and earth to save the one he loved still burned bright.

The journey was far from over, but in that suspended moment, the shadows seemed to retreat, granting respite to the weary souls who dared to defy the darkness.

As the adrenaline of the battle faded, Avery's strength waned, and she collapsed into Lucien's waiting arms. He cradled her tenderly, love and concern evident in his touch, understanding the burden of her exhaustion and the haunting echoes of her suffering.

Lucien's gaze never left Avery's face, as if he could shield her from any lingering shadows with the sheer intensity of his protective stare. The others, their expressions weary, stood a respectful distance away, giving the reunited couple a moment of quiet connection.

Amid this poignant scene, Ash stepped forward. Understanding the need for a swift return to the academy, he wove the elaborate patterns of magic that opened the gateways between realms.

A soft, ethereal glow enveloped the group as the threshold manifested before them. Ash, his eyes focused and hands steady, maintained the spell. The portal became a doorway, a shimmering passage leading back to the familiar grounds of the academy where the war had initially begun.

With utmost care, Lucien lifted Avery into his arms, her head resting against his shoulder. Momentarily setting aside their fatigue, the rest of the group congregated around the couple, united by the triumph they had achieved.

Ash broke the silence. "Let's head back." His suggestion, simple yet comforting, pointed them towards the academy, a place now akin to a sanctuary in their minds compared to the sinister shadows they had just escaped.

As they crossed the threshold of the portal, the dilapidated castle and the echoes of their battle faded into nothingness. The journey between worlds was a mere instant, a swift blur of transition. Then, just as quickly, they were enveloped by the recognisable surroundings of the academy. Here, the air was different. It hummed with a sense of security and a soothing familiarity.

Avery, still cradled in Lucien's arms, smiled.

The portal closed behind them, leaving no trace of the harrowing journey they had undertaken. The school stood silent, but within its walls echoed the heartbeat of those who had faced the shadows and emerged, if not unscathed, then undeniably triumphant.

CHAPTER 12

WITH A SENSE OF URGENCY, LUCIEN CARRIED AVERY through the familiar halls of their sanctuary, his strides purposeful yet gentle. The heft of her body nestled in his embrace served as both a comforting presence and a stark testament to the trials she had faced. As they reached his chamber, he gently laid her down on the bed, a haven far removed from the malevolence they had left behind.

Alessandra, ever practical and composed, entered the room after them. Her keen eyes assessed Avery's condition, registering the cuts and bruises that marred her once pristine skin. Without hesitation, she moved to a nearby cabinet, retrieving clean bandages, salves, and other supplies.

"We need to clean her wounds," Alessandra stated, her hands deftly organising the healing implements. Lucien nodded in agreement, concern etched on his face.

Avery's gaze lifted to meet Lucien's, a soft glimmer of thankfulness flickering in her eyes despite her physical exhaustion. In the wake of the turmoil she had faced, his nearness brought a semblance of calm to her frayed nerves. Lucien's eyes conveyed a wealth of unspoken feelings, delivering a wordless pledge of assistance and tenderness despite the trials they had endured together.

Alessandra approached the bedside, her movements graceful and assured. "Brother, help me lift her a bit," she instructed, positioning herself to tend to Avery's wounds.

As they worked together to cleanse and dress Avery's injuries, a palpable atmosphere of camaraderie and shared purpose filled the room. Lucien's fingers brushed against Avery's, a silent reassurance passing between them. Alessandra, despite her no-nonsense exterior, carried out her healing duties with a gentle touch that spoke of both skill and compassion.

The room, bathed in the soft glow of flickering candles, became a sanctuary of recovery. Outside, the academy's walls stood as a fortress against the unknown, proof of resilience to those who called it home. In the quietude of that moment, they found solace, knowing that even in the face of darkness, the bonds forged between them could withstand the harshest trials.

After the final bandage was delicately secured, Alessandra gathered her supplies, leaving the room in respectful silence. Lucien lingered beside Avery, his eyes reflecting relief and lingering concern.

Tears burst forth from Avery, unchecked and heavy with the pent-up anguish of her recent ordeal. Each sob was a release of the physical scars, the deep-seated pain, and the swirling uncertainty of the future. Beside her, Lucien's presence was a steady anchor. He sat close, his arms wrapping around her in a protective cocoon, his own heart echoing each of her emotional quakes. His whispers of comfort mingled with her cries, words of solace that sought to soothe the ache within her.

As Avery clung to him, her tears leaving damp trails on his shirt, the room seemed to hold its breath. It absorbed the soft, sorrowful sounds of her weeping, bearing silent witness to the profound impact the events had left on her soul.

Her voice quivered as she spoke. "I... I thought I'd never see you again. When Darmon—"

Softly, Lucien responded, "We don't have to talk about it now. Just know that I'm here, always."

He continued to hold her, a steady anchor in the tempest of her emotions. The love between them was a sanctuary that transcended the horrors they had faced. Lucien's heart ached witnessing Avery's pain, yet he remained resolute in being her steadfast support.

Through her sobs, Avery whispered, "I was so scared, Lucien. I thought I'd lost everything."

"You have lost nothing, Avery. We'll face whatever comes together. You're the love of my life, and nothing will ever change that."

His sincere words carried the weight of a deep commitment. In that vulnerable moment, amid the scars and tears, they discovered a profound connection that no darkness could extinguish. Together, they would heal, rebuild, and forge ahead, bound by a love that had withstood the test of shadows.

Avery's eyes held an otherworldly gleam as she looked at Lucien. The transformation into a demon had left its mark, and uncertainty twinkled in her gaze.

Lucien met her questioning look with a tenacity that transcended the supernatural abyss that separated them. "We'll fix this, Avery. I promise you. You're not alone in this, and I won't rest until we bring you back."

Avery's expression shifted between disbelief and a glimmer of hope. Undoubtedly, the seriousness of her demonic condition was clear, but Lucien's determination kept her steady amidst the sea of uncertainty.

"The manuscript..." Lucien explained, his voice carrying a note of urgency. "It holds secrets that might help us. Ash, with his extensive knowledge of arcane arts, can decipher it. Together, we'll undo what Darmon did to you."

As Lucien spoke, he held her gaze, trying to convey both reassurance and the unyielding commitment to restoring her humanity. The Manual of Demonic Magic, a tome steeped in dark mysteries, became a glimmer of anticipation in the face of despair.

Avery nodded slowly. In that shared moment, a silent vow passed between them—a pledge to defy the demonic chains that bound her and rediscover the light that had once defined her essence.

As Avery succumbed to exhaustion, Lucien gently tucked a strand of hair behind her ear. His gaze held a blend of affection and worry as he observed her serene yet delicate slumber.

Lucien exited the room, each step measured and deliberate, embodying a quiet determination. As he gently closed the door behind him, the muted click resonated softly in the corridor. The academy's halls, which had once reverberated with the ominous presence of the Order, now lay in a respectful hush. With purpose, Lucien navigated the silent passageways, making his way to where the rest of the team was gathered.

Entering the dimly lit chamber, he was met with the concerned gazes of his companions. Ash, Jade, Vlad, and Madame Leana formed a tightly knit circle, their expressions mirroring the seriousness of their recent ordeal. They each carried the weight of the recent chaos in their own way, their faces revealing a combination of concern and the weariness that accompanies a hard-fought victory.

Lucien addressed them, his voice a mix of weariness and resolution. "Avery's resting for now. We need to make haste. The Manual of Demonic Magic might be our key to reversing what's been done to her. Ash, your expertise is crucial for deciphering this."

Ash nodded solemnly, understanding the gravity of their quest. "I'll get started right away. This is delicate work, and we can't afford mistakes."

Madame Leana spoke next, her gaze piercing through the shadows. "Time is of the essence. The longer we delay..."

Jade, her eyes reflecting empathy, added, "We're with you, Lucien. Whatever it takes to save Avery."

Vlad, usually the calm voice of reason, chimed in. "Let's not forget the dangers that lie within the Manuscript. It's a path of shadows we tread."

Lucien nodded. "We face the uncertain, but Avery deserves every effort. We won't let her slip away into darkness."

As the group prepared to delve into the mysteries of demonic magic, a collective tenacity replaced the earlier discord. The manuscript awaited, its pages holding the promise of redemption or the hazardous depths of the unknown.

As Ash meticulously deciphered the cryptic passages of the manuscript, an electric tension gripped the chamber. The ancient symbols responded to his expertise, their luminescence pulsating with an otherworldly energy. An atmosphere of anticipation enveloped the surroundings, with every heartbeat resonating the significance of the moment.

Lucien couldn't tear his eyes away from the unfolding

magic, a kaleidoscope of colours dancing in the room. The tome seemed alive, its secrets eager to be revealed. It was both a spectacle and a conduit to the unknown.

When the magical tempest subsided, a figure materialised at the heart of the room, enveloped in a wispy cloud of smoke. Slowly taking form, the silhouette transformed into the familiar visage of a man in an antiquated suit—Jarvis de Winter.

Alessandra gasped, her hand instinctively covering her mouth. Lucien remained fixed in place, surprise and happiness dancing across his expression. The others shared glances of incredulity, attempting to grasp the reality of the miraculous scene.

With a hesitant step forward, Lucien's voice trembled with emotion. "Father, is it truly you? How... how can this be?"

Jarvis cast a sombre smile toward his children. "The dark forces inadvertently forged a link between us through the Manuscript. I've witnessed your struggles, your victories. The untiring spirit that has kept you fighting."

Tears glistened in Alessandra's eyes as she approached her father. "We thought we had lost you. Did the tome somehow bring you back to us?"

Jarvis nodded, a hint of sorrow in his gaze. "Yes, my daughter. The Manuscript, originally a tool of darkness, became an unintended vessel for me to communicate with you. But this connection is fragile, and my presence here is fleeting."

Madame Leana's perceptive gaze mirrored the significance of the moment. "What is the path forward, Jarvis? How can we liberate you from this state of limbo?"

Jarvis turned his gaze toward the Manuscript, determination mingled with sadness in his eyes. "To sever the bond, you must perform a ritual outlined in the book. But be cautious, for it is fraught with danger. The forces that ensnared me are not easily trifled with."

His grave expression deepened as he continued to impart crucial information. "When you release me, other entities from the realms beyond may attempt to breach through the opening. It is imperative that you act swiftly. Once I am fully present, destroy the tome to seal the gateway and prevent any malevolent forces from entering."

The room fell into a contemplative hush. The burden of the responsibility they shouldered weighed heavily on every member of the group.

Lucien, his voice steadying, addressed his father. "Father, we've faced formidable challenges, and Avery, the love of my life, is ensnared in a web of darkness. We must save her before we proceed with the ritual. Can the Manuscript guide us to break her transformation into a demon?"

Jarvis nodded, acknowledging the urgency of Lucien's plea. "The Manuscript holds the answers you seek. Use its guidance wisely, for the forces that ensnare Avery are likely entwined with those that bound me."

A renewed sense of purpose swept through the room as Ash and the others focused on deciphering the book's passages related to Avery's predicament. Lucien's thoughts raced, torn between the joy of his father's return and the urgency to rescue Avery.

In the quiet intensity of the chamber, plans took shape. Lucien, Alessandra, and their allies prepared to confront the looming challenges that intertwined their fates with forces beyond the mortal realm. The Manuscript, a key to both salvation and peril, awaited their next move in pursuing light within the shadows.

Lucien's gaze bore into Jarvis, seeking answers within the

depths of his father's spectral visage. "Do you know who bound you into that book?"

Jarvis sighed, a haunting echo of breath within the ethereal space surrounding him. "The one who did this to me is a formidable practitioner of dark magic, veiled in shadows. I could never find out their true identity. The cloak of anonymity was their greatest weapon."

Lucien clenched his jaw, frustration coursing through him. The enigmatic nature of his father's captor added another layer of complexity to their treacherous quest. The Manuscript lay open before them, its arcane secrets waiting to be unveiled.

Alessandra, standing beside Lucien, sensed his turmoil. She placed a reassuring hand on his shoulder, silently communicating solidarity and strength. Lucien acknowledged her gesture with a brief, grateful glance before turning back to Jarvis.

"Avery was transformed, not cursed?" Jarvis mused, his spectral form seeming to shimmer with realisation. "I had some suspicions about him back when I was still part of the Order. The darkness that surrounds him is ancient, and his ambitions are boundless."

Lucien took a deep breath as he addressed Jarvis. "There's something you need to know. Lord Darmon is no more. He met his end in the shadows he sought to command."

The silence that followed Lucien's revelation seemed to stretch into eternity. Jarvis, enveloped in the residual magic of the tome, took in the gravity of the news. The room held its breath, waiting for Jarvis to respond to the demise of the malevolent figure who had orchestrated so much suffering.

Finally, Jarvis spoke, his spectral voice carrying a mixture of relief and contemplation. "Darmon's passing marks a significant turn of events. Yet, be wary, for the echoes of his darkness may still reverberate in unforeseen ways."

The gravity of the situation hung in the air, intertwining the destinies of the de Winter family with the malevolent forces seeking dominion. Lucien's mind churned with concern for Avery.

CHAPTER 13

Lucien felt the weight of responsibility pressing on his shoulders as the tome lay open before them, its pages filled with esoteric symbols and cryptic incantations. The room, awash in the gentle flicker of candlelight, appeared to be suspended in a moment of expectant silence.

Vlad, his stoic demeanour betraying a glimmer of confidence, exchanged a knowing glance with Ash. "We've faced difficult challenges before. This will be no different. We'll be fine."

Ash, with a subtle nod, echoed Vlad's assurance. "Dark magic can be unravelled, especially with the right guidance. We've got this."

Jarvis, the ethereal presence hovering beside the open Manuscript, spoke with a spectral calmness. "The spell you seek lies within these pages. Turn to the section marked by the heavenly symbol."

Lucien, his fingers tracing the strange characters, found the designated page. His gaze locked onto the celestial symbol that marked the crucial page and took a steadying breath. The book's ancient pages rustled softly as if whispering secrets that only he could comprehend. The symbols glowed faintly in response to the group's collective intent.

Clearing his throat, Lucien recited the intricate spell, each word carrying the weight of centuries-old magic. The incantation flowed from his lips, a dance of syllables that resonated with the energies swirling around them.

"By the moon's silver light and the sun's golden embrace, we beseech the realms of magic and grace. Shadows that bind, shadows that veil, unravel their hold on this cursed shroud."

The Manuscript responded to his words, the markings on the page shimmering with ghostly luminescence. Alessandra, standing beside him, mirrored his focus, her own power intertwining with his as they cast their combined force into the incantation.

Vlad and Ash, the experts in the dark arts, observed with keen concentration, ensuring the precision of Lucien's recitation. The air became charged with a palpable tension, a symphony of magical currents converging in the small chamber.

Madame Leana, her eyes closed in deep meditation, emanated a spiritual aura that augmented the potency of the spell. Her connection to the ancient forces lent an additional layer of strength to the unfolding ritual.

Lucien continued, his voice resonating with resolve. "By the Earth's steadfast might and the winds that weave through day and night, break the chains that bind this soul, restore the one who's lost control."

As Lucien's voice filled the room, the pages of the book fluttered of their own accord. Each turn revealed new symbols that seemed to dance in time with his words. The air pulsed with the gathering of magical forces, creating a palpable tension as if reality itself was warping in response to their efforts to counteract the dark transformation.

Alessandra, her eyes shimmering with a faint, silvery light, channelled her own magical essence into the chant. The bond between her and Lucien deepened in that shared moment of arcane communion.

At the peak of Lucien's incantation, the celestial symbol in the page's centre glowed with a luminous otherworldly light. The culmination of their efforts hung in the balance, and the fate of Avery rested upon the convoluted dance of words and symbols woven by the group's collective magic.

"In the name of love that transcends the darkest abyss, let the transformation be broken, let the light reminisce. By the power within and the bonds we defend, let Avery's true self ascend."

As the chamber echoed with the last words, the remaining syllable hung in the air like a spell waiting to unfold. The Manuscript's pages returned to stillness. The group waited in silence, expecting the spell's effect on Avery's soul.

The room held its breath as a gentle tremor seemed to pass through the air. It was as if the unseen forces had caught the intangible echo of Lucien's spell and the magical currents resonated with the intent woven into the incantation.

A hushed anticipation lingered. Lucien's heart pounded in rhythm with the shared hope of the group. They stared at the tome, their eyes searching for any sign of change.

Then, a soft glow emanated from the pages of the ancient book, casting a warm light that bathed the chamber. The celestial symbol at the centre of the spell pulsed, its radiance expanding like ripples on a tranquil pond.

Alessandra, her hand still resting on the Manuscript, felt the subtle shift in energy. Her eyes grew wide in awe. "It's working," she murmured, her voice tinged with wonder.

Vlad, ever composed, nodded with a knowing smile. "The magic is taking hold. Now we must wait and trust in its course."

Madame Leana, her spiritual senses attuned to the mystical realms, muttered, "The threads of fate are weaving a new pattern. Let us be patient and steadfast in our vigil."

As the glow intensified, a serene warmth enveloped the group, a reassurance that their consolidated efforts had set in motion forces beyond their immediate comprehension.

Then, in a delicate cascade, the light extended beyond the Manuscript, forming ethereal tendrils that floated towards the centre of the room. The magical threads converged, swirling together in a mesmerising dance.

Amid this arcane ballet, a figure materialised. It was as if the very essence of the chamber had coalesced into a form, slowly taking shape with each passing moment.

A gasp escaped Lucien's lips as the silhouette solidified into a familiar figure. Avery stood before them, bathed in the soft radiance of the magical light. Her eyes, once clouded by demonic influence, now sparkled with recognition and clarity.

A hush fell over the room as the group beheld the wondrous transformation. Avery, freed from the shackles of the demonic curse, looked around with confusion and wonder.

Lucien, his heart overflowing with relief and joy, took a tentative step forward. "Avery?" he called, his voice a gentle inquiry.

She turned to him. Their eyes met. The connection between them, tested and tempered by the trials of darkness, radiated with an unbreakable strength. Avery's gaze, filled with love and gratitude, spoke volumes that words could not convey.

"You've done it," she said, her voice carrying the echoes of a soul reborn.

As the group basked in the glow of their success, a subtle tremor passed through the spectral form of Jarvis de Winter. His translucent figure wavered, and a hint of weariness etched into his features.

Madame Leana, perceptive to the nuances of the spirit realm, sensed a shift in the force. She stepped forward with concern and asked, "Jarvis, are you all right?"

Jarvis managed a faint smile, but his voice carried both gratitude and farewell. "Releasing me has taken a toll on my soul. The connection to the Manuscript sustained me, but its purpose is fulfilled. I am grateful for this moment of freedom."

Lucien, realising the sacrifice Jarvis had made for Avery's sake, felt a mixture of gratitude and sorrow. "Thank you, Father. You've played a crucial role in saving Avery."

As Jarvis faded, he extended a spectral hand toward Lucien. "Protect her, son. The darkness is not fully vanquished. Be vigilant."

With those parting words, Jarvis dissipated into a soft mist that merged once more with the Manuscript. The room, once again steeped in quiet stillness, held the lingering essence of a soul that had returned to the confines of the enchanted book.

As the ethereal mist of Jarvis de Winter dissolved once more into the tome, Lucien's gaze lingered on the closed book, a deep sense of gratitude and determination welling within him. Turning to the group, he spoke with resolute conviction.

"I promise you all, I will find the spell or any means necessary to release him permanently. His sacrifice won't be in vain. Father deserves the peace he sought for so long."

Avery, now fully restored, looked at Lucien with a profound understanding. "He did save me," she whispered, her eyes reflecting the depth of emotions stirred by the moment.

Lucien nodded, his heart heavy with the weight of the responsibility ahead. "The darkness may linger, but together, we'll face whatever comes our way."

The group, unified by the bonds forged in adversity, stood in silent acknowledgment of the events that had transpired. The Manual of Demonic Magic, now closed, held the secrets of both peril and redemption, the intricate dance between light and shadow that defined their journey.

The End

THE SHADOWBOUND KNIGHT

CHAPTER 1

UNDER THE SHROUD OF WINTER'S DARKNESS, THE MOON hung low in the ink-black sky, casting a radiant shimmer over the snow-laden grounds of Hajun Temple. The ancient structures stood in solemn silence; their centuries-old tales whispered only by the soft crunch of Casimir Thorne's footsteps on the snow-covered path. The air held a biting cold, seeping into bones and echoing the stories of long-forgotten warriors.

A surge of brilliant lightning forked across the sky, illuminating the once-veiled surroundings with an ethereal glow. With a ferocious display of power, the storm, a combination of arcane and elemental forces, unleashed its fury upon the onyx gates. These gates, designed to guard the temple's sanctity, now faced an onslaught like never before.

The snow-covered gate, once a symbol of the temple's strength, now crumbled under the magical storm, shattered into pieces. The sheer might of the arcane energies shattered the onyx into myriad fragments, each bearing the burden of enchantments woven over centuries.

Cloaked in shadows, Casimir moved with the stealth of a

phantom, his destination? The temple. Its architecture bore witness to centuries of spiritual contemplation, now glistening under the spectral touch of the moonlight.

Another explosion erupted from the heart of the temple, magical energy tearing through the night. The shockwave sent plumes of snow into the air, and the gate crumbled under the force, its destruction revealing figures clad in dark robes against the eerie backdrop.

Recognition quickened Casimir's pulse. The Order of the Dragon, relentless seekers of occult artefacts, had found him. The sanctuary he sought for solace lay in ruins, the calmness of Hajun Temple torn asunder.

Charging forward, his steps heavy with grief and rage, Casimir witnessed the aftermath of the second explosion. The crimson-stained snow told a tale of tragedy, and the sacred grounds had transformed into a graveyard for the old monks who had once welcomed him with open arms.

No longer hidden in the shadows, Casimir faced the devastation with a heavy heart. The tempest of destruction had not only claimed the temple but also extinguished the lives of those he had considered family. In the haunting gleam of the moon, Casimir charged forward, fuelled by grief and a determination to confront the shadows that had not only pursued him but had also desecrated the sacred legacy of Hajun Temple.

He surged forth, wielding a broadsword that cleaved through the rubble without breaking stride. The spiked guard of the blade bore twin demonic wings, casting ominous silhouettes against the tumultuous backdrop. Unfazed, he confronted the dark-robed enemies that emerged from the wreckage, their intentions clear.

"Looks like the Order sent their finest," Casimir remarked with a bitter edge to his voice, his eyes locked on the commander leading the knights. The fallen snow crunched beneath his boots as he closed the distance, his blade drawn and gleaming with an ethereal light.

The commander, a stoic figure in ornate armour, raised a gloved hand in a halting gesture. "Casimir Thorne, you are to surrender peacefully. The Order seeks justice."

"Justice?" Casimir scoffed, a derisive smile playing on his lips. "You burn down my sanctuary, slaughter the only family I had left, and you talk about justice?"

The commander maintained a steely composure. "You were a threat. The Order acts to protect the realms from those who would misuse ancient powers."

Casimir's eyes gleamed with a mixture of defiance and sorrow. "You mean the kind that just obliterated a temple and left monks dead in the snow? Your Order has a twisted sense of protection."

With a swift, fluid motion, he engaged the first of the knights. His blade clashed against the spiked wings of the leader's sword, each strike echoing with the intensity of his emotions. "You really think you can bring me in, drag me back to your righteous fold? The Order might have been my family once, but that died with the people you slaughtered."

The commander, undeterred, parried Casimir's attacks with calculated precision. "You've betrayed our trust. The relic you carry is a danger to us all."

Casimir's laughter rang out bitterly amid the chaos. "The relic is the least of your concerns. You bring destruction in the name of protection. Tell me, how many innocents have you sacrificed for your Order's so-called righteousness?"

As the battle raged on, Casimir fought not just against the knights but against the very ideals that had once bound him to the Order. His every move was a testimony to the gale within him, a storm of grief, rage, and an unyielding determination to defy the twisted version of justice that now stood before him.

The sword, with demonic wings, pulsated with an otherworldly energy, its dark power clear in each swing. The leader, undeterred, pressed forward with resolve.

"Hand over the artefact, Casimir," his opponent demanded, parrying a strike with practised ease.

Casimir's lips curled into a sardonic smile. "You mean this little trinket?" He swung the sword with deceptive grace, deflecting the commander's attacks. "I'd say it's doing wonders for me. Dramatic on the destruction, though."

"It's not a plaything. It's a danger, both to you and everyone around you."

"Danger? Coming from the Order's finest? That's rich," Casimir retorted, delivering a swift kick that sent a knight stumbling backward.

The clash continued, a dance of blades beneath the haunting moonlight. Casimir's movements were fluid, each strike a blend of finesse and the raw power emanating from the demonic relic. "You act like I'm the threat here. Meanwhile, your organisation has left a trail of destruction that would make demons blush."

The leader parried, his tone steadfast. "We seek to maintain balance. Your actions jeopardise that."

As the battle escalated, Casimir's sharp wit proved equal to his skill in combat. He moved with swift agility, capitalising on the commander's brief pause. "Perhaps this artefact is what's keeping me sane amidst your Order's idea of 'balance,'" he quipped.

His opponent, undeterred, struck back. "Surrender, Casimir. There's still a chance for redemption."

Casimir's laughter echoed across the battleground. "I'll pass. I've seen enough of your Order's brand of redemption."

With a sudden, powerful swing, he disarmed his enemy, the demonic sword gleaming ominously in the moonlight.

The commander, now defenceless, faced Casimir's unwavering gaze. "This isn't over, Thorne."

Casimir smirked. "Oh, it's just getting started." Holding the relic high, he plunged back into the fray with a renewed fervour, leaving his superior and the knights to regroup amid the wreckage of Hajun Temple, the snow now stained with both blood and the echoes of their confrontation.

CHAPTER 2

Casimir's breath billowed in the chilly night air as he ran through the frozen landscape, each step leaving imprints on the icy ground. With each step, the weapon in his hand felt increasingly burdensome. Finally, he came to a stop, his chest heaving, and his gaze fixed on the ominous glow emanating from the sword.

In a hushed tone, barely audible over the biting wind, Casimir uttered an incantation, his words a whispered secret shared only with the enchanted blade. As his fingertips grazed the gleaming metal, the air crackled with an otherworldly energy. The steel responded, pulsating with a luminescence that intensified with each passing second.

A surge of hellfire erupted around Casimir, engulfing him in swirling flames that danced with an unholy fervour. The snow beneath him melted away, leaving only scorched earth in its wake. The flames licked at his form, casting an ethereal glow on his hooded figure as he became a transient silhouette within the inferno.

In the blink of an eye, the blaze swallowed him whole, and the searing heat of the underworld replaced the frigid cold of the winter night. After the hellfire dwindled, Casimir found himself in front of Roslyn Academy's ornate gates. The shift from the desolate ruins of Hajun Temple to the majestic grounds of the institute was startlingly swift and surreal.

The entrance, adorned with intricate designs and symbols, loomed before him, a threshold between worlds. The air held a distinct energy here, one that resonated with the mystical aura of the academy. Despite the absence of falling snow, the cold still gripped the surroundings, adding an extra layer of mystique.

The demonic relic, now dormant in his grip, still echoed with the traces of hellfire. As Casimir surveyed his surroundings, the resolute gleam in his eyes revealed the weight of his journey. Roslyn Academy, with its secrets and mysteries, awaited his presence, and the hooded figure prepared to confront the challenges that lay beyond the ornate gates.

In a flash of speed, a swarm of vampire knights materialised, filling the courtyard before Casimir. The glimmer shone off their armour as they formed a commanding aura, their eyes glowing with a crimson hue.

As the gates creaked open, revealing the regal figure within, Casimir couldn't discern the identity of the imposing presence that stepped forward. The figure's dark eyes met Casimir's, and, for a moment, the world seemed to pause.

Wavy, shoulder-length black hair gleamed in the moonlight, framing a handsome, pale face. The noble figure appeared slightly older, adorned with a neatly trimmed beard that added a touch of sophistication. A warm smile played on his lips, revealing perfect white teeth behind the deep red tone.

"You dare trespass?" the older vampire asked, his voice carrying a regal weight that echoed through the courtyard.

Casimir's hooded gaze met the piercing eyes of his adversary as he spoke, smirking. "More like a fashionable entrance, wouldn't you say?" He gestured theatrically at the surrounding courtyard, emphasising the swarm of knights. "Quite the welcoming committee you've got here."

The vampire's eyes flickered with a mixture of curiosity and amusement. "Indeed," he replied, a subtle nod acknowledging the orchestrated display. "But it is not every day we have a member of the Order of the Dragon gracing our presence. To what do we owe this unexpected pleasure?"

As Casimir's hooded silhouette stood tall, the gravity of his heritage hung palpably in the air. "Former. Well, you know how it is." He paused, allowing a moment of dramatic tension to linger. "Casimir Thorne, heir to the House of Thorne, at your service. Just trying to make an entrance worthy of my bloodline."

Vlad's dark eyes crinkled with a knowing glint. "Thorne, you say?" His tone carried a subtle acknowledgment of the lineage. "A name with a history. I've heard tales."

Casimir chuckled, a smirk tugging at the corners of his lips. "Ah, tales. They exaggerate, don't they? But I assure you, I'm as real as the moonlight that graces this courtyard."

Vlad offered a courteous hand. "Vlad Drakulya, pleased to make your acquaintance." His deep green eyes seemed to glint with amusement, acknowledging the wordplay. "It's rare we encounter a Thorne here. What has brought you to Roslyn Academy, Casimir Thorne?"

Casimir's hooded figure took Vlad's hand, the firm shake reverberating with an undercurrent of unspoken understanding. "I'm just a wanderer seeking a bit of warmth in this unfriendly world, Vlad Drakulya. I heard this place had an open-door policy for lost souls."

Vlad's laughter resonated in the courtyard, blending with the ambiance of the night. "Our open-door policy extends beyond just providing shelter. It offers lost souls not only warmth but also a sense of purpose," he remarked with a mysterious smile, hinting at the possibility of unexpected discoveries along the way.

"I hope you won't feel offended if I ask you to prove your intentions," Vlad stated, his dark eyes scrutinising Casimir. Vlad swiftly covered Casimir's extended arm, pulling him closer in a controlled yet authoritative manner. The gesture was more a declaration of caution than an intimate connection, a subtle reminder of Vlad's command.

Casimir met Vlad's gaze confidently. "My blood is toxic to vampires, so you can't use that to read my mind," he replied, smoothly extracting his arm from Vlad's grasp. "I am willing to surrender this to your care instead." He raised the demonic sword, its malevolent glow casting an eerie ambiance between them.

Vlad's eyes lingered on the weapon, the play of shadows emphasising the gravity of the moment. "An intriguing offer. A Thorne willingly parting with a relic. There's a story there, I'm sure," he remarked, his tone thoughtful.

Casimir's smirk remained steadfast. "Oh, many stories. But for now, consider it a token of goodwill. I'm not here to cause trouble; just seeking a place where I won't have to constantly look over my shoulder."

"Your honesty is appreciated. Roslyn Academy welcomes those with a desire for redemption and a willingness to embrace a new purpose."

Casimir extended the sword toward Vlad. "Redemption,

purpose, and perhaps a few surprises along the way, as you said."

Vlad nodded in acknowledgment. "Indeed. You may find more than you seek within these walls." The vampire knights subtly shifted in response to Vlad's unspoken command. "Welcome to Roslyn Academy, Casimir Thorne." However, Vlad declined the offered sword with a simple yet firm, "Keep it. You might need it later."

CHAPTER 3

As soon as Vlad finished talking, another vampire opened the main door, ushering them into the halls of the academy. Vlad turned towards him, a gleam of familiarity in his eyes.

"Allow me to introduce Lucien de Winter, my nephew."

Casimir inclined his head in acknowledgment. "Pleasure to meet you, Lucien," he said, his voice laced with a casual warmth.

Lucien nodded in return, a hint of a smile playing on his lips. "Likewise, Casimir. Welcome to Roslyn Academy."

Vlad, his eyes gleaming with mischief, chimed in, "And to make our family connections even more convoluted, the Thornes are essentially distant cousins of the de Winters."

Lucien and Alessandra exchanged knowing glances. Vlad, gesturing towards Alessandra, continued, "And speaking of family, allow me to introduce Alessandra de Winter, the love of my eternal life."

She stepped forward, her gaze meeting Casimir's. "It's a pleasure."

Casimir offered a genuine smile. “The pleasure is mine, Alessandra.”

Vlad led the guest through the grand halls of the academy, guiding him towards the council room. “Let’s discuss your business first, and then someone can give you a tour.”

Turning to Alessandra, Vlad added with a charming smile, “Darling, please summon the others.”

Alessandra nodded and gracefully left to gather the remaining members, leaving Vlad, Lucien, and Casimir to delve into the matters at hand.

As they waited in the council room, the air was soon filled with the hushed sounds of approaching footsteps and lively chatter. In a seamless ballet of entrances, three additional figures joined Alessandra.

Vlad, with a gracious sweep of his hand, began the introductions. “Allow me to present the esteemed members of our assembly. Avery Darmon, Lucien’s beloved, who adds a touch of grace and resilience to our endeavours.” Avery offered a warm smile, acknowledging Casimir’s presence.

“Next, we have Jade Nicolay, a skilled witch with a heart as fierce as her magic,” Vlad continued. Jade nodded in greeting.

Vlad’s gaze then turned to the last member. “And last, but certainly not least, Ashley Rex, or Ash, the Prince of Hell and my esteemed adoptive father. His wisdom and experience have guided us through many challenging situations.” Ash inclined his head with a regal air, acknowledging Casimir with a nod.

“Now that our assembly is complete, let us delve into the matters that bring you to Roslyn Academy,” Vlad declared.

“For several years, I had been living in seclusion, finding sanctuary within the walls of Hajun Temple, under the compassionate guardianship of the monks. However, just two hours ago, the temple fell victim to a brutal assault that resulted in the ruthless slaughter of its residents, my makeshift family. The Order, under the guise of retrieving me, tried to lay claim to this artefact," he explained as he rested the sword on top of the table.

As the weapon made contact with the surface, Ash's eyes widened in what looked like recognition, a glint of astonishment shining in his gaze. A brief hush enveloped the room, as if Casimir's revelation cast a weighty challenge to the fates that had united them.

"What made you hide in the first place?" Jade asked.

Casimir, wearing a solemn expression, met Jade's inquisitive gaze. "I hid from the Order because they wanted to manipulate and control supernatural beings, including myself. They sought to harness our powers without considering the consequences. I refused to become a pawn in their twisted game, so I chose a life of seclusion and anonymity."

Casimir continued, a solemn tone underscoring his words. "This sword is not merely a weapon; it's a part of who I am. As a half-demon, it's essential to my existence. Without me, it would become dormant, and without it, I wouldn't survive."

"So, when you presented it to me..." Vlad trailed off.

Casimir met Vlad's gaze with a nod, confirming the gravity of the situation. "Yes, Vlad. Offering the weapon was not just a gesture; it was an acknowledgment of the symbiotic bond between me and this artefact. Without it, my existence is precarious, and the Order's pursuit of me would become relentless. But, considering the recent events, it seems the Order is determined to have both me and the sword. Consequences be damned."

A contemplative hush descended upon the room, the gravity of Casimir's disclosure lingering in the midst of the gathered allies. The sword, now at rest on the table, bore witness not only to its own history but also to the uncertain path of its wielder.

As the silence lingered, Alessandra spoke up, her voice carrying a mix of concern and determination. "Casimir, we won't let the Order take you or this artefact. We stand together against their tyranny."

Vlad, his gaze still fixed on the sword, broke the quiet. "Casimir, your predicament is now our shared challenge. We'll find a way to thwart the Order's plans and ensure your safety."

Lucien stood by his uncle and added, "We've faced the Order before, and we've prevailed. We won't let them take another life without a fight."

Jade's eyes reflected a spark of defiance. "The Order's reign of manipulation ends here. We'll uncover their motives and dismantle their schemes."

Ash, the Prince of Hell, leaned back in his chair, a sly smile playing on his lips. "Well, this promises to be quite the adventure. I enjoy a good challenge."

Casimir, moved by the authentic sense of unity that enveloped him, was overwhelmed with gratitude. "I appreciate every one of you. Your backing is invaluable. Now, let's strategize our next steps and bring an ultimate conclusion to the Order's pursuit."

"So, who's leading the Order now? With both Azaroth and Darmon out of the picture, there can't be many left capable of taking control," Jade remarked.

Casimir pondered Jade's question, reflecting on the complex structure of the Order's hierarchy. "The Order of the Dragon thrives in secrecy, with leadership often as changeable as the wind. The last heads were key players, but their absence likely sparked a power struggle within the ranks. Identifying who's taken the helm now isn't straightforward.

We'll have to collect information to understand their current chain of command."

Vlad tapped his fingers thoughtfully on the table. "Indeed, the Order's internal dynamics are intricate. But we have contacts and resources. We'll exploit any weaknesses and unearth their secrets. Our goal is to dismantle the Order, root and branch."

The group nodded in agreement, recognising the formidable challenge ahead. The struggle against the Order encompassed more than just ensuring Casimir's well-being; it was a larger conflict against an organisation determined to manipulate and dominate supernatural entities.

Vlad, addressing the group, suggested, "Ash, I believe you're better suited to show Casimir around. He can stay in the guest wing. Familiarise him with our surroundings and ensure he has everything he needs."

Ash stood up with a nod and a mischievous glint in his eyes. "Consider it done. Casimir, follow me. I'll fill you in on the more 'colourful' aspects of our academy."

Casimir, acknowledging the offer, followed Ash out of the council room.

CHAPTER 4

As Ash led Casimir through the labyrinthine corridors of Roslyn Academy, the grandeur of the institution unfolded before them. The academy, with its centuries-old architecture, seamlessly blended the mystique of the supernatural with the elegance of a bygone era.

They passed through ornate halls hung with tapestries depicting ancient battles and noble creatures, the flickering candlelight casting a ghostly glow on the polished marble floors. Stained glass windows depicting scenes of magic and myth allowed streaks of coloured light to dance across the walls as they moved through the building.

Casimir couldn't help but be captivated by the juxtaposition of the mystical and the scholarly, each room telling a story of a different era.

They reached the central courtyard, where the moon's soft glow illuminated the architecture. Stone pathways crisscrossed between well-maintained gardens, and ancient statues stood as silent sentinels, their expressions frozen in time. The air was filled with quiet serenity, a stark contrast to the turmoil Casimir had recently escaped.

As they strolled through the academy, Ash pointed out notable landmarks—the library with its towering shelves housing ancient tomes, the training grounds where supernatural beings honed their skills, and the main hall where important gatherings took place. The academy, a shelter for those who sought refuge from the Order's grasp, revealed itself as a haven steeped in both history and magic.

Absorbed in the enchanting atmosphere, Casimir couldn't shake the sensation of belonging in this mystical sanctuary. The academy, with all its hidden mysteries and protective entities, held a deeper significance; it stood as a stronghold against the encroaching darkness, a defender of the supernaturals' enduring light.

"So, how did you end up being Vlad's adoptive father?" Casimir asked.

Ash's laughter echoed through the corridors as they continued their walk. "Well, you could say I played a hand in creating him. Vlad was at a crossroads, struggling with the complexities of morality. He needed a reason to embrace his existence, and I offered him that purpose."

He paused, a hint of nostalgia in his eyes. "In a way, I breathed life into him when he needed it the most. He became more than just a fledgling vampire; he converted into a force to be reckoned with. The bond we share goes beyond the conventional. I gave him a reason to live, and he became the formidable vampire prince you see today."

Casimir nodded, absorbing the significance of the tale. The connection between Ash and Vlad, a creator and his progeny, added another layer to the dynamics of the supernatural realm within the academy's walls.

"I remember from the history books that Vlad is the son

of one of the main founders of the Order. It's a shame that they turned against him like they did."

Ash's eyes reflected the shadows of a complex history as he shared further details. "It was Matthias Corvinus, Vlad's father's best friend, who ultimately turned against them. Friendship's bonds splintered beneath the weight of power and ambition. Corvinus, seduced by the Order's promises, betrayed not only his friend but also Vlad's entire family. The betrayal ran deep, tearing apart the foundations of trust that once bound them together. His defiance against the Order is not just a personal vendetta; it's a quest for justice against those who deceived his family. And now, with allies like us, he's determined to rewrite the narrative that the Order seeks to impose upon the paranormal world."

They continued their walk through the moonlit courtyard, the atmosphere heavy with the echoes of a past stained by treachery.

"Casimir, it seems there's more to your tale. Why does the Order want you and that sword so desperately?"

"The Thorne family, my kin, were once the procurers of artefacts for the Order. The blade I carry, imbued with ancient power, was one such article. But when I realised the Order's true intentions—to wield both the sword and me as weapons against their enemies—I broke free."

Ash's gaze shifted from the moonlit waters to Casimir, a silent acknowledgment passing between them. "The Thorne family's ties to the Order are deep-rooted, and your defiance has disrupted their plans. The artefact you carry, this sword, holds a power they seek to exploit. But your choice to resist them has severed the chains that bound you to their dark designs."

Casimir's eyes reflected a mixture of determination and weariness. "I never wanted to be a pawn in their game. The blade, as much a part of me as my blood, holds secrets that the Order aims to weaponize. Now, with the temple destroyed and the monks slain, they won't rest until they reclaim both the artefact and its unwilling bearer."

"Here, within the academy, we stand against the shadows of our pasts. Together, we'll thwart the Order's ambitions and reclaim our own destinies." Ash's voice resonated with a quiet resolve.

As they resumed their walk, the moonlit courtyard embraced the unfolding stories, weaving them into the tapestry of defiance that marked the academy as a sanctuary for those who dared to challenge the Order's oppressive grip on the supernatural world.

Ash swung open the door to a chamber adorned with rich burgundy velvet curtains that framed tall, narrow windows. Moonlight filtered through, casting a soft glow on the polished wooden furniture.

"Here's where you'll be staying."

Casimir stepped into the room, eyes wandering over the lavish furnishings and the intricately patterned wallpaper. "Impressive."

A massive four-poster bed, draped with heavy brocade curtains, stood as the centrepiece. The bed's dark mahogany frame showcased craftsmanship from a bygone era, and the bedding, a blend of deep blue and gold, exuded a regal charm. A small writing desk with a quill and inkwell sat against one wall, adorned with aged volumes and mysterious trinkets.

Ash chuckled. "Victorian times meet the supernatural—it's the academy's unique blend. That bed, by the way, is more comfortable than it looks. The velvet curtains can be dramatic, but they do the job of keeping out the prying eyes of the night."

The room breathed an air of antiquity, with a fireplace

decorated with marble mantelpieces and embellished with mystic symbols. The crackling flames promised warmth on the cold December nights.

Casimir inspected the four-poster bed with a smirk. "I've slept in worse places. And the fireplace, a nice touch. Is it magically enchanted?"

Ash nodded. "You catch on quickly. Now, get some rest. Tomorrow, we'll delve into the mysteries the academy holds."

Once the door shut behind Ash, Casimir was left in solitude, enveloped by the room's lingering echoes of bygone days. The walls of the academy seemed to murmur ancient secrets, while the night air hinted at a blend of restful peace and impending revelations.

CHAPTER 5

In the ethereal realm of dreams, Casimir found himself ensnared in the clutches of his own nightmares. The moonlit room transformed into a chaotic battleground, shadows dancing in a macabre ballet as the relentless knights of the Order hunted him.

The air crackled with an ominous energy as the knights closed in, their dark figures blending with the night. Casimir's heart pounded in his chest as he desperately evaded their attacks, each strike resonating with a malevolent force. The haunting echoes of clashing swords and anguished roars filled the dreamlike landscape.

Trapped and cornered, Casimir fought valiantly, feeling the burden of his history and the weighty responsibility of the artefact he carried. The unyielding determination of the knights pursuing him mirrored the ceaseless pursuit of the Order in the waking world. Each parry and counterattack resonated with the real-life battles he had experienced.

As the nightmare unfolded, the knights closed in, overpowering him with their numbers and supernatural prowess.

Casimir felt the burden of imminent doom bearing down on him as their icy, pitiless gaze bore into his soul. Despite his brave attempts, he found himself overpowered, ensnared by the suffocating hold of the Order tightening its grip around him.

The knights prepared to deliver the final blow. Casimir struggled against the invisible chains that bound him, his breath ragged with exhaustion and fear. The atmosphere thickened with an impending sense of doom.

Just as the dream threatened to consume him entirely, Casimir's eyes snapped open. Beads of sweat clung to his forehead, and he gasped for breath, realising he had been pulled from the clutches of the nightmare.

The return to reality was gradual, and the remnants of the dream slowly dissipated. However, the haunting spectres of his past and the Order's relentless pursuit left a lasting imprint, serving as a reminder that they loitered not only in his waking life but also intruded upon the sanctuary of his dreams.

Casimir's eyes flickered to the bedside table, where the clock's cold digits revealed that only a mere thirty minutes had passed in the realm of troubled dreams. With a silent sigh, he rose from the bed, the persisting echoes of the nightmare still dancing at the edges of his consciousness.

Determined to shake off the persisting unease, Casimir left his chamber, the moonlit corridors of the academy welcoming him back to the waking world. As he navigated the quiet halls, the familiar path to the council room drew him forward, each step a deliberate stride toward the heart of the institute.

Casimir lingered by the slightly ajar door, the muffled voices within drifting to him like elusive whispers of an unfinished tale. The air within the room crackled with tension, each spoken word a strategic move in the unfolding chess game between the realms of light and shadow.

A familiar voice—Lucien's—authoritative and powerful, broke through the hushed conversations. "My father comes first. After that, we address the new leader of the Order." His words held significant gravity, setting a clear course through the prevailing uncertainty in the room.

Jade's voice pierced the council room's quiet, sharp and clear, her words laden with the insight gained from countless battles and uncovered secrets. "The Order is much like a Hydra. You cut off one head, and more spring forth," she observed, her eyes mirroring the resilience shaped by their collective trials.

Still remaining just beyond the threshold of the council room, Casimir listened as Alessandra's voice pierced through the air, injecting a note of urgency into the ongoing discussion. "What about Casimir? He needs us," she emphasised, her words echoing with a resolute loyalty that spoke volumes about the unbreakable bond forged in the ordeal of their shared trials.

Entering the room, Casimir's presence was signalled by the faint creak of the door. As he moved further inside, his voice carried a determined tone. "I'll assist in locating your father, and afterward, we can collectively focus on addressing the Order."

Lucien's voice cut through the room, injecting a note of realism into the collective determination. "That will be harder than you think. He's been gone for ages, and now his soul is bound in this book." He raised the Manual of Demonic Magic into the air.

"Okay, so you have the real deal. May I?" Casimir's question hung in the air.

Lucien nodded and passed the book to him.

"The story goes that only certain people can use this manuscript to its full extent. My family being one of them. Half demons and all. I guess this is the perfect time to test the theory," Casimir said, his words carrying a mix of resolve and a touch of anticipation.

His eyes focused on the Manual of Demonic Magic, Casimir whispered something under his breath. With deliberate intent, he used his index finger to draw a series of symbols on the cover of the manuscript. In response to the arcane touch, the tome opened, revealing the first page, which seemed intentionally left blank. To the astonishment of those gathered, golden writing began to materialise on the once-empty page. An invisible hand, guided by forces unseen, etched the words into existence.

The air crackled with a subtle energy, as if the very essence of the manuscript responded to Casimir's bloodline, unveiling secrets long guarded by the pages of the magical tome.

"So, your family is the owner of this book?" Ash asked, curiosity etched in his features.

"In a way," Casimir responded, his gaze fixed on the golden writing now adorning the manuscript. "This was produced by a family friend after supposedly returning from hell. His peers thought of him as a lunatic, as he experimented with the spells. My family identified this manuscript as dangerous to humankind and put a seal on it. Over time, witches and warlocks tried to break the seal, but only partially managed. Hence, some spells could be used."

"How's this going to help my father?" Lucien questioned, a note of scepticism in his voice.

"It could lead us to where your father is actually being kept. There must be a reason he is bound but not killed," Casimir suggested.

"So, are you implying that this book contains just a fragment of his soul?" Lucien enquired.

"Imagine it as a lifeline. By tracing the magical threads, we may eventually locate the core, the primary focal point where the bulk of his essence is confined. It's a daring undertaking, but it stands as our most promising approach to solving this enigma."

Casimir took a small dagger from his pocket and, cutting his palm, he let a few drops of his blood drip on the first page. "It's just an offering. I may be the master of this book, but I still have to coax it into helping me."

The room fell into a hushed silence as the crimson droplets merged with the golden script, a ceremonial interplay of the ordinary and the mystical. It appeared that the Manual of Demonic Magic acknowledged the offering, its pages reacting to the contact with Casimir's blood by emitting a gentle, otherworldly radiance.

The crimson liquid vanished in an instant, bringing a smile to Casimir's face. He murmured an incantation and gently blew on the cut, causing the wound to vanish. The room, steeped in the enchantment of age-old magic, bore witness to the interaction between the heir of the House of Thorne and the mystical grimoire.

He then took the same palm and rested it on top of the golden writing, closing his eyes. "I see trees. A park maybe. An old house and a cemetery." The words escaped Casimir's lips, each vision carrying a weight of significance as if the landscape glimpsed through his senses held the key to Jarvis's hidden whereabouts.

"Prior Park Mansion?" Lucien asked, his curiosity piqued. "You've explored that place, looking for him." He shifted his gaze to Alessandra, and suddenly, the room was suffused with a palpable sense of realisation, akin to a dense fog settling over everything. The connection between Casimir's vision and Alessandra's first-hand encounters added a new dimension of intricacy to the emerging enigma surrounding their father's imprisonment.

"Now that I think of it, I don't think we actually stepped foot in the mansion last time. I believe Azaroth nabbed us in the chapel," Alessandra pointed out, her words threading a tapestry of memories intertwined with the sinister events that had unfolded during their previous encounter with the Order.

"I think you might be onto something. Him whispering to the flames is the last thing I remember before waking up in chains," Ash chipped in, his acknowledgment lending credence to the significance of Casimir's vision.

"Same here. I think we should give this trail a chance," Jade added, her voice carrying a note of cautious optimism.

"I hate to interrupt your reminiscing, but I think this might be wrong. Father hated that place. The place closest to his heart was the home he lived with Liliana, your mother. The place where you were born." Lucien looked at Alessandra, his revelation injecting an additional dimension of complexity into the unfolding narrative.

"You know about that? That we don't have the same mother?" Alessandra asked.

"Yes. Father informed me about the Order killing Liliana. Unfortunately, people who get close to the de Winters die. It's a universally acknowledged truth," Lucien added with a wry smile, recognising the grim reality that seemed to haunt his family.

"Haerford House. It's not just a park; it's a forest with a small private cemetery. You're correct. It was selfish of me to assume that the place where we experienced childhood joy would hold the same significance for our father. His happiness died along with mother," Alessandra remarked.

"Then it's settled," Vlad stated. "Tomorrow, we assemble a team to go to Haerford House. We need to do this right, without alerting the Order."

As the night progressed, the group laid plans and forged a pact bound by shared purpose. The looming spectre of the Order cast a shadow over their resolve, but within the hallowed halls of Roslyn Academy, a friendship of extraordinary beings united against a common foe.

CHAPTER 6

The morning air was crisp as Casimir and the others gathered in the courtyard of the academy. The daunting journey to Haerford House loomed over them, a mission fraught with danger, yet vital to their cause.

"We can't risk using the usual ways of getting there," Lucien remarked, his gaze sweeping across the assembled group. "The Order maintains an extensive network of spies."

Jade stepped forward, her expression resolute. "I have an idea, but it will require trust and a bit of... unconventional thinking." She held up a sword, its blade glinting in the early light. "I can enchant these to carry us through the air. It's risky, but it's our best shot at staying undetected."

Casimir raised an eyebrow, a mix of scepticism and intrigue in his eyes. "That's... certainly brilliant."

"Do we have a choice? It's that or walking into the Order," Alessandra chimed in.

As Jade began her enchantments, the swords hummed with a newfound energy, levitating slightly above the ground. Vlad stepped up, his hands outstretched as he summoned his powers. A shimmering barrier formed around them, bending light and rendering them invisible to any prying eyes.

"Everyone, secure a weapon and grip it firmly," Vlad directed, maintaining a steadfast tone even in the face of the unknown challenges that lay ahead.

One after another, they stepped onto the hovering swords, a rush of excitement tinged with novelty washing over them. Casimir, unfamiliar with such feats of magic, couldn't hide his amazement. "Definitely not your everyday commute," he joked.

Lucien glanced over at Casimir, a hint of camaraderie in his gaze. "Not the worst way to travel, huh?"

Casimir laughed, the sound lost in the wind.

"Stick together. This magic won't stretch far, and we can't lose anyone enroute," Jade instructed.

Gliding through the sky, the world beneath them appeared like a far-off recollection, a canvas of terrain and existence unfurling beneath their imperceptible barrier.

Haerford House, a mere two hundred miles away, was their destination. But what awaited them there, wrapped in the shadows of their quest, was a mystery that only time would unveil.

After a journey fraught with silent tension and the rush of wind, the group descended gracefully into the dense forest that enveloped Haerford House. The ancient trees stood like silent sentinels, their leaves whispering secrets of the past as the enchanted swords gently lowered them to the forest floor.

Before them, nestled within the woods' embrace, lay Haerford House. Its Jacobean architecture stood as proof of a past era marked by exquisite craftsmanship and grandeur. The house, adorned with elaborate gables and windows framed in stone mullions, possessed a commanding yet magnificent aura.

A short distance away, nestled in the quiet solitude of the forest, lay a small private cemetery. Its weathered tombstones leaned at odd angles, marking the last resting place of those who had once walked the halls of the manor.

"Remarkable," Casimir murmured. "It's like stepping back in time."

Alessandra nodded in agreement, her gaze scanning the surrounding area. "Let's not forget why we're here. This place might hold more secrets than we expect."

They approached the house cautiously, aware that the Order's spies could lurk anywhere. The ancient oak door creaked open at their touch, revealing the dimly lit interior. Dust motes danced in the shafts of light that filtered through the stained-glass windows, illuminating the rich tapestries and aged furnishings that adorned the rooms.

Inside the venerable walls of Haerford House, the atmosphere was thick with the essence of centuries past.

Casimir, despite his own family's enigmatic past, knew their priority was to unravel the mystery of Jarvis. As he wandered into the study, the room seemed to echo with whispers of secrets long kept. Shelves of leather-bound books lined the walls, and the heavy curtains added to the gloom that hung in the air.

It was in a dust-covered desk he found them—a bundle of old, brittle letters bound by a faded ribbon. He carefully untied it, revealing the elegant script of a bygone era. Each letter addressed Jarvis de Winter, speaking of clandestine meetings, cryptic plans, and alliances with shadowy figures.

"Lucien, Alessandra!" Casimir called out, his voice echoing through the halls. "I've found something."

They gathered around, their eyes scanning the faded ink. The letters offered glimpses into Jarvis's dealings, hinting at a network of alliances that were as complex as they were secretive.

"This one mentions a gathering at the old cathedral ruins under the full moon," Lucien read aloud, his brow furrowed. "It speaks of a pact being formed."

Alessandra's fingers traced the words. "And here, a reference to 'the binding of the bloodline'. Could my father have been part of something that bound him to the Order, or perhaps against it?"

Jade, joining them, added, "These letters could be the key to finding him. They suggest he was deeply involved in the supernatural community, possibly in ways we never imagined."

Vlad, with his back against the bookcase, remarked, "Jarvis held a role beyond merely being a part of the Order or a father figure to both of you. He was a participant in a centuries-old game."

As they continued to sift through the letters, each one exposed more details of the elaborate web that Jarvis de Winter had become entangled in. Some spoke of debts owed, others of favours granted, and some were warnings—all painting a picture of a man who lived amidst secrets and danger.

"We need to follow these leads," Lucien decided. "Each one could bring us closer to finding him."

Vlad gathered everyone in the softly illuminated drawing room, directing their attention to a prominently displayed portrait. It showcased Jarvis de Winter and his deceased wife, both immortalised during their youthful peak.

"Look at this," Vlad said, pointing to a small, almost imperceptible detail in the background. Behind the couple, partially obscured by shadows, was a painting of a landscape. It was an unusual choice for a backdrop.

Lucien moved in for a closer look, his eyes focusing

intently on the details. "That scenery is familiar. It resembles the cliffs along the shore," he observed.

Alessandra leaned in, her gaze following Lucien's. "You're right. And there's something written on the ship's sail. It's hard to make out, but it looks like coordinates."

Jade, her interest piqued, added, "Coordinates? That could be a meeting point, or a hidden location Jarvis used. It's too precise to be a mere artist's fancy."

Casimir observed, "Someone must have commissioned this portrait to convey a message."

"We should investigate this," Vlad proposed. "It's the best lead we have on Jarvis's whereabouts or his activities."

They decided to venture to the shore. The night had deepened around Haerford House, casting long shadows across the ancient stones and the silent, watchful trees. The portrait, with its hidden message, seemed to approve of their course of action, the painted eyes of Jarvis and his wife following them as they prepared to leave.

CHAPTER 7

Arriving at their target, they found a secret cove, its entrance cleverly hidden by both natural and intentional means.

Treading carefully across the hazardous ground, Casimir spotted faint symbols. "Jarvis might have left these as clues," he theorised, guiding them forward.

Their path led to an ivy-draped cavern entrance. Within, the cave split into multiple passageways, winding further into the cliff's core. The atmosphere was chilly and humid, enveloped in deep silence.

"It feels like a maze," Jade remarked, her hand tracing the rough cave walls.

Lucien nodded in agreement, squinting to make out the faint symbols etched into the rock. "Alessandra, look," he called out, pointing to a marking. "These symbols... they're from Father's notes."

Alessandra stepped closer, her eyes narrowing as she studied them. "You're right," she confirmed, a hint of excitement in her voice. "He was leaving us breadcrumbs to follow."

"We need to keep going," Lucien urged, his voice echoing through the cavern. "He wouldn't have led us here without a reason. There's something important waiting for us at the end of this maze."

Finally, they arrived at a chamber, secluded and untouched by time. It was empty except for a stand in the centre, upon which lay a single, cryptic letter. The handwriting was unmistakably Jarvis's.

Lucien picked up the letter, his hands trembling slightly. "It's from him," he said, his voice thick with emotion. The letter spoke of Jarvis's journey, of secrets uncovered and dangers faced. It hinted at a hidden location where he had left something of great importance.

"The letter mentions a well," Alessandra noted, her eyes scanning the text, "hidden in the forest's heart, near a place he refers to as 'the weeping willow.'"

Vlad closed the letter, deep in thought. "We need to find this. It could be where Jarvis hid something crucial—perhaps even the key to locating him or understanding his fate."

Emerging from the cave, their quest led them deeper into the woods encircling Haerford House. Wading through thick undergrowth beneath towering trees, they sensed the land's ancient stories murmured by the breeze.

Huddled around the well's edge, anticipation hung heavy; they were on the cusp of a pivotal revelation. Hidden by Jarvis, the clue was crucial for unravelling his vanishing and the mysteries he'd unearthed.

The forsaken well, now dry and engulfed in gloom, beckoned. Lucien, resolved in his gaze, chose to brave its depths. His companions watched, hearts in their throats, as he navigated the deteriorating stones, a lone lantern illuminating his descent.

At the base, enveloped in a musty air fragrant of old earth

and forgotten times, Lucien surveyed his dimly lit environs. It was then he discovered something—a complex etching on the stone, veiled in shadow.

The carving was a detailed sigil, one that Lucien recognised from Jarvis's notes. It was a symbol associated with a secret society that Jarvis had been investigating—one that was rumoured to have deep connections with the supernatural world and possibly even the Order.

Lucien traced his fingers over the carving, feeling the grooves and ridges of the ancient stone. Embedded in the centre of the marking was a small, metallic object. He carefully pried it loose, revealing a peculiar key, its design ornate and unlike any he had seen before.

"This could be what we've been looking for," Lucien called up to the others, his voice echoing in the confined space.

BACK ON THE SURFACE, THE GROUP GATHERED AROUND Lucien to examine the key. It was clearly old, possibly as old as Haerford House itself, and seemed to be fashioned specifically for a unique lock.

"This key must open something important. Maybe a hidden room or a chest in Haerford House?" Alessandra said.

"Or perhaps something in one of the other locations Jarvis mentioned in his notes. We need to cross-reference this design with everything we know," Jade added.

Vlad, holding the key up to the light, mused, "This isn't just a key; it's a statement. Jarvis was leaving us a trail to something that he deemed crucial."

The discovery invigorated the group. They knew they

were one step closer to unravelling the mystery of Jarvis's disappearance. The key served as a concrete connection to Jarvis's clandestine undertakings, a fragment of a mystery that unfolded over many years and explored the depths of the paranormal realm.

As night fell over the forest, the group made their way back to Haerford House, their minds racing with possibilities.

Ash, Jade, and Casimir stepped into the study, a space steeped in history, as the rest of the group dispersed to explore elsewhere in the house. Rows of bookcases adorned the walls, housing tomes that whispered of centuries of wisdom. The air was tinged with a subtle aroma of aged paper and wood, an indication of the room's enduring presence over the years.

In the centre of the study stood a grand, old desk, its surface cluttered with papers and artefacts that hinted at Jarvis de Winter's extensive research and complex interests. Ash ran his fingers over the desk, feeling the grooves and scratches in the wood, each a silent witness to Jarvis's tireless work.

"It's got to be here somewhere," Jade murmured, her eyes scanning the room. Her gaze settled on a tall, ornate cabinet tucked away in a shadowy corner. It seemed out of place, more secretive than decorative.

Approaching the cabinet, Jade noticed it was locked, the keyhole an intricate design that suggested it guarded something valuable. She glanced at Ash, a spark of determination in her eyes. "This could be it."

Ash produced a small set of lock-picking tools from his pocket. With deft fingers, he set to work on the lock, a skill he had honed out of necessity in his earlier adventures. After a moment, there was a soft click, and the cabinet door swung open.

Inside, they found a collection of personal items, scrolls, and small artefacts. But what immediately drew their attention was a leather-bound journal, its cover worn, and the pages yellowed with age.

"This has to be Jarvis's journal," Jade said, her voice tinged with excitement. She delicately lifted it from the cabinet, sensing the gravity of history within her grasp.

As they flipped through the pages, the dim light from the study's lamps cast flickering shadows over the words. The journal was filled with Jarvis's elegant handwriting, detailed drawings, and coded notes. It was a window into his mind and his clandestine activities.

"This could be the breakthrough we need," Ash said, leaning closer to examine a cryptic entry. "Jarvis's personal notes. This might tell us everything we need to know."

Casimir stood silently in the dimly lit room of Haerford House, his eyes fixed on the pages of Jarvis de Winter's journal as Jade and Ash examined its contents. The words on those aged pages seemed to reach out to him, offering glimpses into a past filled with secrets and quiet rebellion.

The journal contained entries about his own family, the Thornes. What struck Casimir the most was the revelation about his late father, Gabriel Thorne. According to Jarvis's notes, Gabriel had begun to question the Order's methods after they had targeted Casimir, eventually turning against the organisation he had once served loyally.

This revelation stirred a complex turmoil within Casimir.

The thought that his father, whom he had always known as a steadfast member of the Order, had secretly harboured doubts and even acted against them, was both startling and sobering. It painted a picture of his father in a light Casimir had never imagined.

"He aimed to protect me," Casimir whispered, his voice hardly perceptible. His father's deeds, veiled beneath responsibilities and allegiance, now disclosed a profound love and selflessness that he hadn't comprehended before.

He watched Jade and Ash as they continued their careful examination of the journal, their expressions reflecting the seriousness of their discovery.

"If only he were here to see this." Casimir felt an acute sense of loss, mixed with a newfound respect for the man Gabriel Thorne had been.

The heavy door to the study creaked open, admitting the rest of the group. Lucien, Alessandra, and Vlad stepped into the dimly lit room, each carrying a palpable sense of disappointment. Their search throughout the rest of Haerford House had yielded nothing, leaving them with more questions than answers.

"We've looked everywhere," Lucien said, his voice tinged with frustration. There was no sign of any hidden compartments or secret rooms where this key could be used.

Alessandra, her gaze sweeping the room, remarked, "It feels as though there's a crucial element eluding us. Every lead we've pursued has reached a dead end."

Vlad nodded in agreement. "This key is unique. It doesn't belong to anything in Haerford House. We're not looking in the right place."

Casimir, holding Jarvis's journal in his hands, felt a sudden clarity. "I think you're right. We need to go to my old home—the Thorne estate." He looked around at the group, his determination clear. "It's the only place we haven't checked, and it makes sense. If my father was working against the Order, he might have hidden something there."

Closing the journal, Jade raised her gaze with contemplation. "It's a slim chance, but it's our most promising lead. Jarvis's journal makes repeated references to the Thorne family. There might be a link we haven't unearthed."

"We should head out immediately," Vlad suggested. "The Thorne estate is widely recognised, but its hidden truths are not acknowledged. We must brace ourselves for whatever lies there."

With the decision reached, they left the study. Casimir lingered for a moment, gazing at the journal in his hand. The journey ahead would bring him face to face with his family's past, a past intertwined with the mysteries they were unravelling. As he turned to leave the room, the shadows of Haerford House seemed to whisper in agreement, as if the old walls themselves were urging him on.

CHAPTER 8

Under the cloak of night, the group prepared to depart from Haerford House, their resolve firm despite the unknowns that lay ahead. The enchanted swords, once more, became their mode of transport, an unconventional yet necessary choice given the urgency of their journey.

As they stepped outside, the cool night air enveloped them, the darkness punctuated by the occasional hoot of an owl and the rustling of leaves in the gentle breeze. The ancient mansion, with its secrets and stories, stood silent behind them, a stoic witness to their quest.

Ash unsheathed his flaming sword, the blade igniting with a mesmerising, otherworldly flame. It cast a warm, blueish glow around them, a beacon in the darkness that both comforted and reminded them of the dangers they faced.

With unwavering concentration, Vlad stretched out his arms, invoking the formidable enchantment he'd employed before. A radiant shield materialised around them, refracting light and rendering them imperceptible to potential onlookers. They were concealed, their existence veiled from casual scrutiny, a vital safeguard against the Order's inquisitive gaze.

Mounted on their levitating swords, the group ascended into the night sky, the blazing sword and magical barrier their only companions in the darkness. They moved swiftly, cutting through the cool air, the landscape below them a patchwork of shadows and silhouettes.

Casimir, taking the lead, experienced a blend of nervousness and eagerness as they approached the Thorne estate. The location held a tapestry of memories for him, some imbued with warmth, while others carried a tinge of discomfort. The prospect of unveiling the enigmas his father had left behind was both formidable and essential.

As they flew, the world below seemed a distant realm, a land of mysteries and stories waiting to be uncovered. The journey was silent, each member of the group lost in their own thoughts, contemplating the significance of their quest and the challenges that lay ahead.

Eventually, the imposing silhouette of the Thorne estate came into view, its grandeur a stark contrast against the backdrop of the night sky. The estate, with its sprawling grounds and ancient walls, held the promise of answers and the threat of new dangers.

They descended quietly onto the grounds, the enchantments ensuring their arrival went unnoticed. Darkness shrouded the estate, with the only light emanating from Ash's flaming sword, which now appeared to burn even brighter in the shadow of the Thorne legacy.

"Let's be cautious," Vlad whispered as they landed. "We don't know what we might find here."

The group approached the main entrance, the heavy oak door standing as a silent guardian to the secrets within.

Casimir, taking a deep breath, reached for the door handle, his hand hesitating for a moment. This was more than just a physical barrier; it was a threshold to his past.

The door creaked open, revealing a grand foyer that whispered of opulence and long-forgotten splendour. Their footsteps echoed on the marble floor, the sound reverberating through the vast, shadowy halls.

The atmosphere carried the weight of time, and the walls were hung with portraits of Thorne ancestors, their eyes tracking the group's movements with silent scrutiny.

Jade, her eyes adjusting to the dim light, noted, "We should search the study or library first. That's where we're most likely to find anything related to the key or Jarvis's connections to the Thornes."

They navigated the corridors, their path illuminated by the flickering flame of Ash's sword.

In the study, a room lined with bookshelves and filled with artefacts from around the world, they began their search. The air was heavy with the scent of leather and wood.

Casimir was drawn to his father's desk, a massive piece of dark wood laden with papers and relics and started sifting through the drawers. His fingers stumbled upon a hidden compartment, a cleverly designed nook that opened with a soft click.

Inside, he found a collection of letters, their seals unbroken, and a small, intricately carved box that matched the design of the key they had found. With a mixture of excitement and trepidation, Casimir inserted the key into the lock. It turned with a satisfying click, the box springing open to reveal its contents.

The group gathered around, their eyes wide with anticipation. Inside the box lay a series of documents and charts. The group found familiar locations marked on the maps, which now held a new significance. They would need time to decipher the documents written in code.

"This could be it. The answers we've been looking for," Lucien said, his voice hushed.

Casimir added, "And possibly the key to understanding Jarvis's disappearance and the role my family played in all of this."

In the study's stillness, surrounded by the opulent remnants of his family's legacy, Casimir felt a connection to his father that transcended time and circumstance. The coded documents in front of him were a testament to Gabriel Thorne's foresight and the cryptic legacy he had left behind.

"My father taught me this," Casimir murmured, his voice a mix of nostalgia and persistence. "He used to say that understanding codes and cyphers was an essential skill for those who tread in the shadows. I never realised how right he was until now."

The others watched in silence as Casimir spread a stack of blank papers across the desk and began the meticulous process of deciphering the documents. With each symbol and character he transcribed, the hidden messages within the documents slowly came to light.

As the code yielded its secrets, the documents revealed a series of correspondences between Gabriel Thorne and various unknown entities. The letters spoke of covert plans, secret alliances, and a deep-seated resistance to the Order's expanding influence. Gabriel Thorne had been a pivotal figure in a clandestine struggle that had remained hidden from the world.

With each line he translated, a picture emerged from the words, a narrative of covert resistance and subterfuge. "These documents detail a long-standing effort by my family and Jarvis to undermine the Order's plans," Casimir said.

The papers contained accounts of thwarted experiments, mysterious disappearances of monsters created by the Order, and leaked locations of secret facilities. Jarvis de Winter and the Thorne family had been deeply involved in a strategic campaign to disrupt and delay the Order's ambitions for global domination.

"This is incredible," Lucien murmured, leaning in to get a better look at the documents. "Jarvis and your family were essentially waging a silent war against the Order."

Alessandra, absorbing the gravity of their findings, added, "They've been working in the shadows, risking everything to prevent the Order from achieving their endgame."

"Their actions might have slowed the Order down, but it's clear the threat is far from over. We need to continue what they started," Jade chimed in.

Vlad, who had been listening intently, nodded in agreement. "The information in these documents could be crucial to understanding the Order's current strategies and how to counter them. We've stumbled upon a goldmine of intelligence."

The revelation that Jarvis and the Thornes had been instrumental in a covert resistance brought a new sense of purpose to their mission. It was a legacy of defiance and courage that they were now a part of, a hidden battle against an enemy that sought to control and dominate at any cost.

As the group deliberated their next moves, a sense of responsibility settled upon their shoulders. They were no longer just chasing the truth behind Jarvis's disappearance; they were the new vanguard in a clandestine war that had been raging in the shadows.

Casimir, reviewing the documents once again, sensed a profound bond with his father's and Jarvis's mission. "We must carry on their legacy. They gave their all to oppose the Order. It falls upon us now to complete their mission."

With the revelations from the deciphered documents still vivid in their thoughts, the team redirected their focus to the enigmatic key discovered at Jarvis's well. It remained a physical connection, a segment of the unsolved puzzle that awaited its rightful position.

Casimir raised the key to the light, examining its elaborate craftsmanship. "There must be an item in this house that corresponds to this key," he mused. "Something we might have overlooked."

Their search led them to Gabriel Thorne's old bedroom, a room that had remained untouched since his passing. The room exuded an air of opulence and complexity, with personal artefacts and furnishings scattered about, each telling a story of a life lived lavishly yet fraught with intricacies. But amidst the grandeur, it was the massive Chinese painting that commanded attention, its vivid hues and elaborate details captivating the gaze.

Casimir watched as Jade, sensing the need for caution, carefully directed a pulse of magic through the room, her senses keenly attuned to any hidden secrets. As the magical energy swept through the space, Casimir's heart quickened with anticipation.

Frowning in concentration, Jade focused her efforts on the area behind the imposing painting, her magic probing deeper in search of hidden chambers. After several tense moments, a subtle shift in the energy caught her attention, indicating the presence of something concealed.

With bated breath, Casimir watched as Jade reached out to the painting, her fingers trembling slightly as she pressed against its surface. Slowly, the painting began to shift, revealing a concealed doorway behind it.

The anticipation in the room grew as Casimir inserted the key in the door and turned it. A soft click resonated, and the door slowly opened, unveiling a narrow, downward-leading passage.

"The key was for this all along," Jade whispered, a hint of excitement in her voice.

The passage was dimly lit and felt untouched by time. Vlad warned, "Stay alert. This was meant to remain a secret; there could be traps."

As they ventured deeper, the hidden passage revealed its secrets under the cloak of an oppressive darkness, thick with the dust of centuries, and seemed to press against their skin.

The path suddenly widened into a small alcove. There, a series of ancient torches awaited them, their heads bowed in silence, untouched by flame for ages.

It was Ash who stepped forward with a grin. With a flick of his wrist, blue flames sprang to life along the line of the torches. The light, ethereal and haunting, cast their shadows against the walls in a dance of azure hues, transforming the passage into a corridor of spectral beauty. The effect was mesmerising, the hellfire's glow painting their surroundings in shades of mystery and magic.

Suddenly, a faint clicking, almost imperceptible against the silence, echoed through the chamber. It was followed by a low, ominous rumble as the floor beneath them began to shift. In that instant, Vlad reacted with supernatural agility. With a swift motion borne of centuries of battle, he leaped to the side, evading the concealed trapdoor that yawned open beneath them. Casimir's heart skipped a beat as he mirrored the move. His own training allowed him to dodge the danger that nearly claimed them.

"Watch your step," Vlad warned, his voice a low growl. His eyes, gleaming in the scant light, were fixed on the path ahead as he extended a hand to aid the others back to safety.

The passage ahead grew increasingly constrictive, the walls seeming to press on them with almost malevolent intent. It was as if the walkway sought to crush their spirits before they could reach their goal. Ash assumed the vanguard, moving with grace. His hands weaved through the air in elaborate gestures that disarmed the traps with an almost casual ease. Arrows, intended to impale, whistled harmlessly by, their deadly intent thwarted by Ash.

Yet, the corridor was fraught with peril at every turn. An unexpected gust of wind blasted through. It kicked up a choking cloud of dust that blinded and disoriented them. They stumbled, nearly lost, as blades sprung from hidden nooks with silent lethality.

In the midst of this tempest of confusion and danger, Jade's composed voice pierced the murk. "Hold on to each other," she instructed, her hands extended to guide them. Her presence was a calm in the storm, a steadying force that led them through the blinding chaos.

They emerged into a vast chamber, the air suddenly clear of dust. Moonlight streamed through unseen apertures, casting an otherworldly glow that bathed the ageless stone in silver.

Here, they were greeted by an assortment of objects and documents, each possibly brimming with valuable insights. The group was drawn towards the room's core, where two ancient sarcophagi lay in silent repose. The air was dense with the presence of untold stories and secrets, enveloping them in an almost tangible shroud of mystery.

Casimir, with a heavy heart, stepped forward towards the nearer sarcophagus. The intricate carvings on the stone lid depicted scenes of bravery and sacrifice, a fitting homage to the man who lay within. Gently, with a reverence borne of deep respect and a son's love, he opened the lid.

Inside, the body of Gabriel Thorne lay in eternal rest. His features were peaceful as if he had merely fallen into a deep slumber. Casimir experienced a surge of emotions—grief, respect, and an overwhelming sense of connection to his father, who had lived a life shrouded in secrets and silently fought against the Order.

Next to him, Lucien and Alessandra approached the second sarcophagus with a similar mixture of respect and sorrow. Opening it, they were greeted with the sight of Jarvis de Winter. His ultimate resting place was a stark reminder of the cost of their clandestine war, the sacrifices made in the name of resistance.

As Casimir observed Alessandra's reaction, a deep sense of empathy welled up within him.

"This can't be true. His soul is still linked to that book," she said. Her words echoed in the chamber, filled with disbelief and a clinging hope. Casimir could see the layers of grief and denial cross her face, a mirror to his own internal turmoil. That Jarvis de Winter, a figure of strength and guidance, was truly gone, was a reality that they all were grappling to accept.

Casimir watched as Lucien moved to comfort Alessandra, his gesture a poignant reminder of their shared loss and mutual support in these trying times. He felt a kinship in their grief, a shared thread of sorrow that connected each member of the group.

Vlad's gentle attempt to ground them in reality resonated with Casimir. "We've all hoped for a different outcome, but this... this is a reality we might have to accept," Vlad said softly. Casimir knew the truth in those words, yet he also understood the difficulty in accepting them.

"Their sacrifice will not be forgotten. We'll honour them

every day," he said, his voice resolute yet tinged with sorrow. The words were a vow, a personal commitment to uphold the legacy left by the two men who had fought bravely in the shadows.

As they moved through the tunnel, retracing their steps back to the estate, a question surfaced in Casimir's mind, echoing the unspoken thoughts of the others. "I am curious. Who buried them?" The practicalities of their final resting place hinted at a deeper network, allies who had ensured that Gabriel Thorne and Jarvis de Winter were honoured in death.

The question hung in the air as they emerged from the passageway. It was a mystery layered upon the many they were already entangled in. Whoever had taken the care to lay them to rest in such a manner knew of their secret fight and shared in their cause.

Lucien, pondering the question, replied, "It must have been someone they trusted implicitly. Someone deeply involved in their plans and resistance against the Order."

Jade nodded in agreement. "It suggests that there are others out there who were part of this struggle, allies we have yet to meet. Perhaps they are still continuing the fight."

Vlad, his expression thoughtful, added, "This could mean that our network is larger than we realised. Finding these allies could be crucial in our ongoing battle against the Order."

Recognising that they had allies in this covert struggle ignited a ray of hope amid their grief. The solemn burial of Gabriel and Jarvis served as a poignant symbol of their common purpose, one that went beyond individual sorrow and persevered.

In the quiet of the early morning, with the first light casting a soft glow over the Thorne estate, Casimir meticulously gathered the journals, maps, and documents concealed within the hidden chamber. Every item represented a portion of the puzzle, a shard of the narrative woven by Jarvis de Winter and Gabriel Thorne. He carried a profound sense of duty to protect these fragments, for they were not mere relics of history but rather crucial instruments for comprehending and unravelling the Order's schemes.

Lucien and Alessandra focused on the artefacts found alongside the journals. These objects, some of which were enigmatic, might hold additional clues or powers that could aid in their fight against the Order. They wrapped them with care, mindful of the secrets they might unlock.

Jade and Vlad photographed each item, ensuring they had digital copies as a safeguard against the loss or destruction of the originals.

"These documents hold invaluable information. It's essential that we thoroughly analyse them once we're back at the academy," Vlad declared in a calm yet determined voice.

"We also have to keep this under wraps. If the Order learns of our discovery, they won't hesitate to do whatever it takes to reclaim it," Jade added.

With the evidence carefully packed, the group took one last look at the Thorne estate. The mansion, with its grand architecture and hidden secrets, had been a silent witness to a legacy of resistance.

In the shadowy light of dawn, the group prepared for their return to the academy. Ash stepped forward, his expression focused as he readied himself to open a portal, a skill he had honed through his unique abilities and connection to the magical realm.

He traced a series of symbols in the air, each movement deliberate and precise. The air around them shimmered, the fabric of reality bending to his will. A swirling vortex of energy materialised, its edges glowing with a spectral light.

The portal stood before them like a gateway between worlds, a testament to Ash's power and their only safe passage back to the academy.

"Everyone, stay close," Ash instructed, his voice steady despite the immense concentration required to maintain the portal. "We don't want anyone getting lost in the transition."

Together, they stepped through the portal, the sensation akin to passing through a thin veil of water. The world around them blurred for a moment, a rush of colours and sounds that were disorienting yet exhilarating.

Emerging on the other side, they found themselves within the familiar confines of Roslyn Academy. The portal closed behind them with a soft whoosh, leaving no trace of its existence. They were now safely back behind the academy's protective walls, a haven amidst the uncertainties and dangers they faced.

The academy, with its ancient stone and ivy-clad walls, was more than just a place of learning; it was a bastion against the dark forces they were contending with. Here, they could study the evidence they had gathered, plan their next moves, and prepare for the inevitable confrontations that lay ahead.

Casimir, holding the collected journals and documents close, felt a sense of relief wash over him. The academy was a stronghold, a place where they could regroup and strengthen their resolve. The journey to the Thorne estate had been revealing, but it was here, within the academy's hallowed halls, that they would uncover the true extent of the Order's plans and how to thwart them.

As the group dispersed to secure the artefacts and documents, there was a shared understanding of the tasks that lay ahead. They needed to analyse the information, decipher the maps, and unravel their secrets. The fight against the Order was entering a new phase, and they were at the heart of it.

In the academy's quiet, with the first light of day filtering through the windows, Casimir felt a renewed sense of purpose. At the forefront of a war that had been waged in the shadows for generations, they drew the battle lines. It was a daunting responsibility, but with the legacy of Jarvis and Gabriel guiding them, they were ready to face whatever the future held.

CHAPTER 9

In the secure confines of Roslyn Academy, the group convened to strategise their next steps. Lucien brought up a subject that had lingered on the edges of their discussions. "Do you think Henry could help?" he asked, directing his gaze towards Alessandra.

Henry, the doppelgänger of Jarvis de Winter, was currently a prisoner in the dungeons of the Academy.

Alessandra pondered the suggestion, her expression contemplative. "Henry's empathic abilities could be useful, especially in understanding the motivations of those we're up against," she said thoughtfully. "And if he has even a fraction of father's time-travel abilities, that could open up possibilities we haven't considered."

Casimir, overhearing the conversation, felt a tinge of curiosity mixed with caution. The idea of utilising Henry's abilities was intriguing, but the implications of involving someone so closely linked, yet so different from Jarvis, were complex.

Vlad chimed in, his tone cautious yet optimistic. "If we

could communicate with him, gauge his willingness to help, it might be worth exploring. His insights as an empath could give us an edge."

Jade nodded her assent. "But let's be cautious. His time in the dungeon could have altered how he sees us. We'll have to establish trust before depending on his skills."

Lucien responded with an understanding nod. "Got it. We'll have a chat with him, see where his loyalties lie. We have to be sure he's with us before we bring him in the loop."

Vlad turned towards the knight standing guard at the door. "Bring Henry in," he ordered, his voice carrying the authority of someone used to command.

The knight nodded, disappearing to fetch their unique prisoner.

When Henry was brought into the room, his appearance was a stark reminder of Jarvis de Winter's legacy. He shared Jarvis's features, but there was a distinct difference in his demeanour. His eyes, though reminiscent of their father's, held a depth of emotion and understanding that was uniquely his own, a trait of his empathic nature.

Lucien was the first to address him, his voice steady but carrying an undercurrent of emotion. "Henry, we need to know where you stand. Jarvis... is dead."

They all watched Henry intently for his reaction. His face registered a momentary flicker of sorrow, quickly masked by a guarded expression. It was a subtle yet telling response, showing a connection to Jarvis that went beyond mere physical resemblance.

Vlad, seizing the moment, pressed on. "We need information about the Order. Anything you can tell us could be crucial."

Henry's gaze shifted across the group, assessing each

member. After a moment of contemplation, he spoke, his voice tinged with the wariness of his imprisonment.

"I know things... about the Order. Things that could help you. But why should I trust you? My experience here hasn't exactly been... hospitable."

Alessandra stepped forward. "We understand your distrust. But we're fighting against the Order, just like Jarvis did. We're on the same side."

Henry's eyes met hers, and there was a long pause as he seemed to weigh her words, sensing the sincerity behind them. Finally, he nodded slowly. "Alright. I'll tell you what I know. You've killed Azaroth and Darmon," Henry said, his eyes scanning the group. "But you're left with one more head of the Order, one as ancient as the organisation itself. To win this war, you need to be ready for sacrifices."

Lucien, his brow furrowed in concern, responded quickly. "Who is this last head? How do we find him?"

Henry shook his head, a shadow of regret passing over his face. "His name is unknown to me. He's like a ghost within the Order, a presence felt but never seen. As for finding him, that will require sacrifices that will test you to your core."

Alessandra interjected, her voice steady yet tinged with unease. "We've all paid the price already. We're prepared for more. What detriment are you talking about?"

"The kind that can break you," Henry replied solemnly. "This war, it's not just fought on battlefields. It's fought in the heart and mind. You'll be tested in ways you can't imagine."

"Whatever it takes, we'll do it. We need to stop the Order once and for all," Vlad added, then motioned to the knight to take Henry away.

Jade nodded in agreement, her expression determined. "To move forward effectively, we must strategise and gather more intelligence."

Avery, who had been listening intently to the conversation, stepped forward with a proactive suggestion. "Let's cross-check the map that I left for you guys in the dungeon with the information from the files we brought over. I bet we can find their strongholds and hit them all in one go."

"That's a solid plan. If we can identify and target their key locations simultaneously, we could cripple their operations significantly," Lucien agreed.

Casimir, already moving to gather the documents and map Avery mentioned, added, "This could give us the edge we need. If we strike decisively, we can take the fight to them before they regroup."

Alessandra, joining Casimir in laying out the map and files, said, "We need to be thorough. Every piece of information could be the key to pinpointing their strongholds."

Jade cross-referenced the locations marked on Avery's map with the data from the files. The room buzzed with activity as everyone pitched in, comparing notes, discussing strategies, and identifying potential targets.

Vlad nodded in approval. "This is good. We're not just on the defensive anymore. We're taking the fight to them, and we're doing it on our terms."

Alessandra and Lucien, standing side by side, surveyed the room with a sense of resolute determination. The path ahead was not just a mission; it was a closure they both needed.

"We're at the point of no return," Alessandra declared with conviction. "The Order's shadow has loomed over us for far too long. We must put a stop to their reign, not only for our sake but for all those who have suffered under them."

"Our struggle goes beyond just opposing the Order. It's about closing a painful chapter of our lives, a chapter that has cost us dearly. The time has come to end it, once and for all," Lucien chimed in.

Casimir, moved by their words, added, "We're all in this together. Whatever happens, we face it as one. The Order has taken enough from us. It ends now."

Vlad agreed. "We've journeyed too long to turn back now. The Order's dominion ends with us. We'll go to any lengths necessary."

Exiting the chamber, their footfalls resonated with the assurance of the approaching showdown. The forthcoming clash with the Order was no longer a remote aim but a tangible reality they were prepared to confront. Armed with steadfast persistence, a sense of unity, and an unyielding resolve, they were poised to bring an end to the oppressive regime that had cast its shadow over their lives.

CHAPTER 10

In the quiet confines of his study, Vlad sat with a sense of purposeful intent, his demeanour that of a leader ready to rally his forces for the impending battle. Casimir was there with him, lending his support to the crucial task at hand.

"We need all the allies we can gather," Vlad stated, his voice carrying the weight of command. "The Order is powerful, but we have strength in numbers and the unity of our cause."

Casimir, fully grasping the seriousness of their predicament, nodded his concurrence. "Each contributes unique strengths. It's crucial we unite them for a common purpose."

Vlad set about composing a letter, selecting each word with care to emphasise the critical nature and significance of their plight. His missive was a rallying cry, a plea for assistance in their final confrontation with the Order.

Once the letters were sealed, Vlad handed them to his most trusted vampire knights. "Deliver these with haste and impress upon our allies the need for immediate action. We will gather at Roslyn Academy to plan our last strike against the organisation. Their allegiance and support are crucial."

The knights bowed, understanding the significance of their mission, and quickly departed to deliver the summons.

With the letters dispatched, Vlad turned to Casimir. "This is it. We're gathering our forces. It's time we put an end to the Order's reign of terror."

Casimir, sensing the gravity of the moment, replied, "We've been ready for this. Our allies understand the danger posed by the Order. They'll stand with us."

Vlad turned his gaze to the window, taking in the vast grounds of Roslyn Academy. "Here, we will stand together in the face of our shared adversary."

They sent out the call to arms, and now those who would answer held the fate of their fight in their hands. Vlad and Casimir, along with their comrades, stood ready to lead the charge, to bring an end to the darkness that had threatened their world for too long.

IN THE COUNCIL ROOM AVERY, JADE, AND CASIMIR WERE deep in analysis, surrounded by maps and documents.

As they meticulously cross-referenced the details from Avery's map with the information from the Thorne estate documents, a pattern emerged, one that was both unexpected and chilling. Casimir, who had been aligning points on the map with entries in the documents, looked up with a realisation.

"Wait a minute," he said, a note of surprise in his voice.

"All the locations mentioned are abandoned mental institutions, and they're spread across Europe," he explained.

Avery leaned over to get a better look, her eyes tracing the locations Casimir pointed out. "That's eerie. Why would the Order choose these places? What's the significance?"

Jade, her mind racing with possibilities, speculated, "These places could provide the perfect cover. They're isolated, steeped in history, and people avoid them because of their pasts. It's an ideal setup for the Order to operate in secrecy."

The realisation that the Order's strongholds were in old, abandoned mental institutions across Europe was a revelation that added a layer of complexity to their fight.

"This is a breakthrough," Avery noted. "If we investigate these institutions, we might uncover critical operations of the Order."

Casimir, already thinking of the implications, added, "We need to share this with Vlad and the others. If we're going to take the fight to the Order, these institutions are where we start."

With the crucial information in hand, Avery, Jade, and Casimir hurried to the headmaster's office, where Vlad, Lucien, and Alessandra were already engaged in deep discussion. The office, usually a bastion of academic leadership, had become the nerve centre for their resistance against the Order.

Upon entering, expectant looks greeted the trio. Vlad, ever the astute leader, immediately sensed the importance of their arrival. "What have you uncovered?" he asked, his gaze shifting between the three.

Casimir stepped forward, spreading the map and documents on the headmaster's desk. "We've found a pattern that could be pivotal. The Order's strongholds... they're all in abandoned mental institutions across Europe."

Lucien, leaning in to examine the map, nodded thoughtfully. "That's a strategic choice. Remote, overlooked, perfect for covert operations."

"This gives us specific targets. We can finally take the fight directly to them," Alessandra added, her eyes scanning the documents.

Vlad, absorbing the new information, responded with a tone of determination, "Then we must make haste. Coordinated strikes on these strongholds could significantly weaken the Order."

"The spread of these locations means they have a wide-reaching influence. Taking them down will disrupt their network," Avery said.

"Timing is crucial. We need to strike all the strongholds simultaneously to prevent them from regrouping," Jade chimed in with a strategic perspective.

Vlad stood up decisively. "Prepare the teams. We'll need all our allies for this. It's time to bring the battle to their doorstep."

"We should also gather as much intelligence as we can at each location. Knowing what we're facing will be key," Lucien suggested.

The headmaster's office buzzed with a new sense of purpose as they planned their course of action. The team studied maps, assigned teams, and defined roles. With the discovery of the Order's strongholds, an opportunity arose to strike a decisive blow against their foe, marking a significant breakthrough.

As the meeting concluded, a shared resolve settled over the group. Although the path ahead was fraught with danger, Vlad, Lucien, Alessandra, Avery, Jade, and Casimir were steadfast in their dedication. Bound together by their common cause, they stood prepared to face the imminent challenges and bring an end to the Order's tyrannical grip.

THE NIGHT WAS A CLOAK UNDER WHICH CASIMIR AND ASH began their critical reconnaissance mission. From Casimir's perspective, the task ahead was clear but fraught with unknown dangers. He felt the familiar weight of his demonic sword at his side, a silent yet powerful ally in their covert operation.

As Ash began the complex incantations to open a portal, Casimir watched the air ripple and warp, a portal taking shape before them. The magic was a spectacle, a dance of light and shadow that never ceased to amaze him. He felt a brief surge of adrenaline as they prepared to step through, a sensation that was part anticipation, part apprehension.

"Let's go," he whispered, the words barely escaping his lips.

The moment they stepped through the portal, Casimir's senses were on high alert. They found themselves on the outskirts of the first abandoned asylum. It loomed like a spectre in the darkness, its dilapidated structure a silent testament to its grim past.

Casimir drew his sword, channelling his power to render them invisible. The blade hummed softly, responding to his command. He felt a deep connection to the sword, an extension of his own demonic heritage, a reminder of the power he wielded and the responsibility that came with it.

As they moved through the shadows, surveying the

grounds and buildings, Casimir's eyes were keenly searching for any sign of the Order's presence. Each location revealed more pieces of the puzzle.

Ash's portal magic was invaluable, transporting them from one location to the next with swift efficiency. Casimir remained vigilant throughout, his sword ensuring their movements were unseen, their presence undetected.

The eerie silence of the abandoned asylums was unsettling, but Casimir pushed any unease aside, focusing on the mission. He noted security details, points of entry, and any signs of recent activity. Their discovery gained significance with each site they visited; it became increasingly clear that the Order had deeply entrenched themselves in these forgotten places.

By the time they made it back to Roslyn Academy, dawn's early light was beginning to streak across the sky. Casimir was awash with a sense of fatigue yet fulfilment. They had secured vital information, a true reflection of their prowess and the unspoken unity that tied them together as allies.

"We've got what we need," Casimir said to Ash, sheathing his sword with a sense of finality. "Now, it's up to us to use this information effectively."

Upon their return to Roslyn Academy, Ash and Casimir, bearing the burden of their exhaustive reconnaissance mission, hurried toward the council room.

As they approached the chamber, the sounds of conversation and the clinking of armour reached their ears. The room buzzed with activity, a clear sign that their allies had heeded Vlad's call.

Pushing open the imposing doors, they were greeted by a scene that was both awe-inspiring and imposing. Allies from various factions, each representing unique strengths and capabilities, filled the space. They pledged their allegiance in the fight against the Order.

At the centre of it all was Vlad, commanding the room from his position at the head of the long table. He looked every bit the prince he was born to be, his demeanour that of a king holding court. His presence was both authoritative and charismatic, a natural leader unifying a diverse array of forces under a common cause.

Casimir couldn't help but smile at the sight. Despite the dire circumstances that had brought them all together, there was something profoundly heartening about witnessing Vlad in his element, rallying their allies with a mix of passion and determination.

Around Vlad, the others – Lucien, Alessandra, Jade, and Avery – were engaged in discussions with the various representatives, each conversation a thread in the tapestry of their collective strategy. The room was alive with the energy of cooperation and shared purpose.

Each ally brought their unique skills and knowledge to the table. From seasoned vampire warriors to skilled witches and cunning strategists, the council room was a microcosm of the resistance against the Order. They listened intently to Vlad, who spoke not just as a leader, but as a unifier, weaving together their disparate strengths into a cohesive force.

As Casimir and Ash made their way through the crowd to join the others, people nodded at them with respect and acknowledgment. The information they had gathered would be a crucial addition to the planning already underway.

In Vlad's capable hands, the diverse group was becoming a singular, formidable force ready to take on the Order. The battle ahead would be challenging, but in that moment, Casimir felt a surge of hope. United in their cause, they were stronger than they had ever been.

CHAPTER 11

Vlad turned to them, his demeanour solemn yet anticipating. "What information have you unearthed?" he enquired, recognising the importance of their discoveries.

Casimir drew in a deep breath before imparting the information they had collected. "The Order's strongholds are situated within deserted mental institutions scattered across Europe. We've pinpointed four crucial sites: The Eichenwald Sanatorium in Germany, the Marek Asylum in Poland, the Voronov Retreat in Slovakia, and the Nyschens Institute in Ukraine."

The room fell silent as the magnitude of the information sank in. Vlad, processing the details, prompted further, "And their defences?"

"The numbers are staggering," Casimir continued, his tone grave. "Forces guard each location in the thousands. Eichenwald Sanatorium alone has close to two thousand guards, both human and enhanced. The Marek Asylum, about fifteen hundred, with heavy magical fortifications. Voronov

Retreat and Nyschens Institute have similar numbers, with advanced surveillance and defence systems."

The news sent a ripple of concern through the room. The scale of the Order's resources and their level of preparation was daunting.

"This changes our approach. We're dealing with a formidable enemy, heavily fortified and deeply entrenched," Vlad responded.

Lucien, joining the conversation, added, "Our assault will need to be precise and overwhelming. We can't afford a prolonged engagement with those numbers."

"Our allies' strengths will be crucial. We have numbers, skill, and surprise on our side," Alessandra spoke up.

Vlad addressed the room, a commanding figure among his gathered allies. "This will be a battle unlike any we have faced. But we stand together, united against a common enemy. We will use the intelligence provided by Casimir and Ash to plan our attack. We will strike hard and fast, dismantling their strongholds and crippling their operations."

The alliance, a varied group of fighters from across Europe, acknowledged with unanimous nods, silently pledging their dedication to the cause. A wave of revitalised determination swept through the room as they refined their plans with the fresh intel in mind.

Casimir, moving to the side, was engulfed in both wariness and resolve. The challenge before them was daunting, yet the solidarity and might of their gathered allies filled him with optimism. They stood poised to confront the Order, to defy its tyrannical grip, and to battle for a liberation from its sinister reach.

He observed Lóthurr Adhils, the bold chief of the Shadowcrest clan, make his way towards Vlad. Casimir knew all too well of Lóthurr's notorious self-assurance, which was evident in his demeanour right then.

"Vlad, my friend," Lóthurr started, his voice laced with the unmistakable tone of overconfidence. "Why spread our forces thin when our clan can single-handedly take one of these strongholds? Give us one, and we'll handle it."

Casimir observed Vlad's reaction. There was a patience there, a leader's tolerance for bravado. "Lóthurr, these aren't simple targets. They're heavily fortified. It's not about individual prowess; it's about a unified strategy," Vlad responded calmly.

But Lóthurr was undeterred. "Come on, Vlad. You know what we're capable of. Stealth, surprise, precision – that's our way. Let us take the Eichenwald Sanatorium. We'll dismantle it before the Order even knows we're there."

Casimir couldn't help but admire Lóthurr's confidence, even if it bordered on recklessness. There was a certain art to the way the Shadowcrest clan operated, a blend of stealth and strategy that had earned them their fearsome reputation.

Lucien chimed in, his voice a note of reason. "This is a collective effort. We can't afford lone-wolf tactics. It's about the bigger picture."

Lóthurr shot a quick, defiant glance at Lucien before turning back to Vlad. "Trust us with this, Vlad. The Shadowcrest clan won't disappoint. We'll be the shadow that cripples the Order at Eichenwald."

Vlad paused, weighing the decision. Finally, he nodded. "Alright. The Eichenwald Sanatorium is yours, but remember, this is a joint operation. We rise or fall together."

A triumphant grin spread across Lóthurr's face. "You won't regret this. The Shadowcrest clan will deliver."

As Lóthurr swaggered back to his group, Casimir felt a mix of apprehension and anticipation. Lóthurr's boldness was a double-edged sword–it could be their greatest asset or a risky gamble. But one thing was certain: the Shadowcrest clan's involvement added a potent, if unpredictable, element to their strategy against the Order.

"Each location poses a unique challenge," Vlad addressed the room, his voice resonant with authority. "And each of your clans brings the expertise we need to overcome them."

Vlad first turned to Maria Kestrell of the Blackwing Guild. Her keen eyes and composed demeanour reflected her guild's renowned skills in stealth and espionage. "Maria, the Marek Asylum in Poland is a key intelligence hub for the Order. Your guild's expertise in covert operations will be crucial in penetrating their network."

Maria Kestrell nodded, her expression one of cool determination. "The Blackwing Guild is prepared. We'll dismantle their operations from the inside, ensuring they're crippled beyond repair."

Next, Vlad's attention turned to Orbin Esson, the formidable leader of the Ironforged Warriors. Orbin's robust physique and battle-hardened countenance bore witness to numerous conflicts. "Orbin, your warriors are indispensable for the assault on the Voronov Retreat in Slovakia. The fortress's defences require the exceptional skill and combat expertise possessed by your warriors.

Orbin Esson responded with a deep, rumbling voice, "The Ironforged Warriors are ready for battle. We'll break through their lines and carve a path to victory."

Finally, Vlad addressed Cara Blackheart of the Dawn Coven, her aura radiating a potent mix of mystique and power. "Cara, the Nyschens Institute in Ukraine is shrouded in dark magic. Your coven's mastery of the arcane will be key to countering and overcoming their sorceries."

Cara Blackheart's eyes sparkled with an intense resolve.

"We accept this challenge. We'll turn the tide of dark magic against them, ensuring their downfall."

Casimir, as he watched the assembly, harboured a profound admiration for the gathered leaders. The Blackwing Guild, Ironforged Warriors, and Dawn Coven, each with their unique strengths and talents, constituted an intimidating coalition united in their battle against the Order.

Vlad concluded, "With your combined efforts, we can strike these strongholds simultaneously, delivering a crippling blow to the Order. Coordination and timing will be crucial."

The room was abuzz with a renewed sense of purpose as leaders and strategists huddled together, discussing plans and tactics. Casimir sensed the growing momentum; the diverse strengths of the clans coalesced into a formidable force poised to challenge the Order's reign.

As Vlad rose from his seat, which had taken on the semblance of a makeshift throne because of his commanding presence, he made his way toward the door of the council room. The meeting had imbued the room with a determined energy, yet beneath it all, Casimir could sense an undercurrent of concern.

Watching Vlad's demeanour, Casimir was moved to make a connection. As Vlad walked by, he gently rested a hand on Vlad's shoulder, silently signalling his desire for a private conversation.

"Casimir," Vlad acknowledged with a nod, an unspoken understanding passing between them. "Follow me. I sense your unease," he said, his voice low, ensuring their conversation remained private.

Casimir followed Vlad out of the council room and into a quieter corridor. The din of strategy and planning faded behind them, replaced by the hushed tones of the Academy's halls.

Once they were alone, Vlad faced Casimir, his expression open and attentive. “Speak your mind, Casimir. I know that look. You have concerns.”

Casimir took a moment, collecting his thoughts. “It’s the scale of what we’re undertaking,” he began. “The strongholds, the numbers we’re up against... I know we have a solid plan and formidable allies, but the risks are immense. I can’t help but worry about the cost of this battle, not just to us, but to all those involved.”

Vlad paid close attention, his gaze steadfast. “Your apprehensions hold merit. Undoubtedly, this is the most formidable trial we’ve encountered. Nevertheless, bear in mind that our battle isn’t solely for our sake. It’s a battle for a future liberated from the Order’s oppression. The dangers are substantial, yet the potential rewards are equally momentous.”

“I understand. It’s just... witnessing everyone uniting, fully aware of the challenges ahead...”

Vlad placed a hand on his shoulder, mirroring Casimir’s earlier gesture. “We all carry that weight. It’s what makes us leaders. But we also carry hope – hope for victory, for peace. We must hold on to that, especially now.”

“Thank you, Vlad. For everything,” Casimir said, gratitude clear in his voice.

Vlad gave a small, encouraging smile. “We’re in this together, to the end. Now, let’s go make our final preparations. The Order won’t know what hit them.”

Back in the bustling environment of the academy, Casimir was filled with a fresh resolve. The road ahead was fraught with peril, but they stood united in their mission, prepared to confront any challenges as a cohesive group.

CHAPTER 12

THE NEXT MORNING, AS THE FIRST LIGHT OF DAWN filtered through the windows of the council room, Vlad gathered Casimir, Ash, Jade, Alessandra, Lucien, and Avery for a final briefing. Outside, the assembled forces of their allies waited, ready to embark on the mission that would define their resistance against the Order.

Vlad's expression was solemn as he addressed Casimir, Lucien, Alessandra, and the others. "This is it," he began, his voice steady and clear. "Today, we strike at the heart of the Order. Each of you will play a critical role in this operation."

He looked at each of them, ensuring his message was received with the gravity it warranted. "You'll join different factions in their assaults, but your mission is twofold. Yes, fight alongside them, but also make sure that we execute our strategies correctly. Monitor the leaders; we cannot afford any missteps."

Responsibility settled heavily on Casimir's shoulders as the success of their plan depended on precision and coordination.

Vlad continued, "Once a stronghold falls, move quickly to support the next. Speed is of the essence. We must maintain the momentum and keep the Order off balance."

Alessandra, with an expression of fierce determination, added, "We will not let you down. We'll ensure that each location falls as planned."

Vlad gave a small, appreciative nod. "I have every confidence in you all. Today, we turn the tide. Today, we show the Order that their reign of terror ends with us."

With the briefing concluded, they rose from their seats, each feeling the enormity of the task ahead. They were not just fighters in this battle; they were leaders, the linchpins in a complex operation against a daunting enemy.

As dawn broke on the decisive day of their assault, the Roslyn Academy grounds transformed into a strategic assembly point. The vampire knights' army, a daunting force in its own right, meticulously divided into four flanks. They assigned the allied clans to each flank and appointed their respective leaders as commanders, who were ready to lead their forces into battle.

The Crescent Clan, renowned for their adept spell-casting and portal-making abilities, had also divided themselves into four groups. This distribution augmented the capabilities of each flank with their magical prowess. Madame Leana of the Crescent Clan had aligned herself with the Shadowcrest Clan, ready to lend her considerable magical skills to bolster their stealth and surprise tactics.

Vlad and Casimir had accompanied the Blackwing Guild, led by Maria Kestrell. Their expertise in covert operations and intelligence gathering would be crucial in navigating and dismantling the defences of their assigned stronghold.

Alessandra and Lucien joined forces with the Ironforged Warriors under the command of Orbin Esson. Their role in the frontal assault would be vital, requiring both courage and brute strength to break through the defences of the Order.

The Dawn Coven, led by Cara Blackheart, paired Jade and Ash, who had their unique abilities. Their combined magical knowledge and skills would be key in countering the dark sorceries protecting the Nyschens Institute.

Vlad addressed the gathered warriors, his voice resonant and inspiring. "Today, we fight not just for ourselves, but for a future free from the tyranny of the Order. Together, we are strong. Together, we will prevail."

With his words resonating in their minds, the groups departed, each heading towards their assigned destination. The synchronised assault on the Order's strongholds represented a colossal undertaking. However, armed with their collective strengths and guided by their commanders, they stood prepared for the daunting mission.

Standing alongside Vlad as they made their way to join the Blackwing Guild, Casimir felt a surge of determination. This marked the culmination of their extensive efforts, a moment where they would put their painstaking planning and thorough preparation to the ultimate trial. The forthcoming battle promised to be intense, yet they were resolute in their commitment to defend themselves, their comrades, and the future they were steadfastly dedicated to safeguarding.

The morning breeze held a crisp tension as Casimir and Vlad, facing the swirling portal, exchanged a meaningful grin. It was a smile born of camaraderie moulded amidst challenges, of past battles and those that loomed ahead. With a mutual nod, they ventured into the portal, the peculiar sensation of traversing it always unsettling, akin to a momentary dip into icy waters.

Emerging on the other side, the grim sight of their target —Marek Asylum under the control of the Order—greeted them, a fortress shrouded in an aura of malevolence. The air was heavy, laden with the anticipation of the impending battle and the unspoken fears and hopes of those about to fight it.

Behind them, the flank of vampire knights and Blackwing Guild members followed with disciplined precision. Each warrior's step was purposeful, their faces set in expressions of steely resolve, yet underpinned by an underlying current of tension. They were ready for battle, yet aware of the dangers that lay ahead.

Vlad's gaze swept across the landscape, calculating and cool. "Stay alert," he murmured, his voice a low rumble that carried both command and reassurance. "Precision and stealth are our allies today."

Casimir felt the familiar grip of his sword in his hand, a comforting presence. The heft of the blade served as a reminder of the battles fought in the past and the imminent struggle ahead. His heart pounded in his chest, a rhythm of both excitement and apprehension.

As they advanced towards the stronghold, the silent, ghostly figures of the Blackwing Guild moved like shadows, slipping through the defences with terrifying efficiency. Casimir and the vampire knights provided a formidable backup, their movements a dance of death and determination.

The clash of steel rang out as they engaged the Order's guards. Each exchange of blows was a deadly ballet, with Casimir at its centre, his blade singing a song of defiance and resolve. Every parry, every thrust, expressed his commitment to their cause, a cause that had become his own.

The stronghold's formidable defences, previously deemed impregnable, succumbed to their well-coordinated attack. The vampire knights fought with a strength stemming from their supernatural essence, their expressions marked by the solemn satisfaction of warriors fulfilling their destined purpose.

The battle raged on, a storm of steel, magic, and will. Casimir could feel the fatigue setting in, his muscles burning, his breath coming in ragged gasps. Yet he pushed on, driven by the knowledge that this fight was more than just a battle; it was a turning point in their war against the Order.

As they fought deeper into the heart of the stronghold, the sense of nearing victory grew.

Exhausted but resolute, Casimir, Vlad, and their allies pressed forward. The stronghold was faltering, its defences breaking under the onslaught. They were on the cusp of victory that would mark a significant blow against the Order's reign of terror.

The battle raged on at the Marek Asylum with ferocious intensity, when suddenly, a flare of magical fire burst in the sky, capturing Casimir's immediate attention. It was a message from Madame Leana, a beacon of urgent, flaming script that read: "Shadowcrest in trouble." The message dissipated into the air, leaving a trail of embers.

A surge of determination flooded Casimir. He knew what he had to do. Turning to Vlad, he said with a resolute tone, "I'll turn the tide here. My sword has power enough to end this swiftly."

Vlad, recognising the direness in Casimir's eyes, nodded solemnly. "Do it. We'll hold our ground here."

Casimir stepped forward, his demonic sword in hand. The ancient blade, a legacy of power and darkness, pulsed with a deep crimson glow. He raised it high; the runes etched its surface blazing with an ominous light. The atmosphere tensed as if the very air expected the unleashing of ancient forces.

With a commanding shout that echoed across the battlefield, Casimir invoked the sword's true power. "By the infernal depths, awaken!"

Above, the sky responded, churning into a maelstrom of dark clouds. A vortex formed, swirling with ash and ember, a portal to realms unspeakable. The air crackled with raw, unbridled energy, the environment responding to the sword's call.

Then, with a powerful downward arc, Casimir unleashed the fury of his sword. hellfire and brimstone cascaded from the vortex above, a spectacular and terrifying rain of blazing destruction. Each meteoric shard of flame that struck the ground exploded with the force of an erupting volcano, sending shockwaves across the battlefield.

Despite its once formidable defences, the Marek Asylum was no match for the onslaught. The ground shook violently with each impact, ancient walls and magical barriers crumbling under the relentless barrage. The air resonated with the roar of fire, the hiss of burning structures, and the distant cries of the Order's forces caught in the inferno.

Casimir, at the epicentre of this cataclysm, was a figure of awe-inspiring power. His sword, now a conduit of primordial chaos, directed the flaming assault with devastating precision. He stood amidst the maelstrom, unflinching, his eyes ablaze with the same fiery energy that he wielded.

The Blackwing Guild and the vampire knights watched in astonishment as the stronghold fell before them, transformed into a smouldering ruin by Casimir's might. The shadows cast by the flames danced wildly, creating a scene of apocalyptic beauty.

As the last of the flames died down, Casimir lowered his sword, the vortex above dissipating. The once impregnable Marek Asylum lay in ruins, a testament to the power he had unleashed.

With the battle won, Casimir didn't celebrate. The Shadowcrest Clan needed him. He stepped through a portal, leaving behind the remnants of his fiery wrath. An obvious message to the Order: their time was ending, and the forces arrayed against them were like nothing they had ever faced.

CHAPTER 13

In the aftermath of the fiery onslaught at the Marek Asylum, Vlad and the remaining forces stepped through the portal and emerged onto a new battlefield. They found the Shadowcrest Clan locked in a desperate struggle. The scene was chaotic, a whirlwind of clashing swords and arcane energies crackling through the air.

Vlad, moving swiftly to Casimir's side, eyed him with a blend of concern and admiration. "Why didn't you unleash the full might of your sword at the outset?" he asked, his voice cutting through the din of battle.

Casimir, his face pale and drawn, revealing the physical toll the sword's power had exacted on him, glanced at Vlad. "Each use of the sword's power comes at a cost to me," he confessed, his voice barely above a whisper. As they advanced towards the enemy, his step faltered, a stark testament to the immense strain on his body.

Vlad's expression softened with understanding, his eyes reflecting a deep concern for his comrade. "Be cautious, Casimir. Your strength is vital to our cause," he urged, his hand briefly clasping Casimir's shoulder in a gesture of support.

Despite the pain, Casimir managed a weak smile. He was buoyed by Vlad's concern but undeterred by the task at hand. "I'll manage. Let's turn the tide here for the Shadowcrest," he responded, summoning a reserve of strength he seemed to have kept hidden.

As one, they charged into the midst of the conflict, where the sounds of clashing steel and the thunderous eruptions of magic enveloped them. The battlefield below bore the scars of intense combat, and the pungent scent of spell-fire hung heavy in the air.

Casimir, pushing through the pain that wracked his body, fought with a grim tenacity. Each swing of his sword was more laboured than the last, but no less effective, cutting down enemy after enemy. Beside him, Vlad was a whirlwind of martial prowess, his movements a lethal dance that left no foe standing.

Casimir, Vlad, and their reinforcements breathed new life into the Shadowcrest Clan's efforts. Madame Leana, amidst the chaos, wove her spells with a focused intensity, her incantations weaving a tapestry of light and shadow across the battlefield.

The Order's forces waned, their ranks breaking under the assault.

In the quiet that followed, Casimir leaned heavily on his sword, his breathing laboured, his body sagging with exhaustion. His face revealed the cost of his power, a combination of pain and fatigue that he could no longer conceal.

Vlad, surveying the scattered remnants of their foes, returned to Casimir's side. "You've done more than enough," he said, respect and concern in his voice. "Rest now. We'll need you for the battles to come."

Casimir nodded, feeling the weight of his exertions more acutely now that the adrenaline of battle had faded. Together, they gathered with their allies, regrouping and readying themselves for the next phase of their campaign. The victory was theirs, but the war against the Order was far from over.

Despite his weariness, Casimir posed a critical question to Vlad, "Where should we go next?" as the dawn broke with a golden hue over the battlefield.

Madame Leana, sensing the urgency, reached out with her mystical senses, her fingers tracing patterns in the air, connecting with her clan members scattered across the various battlefronts. Her eyes, closed in concentration, suddenly snapped open with clarity. "Alessandra and Lucien, with the Ironforged Warriors, have successfully overtaken their target. No casualties."

Vlad, his face etched with a warrior's intuition, frowned. "Something's amiss. The Order's leader should have surfaced by now. This feels too... orchestrated."

With a collective sense of foreboding, the group quickly moved through a portal, emerging at the last stronghold – the Nyschens Institute in Ukraine. A scene of unbridled chaos greeted them. Jade, Ash, and the Dawn Coven were engaged in a ferocious battle against the Order, their magical assaults clashing with the surprisingly formidable defence mounted by their opponents.

The atmosphere was laden with the scent of burnt soil and the sizzling of unbridled magical power. Spells streaked across the heavens, casting brief, destructive bursts of splendour upon the battleground. The scattered remnants of the fallen strewn across the terrain stood as a sombre statement to the price paid in this conflict.

Without hesitation, Casimir, Vlad, and the others plunged into the heart of the conflict. Their arrival turned the tide, their fresh strength tipping the scales in their favour. Casimir's sword, glowing faintly with residual power, cut through enemy ranks, each swing an indication of his steadfast spirit.

As the battle at the Nyschens Institute reached a fever pitch, an unknown figure emerged from the stronghold, cutting an imposing figure against the backdrop of chaos. Dressed in dark robes that seemed to absorb the surrounding light, the leader's presence instantly shifted the tide of the battle. Casimir's eyes narrowed, focusing on this new adversary, sensing the surge of power that accompanied him.

Vlad, catching sight of the figure, stilled mid-strike. His expression morphed from battle-hardened determination to stunned recognition. "Matthias Corvinus," he uttered under his breath, a mix of disbelief and realisation colouring his tone.

Casimir glanced at Vlad, noting the shock on his face. "You know him?"

Vlad's eyes remained locked on Matthias. "He was the head of the Order during my human years, over five hundred years ago. He hasn't aged a day."

Matthias Corvinus stood at the forefront of the stronghold, his gaze sweeping over the battlefield with an air of haughty arrogance. He looked the same as he had in Vlad's memories, a timeless spectre from a past long gone. His eyes, dark and piercing, finally settled on Vlad.

"So, the prodigal son returns," Matthias's voice boomed across the battlefield, laced with venomous sarcasm. "I thought I had rid the world of your treachery centuries ago, Vlad."

Vlad clenched his jaw, his hands tightening around his sword. "You failed then, Matthias, as you will fail now. Your reign of terror ends today."

Matthias chuckled, a sound that echoed ominously. "Bold words for a traitor. Let's see if you can live up to them."

With a swift motion, Matthias unleashed a barrage of dark magic towards them. The air crackled with energy. The ground beneath them trembled, and Casimir felt the hair on his neck stand on end. They dodged, narrowly avoiding the onslaught.

Casimir and Vlad moved in unison, flanking Matthias. The surrounding battle seemed to blur into the background as they focused on their formidable foe. Matthias was a whirlwind of dark energy, countering their every move with a grace that belied his age.

The clash was intense, a battle not just of swords but of wills. Vlad fought with a personal vendetta, each strike a culmination of centuries of betrayal and anger. Casimir, fighting alongside Vlad, sensed the gravity of history with every blow they exchanged with Matthias.

In a swift exchange, Vlad found an opening, his sword slicing through Matthias's defences. But Matthias was quick to recover, countering with a powerful spell that sent Vlad reeling back.

Casimir leaped forward, his sword raised, but Matthias turned, meeting his attack with a sinister smile. "You are a strong, young one, but you are no match for me," Matthias taunted.

Amid their fierce battle, Vlad, while expertly parrying and thrusting against Matthias, grappled with a question that gnawed at his mind. "How have you stayed alive all these centuries, Matthias? Time has not touched you," he asked, his voice strained with both effort and curiosity.

Matthias, deflecting a strike with a dark chuckle, didn't miss a beat. "Ah, Vlad, always the inquisitive one. The ancient Chinese alchemists had the right idea about the elixir of life. They were so close, yet they lacked some crucial elements."

Vlad dodged a blast of dark energy. "So, you found what they were missing?" he pressed, his sword cutting through the air in a swift arc.

Matthias spun around, narrowly avoiding Vlad's blade. "Indeed, I did," he replied with a sinister smirk. "After centuries of searching, I uncovered the missing pieces of the puzzle. The perfect recipe for eternal life."

Casimir, fighting alongside Vlad, overheard the exchange. The thought of their enemy possessing such a power was chilling.

The battle raged on, with each participant keenly aware of the stakes. Matthias's revelation about the elixir of life hung over them, a dark cloud that added urgency to their efforts to bring him down.

Vlad, his face a mask of persistence etched with years of hidden pain, engaged Matthias with a series of relentless strikes, each swing of his sword cut through the air with a hiss. Matthias parried with ease, his dark magic a swirling vortex around him, absorbing and deflecting Vlad's furious onslaught.

Casimir brandished his infernal sword with resolute determination, the blade throbbing with an unearthly blaze. With every swing, he released torrents of scorching hellfire, transforming the battleground beneath them into an incinerated field. The atmosphere hung heavy with the scent of sulphur and singed earth.

Matthias, with a sneer of contempt, countered Casimir's fiery attacks with dark spells that twisted the air and tore at their senses. The clash of their powers sent shockwaves rippling through the air, a cacophony of light and shadow that painted the battlefield with a surreal palette.

"The power of your sword is impressive but futile against me," Matthias taunted, his voice an icy whisper that seemed to chill the very air around them.

Casimir, feeling the physical toll of wielding such immense power, gritted his teeth and pushed through the pain. He could feel the sword draining his energy, yet he knew the importance of their mission. He raised his sword high, channelling every ounce of his will into the blade, and brought it down in a mighty arc, unleashing a torrential inferno towards Matthias.

Matthias conjured a shield of swirling dark energy, but the hellfire, fuelled by Casimir's sheer tenacity and the ancient force within the sword, shattered it. The dark sorcerer staggered, his cloak catching fire at the edges, his face contorted in a mix of surprise and rage.

Vlad, seizing the moment, lunged forward with a warrior's cry, his sword cutting through the dissipating dark magic. Their blades met with a resonant clang, sparks flying as they struggled in a test of strength and will.

In a moment that seemed to hang in time, Vlad's eyes locked with Matthias's. Years of betrayal, loss, and pain were reflected in Vlad's gaze, a silent testament to the journey that had led him to this moment. With a final, desperate effort, he pushed forward, his blade piercing Matthias's defences and striking true.

Vlad intensified his attacks. "You may have cheated time, Matthias, but you cannot escape justice," he declared, his blade moving in a relentless dance of silver.

Matthias, though seemingly invincible, showed signs of weariness under the unyielding assault. His movements, once fluid and confident, became slightly more laboured, his spells less frequent.

In a climactic moment, Vlad and Casimir coordinated

their strikes, exploiting a brief lapse in Matthias's defences. Vlad's sword connected, a decisive blow that pierced through the dark magic and struck Matthias.

The leader of the Order staggered, his eyes wide with disbelief. He fell to his knees. The elixir of life had prolonged his existence, but it could not save him from the consequences of his actions.

Vlad towered over him, his blade still in hand. "Why all this, Matthias? What was the endgame?" he demanded, his voice heavy with emotion. "Was leading a chivalrous Order not enough for you, that you had to corrupt it so thoroughly?"

Matthias, weakened and defeated, kept a hint of his defiant spirit. He looked up at Vlad, his eyes glinting with a mix of resentment and pain. "After your wife died, I saw the power that you possessed," he spat. "That was when I realised that being the head of some mere knights meant nothing. The true power, the kind that could shape the world, was what I craved."

Vlad's grip on his sword tightened. The memories of his past and the loss he had suffered flooding back. "You let your ambition poison everything the Order stood for," he accused, his voice a low growl.

Matthias coughed, the effort of speaking seeming to drain the last of his strength. "I don't expect you to understand, Vlad," he sneered. "All your life, you had everything handed to you on a silver platter. I fought for everything I've got. I made myself into what I am today."

The surrounding air was thick with the presence of their shared past, a history marked by ambition, power, and loss.

"Your fight ends here, Matthias," Vlad said quietly, a sense of finality in his voice. "Your quest for power, for immortality... it's over."

Matthias' gaze faltered, and for a moment, there was a

flicker of something else in his eyes—perhaps regret. Perhaps a realisation of what his ambition had cost him.

Matthias gasped, his eyes widening in disbelief as he felt the mortal blow. He crumpled to the ground, his fall marking the end of an era, the collapse of a reign built on darkness and ambition.

As silence descended upon the battlefield, Vlad and Casimir stood side by side, their breaths heavy, their bodies weighed down by exhaustion and the emotional toll of their victory. They had faced a formidable foe, a spectre from Vlad's past, and emerged victorious. But the triumph was bittersweet, filled with the echoes of confrontations and the cost of the war they had waged.

The fight against the Order had come to an end, but as they gazed at the fallen Matthias, they understood that the wounds from this conflict would persist, serving as a poignant reminder of the cost of power and the enduring strength of the human soul.

As the last echoes of the battle faded into an eerie silence, Casimir's grip on his demonic sword loosened. The overwhelming exertion of channelling such immense power, combined with the fatigue of the combat, finally took its toll. His vision blurred, the sounds of the battlefield receding into a distant hum. His legs buckled beneath him, and he felt himself falling, the world around him spinning into darkness.

Vlad, who had been standing beside him, victorious yet sombre, reacted swiftly. Seeing Casimir's collapse, he reached out, catching him before he hit the ground. Casimir's sword clattered to the side, its hellish glow fading as it left his hand.

CHAPTER 14

Casimir's return to consciousness was gradual, a slow emergence from the depths of darkness that had enveloped him. His first sensation was one of weightlessness, as if he were floating in a void. Slowly, muffled sounds penetrated the fog that shrouded his mind, gradually becoming clearer and more distinct.

As he opened his eyes, the blurred figures around him slowly came into focus. He was back at Roslyn Academy, lying in a bed with soft sheets; a stark contrast to the harsh battleground he had last remembered. Concerned faces filled the room as his allies and friends gathered around him, their expressions reflecting a mix of relief and worry.

Vlad was there, standing by the bedside with his arms crossed, a look of genuine concern on his usually stoic face. Madame Leana was close by, her magical energy visibly depleted, yet her eyes conveyed a gentle reassurance.

Alessandra, Avery, Lucien, Jade, and Ash were also present, each showing signs of relief as they noticed Casimir's awakening. Their battle-worn appearances spoke volumes of the ordeal they had all been through.

"Welcome back," Vlad said, a rare smile breaking through. "You had us worried for a moment there."

Casimir tried to sit up, but a wave of dizziness forced him back onto the pillows. His body felt incredibly heavy, as if he had been carrying mountains on his shoulders. "What happened?" he asked, his voice hoarse.

"You collapsed after the battle," Lucien explained. "The power you wielded... it took its toll on you."

Madame Leana added, "You've been unconscious for nearly a day. We were all concerned, but I assured them you would recover."

Casimir's gaze swept across the countenances encircling him, all displaying signs of battle-weariness but also gleaming with the spark of triumph. "Have we... have we emerged victorious?" he enquired, seeking affirmation.

Alessandra's visage broke into an expression of weariness tinged with triumph as she confirmed, "Yes, we did."

Relief flooded through Casimir, blending with the weariness that had settled into his body. Every individual in this chamber had fulfilled their role. They had confronted overwhelming challenges and emerged as conquerors.

"There will be time for stories later," Jade whispered. "For now, you need to rest and recover. We all do."

The room filled with quiet agreement, the tension of the past days finally giving way to a sense of peace. They had done what had seemed impossible. The Order was no more, and though the future was uncertain, they faced it together.

As his friends and allies left the room to allow him to rest, Casimir lay back, closing his eyes. The echoes of battle still rang in his ears, but there was also a profound sense of accomplishment. They had turned the tide, fought back the darkness, and now, the path ahead was theirs to shape.

Lying in the quiet solitude of his room at Roslyn Academy, Casimir found himself enveloped in a sea of thoughts and emotions. The soft rustle of the sheets and the occasional distant murmur of voices in the corridors were the only sounds that accompanied his contemplation.

For hours, he lay there, staring at the ceiling, the events of the past days replaying in his mind. The Order, which had been an ever-looming shadow over his existence, was finally gone. The relentless vigilance, the constant looking over his shoulder, the clandestine living—all of it was over. A chapter of his life, defined by conflict and purpose against a clear enemy, had closed.

But in the wake of this monumental change, a profound sense of emptiness settled in. What was his purpose now? The driving force that had propelled him through danger and battles was no longer there. For the first time in what felt like forever, Casimir felt directionless, unmoored in a sea of newfound peace.

It was an ironic twist—he had yearned for freedom from the Order's threat, but now that he had achieved it, he grappled with the question of what came next. His identity had been so intertwined with the fight against the Order that its absence left a void within him.

Casimir's eyes were drawn to the window, where the tranquil twilight painted the sky in shades of orange and purple. The serenity of the view stood in stark contrast to the turmoil raging within him. He came to understand that in triumphing over their war; he had sacrificed a piece of himself—the part that had always been in battle, always in defiance.

There was a knock on the door, gentle but firm. It was

Vlad, stepping in with a look of concern. "You've been in here for a while. How are you feeling?"

Casimir sat up, offering a half-hearted smile. "I'm fine, physically. Just... thinking."

Vlad nodded in understanding. "It's a lot to process. We've all been through a great ordeal. But remember, Casimir, finding a new purpose takes time. This is just the beginning of a unique path."

Casimir sighed, the wisdom in Vlad's words resonating within him. "A journey without a clear route," he mused.

"Perhaps," Vlad replied, "but of your own making now. You're not bound by the shadows of the Order anymore. You have the freedom to choose what comes next."

Vlad's words lingered in the air, offering a glimmer of hope amid Casimir's uncertainty. He was right – the future was an open book, waiting to be written. It was a daunting thought, but also liberating.

As Vlad left him to his thoughts, Casimir realised that while one chapter of his life had ended, another was waiting to begin. The road ahead was uncharted, but it was his to explore. For the first time in a long time, he had the chance to discover who he was beyond the battle, beyond the resistance. It was an opportunity to redefine himself, to find a new purpose in a world that was no longer overshadowed by the Order.

With a deep breath, Casimir rose from the bed, a sense of determination slowly taking root. The path ahead might be unclear, but it was his to forge, and that was a journey worth embarking on.

Casimir, with a newfound persistence to explore his path forward, wandered through the hallowed corridors of Roslyn Academy. The walls, lined with rich tapestries and portraits of long-gone figures, echoed with the history and mysteries of the ancient institution. As he walked, the sound of laughter and light-hearted conversation drew him towards the common chamber.

Entering the chamber, Casimir found himself enveloped by its Victorian charm. It was a faithful representation of the era, featuring lofty ceilings adorned with intricate mouldings and walls covered in richly patterned wallpaper. Lavish velvet curtains framed the tall windows, their hues of deep red and gold harmonising with the gentle radiance emanating from the crackling fire in the ornate fireplace.

The furnishings comprised a selection of opulent, generously cushioned sofas and armchairs, upholstered in sumptuous fabrics that beckoned for comfort and repose. Illumination within the room was a blend of the fireplace's inviting warmth and the gentle radiance cast by crystal chandeliers suspended from the ceiling, their light reflecting off the gleaming polished wooden floors.

A group of people surrounded the large, elaborately carved wooden table in the centre of the chamber, filling the space with their laughter and smiles. It was the first time since their victory that everyone had gathered there, a moment of shared happiness and relief.

Vlad and Alessandra snuggled together on one sofa, their faces close, whispering and laughing in a world of their own. Their comfort with each other was clear, a bond forged through shared battles and experiences.

Nearby, Lucien and Avery sat together, their hands entwined, the joy in their reunion palpable. Avery's laughter, light and carefree, was a sound that seemed to bring even more warmth to the room.

In a cosy corner, Ash and Jade were engaged in a quiet conversation, their eyes locked, smiles on their faces. Their connection, once tentative, had grown stronger, an indication of the trials they had faced together.

Casimir lingered at the entrance, absorbing the tableau that unfolded before him. The room, resplendent in its grandeur, stood in sharp juxtaposition to the battlefields they had departed recently. Amidst the academy's inner sanctum, encircled by the mirth and felicity of his companions, Casimir encountered a profound tranquillity.

As he ventured further into the inviting common room, the voices of his friends coalesced into a harmonious chorus. "Welcome back," their collective voices chimed, countenances aglow with heartfelt smiles.

Joining them, he realised that this was what they had been fighting for – moments of simple, unguarded happiness. The battles they had waged were not just for survival, but for the chance to live, to love, and to find joy in each other's company.

Feeling a sense of belonging and relief, Casimir returned their greeting with a heartfelt expression. "It's good to be back. For a moment, I thought that was it," he replied, his voice tinged with reflective honesty. The recent brush with mortality had left its mark, making this moment of camaraderie even more precious.

The room settled into a comfortable quiet, the crackling of the fire and the soft hum of conversation filling the space. Jade, her eyes thoughtful, turned to Casimir. "So, what now?" she asked, her question hanging in the air, reflecting the uncertainty they all felt in the wake of their victory.

Casimir, feeling the weight of her question, took a moment before responding. "I think I'll stay here for a bit," he said, his gaze drifting around the room, taking in the familiar sights of the academy. The decision felt right; the academy had been a sanctuary in their time of need, a fortress against the darkness. Now, it could be a place of healing and reflection, a starting point for the fresh paths they would each carve.

Vlad, leaning back with a sense of contentment, added, "This place has been more than just a battleground for us. It's been a home, a place where we've grown and forged unbreakable bonds. Staying here, even for a while, feels like the right thing to do."

Casimir, leaning back comfortably, turned to the rest of the group. "What about you guys? Any plans?" he enquired, genuinely interested in what paths they might choose now that the dust of their long struggle had settled.

Vlad, with a slight smirk, replied, "I think we'll stay here for a little while." His gaze shifted to Lucien, a twinkle of mischief in his eyes. "Someone needs to put his big boy pants on and take over the reins of the academy. It's time for me to step back and perhaps enjoy the peace."

Alessandra snuggled next to Vlad and playfully nudged him, laughing. "Hey, don't be mean," she teased, her eyes sparkling with mirth.

Lucien, who had been listening with a growing sense of apprehension, protested. "What? You're trying to palm off your responsibility on me so you two can go off and be lovey-dovey together? I think not." His tone carried a lightness, yet beneath it lay a subtle seriousness, acknowledging the gravity of such a responsibility.

The room erupted in laughter, the tension and stress of their recent battles momentarily forgotten. Then everyone suddenly hushed as Vlad turned to Alessandra with a meaningful look in his eyes. "The Order used to stand for chivalry, for noble causes," he began, his voice reflecting a blend of nostalgia and hope. "I don't intend to revive it, but I do want to pick up the pieces. Setting up more academies for supernatural students seems like the right path. And Corvin Castle could be one of them if my viscountess agrees?" He gave Alessandra a playful yet earnest look. "Alessandra Elaina Chambord, Viscountess D'Auvergne. It has a nice ring to it, don't you think?"

Everyone's eyes were on Alessandra, waiting for her reaction, filling the room with an anticipatory silence. Before she could respond, Vlad added with a soft chuckle, "Actually, I have something else in mind. Something I've been keeping a secret. But this feels like the right place and time."

With a graceful movement, Vlad reached into his coat pocket and pulled out a ring. The room gasped collectively as he knelt before Alessandra, the mediaeval engagement ring catching the light from the chandeliers above.

The ring was a stunning piece of craftsmanship, its design a tribute to a bygone era. In its centre sat a large ruby, its deep red hue like a drop of blood crystallised in time. The ruby sat in a band of gold, which a skilled artisan crafted and ornamented with delicate filigree, resembling twisting and turning vines. Surrounding the ruby were smaller diamonds, their brilliance complementing the deep red of the centre stone. The diamonds sparkled with a fire that seemed to capture the essence of their love—bright, enduring, and unyielding.

"Alessandra Elaina de Winter," Vlad said, his voice steady yet filled with emotion. "Would you do me the honour of becoming my wife?"

The room held its breath as Alessandra looked at Vlad, her eyes shining with unshed tears and a smile spreading across her face. The ruby in the ring glowed warmly in the firelight, a symbol of the passion and depth of their relationship.

Her response was a whisper, yet it resonated with the depth of her love and commitment. "Yes, my love. I will."

A cheer erupted in the room, breaking into applause and laughter. The moment was a celebration, not just of their victory over the Order, but of love, of new beginnings, and of hope for the future.

As Vlad gently placed the ring onto Alessandra's finger, the ruby sparkled brilliantly, a symbol of the path they were embarking on together. In the midst of Roslyn Academy, enveloped by friends and the reverberations of their shared history, Vlad and Alessandra's engagement signified the commencement of a fresh chapter, brimming with potential and the assurance of a future constructed side by side.

"Don't tell me you're sitting on some old Wallachian treasure you have told no one about," Ash teased, casting a mock suspicious glance at Vlad, and the room erupted into more laughter.

Vlad, with a twinkle in his eye, played along with the jest. "Why, Ash, are you looking for a funding source for when you and Jade decide to tie the knot?" His counterchallenge, delivered with a knowing smile, drew another round of laughter and playful banter from the group.

Ash's response came with a confident grin, his eyes twinkling with mirth. "Nah, I made my fortune ages ago. You can keep your little pile of gold. I'll make sure my little Princess Consort will have everything she needs as we travel the world." His tone was playful yet underscored with the sincerity of someone who had lived many lifetimes and had learned the value of making his own way.

Jade, however, was quick to counter, her voice laced with humour but also a hint of independence. "Hey, I haven't agreed to any of that," she said, raising an eyebrow at Ash. Her expression was one of mock indignation, but her eyes danced with affection. The teasing between them was light-hearted, yet it spoke of a deep understanding and partnership that had grown.

The group erupted into laughter again, enjoying the easy back-and-forth bantering among friends. It was a refreshing change from the intensity of their recent experiences, a reminder that amidst the grand narrative of their lives, there were moments of simple joy.

Vlad, joining in the laughter, added, "Well, Ash, it seems you'll have to negotiate terms with your Princess Consort." His voice was rich with amusement, and he winked at Jade, acknowledging her spirited nature.

Alessandra, smiling at the playful exchange, leaned in closer to Vlad. "It seems we're not the only ones preparing for a future together," she whispered, her voice filled with happiness.

Casimir, with a dramatic flourish, feigned sickness from the overload of heartfelt sentiments. "Yeah, that's for sure. I plan to get out of here. This is way too much sugar for me," he said, mockingly clutching his stomach.

People responded to his playful jab with immediacy and spirit. In a blur of vampire speed, Vlad and Lucien, both grinning widely, tackled him to the floor in a friendly ambush. The room erupted in laughter as the trio scuffled playfully on the ground, their movements a whirlwind of mock combat and laughter.

Ash, seizing the opportunity to join the merriment, leaned over Casimir with a playful twinkle in his eyes. "Who said you could leave?" he quipped rhetorically, unleashing a tickle assault. Casimir's laughter, mixed with his futile attempts to break free, drowned out his playful protests.

Avery, laughing along with the others, shouted playfully, "Don't hurt him too much! We might need him in one piece!"

Amidst the glee and mischievous wrestles, the group

shared a sense of unity and relief. They were not just warriors who had fought side by side; they had become a family, united by shared experiences and a deep bond of trust and affection.

As the spirited tussle wound down, Casimir lay on the floor, still chuckling, surrounded by his friends. Looking up at their smiling faces, he realised that this moment, this feeling of belonging and joy, was something he had been missing for a long time.

In the heart of Roslyn Academy, amidst the echoes of a past marked by struggle and triumph, a new era dawned. A time of peace, exploration, and building a future where the shadows of the past no longer held sway. Together, they stepped into this new world, their hearts full of hope, their spirits unbroken, and their bonds unshakable.

People would remember the story of their fight against the Order as an account of bravery and resilience. But more importantly, it was the tale of their journey together, evidence of the enduring truth that in unity lies strength, in friendship lies solace, and in love lies the greatest power of all.

THE END.

BONUS SCENE 1

Journey Through Otherworldly Realms

As the fiery sails billowed in the wind, Ash and Jade stood at the helm of their ship, the Infernal Voyager, embarking on a journey fuelled by the flames of adventure. Guided by the unearthly power of demonic fire, they set sail across the vast expanse of the ocean, their destination unknown but their spirits ablaze with anticipation.

Amidst their travels, Ash and Jade ventured into the enchanting realm of Eldoret, a land of ethereal beauty and mystical wonders. As their ship glided gracefully across the shimmering waters of the Crissal Sea, they beheld a breathtaking sight: the Floating Gardens of Lunima.

The gardens stretched as far as the eye could see, a mesmerising tapestry of vibrant colours and lush greenery suspended in the air by delicate strands of magic. Each floating island was decorated with exotic flora that seemed to glow with an otherworldly radiance, casting a soft, iridescent light that danced upon the surface of the crystal-clear waters below.

As they drew nearer, they marvelled at the complicated network of bridges and walkways that crisscrossed the gardens, connecting the various islands in a delicate web of enchantment. Crystal-clear streams meandered through the verdant landscape, their gentle murmur echoing softly in the air.

But it was the flora of the Floating Gardens that truly captivated their hearts. Towering trees with iridescent leaves swayed gently in the breeze, their branches adorned with delicate blooms that shimmered like stars in the night sky. Exotic flowers of every hue and shape carpeted the ground, their sweet fragrance filling the air with a heady perfume.

As they wandered through the gardens, Ash and Jade felt as though they had stepped into a world of pure magic, where every flower, every tree, and every blade of grass was touched by the hand of the divine. And as they gazed upon the breathtaking beauty that surrounded them, they knew that their journey through Eldoret had only just begun and that the wonders of this enchanted realm would forever remain etched in their hearts.

They followed winding pathways adorned with delicate faerie lights that twinkled like stars in the dusky sky, leading them to a hidden glade nestled at the heart of the gardens.

As they entered the glade, they were greeted by a symphony of songbirds whose melodic tunes filled the air with a sense of serenity and joy. Sunlight filtered through the canopy of towering trees, casting dappled shadows upon the forest floor and illuminating the vibrant hues of the flowers that carpeted the ground.

In the centre of the glade stood a magnificent fountain, its waters shimmering with an iridescent glow that seemed to dance with the light of a thousand stars. As Ash and Jade approached, they saw that the fountain was embellished with intricate carvings depicting scenes from Eldoret's ancient legends and lore.

Drawn by the fountain's ethereal beauty, they reached out to touch its waters, feeling a surge of magic coursing through their veins. In that moment, they knew that they stood at the nexus of Eldoret's power, surrounded by the untold mysteries and wonders of this mystical realm.

“Should we stay here for a while?” Jade finally asked, her voice a whisper amidst the rustle of leaves.

The setting bathed the lush forest in a golden glow, casting long shadows across the forest floor. The air was filled with the sweet fragrance of wildflowers, and the distant sound of a babbling brook added to the tranquil ambiance.

Ash gazed into Jade's eyes, seeing the reflection of the sunset dancing in their depths. He reached out and took her hand in his, the warmth of her touch sending a comforting shiver down his spine.

“I think we should,” he replied, a soft smile playing on his lips. “This place is too beautiful to leave just yet. Let's stay and enjoy the peace and quiet together.”

Jade’s eyes sparkled with delight as she nodded in agreement. Hand in hand, they ventured deeper into the forest, their hearts filled with love and contentment as they embraced the serenity of their surroundings.

BONUS SCENE 2

Guardians of Roslyn

As the sun set, casting long shadows over Roslyn's courtyard, Lucien and Avery stood together, watching students head back to their dorms.

"It's hard to believe we're finally here," Avery said, her voice tinged with disbelief. "You as the headmaster, and me as your assistant. Who would have thought?"

Lucien smiled, his eyes scanning the courtyard with pride. "It's been a long journey, but we made it," he replied. "And I couldn't have asked for a better partner to share it with."

Avery blushed at his words, feeling a warm glow spread through her chest. "Thank you, Lucien," she said softly. "I'm just happy to be here with you, making a difference in these students' lives."

Despite the challenges they had faced along the way, they

had finally found their place at Roslyn Academy, shaping the minds of the next generation of supernatural beings.

With Lucien at the helm, they were confident that the academy would thrive, providing a safe haven for students to learn and grow under their guidance. And as they stood together under the starry sky, they knew that their journey was far from over, but they were ready to face whatever challenges lay ahead together.

As the moon cast its silvery glow over the sleeping academy grounds, Lucien's voice broke the stillness of the night. "It's time," he declared, his tone firm and resolute. With a swift movement, he retrieved their swords, the blades catching the moonlight with a glint.

Avery nodded in silent agreement, her eyes gleaming with determination as she prepared herself for the task ahead. The students were safely tucked away in their beds, oblivious to the world beyond the walls of the academy. It was their duty to protect them, to ensure their safety from the lurking shadows.

With a nod between them, Lucien and Avery slipped out into the night, their steps light and purposeful. Under the cover of darkness, they moved with silent grace, their senses attuned to the slightest hint of danger.

Guided by Vlad's teachings and Lucien's growing mastery of his powers, they ventured forth into the darkness. Lucien's abilities, honed through centuries of guidance, allowed him to tap into the ancient lineage of the first vampire. With a whispered incantation, he summoned an invisible barrier to cloak them from prying eyes, concealing their movements from any who might seek to interfere.

Rising into the air with a gentle levitation, Lucien effortlessly lifted Avery into his arms, her weight feeling like nothing against his newfound strength. Together, they ascended into the night sky, their figures silhouetted against the backdrop of the moonlit clouds.

As they soared above the academy, their senses heightened, alert for any sign of danger lurking in the darkness below. With Lucien's guidance and Avery's unwavering resolve, they stood as guardians of Roslyn, ready to face whatever challenges the night might bring.

BONUS SCENE 3

A Day of Wonder at Corvin Castle

Under the warm embrace of the midday sun, the sprawling grounds of Corvin Castle blossomed with life and laughter. Vlad, towering yet gentle, found himself amidst a lively group of younger students, their youthful energy contagious as they scampered across the lush green expanse near the castle's moat.

As the children darted about, their laughter echoing through the air, one of them, a bright-eyed youngster with tousled hair, approached Vlad with a curious glint in his eye. "Have you ever seen a real dragon, Godfather?" he asked, his voice tinged with wonder and excitement.

Vlad's lips curved into a tender smile at the child's question, his eyes alight with fondness as he crouched down to meet the young one's gaze. "Ah, my young friend," he began, his voice gentle yet filled with a hint of mystery, "dragons are elusive creatures, rarely seen by mortal eyes. But they exist in the realms beyond, where magic and myth intertwine."

The child listened with rapt attention, his imagination ignited by Vlad's words as he envisioned the majestic creatures soaring through the skies. With a wide grin, he turned to his companions, regaling them with tales of dragons and daring adventures.

Meanwhile, Alessandra stood nearby, her heart warmed by the sight of Vlad's interactions with the children. Her gaze lingered on him, her love and admiration for him shining brightly in her eyes. In this moment, amidst the joy and innocence of the young ones, she couldn't help but feel grateful for the life they had built together at Corvin Academy—a place where magic thrived, and every day held the promise of new wonders and discoveries.

"Do you ever wish your own children were still alive?" Alessandra asked as she drew near.

Vlad paused for a moment, his gaze lingering on the children playing in the sunshine. Memories stirred within him, memories of a time long past when his own children roamed these halls, their laughter echoing through the corridors.

"Yes, occasionally," Vlad replied softly, his voice bearing the depth of centuries. "But then I remember that they are at peace now, free from the burdens of this world."

Alessandra nodded in understanding, her eyes reflecting a mixture of sorrow and empathy. She placed a comforting hand on Vlad's arm, a silent gesture of support.

"They live on in our memories," she said gently. "And in the lives we touch every day."

Vlad smiled gratefully at Alessandra, a sense of warmth spreading through him despite the melancholy of their conversation.

“They’re my children now. I’ll protect them until my last breath.”

Vlad’s voice held a quiet determination as he spoke those words, his eyes filled with a fierce resolve. Alessandra nodded, understanding the depth of his commitment to the young ones under their care.

“Together, we’ll ensure they have a future filled with hope and safety,” she affirmed, her tone echoing Vlad’s tenacity.

With a shared understanding and a bond forged through shared responsibility, Vlad and Alessandra stood side by side, ready to face whatever challenges lay ahead in their role as protectors of the children at Corvin Academy.

BONUS SCENE 4

The Half-Demon's Quest

Casimir stood atop a rugged cliff, the wind whipping through his dark hair as he surveyed the vast expanse of the world below. His demonic sword gleamed in the sunlight, a deadly reminder of his mission to rid the world of monsters.

With steely determination in his eyes, Casimir embarked on his quest, traversing desolate landscapes and treacherous terrains in search of his next target. Each step forward brought him closer to his goal, his keen senses honed to detect even the slightest hint of supernatural presence.

As night fell, he found himself deep within a dense forest, the ancient trees casting long shadows in the moonlight. Suddenly, a guttural growl echoed through the darkness, signalling the approach of his prey.

With lightning reflexes, Casimir unsheathed his demonic sword, the blade pulsating with dark energy. As the creature lunged towards him with feral intent, Casimir met its charge head-on, his movements fluid and precise.

With a swift strike, he severed the monster's head from its body, the demonic sword slicing through flesh and bone with ease. As the creature fell lifeless to the forest floor, Casimir knew that his mission was far from over.

As dawn broke over the horizon, Casimir emerged from the forest, his body weary but his spirit undaunted. With each victory against the forces of evil, he felt a sense of purpose coursing through his veins, driving him ever onward in his quest.

With his demonic sword at his side, Casimir traversed vast deserts, towering mountains, and ancient ruins, hunting down monsters wherever they lurked. Along the way, he encountered brave souls who joined him in his crusade, their strength bolstering his own.

Yet, amidst the chaos and danger, Casimir never forgot his ultimate goal: to rid the world of darkness and protect the innocent from harm. With every swing of his sword and every battle won, he drew closer to achieving that noble aim.

As he journeyed across the world, Casimir's legend grew, his name whispered in hushed tones by those who had witnessed his feats of bravery. Though his path was fraught with peril, he remained steadfast in his resolve, knowing that his quest was far from over.

And so, with the sun shining overhead and the wind at his back, Casimir continued his journey, his heart filled with hope and his spirit aflame with purpose. For in a world consumed by darkness, he was the light that shone brightest; a beacon of hope for all who stood against the shadows.

ABOUT CORINNE M. KNIGHT

I was born in the mystical land of Romania, a place where legends come alive and magic runs deep. As a child, I was entranced by the stories of the supernatural creatures that roamed the Carpathian Mountains. It was no surprise that I fell in love with writing paranormal romance novels, infusing them with the enchanting magic of my motherland.

While I currently reside in the bustling city of Cardiff with my beloved husband, my heart yearns for the rugged wilderness of Scotland. It's a place that ignites my imagination and inspires me to create stories that transport readers to far-off lands, where love, passion, and the supernatural intertwine.

As a fervent student of history, I find inspiration in exploring the secrets of the past. My dream is to one day live in a grand castle where I can immerse myself in the rich tapestry of historical tales and draw upon them to create new and captivating stories.

To keep up with my latest literary adventures and my upcoming trip to the Scottish Highlands, join my newsletter. And for a chance to win magical giveaways and be the first to hear about my latest book releases, come hang out with me!

Also by Corinne M. Knight

Of Knights and Monsters series – Supernatural Paranormal Fantasy

The Dark Heir

The King of the Undead

The Demon Prince

The Assassin Heiress

The Veiled Huntress

The Shadowbound Knight

Of Knights and Monsters: Complete series

Veil of Dusk series – Supernatural Paranormal Fantasy

House of Shadow and Bloom (November 2024)

Kingdom of Twilight and Thorns (2025)

Empire of Nightfall and Petals (2025)

All news regarding upcoming books is shared via Corinne's newsletter. Subscribe to be the first to know.

Milton Keynes UK
Ingram Content Group UK Ltd.
UKHW032003230824
447235UK00001B/73